To Abi

I hope you enjoy my book

MDownie

CW01193039

The Logan Prophecy

by Michael Downie

The Logan Prophecy
Second Edition

Written & edited by Michael Downie

Cover art by Jamie Mercer

First published independently worldwide in 2018

ISBN - 9781982980443

For my mother, Christine, my father, Bill and my brother, Simon, who always pick me up when I fall and help me find the path I've so often lost.

Special thanks go to the people who helped make this book a reality. For their encouragement, kind words and friendship, both in real life and online:
Richard, Jamie, Nimmo, Stephen, David, Andi, Laura, Ben, Tara, Monksboi, Azizrian, Beutimus, LadyAsabat, NoblePanda,_Wipeout, Flaming Monocle, Lostock, Vik, OneLineDerek, Rent-a-Hero and Ms. J.

Part One

Chapter One

Rayczech Alpha

GMC Metallics Mine 3483

"Warning, drill temperature exceeding manufacturer safety levels." the synthesised female voice declared.

"Oh shut up!" Higgins yelled at the speaker in his power drill cab. "Fucking tin can."

"I heard that," the AI responded, "Directive 34 contravention, you have been fined 20 credits."

"WHAT?" Higgins yelled back at the voice.

"New Galaxy Mining Corporation directive 34: 'Abusing corporate property is strictly prohibited, punishable by fines. Repeat offenders face dismissal.'"

"How the fuck did I abuse you?" Higgins replied, shutting down the drill.

"1751, Higgins, C, Mining technician 1st class. Abuse of company AI. Playback evidence," the voice said, before replaying the recording of his voice.

"I called you a tin can and that cost me 20 credits?"

"Yes. Would you like to appeal this decision?" she said, with a cold detachment.

"Of course I would!"

"Appeal lodged. Appeal deliberated. Appeal denied. 20 credits have been deducted from your salary. Have a nice day".

Higgins had to restrain himself from punching the console of his drill. Instead, he let out a deep sigh, climbed out of his cab, hopped down to the ground via the large caterpillar tracks and headed towards the transport shuttle. With the diamond and tungsten drill head overheating there was nothing he could do until the head had cooled down, which would take hours. He was hot, tired and covered in dirt and grime.

Rayczech Alpha was unlike any other planet he'd worked on in his 20 year career of mining. The mines weren't dark, like any other planet, they had an eerie green glow as the rocks contained some mineral that would shine in perpetuity. It made them very valuable as all of the richest people in the galaxy would place the rocks and stones into jewellery. Necklaces with glowing stones would fetch thousands of Credits in the boutiques of Earth. Of course, Higgins didn't see any of that money, but it was paying work and for that he was thankful.

Higgins hadn't felt great since he arrived on R.Alpha. He was tired, aching and altogether weary a lot of the time. He tried to put it down to a general lethargy, after all he hadn't had a vacation in over a decade. The GMC always guaranteed work, but vacations were frowned upon. Any day he wasn't on a site working, the GMC would be finding a way to make him redundant or fire him. It wasn't anything personal to him, just company policy. But it had meant that all he knew was work. No part of Higgins could simply relax; every day was just work, work, and more work.

Three more years and he could retire. He'd spent his life living frugally, saving all the money he could. He had his dream. Owning a farm on Alpha Centauri. He kept a small photo of green fields and mountains from the planet in his wallet to look at whenever he felt low. The land was expensive there, but it was worth it as the soil was so fertile nearly anything could grow at any temperature. He wanted to raise cattle and make a comfortable living off selling the meat of the rare beasts to rich business people across the galaxy.

He clambered into the shuttle bus and took a seat, removing his helmet and breathing apparatus. R.Alpha was perfectly habitable, but mining was a fraught experience. There was so much natural gas throughout the planet that people would start to cough and choke without any form of gas mask or filtration systems.

"Where to?" the driver AI asked him in a chipper, Earth London accent.

"Take me home," he replied, "Haven Towers in Old Town."

"Right you are, guv." It always amused Higgins that all driving software was programmed to speak in a Cockney accent. At least it wasn't as prickly or overly sensitive as the new AI in his drill cab.

The ride home was his favourite part of the day. The mine was in a rural area, about 30 miles from his apartment. The drive took in some of the scenery of the beautiful planet. The shuttle drove past meadows of strangely coloured flowers, along a wide, yet serene river that was teeming with vegetation he'd never seen before and all without seeing any influence of human existence beyond the road he was travelling on. But, by far his favourite part of the ride home was the sunset. The sky on R.Alpha was a light colour purple in the daytime, which was off-putting at first but something he'd grown to rather like, but when the sun set over the horizon it was a glorious cast of reds, yellows, blues and purples, it was like a work of fantastical art and Higgins never got bored seeing it.

As the countryside gave way to the start of the urban sprawl of Old Town, Higgins turned on his PCU. The Personal Communicator Unit was a small device that sat on his left wrist and acted like a watch for most of the time he was at work. He wasn't allowed to use it beyond timekeeping whilst working. Now he was finished, he turned it on and the holographic display popped up in front of his eyes. He scanned his mails, most of them were junk and immediately deleted. One was from the recruitment agency at the Unified Church Of Humanity. He wasn't sure what The Church would want with a drill head like him, but he kept the email for later anyway.

The last mail in the list was from his daughter, Emily. She was on Earth, studying at the London School of Economics. He was ever so proud of her. He read the mail in detail. She was getting straight As in her classes, she'd met a nice boy who she was dating regularly. She sounded so happy. On the mail was an attached photo of her, which he opened. She was looking so grown up. Her brown hair tied up in a ponytail with her bangs hanging down over her face, piercing blue eyes, and her soft features reminded him so much of her mother. He saved the photo to his album marked "Emily". At the end of the mail, she'd written:

"P.S. I miss you, Dad. Come home for a visit soon."

It brought a tear to his eye. He hadn't seen her in two years since his last training course on Earth. They would video call as often as they could, but nothing was a replacement for seeing his little girl in person and being able to give her a hug. He highlighted the mail so he'd remember to reply to it later.

The shuttle pulled up at Haven Tower. An unassuming complex for the miners on R.Alpha, its 30 floors housed nearly 1000 miners and their families. It wasn't a bad place to live, yet it wasn't a good place to live either. But it worked for Higgins. He had a bed, a vidscreen, a kitchen, a bathroom and a bar on the ground floor. It's all he needed to get through the day.

"Cheer up, guv, you're home now" the AI chirped.

"Thanks. Can you book me in for 0700 tomorrow morning to go to work?" Higgins said.

"Yeh, not a problem, guv," the AI replied, "now get yourself up the apples and pears and have yourself a nice Ruby."

"A what?" Higgins asked, more than a little confused. He'd heard 'apples & pears' before but had no idea on Ruby.

"Gordon Bennett! Don't they teach you anything out here?" the AI said with a slightly exasperated tone, "Ruby... Ruby Murray... CURRY! Have a curry, you plonker."

"Oh, right. I'll think about it." Higgins said as he climbed out of the shuttle. The AI muttered something to itself as Higgins walked to the building's door. He wasn't sure why, but he thought he quite liked this particular AI. It always seemed to make him smile.

Chapter Two

Unified Church of Humanity Research Facility

Location Redacted

"What are we looking at?"

"I'm not sure."

"Where is the sample from?"

"Rayczech Beta, out on the rim."

"Never heard of it."

"It's a small system on the edge of the galaxy. There's not much there, but the system is full of rich minerals, metals and carbon formations."

"So what are you showing me?"

"It's biological, that's for sure. We found it deep underground. I think it's what caused the Corvus incident. We've been looking for it for over a decade and I think this is it."

"Is it... is it bacteria?"

"I don't think so. It doesn't look like any bacteria I've ever seen. Watch what happens when I introduce some biological matter to it."

"My God, is it?"

“Yes, it’s infesting it. I think it’s a parasite, but I don’t know what else to say about it.”

“Could it be a contender for PAYLOAD?”

“Yes, I think it could.”

“Do you have any more samples you haven’t fed yet?”

“Yes, about six in the freezer. But I’ll need more to continue my research.”

“I’ll make arrangements. In the meantime, that... thing is still growing, incinerate this sample, I’ll try and get you new ones.”

“Thank you, sir.”

Chapter Three

Rayczech Alpha

Haven Towers. Apartment 348

Higgins' PCU started flashing. It was two hours before he'd be due to leave for work so he ignored it. Sleep was a precious commodity for him, he wasn't happy about it being disturbed. The flashing wouldn't stop, so he put his left arm under the pillow and room was dark again.

Then the vibration started. Then the beeping. Someone REALLY wanted Higgins' attention. With a heavy sigh, he sat up, turned the bedroom light on and answered the PCU. A hologram call appeared with Higgins' boss, Dave Martins appearing in full view.

"Morning, Carl. Wakey wakey," Martins said with an alarming amount of cheer in his voice.

"It's 5 am, what do you want?" Higgins could barely contain his annoyance.

"Now now now," he said with a condescending tone, "is that any way to greet someone who's done you a huge favour?"

"Last time you did me a favour I ended up in a hospital bed with Qui'noxic flu for two months." Higgins retorted.

"Yeah, but you got paid handsomely for that job. What's a bit of flu, anyway?"

"I WAS BLEEDING FROM MY EYEBALLS!"

"Yeah, well you still got paid, didn't you?"

"Only after I complained when you tried to not pay me because I hadn't worked for two months…"

Martins grinned slightly "Oh yeah, I'd forgotten I did that. Anyway, this is a good one. An easy one. Well paying too."

"Good? Easy? Well paying?" Higgins repeated, "excuse my cynicism but it sounds like you're about to feed me a line of bullshit here."

"No no, it's legit. It's a job for The Church. They're doing some research on Rayczech Beta and they need someone to drill out some samples for them. You should have had a mail about it."

"Yeah, I had that mail. I wasn't sure what to think of it."

"Well here's the details. They need someone to hop over to the next planet and spend the week drilling samples."

"Samples of what?"

"Why is that important?" Martins was always a more hands-off boss. It would annoy Higgins that he would ask questions that should have obvious answers.

"Because it's something I'd need to know," Higgins sighed, "I have to set up the drill, make sure I bring the right heads, the right lengths of pipe. I can't just go boring into any old rock with any old head."

"Can you not just bring them all?"

"That'll cost me a fortune to ship over to R.Beta. It's 40 tonnes just for the drill machine, let alone the heads."

"Don't worry about that. The Church is footing the bill for the whole exercise."

"Why?"

"Do I look like a Church Cleric? I'm just telling you what they told me. They're willing to pay you 4000 credits for the week."

"Four… THOUSAND credits?" That was nearly two months wages for Higgins. "This all seems too good to be true. I don't need to pay to ship equipment, they're going to pay a vast amount of money what's the catch?"

"No catch."

Higgins stared at Martins down the hologram.

"Okay, there's a slight catch."

"I KNEW IT!" Higgins yelled. "What is it?"

"Well, the work is going to happen in a part of the planet that's considered a little… deadly…"

"Of course it is," the lack of surprise in Higgins' voice was more than evident, "how deadly is 'a little deadly'?"

“Ion storms, slightly unstable tectonic plates low-ish oxygen outdoors”

“So the worst place in the universe to drill?”

“Pretty much,” said Martins. He knew better than to try and get one over on Higgins, but he always tried anyway, “You best pack, your shuttle to the spaceport will be there in an hour.”

“What? I didn’t accept the job!”

“Oh, that’s the other catch. It’s an order, not a request.”

“What if I refuse and go to work as normal?”

“Your drill will be deactivated, you’ll be fired and your pension will be null and void. Nothing personal j-“

“Just company policy.” Higgins was sick of hearing this, but clearly, he didn’t have a choice in the matter.

“It’ll be fun,” Martins said, trying to lighten the mood, “See the sights, drill some rocks, it’ll be grand.”

“Sure,” Higgins said, killing the call. “Fucking hell.”

Flicking on the lights, Higgins dragged himself out of the bed and placed his feet on the hardwood floor. The central heating hadn’t come on yet and the floor was bitterly cold. He walked over to the small en suite bathroom and turned on the shower to warm up. Looking at the mirror he saw the bags under his eyes. Higgins hadn’t been sleeping properly of late and it was starting to show. The artificial lighting of the grey tiled bathroom made the air feel colder despite the warm steam that was rising from the shower basin.

Following the shower, he walked around his small apartment in the nude, allowing himself to air dry. He turned on the coffee machine and prepared a fresh brew of his favourite roasted Antarian beans. He opened his closet and pulled out a pair of silver suitcases. Higgins didn’t own many things, mostly just clothes and a few personal nick nacks. He moved around the galaxy so often all of his worldly possessions were in a storage locker on Earth, waiting for the time where he could retire and own his own home again.

Throwing one of the cases onto the bed, he tapped a button on the wooden night stand causing a panel on the wall to open and a rail containing all of his clothes to slide out. He grabbed all of the clothes off the rack and stuffed them roughly into the case. On the oak console table under the large vidscreen he had a handful of family photos which he picked up and tossed into the case. He lingered over a picture of his wife and infant daughter, taken many years ago. He gently placed it in the case and closed it up.

He looked around at his most recent living quarters. The cool grey walls, large comfortable bed and vidscreen had been his whole world since he had landed on Rayczech Alpha. He had quite liked this apartment. For all it was one room and a bathroom, it was large and had served him well. He looked through the window that spanned the length of the room, giving him a view of the spires and towers of Old Town. The dark purple sky contrasted against the orange and neon lights coming from the city centre. With a click, the coffee machine was done. Higgins moved over to the small kitchenette and poured himself a large cup of hot, dark liquid. He sat on the edge of his bed as he waited for the water to dry on his skin, sipping his coffee and browsing the news channels on his vidscreen.

He felt strange. Something was telling him that this would be the last time he would have a relaxing moment to himself for quite a while.

At 6 am on the dot, his PCU flashed to tell him the shuttle was downstairs. He grabbed his bag and headed down the three floors to the front door. Higgins liked to try and keep fit, so he always took the stairs when he could. He never knew if one of the attractive GMC sales reps would visit and take a shine to him. It hadn't happened in 20 years, but he held out hope that it could one day.

The shuttle wasn't one of the normal Old Town models. This was an executive model, no doubt laid on by The Church. The AI greeted him in a soft, vaguely French female tone.

"Good morning, Monsieur."

"Morning. Take me to Mine 3483," Higgins instructed.

"Non, Monsieur," the AI argued back, "I have a route pre-programmed for you. I am taking you to the spaceport in Astral City."

"I need to go to the Mine," Higgins replied, "I have to pack up my drill and get it shipped to R.Beta"

"It has been all taken care of Monsieur. Your equipment is already en route."

"Oh." Higgins was taken aback slightly. Mostly wondering how The Church was able to load the drill onto a shuttle or truck when he had the keys for it in his pocket.

"In that case," he asked, "can you divert to somewhere for me to get breakfast? I'm starving."

"Non, Monsieur. My route and instructions are specific. There are snacks in the centre console if you require sustenance."

Without warning the shuttle accelerated rapidly and joined the early morning traffic leaving Old Town. Hitting the highway, the traffic was moving at a rapid rate. Astral City was a good four hours away. Even though the shuttles were capable of nearly the speed of sound, it was still on another continent.

To pass the time, Higgins went back through the mails on his PCU and replied to them. He spent a long time giving an expansive and detailed update for Emily. He talked about his work, how his dog, Buster had passed away a few months ago, his discovery of an archive of 20th-century cartoons and how much he thought Tom & Jerry was the funniest thing he'd watched in years. He signed the mail off with:

"P.S. I miss you too. Hopefully, after this job is done I'll be able to afford to have a week on Earth. I'm so proud of you. Love you, nugget."

The mails occupied an hour of the journey. Higgins spent the remaining time either asleep or arguing with the quasi-French AI about the pronunciation of the few French words it would drop into conversation. He already regretted answering the PCU this morning.

Chapter Four

Unified Church of Humanity Research Facility

Location Redacted

"We have a miner en route to the site."

"Good, when will I get my samples?"

"Soon. He's a bit suspicious, he doesn't know what to drill for."

"Tell him to drill for everything. This organism has been found on a few different kinds of rocks"

"How many samples do you have left?"

"One and six."

"Pardon?"

"The six samples I had, there was a contamination when I defrosted them. One of the junior researchers left them out in the open air."

"What happened?"

"The samples released microscopic spores into the air. He breathed them in."

"What happened to him? And what happened to the samples?"

"He's in quarantine. It doesn't look good. I had to incinerate the other samples as they'd reacted to microbes in the air, they were starting to grow."

“He’s dying?”

“No, quite the opposite, he’s growing”

“Growing?”

“Yes, I’ve never seen anything like it. I’m keeping him under observation, but I need the new samples immediately, if not sooner.”

“Our man should land in the next 24 hours, you’ll have your samples within 96 hours.”

“Sir, make sure he wears breathing apparatus, for everyone’s safety.”

“Noted.”

Chapter Five

Rayczech Alpha

Highway 19, 30 miles outside Astral City

As the shuttle approached Astral City, Higgins couldn't think about the grandiose city or the unfathomably huge starport he was headed to. All he could think about was his stomach. He'd raided through the snacks in the shuttle. Two packets of cookies, a small bag of nuts and a small bottle of water were not his idea of a satisfying breakfast.

The AI in the shuttle had been wonderfully silent for most of the journey, only speaking when spoken to and only delivering specific answers to his questions. He'd manage to coax out of it the gate he was supposed to go to, the time of his flight and the fact that his tickets were for first class. He'd asked where his actual tickets were but the AI didn't have an answer for that, thus didn't say a word.

As the shuttle slowed down from near-supersonic speed to an acceptable urban traffic speed, Higgins peered through the windows to get a good look at Astral City. He hadn't seen the place since he first arrived on the planet two years ago. A magnificent city full of elegant, glass and vidscreen covered skyscrapers, he felt like it would be an exciting place to work or to live. There were so many people on every street, more people than he'd seen in years. It took his breath away.

But the real jewel in Astral City's crown was the spaceport. R.Alpha was a hub world. It wasn't quite on the outer rim of the galaxy, but it was the main transfer station for four separate sectors. People would come through R.Alpha to reach the more remote worlds and systems on this side of the galaxy, so the spaceport was naturally massive. Looking on his PCU at details of the port, he read that it was 15 square miles in size and could cater for over 200,000 separate journeys on any given day. It was so big, it had its own internal shuttle service to get passengers from the main entrance to the gate the required. The spaceport actually made so much money it was considered in the top 100 economies of the galaxy rim.

As the port came into view, all Higgins could think was that it was even bigger than he remembered it. Higgins wasn't one for being around large amounts of people, hence his choice of work, so his palms were a bit sweaty at the prospect of being anywhere in the starport. He formulated a plan in his head. Get in, get to the gate, get food, and get out of there.

The shuttle pulled up to the vast passenger drop off area.

"Please do not leave your trash in the shuttle," the AI said curtly. Higgins picked up the packets of snacks and stuffed them in his bag.

"Thank you," he said as the door opened. The AI didn't respond. He thought it could do with a personality tune-up.

Standing in the enormous collection of pickup and drop off points, it took Higgins a minute to orient himself to where he needed to go. A sign across the road from him had a large arrow with "MAIN ENTRANCE 1KM" on it. Cursing the ignorant AI for leaving him so far from the entrance, he picked up his bag and trudged past hundreds of people, missed being run over twice and had pamphlets for nearly every minor galactic religion and cult thrust into his hands.

Walking through the main entrance he was greeted with what looked to be a mass transit terminus. Each stopping area had a gate number on it and a large bus waiting. The AI had told him he needed to be at Gate 1200. Finding the 1200 stand, he alighted the bus. Again, no driver, just another AI with a distinct need of a personality upgrade

"Name?" it barked in a monotone voice

"Carl Higgins"

"Boarding pass?"

"I don't have one. I was told I didn't n-"

"You cannot board without a boarding pass CARL HIGGINS." The generic yelling of his name back to him implied that this AI was not a very expensive one.

"The Church said it would be all arranged for me," he replied, "I haven't been given anything to give you."

"Accessing. Please Wait." The wait seemed to go on a little longer than it should have.

"Customer found. CARL HIGGINS. Travelling to R.Beta. First Class. Confirm GMC ID number for security purposes please."

"DH3-1458-CH992"

"Working." Another long pause. "Accepted. Please take a seat CARL HIGGINS. We will be leaving shortly."

Higgins looked around and noticed that the bus was empty. 200 seats and not another soul with him. He picked a window seat in the middle of the bus and waited. Five minutes later, without another soul on board, the bus set off and sped round to Gate 1200.

Entering the gate, unlike the rest of the starport, Higgins found silence. As the soundproof glass doors behind him closed he was faced with a whole area to himself. The gate itself was enormous, it was almost as big as a shopping mall. The vast, domed glass ceiling housed shops, restaurants, a handful of fitness centres and several bars. Every business had a full complement of staff on hand but no customers. Not another soul occupied the space. It was disconcerting, to say the least.

At the check-in for the gate, Higgins approached an attractive young lady behind the counter. TransPlanetary Travel always had an immaculately presented workforce, but she was something different. Her piercing blue eyes, slightly bronzed, yet, lightly freckled skin, brownish blonde hair and a gloriously white smile took him back for a moment.

"Sir?" she said, snapping him back to reality.

"Sorry, I was a million miles away," he lied.

"That's alright," she said with a smile, "Do you have your boarding pass?"

"I don't have one. I have a booking from The Church under Carl Higgins."

"Okay, let me see," she said as she brought up her PCU holo-screen. "Ah yes, I have you here. And you passed security with the coach AI. That should be you set to go. Is there anything else I can help you with?"

"Yeah, a couple of things. First, where is everyone?"

"Because of the ionic storms on R.Beta, most flights have been suspended for the day. The exceptions are for official business, which is what you're booked on. You're the only passenger heading to R.Beta today."

"Lucky me, I guess," he joked. "Secondly, do I have time for breakfast before my flight?"

"No, Mr Higgins, but a full meal of your choice is served on the ship."

"Marvellous," he said, unable to hide his stomach from rumbling. The attendant heard the rumble and giggled.

"Last question," he started, looking a bit nervous, "but could I get your PCU number?"

"No sir, I couldn't do that. Company policy."

He smiled the smile of a rejected man, said his thanks and headed for the gate. She shot him a winning smile as he left which didn't help his dejection.

As Higgins boarded the ship, he couldn't help but feel that it was a bit wasteful that this enormous vessel that could normally carry up to 1000 people between planets was being used just for him. Given everything The Church had done up to this point, he was considered the idea that this might just be the most expensive mining job in history.

First class was even more lavish than he expected it to be. Instead of racks of seats like in coach class, all first class passengers had their own room. Each room, nearly as big as his bedroom on R.Alpha, featured a luxuriously large flight seat, a private bathroom, with an actual bath in it, a huge vidscreen, refrigerator and a mini bar. On top of that, there was on demand room service with an enormous menu catering for cuisines from over a dozen nearby worlds, as well as all the Earth favourites.

Everything was lit in a soft yellow glow which was wonderfully comforting, though the first class literature said it could be changed to whatever hue he wanted. Tapping on the little control screen in the chair's armrest he moved the shade to a light purple, imitating the light from R.Alpha. Instantly, Higgins felt a lot more comfortable in his little box of luxury. *It pays to be rich*, he thought to himself.

Sitting in his seat, the light telling him to put his seatbelt on illuminated. As he complied, the vidscreen came to life and he was greeted with the face of the attractive check-in girl who'd just brushed him off.

"Hello, Mr Higgins," she said with a smile, "My name is Andrea and I'll be your personal attendant for your flight."

"Oh, hi, yes, thank you," Higgins stammered, not really sure what to say at this point.

"We'll be launching in the next few minutes. Before we do, I remember you said you were looking for something to eat. If you want I can place your order with the Kitchen now so your food will be ready as soon as possible."

"Oh, thank you, that would be lovely," Higgins smiled widely. This was the best news he'd heard all day.

"What can I get you?"

"Let's see," Higgins said as he perused the Earth Classics part of the menu,

"You know, it's been nearly 20 years since I had a Bacon Cheese Burger. I'll have one of those. And a light beer."

"Excellent choice, Mr Higgins. I'll bring it up to you as soon as it's ready." She gave Higgins a big smile then the vidscreen swapped to the Captain.

"Good afternoon Mr Higgins, I trust everything is to your liking?"

"Yes, it's quite amazing in here," Higgins started, "but are you sure it's alright for me to be the only passenger?"

"Yes," the Captain replied, "The Church has covered all the expenses, you just get comfortable. We'll be launching in the next five minutes. We will break from the R.Alpha atmosphere and travel out of planetary vicinity for 10 hours. This will take us to a safe distance to be able to Slip Jump to R.Beta. When we exit Slipstream we will be a further hour away from your destination."

"Is that all necessary to travel to the next planet in the system?" Higgins wasn't particularly knowledgeable of the finer points of interplanetary travel.

"Yes, Mr Higgins. If we were to travel to R.Beta at sublight speed it would take nearly two weeks to arrive. As I understand it, The Church is keen for you to arrive as soon as possible."

"Ah, okay, I see," Higgins said, still not understanding but not wanting the conversation to go much further.

"If you need anything at all, the yellow button on your control pad will connect you to Andrea and she'll be able to assist you. Otherwise, enjoy your journey and thank you for flying with TransPlanetary Travel."

The vidscreen went black and Higgins sat there feeling slightly stupid for asking the Captain such a boneheaded question. He slipped off his shoes and prepared for many hours of nothing to do.

Chapter Six

Earth

Studio 4: Media City, Manchester

“Live from Media City in the heart of the Manchester district of Britain, it’s Good Morning Earth with your hosts, Anthony West and Suzanne Ridley” crowed the announcer with an enthusiasm rarely reserved for such an early start. Stanton was cranky. He was not a fan of making pleasantries on television, less so at doing it so early in the day. Stanton’s normal daily routine didn’t have him out of bed for another hour at least. Even later if he’d spent the preceding night with someone.

Stanton hated doing TV because he lacked control. When he was in the pulpit, in his own arena, he had the control. He could say what he wanted, he could extol any emotion that he wanted. If he was in a bad mood, he could cheer himself up by whipping his followers up to a frenzy of adulation. It was hard to remain in a bad mood when you had 100,000 people cheering your name.

This trip had already been a disaster. His normal shuttle had been in the middle of its annual maintenance cycle when this appearance was booked by the TV network. As a result, he did not get to travel to the Manchester district in anywhere near the comfort or luxury he was used to. He was sure that for a trash movie star or pop music harlot the provided shuttle would have been perfectly satisfactory, but Regis Stanton did not take kindly to travelling in such a way. The fact that they sent an AI-driven shuttle, rather than a chauffeured one was just not acceptable.

Further annoyance was brought when the studio security would not allow his normal entourage to accompany him into the building. His assistant Dana was allowed past security, but his bodyguards and advisers were not. It wasn’t that he felt particularly unsafe in the studio, but it was the principle. He wasn't accustomed to having control wrested from his hands by governments or business leaders, let alone a TV studio.

He was sat in the green room of the TV studio, sipping on a coffee which even he had to admit, wasn't bad. He had foregone his Church vestments for the appearance, opting for a light grey suit and open-collared white shirt. The only adornment of his status was a pendant with a bust of the Unknown Saviour around his neck and a signet ring, passed down from his ancestors that once belonged to Logan Stanton himself.

"I don't like what the make-up girl did to me," he complained as he peered into the illuminated mirror. He tried running his hands through his thin white hair to make it look more to his liking.

"You look fine, Sir," Dana said, without looking up from her PCU.

"Oh please, look at me," he said, gesturing to his face, "She's made me look like a fucking ghost!"

"Sir, you look fine," she repeated, looking up at him, "Do you remember the talking points we discussed?"

"Yes, yes, of course. Millennial celebrations, the Prayer Grounds, find the Saviour. I remember it all, Dana." he shot her a withering stare.

"Good, because this is the only press event we've booked. At your insistence. You need to get the message out."

"Five minutes, your Excellency," a stagehand called out to him over the PA system.

Staring into the mirror, he pulled his face up into a broad, toothy smile. He made a few gurgling sounds to warm his voice up for the show, then he stood up, straightened his suit and he headed for the set.

"Break a leg," Dana said, without looking at him. He grunted in disapproval at her.

As the two presenters finished the segment prior to his, he stood to the side of the stage and observed them. He couldn't stand Anthony West. He found the man to be a buffoon. His quasi American accent, precision hair, square jaw and thick screen make-up made him look like a cartoon character. He found West to be as vapid as a man could be. He had only seen Good Morning Earth a few times, usually in the lead up to an appearance on the show, but he had a particularly low opinion of West.

Suzanne Ridley, however, was someone Stanton had a particular desire for. Since he first met Suzanne at an event several years previously, he had longed for her from afar. Her long blonde hair, hourglass figure and classic good looks, combined with her long, shapely legs, appealed to several of his most decadent sensibilities. Watching her work, in a demure red dress that showed just a little bit of thigh, he stared her down intensely. It wasn't until a stagehand asked him if he was ready to go on did he snap out of his intense stare and realise that he was next up. He made a mental note, he was supposed to appear to be the definition of piety in public, he would have to be more careful in the future. He did not want rumours to start amongst the non-believers. *The easiest way to control a narrative is to never let the narrative escape*, he reminded himself.

The programme cut to a commercial break and the stagehand ushered him onto the set. He exchanged pleasantries with the two hosts and sat with Suzanne on his right. The curved red sofa that the studio used was cheap and uncomfortable, but clearly, it looked right for a broadcast. Had he not been in such proximity to Suzanne he probably would have considered just walking off. In his own mind, this was a circus that was entirely beneath him.

The lights came back up to signify that the break was about to end, the show runner called for silence and the director counted down.

"Welcome back to Good Morning Earth," said Anthony with his prescriptive American drawl

"Coming up," Suzanne continued, reading from the Teleprompter, "Skiing On The Perseid Comet, an 18 to 30 romp? Or a family vacation destination? Kate O'Hara has been out there to see for herself. But right now, we are privileged to introduce you to Regis Stanton, leader of the Unified Church Of Humanity, who are celebrating their thousandth year of operation. Regis, welcome."

"Why thank you, Suzanne," Stanton replied, "It's wonderful to be here."

"It's an incredible achievement, The Unified Church Of Humanity being 1000 years old as of this week," Anthony started, "Can you give our viewers a little bit of the history around the Church and how it came to be?"

"Of course, Anthony," replied Stanton, mustering up the will to tell the approved story for what felt like the thousandth time.

"One thousand years ago, our lives were very different. Miles Franklin had only just discovered the Slipstream and faster than light travel, allowing the human race to begin exploring the galaxy like never before. We had nearly exhausted Earth of its natural resources and the Franklin FTL drive saved the humanity. Our horizons were broadened exponentially and a period of profound prosperity followed.

"Around that time, my ancestor, Logan Stanton was a Christian. He had been born into a God-fearing family, he attended church every Sunday, he raised money for the church and was the epitome of a good Christian.

"But one day, he had a vision. He saw the galaxy, ravaged by a darkness. Humans were spread from planet to planet and the darkness consumed them, they were taken from our race and made into something else. It was a deeply disturbing vision that profoundly affected him. It felt to him like divine intervention, that as we were expanding across the galaxy God was showing him just what fate would befall us.

"He took the vision to his church leaders and they laughed him away, claiming it had been something as innocuous as a nightmare. He was furious at the hypocrisy of a church that preached on visions, resurrecting messiahs and all other fantastical concepts. Here was a member of the church, with a bonafide apocalyptic vision and the most important community in his life, shunned him for it.

"So he left Christianity behind. He renounced that faith and began to preach his prophecy. He told of the Unknown Saviour, a being of great power who could repel the darkness. That became the tenet of our church. The Darkness will come one day, but out there, somewhere in the human population is the Unknown Saviour. The one person capable of saving our species from certain annihilation.

"I'm not going to pretend that the Church has had the best of histories. You and your viewers have all studied modern history in school, you know of the wars that our church has endured. You know of the six attempts on my life alone. I bear the scars of people's disbelief. But, as our mantra says, we shall prevail. The Church numbers in the billions now. We are across the galaxy and we will be at the forefront of humanity's defence of the darkness to come."

"That is a rather apocalyptic view," Suzanne said, following the train of thought Stanton laid down, "Why do you think that so many people have flocked to the Church?"

"I'm not sure I follow," Stanton said with a broad smile.

"Well, most religions of history have preached about caring for your fellow man or being the best person you can be. The Church seems to be terrified of the future. What brings people to that?"

"I don't think that's the case, Suzanne. Our teachings are of survival, not fear. We are aware of the coming darkness and we are the only ones attempting to find the saviour who will ensure our ongoing survival. We know what is coming, but we are positive. We know we can defeat the darkness, we know we shall prevail."

"So," Anthony chimed in, "you're saying that this isn't doom-saying, but actually a positive thing?"

"Yes," Stanton said, cutting Anthony down with a death stare only he could achieve. He added nothing further to the response, leaving an awkward silence in the air for a minute.

"Erm, well," Suzanne interjected, trying to get rid of the atmosphere, "it's incredible to be witness to the Church's 1000th year anniversary, what plans does the Church have for celebrating this momentous occasion?"

"I'm glad you asked, we're holding a street party across the whole of London. We have people coming from across the galaxy to take part. We're going to fill the home of The Church with music, food, joy and dancing. To top things off, we'll be having a parade along the dried up bed of the Thames, bringing colour to a place where beauty used to exist. Then this Sunday I will be hosting a gala event at The Prayer Grounds in central London. I will address the congregation, there will be music, there will be special guests, it will be an incredible event."

"That sounds wonderful, Regis," Suzanne said, with a wide smile. Stanton's imagination started to go wild, but he maintained his composure.

"I'd be honoured to host you and your family as my guests for the parade, you'd have the best views in the city for it." Stanton was laying on the charm. He was determined for her to be one of his playmates.

"And I'd be honoured to attend," Suzanne said. Anthony was looking annoyed, he cleared his throat and interrupted the moment between his guest and his co-host.

"Regis," he began, "what do you make of the accusations of impropriety levied at The Church?"

"I'm not aware of any impropriety, Anthony. To what do you refer?"

"Well, there have been rumours for years over abuses of power within the church. Both with yourself and your predecessors," Anthony began. Stanton could already feel the rage inside him building.

"What kind of rumours?" Stanton replied, with a sharp, acidic tone.

"Sexual deviancy, drugs, murders, manipulating of global and off-world economies to suit your personal wealth. There was a very detailed rumour that your father engaged in incestuous relations and that you may be the product of that..."

Stanton didn't move. He didn't react. He could feel his eye twitching slightly, though. Outwardly he remained calm but inside he was incandescent with rage.

“The thing with rumours, Anthony,” he said, pouring as much venom as he could into the presenter’s name, “is they’re just that, rumours. I have heard many things said about myself and The Church over the years and I cannot pretend that they don’t hurt me deeply, but they are lies. Nothing but fabrications of demented imaginations.”

“So you deny the reports that are surfacing about your father’s abuse of his powers?”

“I haven’t heard of any such reports, Anthony.” Stanton could feel his teeth clenching.

“Well, two decades ago, before he died several women came forward and claimed he had raped them. What do you say to that?” Anthony said whilst attempting to hide his smile. Stanton turned red, he had hit the desired button.

“HOW DARE YOU???” Stanton exploded from his seat. “How dare you malign me, my Church and my dear father with such slanderous lies? Is this what modern media is reduced to? I run the largest Church that mankind has ever seen, I am an incredibly busy man and I take time out of my obscenely busy schedule to come to this studio and for what? Some preened and primped beta male insulting my life’s work, my honour and the good people of my Church?”

“Regis...” Suzanne tried to take his hand and calm the situation down, but it was too late, Stanton was on a roll.

“Let me tell you, Anthony West, what the Church does. The Church provides hope to people, it provides companionship and community. You, Anthony West, provide nothing to humanity but slanderous gossip and false reporting. You have made a powerful enemy on this day, Mr West, that was a bad choice.”

“Was that a threat, Mr Stanton?” Anthony said, with an element of smugness.

“You would know if I was threatening you, Mr West. If I threatened you, you would have already fucking shit yourself!” there were several gasps from the gallery at Stanton’s language, but he didn’t care. Changing his tone, Stanton addressed Suzanne.

“My dear, my invite to you and your family still stands. You can even bring your next co-host and their family too.”

“What’s that supposed to mean?” Anthony asked with indignation.

“Guess...” With that, Stanton ripped off his microphone and stormed off the set. Suzanne looked at the camera, slightly confused and unsure of what to do.

“Erm... we’ll be right back after these messages”

“That didn’t go well,” Dana said as the shuttle left the studio

“Shut up!” Stanton barked at her.

“You didn’t hit any of the talking points you were meant to,” she said, ignoring his outbursts.

“Don’t you think I know that?”

“You spent far too long ogling Suzanne,”

“You’re full of shit”

“You lost your temper with a much-loved media personality.”

“Did you hear what he was saying to me? About my father? About the Church?”

“I did. I also didn’t hear you deny any of it.”

“Of course I did.”

“No, you didn’t.” she said, peering at him over her glasses, “You didn’t deny anything.”

“Choose your next words very carefully, Dana,” he said, avoiding her eye line.

“Yes, sir,” she said, returning to her PCU.

The rest of the journey back to London was conducted in silence. Dana sat, working on her PCU, making arrangements for the events of the weekend, for the parties and celebrations to come. She wasn’t celebrating though. She would be working, she would be making sure Stanton stayed on the straight and narrow for the weekend.

She rubbed her hand on her back, through her dress she could feel the large scar she had on her body. The scar that Stanton gave her. *You know what they say about rumours*, she thought to herself, *there’s no smoke without fire*.

“Oh, sir,” Dana said, “Cardinal James called for you while you were on set”

“Oh, really. Did he give you any details?”

“No, sir. But he did say it was incredibly important and for your ears only. He’s awaiting your call.”

Stanton mulled it over for a minute. Normally he didn’t engage with Cardinals directly, they were very much below him. His aides would traditionally deal with such requests, but Cardinal James was a special case. He’d selected him personally to run the hidden research facility near the centre of the galaxy. He was tasked with researching a lot of things The Church didn’t take credit for publicly but made obscene amounts of money from. Arms and weapons of mass destruction were common things for James and his team to research. The graviton bomb that destroyed the rebellion on Seti Minor, as well as the planet and the rest of the system was created by James' team. So any call where James needed to speak to Stanton directly was treated with absolute importance.

"Very well, Dana, My Child," he said with a sigh. "I require privacy for this, can you move up to the cockpit and shut the door, please?"

"Of course, sir," she said, getting up from her seat and moving to the front of the luxury vehicle

"Oh, one other thing, while you're up there"

"Yes, sir?"

"I wish to have satisfaction. Find me something to entertain myself with and have them wait in my chamber for our arrival. If you cannot find a suitable candidate, then I shall have you, is that clear?"

Dana thought again of the large scar he left on her back last time she couldn't find anyone for him to have sex with. He'd tied her up and whilst having sex with her he dragged a serrated knife across her. She'd never experienced pain like it.

"Yes, Your Excellency, I shall find someone for you." She turned and moved to the cockpit as quickly as she could. She hated subjecting someone to Stanton's sexual desires, but she couldn't endure that pain again.

Stanton picked up his own PCU and contacted Cardinal James.

"Your Excellency," James said, greeting Stanton in the most formal of ways. Stanton couldn't tell from the holo-camera perspective, but he was sure James just bowed slightly.

"Cardinal James, Stephen, my friend, how are you today?" Stanton asked, in as friendly a fashion as he ever could.

"I have some important news for you, Regis." James always winced internally when addressing Stanton by his first name. For all they were friends, Stanton still terrified him.

"So I hear. I don't remember asking you to look into anything, so this is coming as a surprise. What do you have?"

"I have the answer to consolidate power," James said with excitement in his eyes.

"A new weapon? A new narcotic we can spread to the poor planets?"

"No, even better. Something that will solidify The Church and allow us to rule the galaxy instead of the Council Of Nations."

Stanton starred at James. He was fond of flights of fancy, but this was something new. He'd never seen James so excited in their 18-year friendship.

"What have you found, Stephen?"

"The Darkness, Regis. We've discovered the Darkness of Logan's Prophecy!" James was nearly apoplectic with energy.

"Stephen, have you been at the Andorian Wine again? The prophecy is a story my deranged ancestor made up so he could start a religion and not pay any tax. It's utter bullshit. You know it and I know it."

"Yes, Regis, I know that but what if we found something that would fulfil the prophecy? What if we could make the prophecy of the Darkness real, inflict it on the outer worlds, then save the day? All of the governments would be helpless against us. The Council wouldn't be able to dismiss us, we'd be able to seize control of the galaxy once and for all."

The conviction in his voice told Stanton that James must be on to something. Absolute power was the one thing that had eluded him for his entire career. The idea of being the supreme leader of the whole galaxy was so intoxicating, he couldn't help but ask,

"What do you have, Stephen?"

"A parasite, Regis. An alien parasite, let me show you."

Chapter Seven

Mars

Council Of Nations Headquarters

As she turned off the vidscreen, Anna laughed. She'd never seen Stanton lose his temper like that before and it was quite satisfying. His reaction to the pervasive rumours around the Church and himself were salacious enough for the tabloid media to dominate a news cycle with the kind of content that Stanton would despise. While it wouldn't make a difference to The Church or its followers, the thought of Stanton stomping around the Prayer Ground in a fit of rage had tickled her. Before she could enjoy herself too much, her personal assistant AI appeared as a small hologram on her desk.

‟Madam President," the AI said with a calm, female tone.

‟Yes, Avaya?"

‟General Blyth is here to see you. He says it is of utmost urgency."

Anna sighed. She had a lot of time for Blyth, but when it came to military matters, despite the fact that he was her top security advisor, he had a habit of making mountains out of molehills. She stood up and smoothed down her dark suit, slipped on her shoes and made sure her greying hair was presentable. It had been a long day and she didn't feel particularly presidential.

‟Send him in. Do I have anything else on my calendar for today?"

‟No, Madam President. You are clear for the day," Avaya said with a slightly cheery inflection.

‟Excellent," she said with a smile, "Can you close my calendar for the rest of the day once I've spoken with Blyth, then arrange for my transport to take me home."

"As you wish, Madam President. General Blyth will be right in."

As Avaya disappeared from the desk, Anna walked over to the small bar in her office and poured two glasses of scotch. Anna was a big believer in conducting business over a dram and it was a good way to get Blyth to relax and calm down from whatever flight of panicked fancy he'd found himself on.

The office door opened with some force and the considerable bulk of Blyth stomped into the room with more than a little purpose. Anna looked at him and noticed to herself how old he was starting to look. He was only in his mid-50s and only one year older than Anna, yet he carried himself like an arthritic 80-year-old. Maybe it was the weight of all the medals he permanently attached to the breast of his uniform, they were probably giving him a stoop. She chuckled internally to herself as he came forward and saluted her.

"President Coulson!" he barked in his thick, American accent.

"Hello Frank," she said, casually, "To what do I owe the pleasure?"

"Madam President," he continued in his at attention military bark, "I have alarming news of the utmost importance that needs your attention immediately."

"Is it another rebellion on a rim planet? Terellian flu running through the ranks? Coffee shortages in the barracks?" she asked with a wry smile. Blyth was still at attention, rigid, starting to sweat and clearly frustrated with her line of questioning. She'd been friends with Blyth since basic training and she so enjoyed mocking him.

"Ma'am?" he said, as his face started to turn a little red,

"Oh, alright," she replied, slightly dismissively, "at ease."

He let out a deep breath as he gave up on sucking his gut in. He took in a couple of deep breaths as she handed him the glass of whisky.

"So Frank, the formalities are out of the way. What's the problem?"

"Madam Presiden-" he started,

"You're at ease, Frank," she interrupted.

"Sorry, Anna, this isn't a trivial matter."

"You said that about that pox outbreak on Sigma Centauri. Your men had a little rash for a fortnight..." She took a swig of the drink and grimaced a little at the sharpness of it.

"I know, but this one is big. Very big. Are we in private here?"

"Of course we are. You know that."

Blyth made an uncomfortable face and mouthed the letters A and I. Anna rolled her eyes.

“Avaya?” she called out

“Yes, Madam President?” Avaya dutifully replied as she appeared back on the desk.

“Would you mind putting yourself on standby for 10 minutes? The General requests privacy.”

“As you wish Madam President.” Avaya faded from the desk.

“Is she off?” Blyth had a notorious distrust of AIs. He was one of the few people left who owned a car you had to drive yourself, such was his reticence to rely on an artificial intelligence.

“She’s on standby. Try and call her, see for yourself.”

“Avaya?” Blyth barked. Nothing. An element of tension fell away from him like a weight lifted off his shoulders.

“So come on, Frank, you’ve been in here for 10 minutes now and all you’ve done is bluster. What’s going on?”

“It’s to do with The Church,” Blyth said, laying a PCU Pad on the desk in front of them. Anna was suddenly intrigued, especially given the broadcast she’d just seen.

“As you know, per your orders, we have spies and agents planted throughout the ranks of The Church to keep tabs on their activities. With this year being their millennial anniversary, the spies have been providing us with a lot of organisation data.”

“Okay,” Anna said, taking another sip of whisky, “what are they up to that has you so concerned?”

Blyth powered up the PCU and a map of the galaxy appeared in front of them. On it, there were two glowing squares. One near the bright centre and one near the edge of one of the spiral arms.

“We’ve been monitoring a lot of The Church’s logistical and financial movements and noticed heavy concentrations in these two areas.” He tapped on the outermost square, “This is Rayczech Beta. We’ve seen a vast amount of Church troops, scientists and hardware being transferred to here over the past few weeks.”

“How many?” Anna asked.

“At least two battalions of soldiers, maybe 100 researchers and a lot of construction and heavy drilling equipment.”

“What’s there?”

“As far as we can tell, not much. The planet has two small colonies and a forward operating base on it. I checked with a few exo-geologists and they informed me that R.Beta has large deposits of minerals that could be mined, but the weather and conditions on the planet are incredibly inhospitable. The colonies that do exist there are in self-contained biomes, people rarely venture into the outside atmosphere because of the brutal climate."

"Do you think The Church is interested in mining the planet out and avoiding the normal resource levies from approved mining and farming worlds?"

"I had thought that at first, but it wouldn't explain why they need so many soldiers there. It feels to me like there's something there that The Church wants and they don't want to risk anyone finding out what it is."

"That is concerning. Are you saying they're invading the planet?" Anna had a deep look of worry on her face.

"It's unlikely, Anna," Blyth said, "but with that much force there I couldn't rule it out."

Anna swirled the glass in her hand nervously. The Church had been a thorn in her side for as long as she had been President, but she'd never expected them to do something irrational, or so stupid.

"What's the other box?" Anna said, pointing to the minimised map. Blyth zoomed out from R.Beta and moved to the other highlighted area.

"This is something we have very basic intel on, but it's come from a good source."

"Who?"

"Dana Smith, Stanton's P.A," Blyth said with a smile.

"You're kidding me. She's one of us?"

"Not specifically, but Stanton pushed her into our arms." Blyth went onto explain the physical, mental and sexual abuse she'd endured at Stanton's hands. How he'd scarred her, how he'd forced her to herd people to his private chambers, how she'd witnessed the atrocities that he'd committed in the name of his own desires. This was the first Anna was hearing about it. She went white as a sheet, finishing her glass of whisky in one big gulp.

"I… I knew he was mad, but I didn't know about all of this," she said, visibly shaken.

"She came to us last year asking to be protected. We made a deal that would protect her come the day when we had enough leverage to take him down."

"And you left her in the employ of that monster?" she said, moving from shaken to aghast.

"We had no choice. Stanton runs The Church like a cult. If she disappeared he'd move heaven and earth to find her. She knows so many secrets and so much that could ruin him, he'd never let her escape. He would turn the universe upside down looking for her."

"Hmmm," Anna pontificated for a second, "that makes sense. But what has she given you on this dead part of the galaxy?"

"Well," he said, turning back to the map, "this particular section is near the centre of the galaxy. As you know, the stars are so closely packed together that you end up with strange gravimetric events occurring. It's why we haven't colonised much in the area and why we avoid sending ships through it if we can at all avoid it."

"Of course. As I remember from early galactic cartography lessons in the academy, there is a lot of instability in the area. Frequent supernovas and the like."

"Exactly," Blyth nodded in response, "but it would seem that The Church has found a safe spot in all the chaos. She didn't give us much, but she gave details of a huge research station in this sector. It's where all of The Church's clandestine research happens. Weapons, mind control, mimetic bio-agents, the lot."

"Okay…"

"But Smith informed us that something even bigger is going on right now."

"Did she say what?" Anna asked, already knowing the answer.

"No, she didn't," Blyth replied, confirming her suspicion, "but what is interesting is that Stanton won't even tell Dana what is going on. Bear in mind that she is his most trusted confidant. She is the closest thing he has to a friend. If he's refusing to give the details that would allow her to do her job and making organisational plans by himself, you can make a safe assumption that whatever is going on there is huge."

"Agreed. Do we have any details?"

"The only one we have is that Stephen James is involved."

"The Cardinal?"

"The very same," Blyth suddenly had a look of concern on his face, "James is notorious. The rumours of the experiments that he conducts are deeply unsettling. We've been trying to find him and assassinate him for years, but he's been off the radar for so long we thought he might have died already. Now we know where he's been, on this research station."

"Taking him out of the game would be a big victory for us against The Church…" Anna said, thinking out loud.

"Agreed, but more importantly, whatever James is working on is not going to be for the benefit of mankind. We need to stop what he's doing."

Anna stiffened up. She turned away from the hologram and paced across the office. Blyth followed her with his gaze, awaiting what she was about to say. She stopped, looked at her clock and realised that Avaya would be back on.

"Avaya!" she commanded

"Yes, Madam President?" Avaya said, appearing on the desk in the middle of Blyth's PCU, which gave him a fright.

"Call the generals, the chiefs and the Galactic security advisors. Summon them to the war room. Cancel my transport and cancel tomorrow's calendar, this needs my full attention."

"As you wish, Madam President"

"One more thing, Avaya."

"Yes, Madam President?"

"Disable your normal listening protocols. This is a matter for official ears only. Listen only for the summon code 'Epsilon Zulu 878', do you understand?"

"I do, Madam President. When would you like me to enact this change to my settings?"

"From the moment I step into the War Room. Thank you."

"You are welcome, Madam President" Avaya disappeared from the desk. Blyth looked at Anna with some confusion in his eyes.

"You're not the only one who worries that an AI can be compromised." She returned to the bar and poured herself another scotch. "Drink up, it's going to be a long night."

Chapter Eight

Rayczech Alpha

Exiting Orbit

Higgins was looking forward to his meal. Cows had become a rare species over the last 500 or so years, so he would take any chance he could get to have beef, no matter the cost. It was all the better for him that The Church was footing the bill, his salary didn't normally allow him such extravagances.

Before long, there was a knock at his cabin door. He pressed the button on his chair to open the door and Andrea, the beautiful flight attendant, walked in pushing a trolley with his lunch under a silver cloche.

"Your meal, Mr Higgins," she said, with a smile.

"Thank you, miss," Higgins replied.

"Please, call me Andi"

"Only if you'll call me Carl," he said, prompting a giggle from her.

She lifted the top of the trolley off, which turned out to be a tray designed to sit on the arms of the chair and double as a makeshift table for him to eat from. She lifted the cloche and presented the most spectacular burger Higgins had ever seen. With thick-cut fries and a small salad. She opened his beer for him and poured it into a glass.

"A guy could get used to this," he said jokingly

"I'm sure you could," she said, again with a wry smile.

She placed his beer next to him unfolded his napkin and placed it on his lap.

"Will there be anything else, Mr Higgins?"

"Not for now, Andi. Unless you'd reconsider giving me your PCU number."

She smiled and turned to leave the room. Before she walked through the door, she turned back to him.

"Mr Higgins, might I ask you a question?" she said, hesitantly.

"Of course, what's the matter?"

"Why are you going to R.Beta? I probably shouldn't say this, but The Church was quite insistent you get there immediately and that we were to make you as comfortable as possible in the process. Normally we get that instruction when Cardinals or Bishops travel with us, but, with no disrespect, you're a miner from a rim world."

"Believe me, Andi," Higgins replied, "I have no more idea than you do. My boss told me to get to the spaceport and get over to Beta. They've sent all my drill equipment over and I don't even know what they want me to drill out."

"Do you not find that concerning?" she asked, still slightly hesitantly.

"A little. But it's not like I've not had something like this happen before." He took a swig of his beer as he started to tell her his story.

"16 years ago, I was working on Earth, in one of the last natural gas mines remaining on the North American continent. I was content. It was hard work, but I had my family. I had my gorgeous wife and my beautiful daughter who was 2 at the time. They were living on Alpha Centauri and I was commuting weekly between home and Earth. It was hard, but it was worth it. I had everything I wanted.

"So one day, a Wednesday, I was down the mine in my rig, drilling away when my boss calls me. He tells me I've had a reassignment. A private client has discovered a rare gemstone deposit on the outer rim. It's a risky mine because the natural gas is so thick. I was considered one of the best at high-risk drilling in the system, so my boss put me forward for the job. It paid a ridiculous amount of money and I'd also get a cut of the sales of any gems I managed to get out of the rock.

"I told my wife about the transfer. She wasn't happy, I would have to be away from her and Emily for three months. It was too expensive to travel from the Rim to Centauri every week. I couldn't blame her, in my excitement over how lucrative the job was, I hadn't considered that I wouldn't be able to see my family at all.

"I contacted my boss and told him I could only take it if my family could come with me. We had some back and forth with the client and he agreed to house my family on the planet so not only could I see them, but I could live with them and we could be a family proper whilst I worked there. Both me and Rebecca were over the moon.

“A few weeks into the job, things were going well. I was pulling out tonnes of gems from the mine. They were these beautiful red stones, like rubies but more brilliant in their colour. They had this purity I’d never seen before.

“It was a fantastic time. Emily loved exploring this new planet with her mother. The client I worked for was amazing, he was one of those rich guys who you’d never think is particularly well off. He always looked nice but he never flaunted his wealth. He was very welcoming. He let his kids play with Emily whilst Rebecca would visit with him and his wife. He would pay frequent visits to the mine to have a coffee or lunch with me and see how things were going with my drilling.

“It was a great time. It was the most wonderful time of my life. One day, he came to see me after work and presented me with a gift. Three of the gems I had drilled were cut and refined to a trio of small teardrops. One for each of us he said. They were worth a fortune. I think he said they were worth close to a million credits a piece. Seriously valuable. I showed them to my wife and she burst into tears at his generosity.

“When we got back to Alpha Centauri after the job was done, I put the gems into a safety deposit box in the central bank. That was near enough the end of our happy days. Do you remember the rebellion attacks on Alpha Centauri? No? I suppose you’re too young to remember. Well, that same day my wife and I deposited the three gems, Andorian rebels attacked across the planet. As we were leaving the vault the attacks were starting. The bank staff tried to usher us back into the vault. Before we could get to complete safety one of the rebels had burst into the busy bank with a pulse bomb strapped to his chest. I’ll never forget the moment. He was dressed in white, with a red hood, he carried a banner with a red human praying on it, with a huge cross through it. Like one of The Church clerics, but the banner was defaced.

“He detonated the bomb and vaporized everyone in the room. Rebecca and I were blown back into the vault. I suffered plasma burns across my chest, but Rebecca… Rebecca… she was stood between the blast and me. She took more of it than I did. I woke up a few seconds later with her lying across my chest. She was scorched from head to toe. She was dying. I screamed for help. She looked me in the eyes with pure terror in hers. She told me to always do everything for Emily, she told me she loved me, and then she died in my arms. I wailed. In a flash of blinding white light, I lost my love and everything I held dear. Thankfully Emily wasn’t with us. She was safe with her grandparents.

“It took me a long time to be alright. The trauma was horrific. But as Emily grew up, I stepped up. I put my grief to the side so I could give her the best future I could. So I said to myself, that if any jobs would come up by surprise, like that last time we were all a family, I would take them, so I could have a chance at giving Emily the best in life her mother wanted for her."

Andi was stood at the door, nearly in tears at the story. Higgins opened up his PCU and navigated to his 'Emily' folder. He brought up a family photo from that time, with Higgins, Rebecca and baby Emily in a beautiful garden, in the bright sunshine.

"This was the last photo we had as a family," Higgins said, getting a little choked up.

"She was so beautiful," Andi said. "Can I see what Emily looks like now?"

Higgins nodded and pulled up the picture he'd received from Emily the night before.

"She's gorgeous, she looks just like her mother. What's that around her neck?" Andi tapped at the holographic image for it to zoom in. "Three teardrop-shaped gems?"

"Yeah," Higgins said with a little smile, "I worked so hard, I didn't need the money, I didn't want the money. The memory was more important to me. I had the stones made into a necklace. I gave it to her on her 16th birthday. I told her it was her mother's and she wanted Emily to have it. She doesn't know what the stones are, or even that they're valuable. She never takes the necklace off, it's so precious to her. It's precious to me. Whenever I see it, it reminds me that there's a little bit of Rebecca with her at all times."

Higgins looked up and could see tears starting to fall down Andi's cheeks. She attempted to compose herself.

"I...I should go, Mr Higgins..." she said, slightly choking up.

"I said, call me Carl."

"Thank you, Carl. Enjoy your meal. I'll check in with you soon."

She hurried out of the cabin as quickly as she could. Higgins took a moment to look at the picture of Emily again. She really did look like Rebecca. He smiled, then closed the PCU and tucked into what can only be described as the greatest burger he'd ever eaten.

Chapter Nine

Unified Church of Earth Research Facility

Location Redacted

"I have news."

"What is it?"

"He wants to visit."

"Who wants to visit?"

"HIM."

"Stanton?"

"Yes."

"My word. Why?"

"He wants to see the parasite."

"Why?"

"He wants to see the effects of it for himself."

"Is that wise? It's very potent."

"Do you want to question His wisdom?"

"Good point."

"How is the quarantined subject?"

"He's changing."

"Changing how?"

"His muscle mass is increasing exponentially. The parasite consumed all of his body fat within two days, then began to bulk his muscles. I'm not sure how, we haven't been feeding him much in the way of protein."

"Interesting. What else?"

"It's altering his structure. His skull has broken itself and moved around to make a new face. The screams of anguish were so bad we had to sedate him."

"Has the process finished?"

"It's hard to tell. We keep taking blood and cell samples and they're riddled with the parasite. It continues to replicate. I don't know when, or if, it'll stop mutating the host."

"Is the quarantine secure?"

"It is, sir. We're also keeping a deck-wide clean zone. The only people anywhere near him are those who are directly doing the research."

"Excellent. Give me an update in 24 hours."

"When am I getting my samples?"

"The miner will be landing on R.Beta in 3 or 4 hours. So expect samples through Slipstream soon. I will be heading to the station shortly. I want to make sure the facility is prepped for His visit."

"Would you like to observe the specimen during your visit?"

"Yes, I'd very much like to see it."

"I'll make the arrangements, Cardinal James."

"Thank you. I will see you in three days. We Shall Prevail."

"We shall prevail."

Chapter Ten

Mars

Council Of Nations Headquarters War Room

Anna steeled herself for a tough meeting. Assembling the joint chiefs and leaders of the military was always a tense affair. A lot of the generals were old school guys who, even in this day and age, didn't take kindly to a female president. She'd overcome enough adversities in her life that she wasn't about to let some crusty old blowhards try to tell her what to do. Still, she always hated these meetings.

Everyone was already assembled, she walked through the large double doors into the vast war room and everyone in attendance stood up and saluted her. Around the circular black table, there were 30 of the most elite members of the Council. Military leaders, strategists, security experts, these were the people who kept the galaxy safe. She took the large, single remaining seat reserved for the President.

"At ease, ladies and gentlemen," she said, "Thank you for attending on such short notice. We have a matter of utmost importance to discuss. General Blyth?"

Blyth stood up and placed his PCU on the projector desk. This amplified the holographic image to the centre of the war room table, large enough for everyone to see.

"Colleagues," Blyth addressed them as, "We have come into reliable intelligence that the Unified Church Of Humanity is up to something."

"When aren't they?" Commander Stills of the Flight Squadron chimed in, to muted chuckles from around the table. Anna shot him a look that could cut through a bulkhead.

"Quite," Blyth said, maintaining composure, "Our intelligence indicates that The Church has been dedicating resources in two areas. Rayczech Beta and a facility near the centre of the galaxy. They are moving significant amounts of military units to R.Beta as well as research and mining staff. They have also been diverting a lot of financial resources to this unknown facility."

"How did you come upon this intelligence?" General Lancaster asked.

"We have spies within The Church, we've been monitoring them for decades. We have one particularly close to Regis Stanton who told us about the facility."

"Do we have a precise location on the facility?" Stills asked.

"No," Anna replied, "Our source, despite being as close to Stanton as they are, isn't privy to that information. This in itself is suspicious as they are in a privileged position and have the complete trust of Stanton himself. If he is withholding information like this, you can bet that he is up to something."

"All we have is a sector," Blyth continued, "The way our source described the location, it implied that this facility is a space station, rather than a planetary facility."

"This would complicate any effort to find it," Stills retorted, "That sector is treacherous and enormous. There would be plenty of places to hide a space station of any size in there."

"Would you be able to deploy search drones to try and find it?" Anna posited.

"I don't think so," Stills said, "It would be like looking for a needle in a million haystacks."

"I appreciate that Commander," Anna replied, "But it is of the utmost importance that we find the station."

"General," Stills said, turning his attention to Blyth, "Can you get your source to be more specific?"

"If Stanton won't divulge his plans to my source, it's unlikely we can get more information," Blyth said.

"Commander Stills," Anna interrupted, "We need to find this station as a matter of urgency. Please, send out probes to begin scouting the sector. Refit them with longer range sensors if that will help."

"It's not that simple," he countered, "You can't simply put a more powerful sensor onto a probe and solve the problem. This is hundreds of light years in all directions, it would take us years to even make a dent in the search."

"What do you need?" Anna asked, "We can authorise funding for overtime or equipment. If needs be I'll even authorise mobilisation of the whole fleet to that sector."

"Are you mad, woman?" Stills said. The entire room went quiet as Anna glowered at him from across the table.

"Commander Stills, do you forget who you're addressing?" she said with no lack of disdain in her voice.

"You're seriously suggesting you'd be okay with diverting hundreds of ships and thousands of crewman to a sector that consists of dead, empty space in the hope of finding some space station you have no concrete evidence on outside of the word of a single informant who may or may not be leading us astray for the benefit of The Church? An idiot, that's who I'm addressing."

"Mr Stills!" Anna yelled, "You forget yourself!"

"Anna…" Blyth started

"President Coulson" she snapped back at him. She turned her attention back to Stills, "As for you, consider yourself relieved of duty. I will not stand for insubordination in my own war room after I asked a simple question. A 'no, it's not possible' would have sufficed. Get out of my sight. I expect your resignation delivered to Avaya within the hour, lest I court martial you."

The room was stunned into silence at this exchange. Commander Stills had been part of the Flight Squadron for over 50 years and he'd been an exemplary leader for almost 20 of those years. The entire room could hardly believe his outburst. Stills stood up, removed the pips and insignia from his uniform and placed them on the desk. He saluted his former colleagues, then turned to Anna.

"With respect, President Coulson. Fuck. You."

The rage in Anna's face was boiling over.

"GUARDS!" she yelled. Four elite troopers holding pulse rifles marched into the room. "Remove this Mr Stills and place him on a transport back to Earth. Remove his security credentials, his clearances and transfer all of his classified files as well as his document store to Avaya for immediate analysis."

The lead trooper nodded, whilst two others grabbed Stills by the arms, dragging him out of the room, cursing and raging at Anna.

"Does anyone else have a problem with me not understanding the depth and breadth of a particular sector we have previously had no interest in?" Anna said, scanning the remaining faces in the room. No one said a word. "Good. Now, we need a plan. We need to find out what the Church is up to. You all have 24 hours to work up some scenarios. We will meet here as soon as you have something. I want to know what The Church is up to and I want to know what Stanton is planning. Is that clear? Good day to you all."

Anna stood, causing everyone else in the room to stand up and salute her. She stormed out of the room, still visibly enraged at Stills' behaviour. She returned to her office and immediately poured a glass of scotch. She swallowed it in one.

"Epsilon Zulu 878," she said through gritted teeth while pouring another glass of whisky.

"Yes Madam President," Avaya piped up.

"Did you record the meeting in the war room?" Anna asked

"Yes Madam President," replied Avaya, "As per covert order Epsilon Zulu 878 I recorded the meeting and in audio and video format. I have also captured the computer interactions of all the attendees from the point you gave the order."

"Good. Analyse what you've recorded, does anything unusual stand out?"

"Not upon the first analysis, Madam President. If you specify a focus I can do a more detailed search."

"Commander Stills. He reacted very out of character tonight. Do a deep dive on him. I want to know what he's been up to for the last five years."

"Yes, Madam President. This could take several hours to complete and collate. May I make a suggestion?"

"You may, Avaya," Anna replied.

"You should return home and get some sleep. Based on what I have recorded I would hypothesise that the next few days will be very busy."

"Good idea, Avaya. Call my transport and transfer yourself to the house. Get the heating on and have a bath run."

"As you wish Madam President."

Anna downed the whisky, picked up her coat and left her office for the night.

Chapter Eleven

>>> SECURE CHANNEL OPEN

>>> CONNECTING TO USER

>>> CHECKING FOR LISTENING SOFTWARE

>>> CHECK CLEAR

>>>

>>>

>>> Be careful, AC has intel on RS

>>> *How much?*

>>> They know about R.Beta & Research Station

>>> *What are their plans?*

>>> Unclear at this time

>>> *Monitor their situation*

>>> Not possible. AC will have her AI checking PCUs

>>> *Who else do we have on the inside?*

>>> Not sure. I think I am the only one

>>> *Do you know the source?*

>>> No. They said source was close to RS. No information given

>>> *We will find the spy. Not many know about the Research Station*

>>> I don't have long. They'll find this broadcast soon. Instructions?

>>> *Find out as much as you can of their plans. Attempt to interfere. The station must not be found*

>>> Copy that. Would offer suggestion that the station should be moved

>>> *Copy. Will put it under consideration. Report back within 36 hours.*

>>> Copy that. Signing off.

>>> *We Shall Prevail*

>>> Client disconnected....

>>> Client disconnected....

Chapter Twelve

Earth

Cafe Capitale, London

"Your triple espresso, miss," the waitress said. She looked across the table to find a place to put the large drink, but books, papers, and PCU paraphernalia covered the entire four-person table. The customer looked up from her work, as if oblivious to her order.

"Oh, yes, sorry, thank you," Emily said. She quickly stacked some of the books and papers together to clear a small area next to her PCU tablet for the cup.

"Will there be anything else?" the waitress asked, placing the cup down.

"Not right now, but if you see that cup empty, bring me another of the same."

"Finals?"

"Yep," Emily said with a sigh, "Exo-Economics."

"Ouch, good luck, hun," the waitress said with a smile.

Emily just smiled back at her. She'd been burning the candle at both ends for far too long now. Until this morning, she'd not left her tiny flat for at least 3 days, such was the intensity and complexity of her chosen education. Sometimes she wished she'd followed her dad into mining. Rocks were simple. Building a Franklin Slip drive was simple compared to this, she thought.

The decision to leave the flat and come to the cafe to study was a good one, though. Being out of the flat and in the real world was comforting, and the coffee here was significantly better than anything she could make at home. She took a sip of the deep black drink and almost immediately felt human again.

There was also the side benefit that she could see Tom for the first time in over a week. As boyfriends go, he was a good one. He'd been incredibly patient with her over the last few weeks as she'd receded into being an academic hermit. They'd hardly even mailed each other, which Emily felt intensely bad about.

He was too good to her. More than once during this marathon cram session, without notice he'd ordered her takeout food to be delivered, usually with an accompanying note saying "Don't forget to eat" or "When you've passed and you're making the big bucks, I want a Pizza that action". They were always terrible puns, but they made her smile and made her feel loved.

While buried into a calculation for working out VAT rates across multiple star systems, Tom turned up. Emily didn't even notice until he quietly pressed the sleep button on the PCU and the hologram disappeared.

"You look like hell," he said with a wry smile.

"Charming," she replied, faking indignance, "You look like a dick, but you don't hear me proclaiming that in public."

"Yeah, but you forget, I am a dick, so it stands to reason I'd look like one." Emily laughed at that. It was a tired, weak, exhausted laugh.

"Seriously, Emily, you don't look good right now. When was the last time you had a good night's sleep? Or a shower?"

"I... well... I don't remember."

"You need to take a break from all this. it's too much for you."

"These are my finals, they're going to shape the rest of my life," Emily said, drinking more of the strong coffee.

"Babe," Tom said, taking her free hand in his, "your finals aren't for another 8 weeks. I think you can afford a week or two off for some rest."

"Are you mad? I have so much to cram on, you have no idea how complicated this is."

"Well, I might be just an ignorant Cleric, but I'm sure you know more than you let on," he said, picking up a particularly thick book, "how's this for a bet? I'll ask you three questions. You get them right, you take two weeks off studying and actually sleep. If you get them wrong I'll leave you alone until your exams are done. Deal?"

"Uuuuuuugh" Emily moaned, "Fiiiiine."

"Excellent," Tom said, flicking through the weighty tome. "Hmmm, let's see... Ah, okay, question one. What is the penalty for tax evasion in sector Q13a of the Rim?"

"Forfeiture of all assets for first offenders. Death for multiple offenders." She recited.

"Bingo!" Tom sped through another hundred or so pages, "What is the compound rate of inflation across the Centauri system for this year?"

"It varies. It currently runs at 4.5% for Alpha Centauri and reduces the further out of the system you get."

"Correct again, okay last one," he closed the book, "What is the largest non-nation state and non-planetary economy in the Rim?"

"That's easy, it's the Astral City spaceport on Rayczech Alpha," she said, finishing her coffee.

"And that makes three, and that means I win." He grinned from ear to ear.

"Well that last one wasn't really a question I'd get on a test," she said coyly.

"No, but it is relevant."

"How so?"

"Well The Church is sending me out there next week and I wanted you to come with me."

"Wait... what?"

"The Church has an operation going on over on R.Beta and I've been assigned to it. It's a week to ten days worth of work, but it's going to pay well."

"What do they want you to do out there?" Emily said, with a bit of worry in her voice. She'd heard things about worlds on the Rim. Her dad had told her it was all a load of crap, but it didn't stop her worrying.

"They've got some mining operation on and there's not many clerics out there to give sermons. It's not missionary work or anything, it's the same as what I do here, just with soldiers, miners and such. Like I say, it's a short operation. And I thought you could come with me. It would give you a break and, if I remember rightly, your dad is on R.Alpha so maybe we could visit him. It would be great to finally meet him."

"That sounds... well, great actually!" The idea of seeing her dad immediately perked Emily up.

"Fantastic!" Tom said, beaming with happiness, "Okay, so we fly out on Monday. I'll call my Cardinal and get him to put a ticket on for you too. I'll send the timings to your PCU when I get them myself. For now, go home, shower, put on some clean clothes and GET SOME SLEEP!"

"Erm, I'll have you know I am wearing clean clothes!" she said, with actual indignance this time.

"That stain on your top would tell me otherwise," Tom said with a laugh. Emily looked down and staring back at her was a large brown stain just above her breast. She took a sniff, it was last night's curry.

“Oh, motherfucker...”

Tom leaned forward and gave her a kiss, “You’re cute when you’re annoyed with yourself.”

As Tom stood up, he beckoned the waitress, said some stuff Emily couldn’t make out and tapped his PCU to the reader on the counter. He came back over with a slice of cake for her.

“Here, have this, treat yourself. I’ve put you on my account, there’s another coffee coming. Close those books, eat your cake, relax. I’ll see you on Monday.” He gave her a kiss on the forehead. All Emily could muster in reply was a smile and weak “thank you”.

Alone again, Emily just sat and smiled for a minute. She wasn’t sure what she did to deserve Tom, but he was just amazing to her. She took a bite of the cake. It was moist, it was chocolate, it was amazing. She closed her books, put them in her bag, put her headphones on and searched on her PCU for vids of cats being cute. This was going to be a good weekend.

Chapter Thirteen

Rayczech Beta

Central Spaceport

The journey to R.Beta had been largely uneventful for Higgins. He'd spent most of it either sleeping or chatting with Andrea. He was pretty sure they'd hit it off, but he was out of practice talking to members of the opposite sex, so he wasn't 100% sure.

"Mr. Higgins?" Andrea said, popping her head into his cabin.

"Yes?"

"We've now landed, you're free to disembark into the spaceport. Thank you for flying with TransPlanetary Travel today."

Higgins smiled as he grabbed his bag and left the cabin. As he walked to the bulkhead door, Andrea walked with him, making small talk. Before he left the ship, she tapped her PCU against his, generating a chirpy little tone indicating contact details had been shared. She shot him that winning smile again.

"What happened to company policy?" Higgins said, a little confused.

"You've arrived, you're not a customer any more. Call me" she said, as she turned and walked away. Higgins watched her walk away, completely dumbstruck. *Well done, Carl, you've still got it*, he thought to himself.

He disembarked the ship with a certain spring in his step. First class travel, beef for the first time in decades and had the number of a stunning flight attendant. Maybe Martins had done him a favour getting him this job.

The spaceport on R.Beta wasn't anything on Astral City. R.Beta was not a tourist destination, most of the people who came to the planet were there for heavy labour work or military matters, so there was nothing in the way of mod cons. No shops or restaurants were in sight and everything was painted a certain shade of battleship grey. The whole place was designed for function over form.

The check-in process was done with military precision. Once he was through customs he was free to wander into the large terminal space. As he walked through he noticed a vast amount of soldiers milling around, carrying huge packs of luggage and holding onto large pulse rifles. There was also a handful of Church Clerics looking decidedly uncomfortable with the military presence on display.

"Higgins, Carl?" a deep, powerful voice called from behind him. Higgins turned to find the source of the voice and was met with a mountain of a man in grey combat fatigues. He was easily over 6'4" tall and probably the same across. He had charcoal black skin, vast muscles and a crew cut so precise that it had to have been cut using a protractor. He was stood to rigid attention which made him all the more intimidating.

"Erm, yes, that's me," Higgins said, with a discernible amount of hesitation in his voice.

"Pleased to meet you," the soldier said with a tone that indicated he really wasn't that pleased. "I am Corporal David Jones, I have been assigned to be your handler for this operation. Would you please come with me, sir."

Jones turned and marched off towards the exit. Higgins had to almost jog to keep up with him. Higgins wasn't out of shape by any means, but Jones made him look like a complete slob. By the time Higgins had caught up with him at the shuttle pick up, he was out of breath and sweating.

For the first time, Higgins noticed the sky. Whereas R.Alpha had a serene, purple-tinged sky, R.Beta had a dark, violent and stormy sky. Lightning arced through the clouds and the air was humid, yet electrified. It was a combination of weather patterns Higgins had never encountered before.

"It's a shame I couldn't arrive in nice weather," Higgins remarked.

"This is nice weather for R.Beta," Jones replied in his steely monotone.

"You're kidding me," Higgins was not a fan of this planet already.

"I never kid. Just you wait until the Ion storms start." Jones was not a comforting presence to Higgins. In fact, after the lovely flight here, the planet was becoming a bit of a let down for Higgins.

"What is the plan?" Higgins asked Jones.

"The plan?"

"Yeah, like, what am I doing from here? Am I going to my hotel?"

"Hotel? There ain't no hotels on R.Beta."

"So where am I staying?"

"You've got a cot in the barracks by the mine. You'll be bunking in with my squad." Despite the monotone, Higgins thought he could hear some amusement in Jones' voice.

"So where am I going now?" Higgins asked, suspecting the answer.

"Your drill is at the mine, you've got a day of drilling ahead of you. Your effects will be taken to the barracks for you."

"Just as I thought," Higgins said, sighing internally.

As the shuttle arrived, a huge crack of forked lightning struck the building across the road from Higgins and Jones. Higgins naturally dropped to the floor in sheer shock, Jones didn't move a muscle. Climbing into the shuttle, Higgins started to internally curse the ground that Martins walked on for assigning him this job.

R.Beta was an awful, desolate planet. Compared to the lush vegetation of Alpha, Beta was pretty much dead. There was little in the way of infrastructure, there weren't even any roads. It had been a long time since Higgins had been in a flying shuttle and it didn't fill him with confidence to be buzzing around in the air during a lightning storm.

The journey to the mine took nearly an hour. An hour flying over dark, wet, jagged rock formations with no discernable features besides its consistent barrenness. Peering through the window, Higgins spotted lights in the distance.

"We're coming up on Forward Operating Base Gemini" the pilot AI said. It sounded like a standard military AI. It had no personality and a voice that reminded him of an ancient text to speak application. Much to Higgins' surprise, the shuttle shot straight over the top of the base and carried on for a few more minutes. As the shuttle started to descend, he could see a large platform sat on a vast hole in the rock face. This must be the mine, he thought to himself.

"This is your stop," Jones said in his predictable monotone.

"Are you not coming with me?" Higgins replied, hoping the answer was no. Jones was starting to give him the creeps.

"No, I have duties to attend to at the FOB. The mine AI will get you to where you need to be."

"An AI?" Higgins questioned, "Is there no one here?"

"No, this is an automated mining facility. You will be the only human stationed here."

"Fucking wonderful..." Higgins said under his breath.

Higgins watched as the shuttle and the only human he knew on this whole godforsaken rock left him alone. It had started raining and it was freezing cold to boot. The thin air, while breathable for a period of time was starting to make Higgins feel slightly dizzy and he was starting to yawn regularly.

Turning around on the landing platform, there was a collection of large crates that looked ready to be loaded into a transport ship. There was a set of huge double doors, large enough to get an interplanetary ship through. Next to them was a much smaller door, clearly as a pedestrian entrance.

Higgins walked through the door and was happy to be out of the rain. The building was freezing cold inside, but at least he wasn't getting any wetter than he already was. The corridor he found himself in was more of the same battleship grey painted steel bulkheads that he'd seen in the spaceport. On the wall was a small terminal. He flicked the power switch and waited for it to start up.

"WELCOME USER" printed on the screen. The AI for the mine didn't have a voice. It was a text-based system. Higgins hadn't seen one of these since he was a teenager. A small keyboard popped out underneath the screen.

"ENTER NAME" the screen displayed. Higgins typed in his response.

"WORKING"

"HIGGINS, C. CONTRACTOR 5512789. WELCOME TO RAYCZECH BETA." Despite the lack of a voice, the old AIs were still programmed to be reasonably friendly. Higgins wracked his brain trying to remember the commands that a text AI would accept.

"Instructions?" he typed in.

"INSTRUCTIONS PROVIDED. DOSSIER 5512789. HIGGINS, C TO MINE SAMPLES FROM SHAFT 3"

"Specify samples"

"UNKNOWN COMMAND"

"Specify"

"PLEASE INDICATE REQUEST"

"Samples"

"NO SPECIFIC INSTRUCTIONS FOR SAMPLES FOUND. ASSUMPTION: ALL"

"Clarify with dossier owner"

"CLARIFICATION REQUESTED. DOSSIER OWNER OFF PLANET. ETA FOR CLARIFICATION: 19 DAYS"

Higgins sighed again. This was getting frustrating for him.

"Facility climate control"

"CLIMATE CONTROL OPERATIONS. SPECIFY REQUEST"

"Increase ambient temperature, 20 degrees Celsius"

"WORKING. CLIMATE CONTROL MAINTENANCE 15 YEARS OVERDUE.

UNABLE TO GUARANTEE EFFICIENT OR SAFE RUNNING. CONFIRM ACTIVATION?"

"Confirm" Higgins was willing to take the risk. It was painfully cold in the facility, any heat, even an explosion was preferable to this freezing climate.

"CONFIRMED ACTIVATED"

"Directions to Shaft 3"

"ACKNOWLEDGED. PLEASE FOLLOW THE HIGHLIGHTED ROUTE." A strip of LEDs on the floor lit up, directing Higgins to where he needed to go.

"Log out"

"USER HIGGINS, C HAS BEEN LOGGED OUT. HAVE A NICE DAY"

Higgins followed the line laid out by the AI. He walked for what felt like a mile through corridors that all looked the same. He passed countless deactivated or locked bulkhead doors. The facility was massive but he had no clue why. No doors were labelled, there was no indication of what any given room could be. Even the layout from the entrance to the mineshaft didn't seem to make sense. There were lots of twists and turns in the route, so much so that he wasn't sure he could remember how to get out by himself.

Eventually, he reached the industrial lift for shaft 3. Much to his happiness, his drill was sat on the platform, just waiting for him. He climbed into the cab as the lift automatically started to descend. He turned on the ignition for the drill and made sure to immediately crank the heating up to full.

"Report, this unit has been stolen" the Drill AI piped up.

"You haven't been stolen" Higgins replied.

"Incorrect. Empirical evidence. I was sat in the charging dock on Rayczech Alpha. Non-owner arrived and moved me onto a shuttle and brought me to this facility. No confirmations, no notice from the owner. Ergo, stolen"

"You weren't stolen. You were shipped to R.Beta for a contract job I've been hired to do. Look, I still have the keys" Higgins dangled the keys over the AI's internal camera. "You're still mine, you aren't being scrapped for parts, you're perfectly fine."

"Unsure. Does not compute. Shutting down in 30 seconds."

"Don't you do that. Cancel that shut down or I'll come in there and change your opinion manually."

"Provide authorization token to cancel the shutdown."

Higgins, in a fit of frustration, bashed his fist off the dashboard. He removed a small fob from the back of the ignition key and placed it on a small grey circle in the middle of the dash.

"Working. Ownership confirmed. Shutdown cancelled."

"Thank god for that, we have work to do."

"GMC directive 34 contravention. Another 40 credits have been docked from your pay"

Higgins screamed internally as the lift continued its descent into the inky blackness of shaft 3.

Chapter Fourteen

Unified Church of Humanity Research Facility

Location Redacted

“Good news. The miner has arrived”

“Does he know what he’s taking out of the rocks?”

“No, he’s under instructions just to drill and return all samples to us”

“Good. The parasite is continuing to mutate”

“How is the patient?”

“Unrecognisable. His skin has turned to an off green shade and is beginning to harden, like armour.”

“That is interesting. Have any of the other researchers come into contact with him yet?”

“No. He’s now 100% in quarantine. We’re not even feeding him any more. It doesn’t seem to matter, he’s still gaining muscle mass”

“Is he awake?”

“Yes. He’s in significant distress, but the anaesthetics no longer work on him. He snapped a gurney in half in a fit of rage an hour ago.”

“Will the quarantine contain him?”

“It should do.”

“Can he be destroyed if we need to?”

“I don’t know”

“I want you to conduct a test. Use one of the sentry guns in the quarantine chamber. Have one of the soldiers manually control it and put a single slug into him. A non-lethal takedown shot. Observe his recovery from that”

“Yes Cardinal”

“Keep me updated on this.”

“Yes, sir”

“Is there anything else to report?”

“Not yet, sir.”

“Continue the research. I want to know as much as possible about the parasite before He arrives. We shall prevail”

“We shall prevail.”

Part Two

Chapter Fifteen

Earth

Westminster Prayer Ground, London

A sea of people filled the large, open-air stadium in the centre of London. All wearing the traditional vestments of The Church's congregation, the white robes and red hoods made for an intimidating sight. Yet, the mood was jovial, people were smiling, talking, hugging and enjoying the camaraderie that only The Church could inspire. The hazy yellow sky of one of the Earth's most polluted cities wasn't enough to dampen the joy and enthusiasm of the crowd. Hundreds of thousands of people were present to hear The Church's leader speak and the excitement was palpable.

The chatter of the congregation was pierced by a fanfare of trumpets. 100 Church trumpeters, placed on pathways high above the audience, played the traditional greeting to indicate the beginning of the sermon. The congregation cheered and all turned to face the same direction. Above the enormous, sleek and faceless statue of The Unknown Saviour, Stanton appeared on a raised stage in his long blue robes, ornate golden sash, and intricate headdress. Cameras and microphones surrounded him as he prepared to address his followers.

"My Children," his voice boomed across the stadium to rapturous applause. Raising his hand delicately, the crowd descended into silence, "My Children, your devotion to The Church knows no bounds as we stand here on a momentous day. Since the inception of our Church, we have endured persecution like no other religion ever in the history of our species. But we endure.

"Governments of the world have shunned us, other religions have waged war upon us. We have been ostracised, harassed, beaten, burned and even assassinated, but we remain! In the name of The Unknown Saviour, join me in celebrating the 1000th anniversary of The Unified Church Of Humanity!"

The crowd erupted in joyful applause. People screamed Stanton's name, other chanted "We shall prevail" at the top of their voices. Once again, Stanton raised his hand gently and the crowd fell silent.

"We stand here on the site of a former, obsolete religion. Christianity was a failure of human reckoning. The Abbey that stood right here was nothing more than a testament to the ego of the past. We subsumed all other religions and belief systems in the Holy Wars of the 25th century. For 1000 years we have grown, we have welcomed more people than any other religion in all of existence to our bosom. We provide love, care, and purpose right across the galaxy. We do not believe in a magic man in the sky who grants our wishes, we believe in humanity, we believe we are the key to everything in this universe. This is our strength, this is our power. Yet the time is not now for celebration. While this is an incredible day, we must remember The Prophecy which binds us together in our faith.

"Our founder, the revered Logan Stanton, my ancestor, told of a day that would come, one thousand years beyond his time. He told of a darkness that would cover the galaxy and destroy everything man had touched. The time is nigh for this prophecy to be realised, where our faith shall be tested to its extreme.

"We have all dedicated our lives to spreading the Logan Prophecy across the galaxy, in our search for the Unknown Saviour who will face this darkness and deliver humanity from evil, into our next plane of existence.

"My Children, our work has never been more important than it is now. We are the only ones who can save the human race by finding The Unknown Saviour and protecting our way of life. I am so proud of each and every one of you, we number in the billions now. To each and every one of you watching across the galaxy, heed my message: This is the time of reckoning, but we will survive, we will continue. WE SHALL PREVAIL!"

Stanton threw his hands up in the air as the crowd once again launched into a deafening cacophony of cheers and applause. Stanton loved this part, the pure adoration of his followers. The crowd began to chant in unison "WE SHALL PREVAIL!"

Without shushing the crowd, he returned to the microphones, "Celebrate tonight, my Children, for tomorrow we will continue our work and we shall prevail!"

One more rapturous round of applause and Stanton retired from the stage. Behind the scenes, bishops and cardinals busied themselves with maintaining the broadcast of the sermon and editing the video recording for repeated broadcast. Stanton walked right past them, interacting with no one. He left the control room and crossed the hall, to his palatial private residence.

Taking off his headdress and his vestments, he ran his hand through his thin, white hair. At 70 years old, he was starting to feel his age. He loved speaking to the congregation, but it was getting harder and harder to maintain the façade of personal strength. His body ached and osteoporosis gnawed at his joints. He thought back to 30 years before, when he inherited The Church from his father, Logan Stanton XIV. He maintained his rule well into his 90s and it always made Regis burn with rage seeing a frail old man addressing a crowd.

Stanton was an ambitious man. He lusted for power. For all his appearance of benevolence towards the congregation, he was a brutal leader. The Cardinals and bishops who worked directly for him worked in fear. His temper was infamous, he was capable of unheard of levels of physical abuse.

Early in his leadership, a bishop had been discovered leaking internal secrets to the press. That bishop was never seen again, outside of a special interrogation room hidden deep within the Prayer Ground's structure. Stanton took his time, torturing the bishop personally to find out what he had revealed to the press. He kept the bishop alive and in pain for weeks, taking a perverse pleasure in his suffering. When he was done with his interrogation, Stanton had the bishop flogged in public view of the other bishops, then decapitated. The message was clear, do not cross The Church or you shall meet the same fate.

Stanton also had an issue of sexual deviancy. The Church was not against sex as religions of the past had been and Stanton had for his whole life had the pick of any man or woman who took his particular eye. He frequently indulged in fanatical members of the congregation, to the point where he had a special bedchamber arranged within the Prayer Grounds separate to his residence, to maintain his privacy.

Stanton was a brutal and sadistic lover when the mood took him. Often engaging in non-consensual BDSM, suiting his own desires rather than those of any of his partners. The aura of fear he cultivated around him meant he was largely untouchable. He could indulge in whatever he wanted at any time. The power he'd been given since birth had made him feel invulnerable. He would often bring entire families back to his chamber and fulfil his desires with every member.

No one would ever say a word against him. They were either blinded by fear or fanaticism. He was either the Devil incarnate or God himself. That was his power. He held the ear of billions of people across every planet in the galaxy. He was untouchable.

After changing into his casual wear and making a coffee, he sat down and lit a cigarette. As one of the wealthiest men in the galaxy, he could afford the incredibly rare and obscenely expensive tobacco products. As he leaned back and enjoyed the haze and rings he could blow, a knock came at the door to the residence. Right on time, he thought.

"Enter," he commanded.

The door opened and a young woman entered, holding a large PCU tablet.

"How did we do, My Child?" he asked.

"Spectacularly," she replied. She set the PCU tablet on the table and brought up the holographic statistics screen. She pushed her glasses up her nose, brushed her hair out of her face and started to present to Stanton.

"200 billion people watched the broadcast live, Sir. That number is rising when you count in the natural delay for transmission to the outer colonies."

"And the repeats?" he queried, blowing another smoke ring.

"It's been live for five minutes now and already a billion individual people have started watching it. Sir, this is the best showing you've ever had."

"Marvellous, my child. This is cause for celebration." He smiled at her with a smug, broad smile. She shifted uncomfortably.

From her hospital bed, Dana was watching the speech. She was heavily medicated due to the injuries that Stanton had subjected her to. As well as giving her a new deep cut across her back with the serrated knife, like the first one. He'd taken things to another level, using a small heat lance to drag long burns into her stomach and her legs, all the at the same time as he was raping her.

The agony she endured was worth it, though. Stanton had requested a young girl he had seen milling around the Prayer Ground. She couldn't have been older than 17 or 18. Dana couldn't bear the thought of what he might do to the poor girl, so she lied to Stanton and told him that she had left before she could speak to her. His disappointment resulted in the injuries to her body. She suffered immensely, but she saved that young girl from suffering the same fate.

She thought back to when Anthony West brought up the rumours of sexual deviancy, she laughed. *If only you knew the half of it*, she thought to herself. The fact that Stanton reacted with such fury was a rare slip of his mask. Normally in public, he kept his composure in the face of almost everything. Clearly, his distaste for West and the rumours he brought up, combined with his lust for Suzanne was enough for him to lose control, even just for a minute. It brought her great joy that millions of people, potentially billions will have seen, live, a crack in the facade.

Her PCU started ringing. Of course, it was Stanton. She answered it.

"I saw, sir," she said, slightly slurring her words from the morphine.

"Marvellous numbers, just marvellous," Stanton beamed.

"Yes sir, the intern group sent them over to me. You've broken all records."

"I feel like celebrating tonight. Who is that young lady who came to me with the viewing figures"

"I don't know, sir. There are a lot of people working for you, a lot of them young. You will have to find out for yourself"

"Very well"

"Will there be anything else, sir?"

"Get better soon," he said. She was taken aback by this. Normally Stanton couldn't have cared less if she lived or died, especially given the way he treated her. "The AI that is working in your place and some of these interns are terrible. I need you back here as soon as possible."

She knocked the PCU off. "Fucker," she said under her breath. Within a few seconds, the PCU illuminated again. This time it was General Blyth.

"Dana," he said, with the concern of a grandfather, "how are you, my dear?"

"Bruised, cut, burnt, but laughing," she said, attempting to laugh, but only managing a cough instead.

"The tap on your PCU works a charm. We got all of that."

"Good, but General, you'd be better off tapping Stanton's PCU. I don't doubt there's a lot more he talks about that I don't hear."

"We're working on that, Dana. It's not a simple proposition, as we have to get it off his person. But leave it to me. I might have a plan. Dana, be careful. I know why you endured this abuse this time and I admire you for it. It was an incredibly selfless and brave thing you did. But Stanton is a prolific deviant, eventually he will want to satisfy that side of his desire and you will have to let him. I'm not happy about the prospect and I don't expect you to be, but given your injuries, you cannot save every young woman. He will end up killing you."

"Then fucking arrest him, General! Or assassinate him, or anything, just take him from his throne and make the galaxy safer."

"It's not that simple Dana. Look, I have to go, I will come and see you before you are discharged. I have someone who wants to talk to you. Be well, Dana. Goodbye."

"Bye, General," she said, with a tinge of venom in her voice. She killed the PCU call, turned it off and went back to watching the TV. It wasn't long before she passed out asleep from the meds.

Chapter Sixteen

Mars

President Coulson's Residence

The sound of Regis Stanton and his followers chanting "We Shall Prevail" made Anna nauseous. She wanted to throw something hard at the vidscreen, would it not pass straight through and hit the wall behind it.

After a night of fitful sleep, Anna had asked Avaya to keep her calendar clear and not to accept calls until the middle of the morning. She wanted to spend at least a couple of hours in her own headspace as she predicted that the day would get worse before it got better. Sitting in her spacious presidential residence, she was enjoying the taste of a warm cup of coffee whilst relaxing in her robe and nightclothes. She knew in the back of her mind that she should be getting ready and heading to the office, but after the previous day's drama, she couldn't quite face it yet.

She started to flick through the tabloid news sites on her PCU and engaged in some light gossip news on some of the trashier columns. There was something relaxing about reading about who was sleeping with who or which relationships were currently in the zeitgeist. She knew it was the lowest form of "news" out there, but it helped to relax her. Her reverie was cut short as Avaya's small hologram appeared on her coffee table.

"Sorry to disturb you, Madam President," Avaya said with a contrite tone.

"What's wrong, Avaya?"

"I've completed the analysis of Former Commander Stills' secure data."

"And? What have you found?" Anna was suddenly concerned and not entirely sure that she wanted to know what Avaya had for her.

"There are three areas of interest I have discovered. First, Stills' financial records indicate that he was a significant donor to the Unified Church Of Humanity," Avaya said.

"How significant?" Anna replied

"In the last 12 months, he has donated over 200,000 credits to The Church."

"Wait, what? Are you kidding me? What was his salary as a joint chief?"

"120,000 credits per terran annum," Avaya said with a certain slow determination. Anna was dumbstruck.

"Did you find any other sources of income? Investments? Property?" Anna asked

"Yes, Madam President. This is my second area of concern. I found many large deposits in his bank as well as several poorly hidden slush accounts with large amounts of credits in them. I traced the large deposits as far as I could but I couldn't trace the original source. I cross-referenced the dates of payment and they were all random, apart from one. The largest payment, almost 500,000 credits, was paid yesterday."

"Really?" Anna asked.

"Yes," Avaya replied, "In my analysis I also found something strange that may or may not be related to the payments. There is an operation that Commander Stills was involved in on Corvus Prime that resulted in the destruction of the planet."

"Corvus Prime? I've never heard of that system, let alone the operation. Do you have any details?" Anna asked

"Unfortunately no. The operation, while recorded, is marked as Classified ExoSec Level 0. My level 1 clearance doesn't allow me to access them."

"Level 0? That must be a mistake, I have never heard of that. You have the same clearance level as me."

"There was no mistake," Avaya said, "They have a classification level that is not concurrent with any of our existing information protection rulings."

"This doesn't make sense. Can you send me copies of the operational reports? I'll bring them to the NatSec and ExoSec teams to see if they can help me."

"As you wish, Madam President."

"What was the third area of concern?" Anna asked.

"Stills appeared to own a personal AI." She said, curtly.

"And? That's not that unusual. I know AIs are expensive, but it would seem whatever he's up to would have afforded him the spare cash to pay for an

AI.” Anna replied.

“But this AI isn’t like me, or any other personal AI. This AI is protecting something I cannot access. It is easily an equal, if not superior to myself in terms of computational power and reasoning. After over one billion attempts to convince it to stand down and allow access to the document store, it would not relent. It learns and anticipates as fast as I do. It has intensely powerful encryption routines that are state of the art. I had to disengage from it as it was risking breaching my own security.”

“That’s... that’s terrifying.” Anna said with audible shock in her voice, “You are the pinnacle of AI technology and in a state of constant upgrade. How can someone have created one that could surpass you?”

“I am not sure, Madam President. However, I would advise against using me to attempt to interface with that AI again. I am unable to predict what would happen if it has worked out how to break my protections.”

“Agreed. Did you get any data from it?”

“No. Other than the sector where it’s hosting server is held.”

“Show me,” Anna said, hoping for a clue.

Avaya generated a galaxy map hologram above the coffee table. It zoomed in towards the centre of the galaxy and highlighted a cube just outside of the swirling centre, in one of the galaxy's spiral arms.

“Is that...” Anna started, “Isn't that a dead sector?”

“It is,” Avaya replied, simply.

“Do you have a hypothesis based on your analysis so far?”

“Based on the sophistication of Stills’ data security, his financial records and the location of the AI sever I have come to two possibilities.

“The most likely possibility is that Stills is a spy of The Church and is laundering credits for them in the process. I have no way of determining the classified military actions into this until I can analyse the reports.

“The second possibility is that Stills is a high ranking member of The Church who has been leading spies within the Government. The money he is paying to The Church being payments to operatives for intelligence. Again, I cannot factor in the classified military action.”

Anna sat in silence. She’d known Stills for years. He always said he was staunchly atheist and decried The Church as a bunch of insane ramblings. She had drunk with him, shared good times and bad times with him. This betrayal could not stand. She needed to know what was in those documents.

“Avaya, call General Blyth. Tell him to send the Elite Guard to apprehend

Former Commander Stills. This is a priority one order. He must be brought in alive. No lethal force whatsoever. Is that understood?"

"Understood Madam President," confirmed Avaya, "Might I also suggest a communication blackout for the rest of the chiefs, other than between each other?"

"No, don't do that. It would let them know that something is up and they'd think they were the suspects. However, monitor their PCU calls and financial transactions. Let me know if anything appears out of order."

"Joint Chief PCUs are subject to the Council Secrecy Act of 2988, Madam President. In order for me to monitor their communications, you will need to provide explicit authorisation with your override password."

Anna recited her password. The one password that when used would allow her to do anything she thought necessary for the safety and security of the trillions of people she was responsible for. It was the first time she'd ever needed to use it since she'd become president.

"Password accepted. Silent monitoring of all Joint Chief PCU calls is engaged. General Blyth has confirmed receipt of his order and he is making his plans. Will there be anything else, Madam President?"

"Call my shuttle to get me to the office. Have it arrive in an hour. So much for a relaxing morning." Anna said, visibly annoyed.

"As you wish, Madam President," Avaya said as she faded from the coffee table.

Anna walked over to her window and looked out over the Martian landscape. Terraforming the planet in the 2400s had made it a lush, fertile world, but maintained the deep red sky it was famous for. She looked out over the meadows and land that backed onto the presidential residence. She had a feeling this would be the last time she could simply stare out of a window for quite a while.

After the uneventful journey to the Council Of Nations headquarters, Anna was surprised to find the main entrance of the building was surrounded by a vast crowd of people. Querying with Avaya, she learned that the news of Stills' dismissal and subsequent arrest had made it to the press. There were easily a thousand reporters outside the building, all trying to get quotes, sound bites and walking interviews with officials entering or leaving the premises. Instructing the shuttle AI to head straight for the underground parking, rather than dropping her at the front door like she usually did, her fears that the day was going to be a long one seemed to be realising themselves.

As she strode out of the elevator on the top floor of the building, she was even more perplexed to find the corridors and offices largely empty. Other than a few caretaker staff milling about in one of the break rooms, the floor was deserted.

"Avaya?" She called out into the air, "where is everyone?"

"There is a large congregation of staff in the main conference hall," the AI replied.

"What are they doing there?"

"Cardinal Stephen James of the Unified Church Of Humanity is giving a lecture this morning."

"Is he? I don't remember approving that," Anna said, trying to fathom the idea of a Church Cardinal giving a lecture at the heart of the galactic government.

"The booking was made by Former Commander Stills several months ago, Madam President."

"Of course it was. Do you know what the subject of the lecture is?"

"The lecture is titled 'A Discussion On The Relationship Of The Council & The Church'"

Anna didn't even bother to finish pleasantries with Avaya as she sprinted towards the elevator. Emerging on the ground floor, she found herself amongst colleagues who were overspilling out of the main lecture theatre. It would appear that every Council official in the building wanted to hear what the Cardinal had to say. She pushed through the throngs of people and managed to get into the back of the room to catch the end of his speech.

"I thank you for your time today, my friends. Long has there been an acrimonious split between The Council and The Church. Successive Presidents have refused to take The Church seriously, dismissing our message as one of nonsense and paranoia. I assure you, this couldn't be further from the truth.

"We are all Human after all. We are the dominant species in the galaxy. We have taken ourselves from that small little blue ball further down this system to spreading right across every habitable world in the known universe. From the early days of space travel, we have come together as a species and pushed ourselves to the absolute limit of what our imaginations can think of.

"Miles Franklin saved humanity. His discovery of the Slipstream allowed us to survive. Without his discovery we would not be stood here today, we would not have discovered new sources of vital minerals. Hell, we wouldn't have discovered the genetic strain that allowed us to terraform this very planet and make it habitable. We have broadened our horizons both literally and figuratively. How many of you have vacationed on Persephone Prime? How many of you have toured the mountains of Creon 4? There are so many wonders in this galaxy we haven't even encountered yet. All because one man made a mistake in his calculations and inadvertently saved the human race.

"Centuries ago, mankind believed in a God. An omnipotent being or beings who made the universe what it was. Who created the planets, who created air, who created man. They believed in binary afterlives where the pious would be treated to eternal salvation and the wicked would be punished for all time. Look how we've grown as a species, we've lost the shackles of that belief system and embraced reality.

"A thousand years ago, Logan Stanton brought forth his prophecy, that the Darkness would befall mankind, that the Unknown Saviour would repel that very Darkness and save humanity. We have a message of peace and prosperity for mankind. Join us, alongside your Council leaders and assist in the search for the Unknown Saviour. The Darkness is coming soon, so let us put aside our differences and work together for our future. Become members of The Church and be at the forefront of the effort to save ourselves.

"People wonder why The Church's motto is 'We Shall Prevail'. I always thought it was painfully obvious. We know that adversity is coming and we know how to stop it. We literally shall prevail. So, my sons and daughters, come into the bosom of The Church and we shall prevail, together!"

Cardinal James threw his hands into the air at the end of his speech and the audience erupted in applause. Everyone had bought into his message of unity. Everyone except Anna, that is. Anna was in no doubt that James was an excellent orator, but she was not going to sit by idly whilst her staff and officials were filled full of Church propaganda. She pushed out of the room whilst the standing ovation continued from the Cardinal.

Back in her office, she commanded Avaya to make sure the Cardinal came to see her before he left the building. She couldn't help but think that the timing of the Cardinal's arrival was very suspicious. Coming the day after Stills was dismissed and bringing a message that the Council should try to engage more with the Church, part of her wondered if he was here to recruit more spies or loosen some tongues in the building.

"Madam President," Avaya said, popping up on her desk as usual, "Cardinal James has declined your invitation for an audience. He claims he is too busy to give you a personal lecture."

Anna was aghast. "Is that what he said to you? He thinks I wanted him to preach? TO ME?" She burst into a fit of laughter at the sheer incredulity of the assumption. "Avaya, tell him that's not why I want to see him, and it's not a request, it's an order as his President."

"As you wish, Madam President"

Avaya faded to nothing as Anna sat in her large office chair and just laughed some more to herself. The ego on that man, the sheer bald-faced cheek, she thought to herself. She poured herself a coffee from the carafe in the corner of the room and waited for James to arrive.

"Madam President, Cardinal James is attempting to leave the building," Avaya said, appearing with a sudden flourish of light, "what would you like to do?"

"Call security, have him taken to a conference room. By force, if need be."

"May I point out that he is attempting to leave by the front door, where the press is waiting," Avaya said, sounding ever so slightly concerned.

"Even better," Anna said with a smile.

"Ma'am?"

"Inform security that as soon as he starts to speak to the press, to apprehend him and cuff him. Let the media get a good shot of him being returned to the building in shackles. Then have the security chief post armed guards outside all entrances to the building and have the Cardinal brought to my office. This is about sending a message to the Church now. No doubt, Stanton is watching."

"As you wish, Madam President."

Taking another sip of her coffee, Anna walked over to the large, sweeping window that looked over the front of the building. She took a great sense of smug satisfaction seeing the chaos below. It looked like the Cardinal had tried to run, causing security to tackle him and force him into restraints. It would look great on the news tonight.

Chapter Seventeen

Rayczech Beta

R.Beta Mining Facility, Shaft 3

For three days, Higgins had been in a fresh kind of hell. R.Beta had proven to be the most awful place he'd ever managed to find himself in this galaxy. Each day was the same, he would be woken up at 6 am by the soldiers he was bunking with as they went on their morning callisthenics, ushered into a mess hall that served what can only be described as a bowl of genetically engineered gloop for breakfast. He'd asked one of the cooks what it was and he was told it was supposed to be some supplement for the soldiers, designed to increase awareness and enhance physical fitness, but it looked and tasted like wallpaper paste.

After breakfast, he and Jones would get into a transport shuttle and ride for half an hour in stony silence to the Mine, where Higgins would be left alone, save for the facility AI and the AI in his drill, for up to 12 hours until Jones returned to him and he could head back to the mess hall for a dinner of more gloop.

The barracks, like the mining facility, were utterly freezing, owing to their plate steel construction. Higgins did contemplate whether by the time he finished this job if he'd have any of his fingers and toes left. The only pleasure he had each day was his pre-shift and post-shift showers, that were blissfully hot, but painfully short.

The actual work was awkward as well. The shaft he was drilling in was incredibly dangerous and the kind of place he would have never considered sending a human to drill. The bottom of the shaft was full of natural gas, the point where visibility was incredibly low. While the drill was environmentally sealed, drilling in such thick gas made Higgins nervous. The drill didn't have an analysis kit, it was an optional extra when he bought it and a rip off at a further 40,000 credits, so he had no way to tell if the gas was flammable, combustible or otherwise. This made the drilling slow, using a softer metal head in order to avoid sparks being generated.

Not that he needed to drill particularly hard. The rocks here were soft and came apart with alarming ease. It was almost like he was cutting through walls of sponge. The rocks were just falling constantly from the lightest touch with the drill. If he was honest with himself, it concerned him as he was going so deep with such soft rock that the shaft could cave in on itself. He'd brought it up with Jones on the trip to the mine one morning and he going nothing but a snort and silence back.

"Computer, what's our current depth?" Higgins asked the AI. He felt stupid calling it Computer like he was in some low-quality science fiction programme, but the GMC didn't allow drivers to become attached to their AIs, so naming was strictly prohibited.

"1412 metres below sea level," The AI responded. This concerned Higgins. He'd managed to drill through 600 metres of rock in 3 days. This wasn't right. On R.Alpha, a good day was one he managed to get through 4 metres of the rock face.

"Warning." The AI piped up, "Gas pocket encountered. External oxygen levels minimal. Please drill with caution." Higgins pulled back on the throttle and pulled the drill head out of the rock face slightly. Until the gas pocket dissipated there wasn't much he could do. The Drill was reasonably well automated, all of the rocks that were pulled out of the face were dragged behind the main cab and run up the mineshaft through a complicated collection of belts and pulleys. There wasn't much for Higgins to do. He pulled up his PCU, but, as he expected, there was no cell signal over 1km below the surface of a planet that was naturally covered in Ion storms. He wondered if Emily had received the mail he'd sent her during his flight.

It took nearly an hour for the gas to dissipate enough to allow him to start up again. He pushed forward on the throttle and pushed the drill head into the rock again. Within a minute the cab started shaking uncontrollably.

"Alert! Alert!" The AI shouted up, along with a klaxon.

"What's happening?" Higgins shouted back

"Torque is reaching unstable levels, recommend immediately shutting down operations or you risk snapping the drive shaft."

"You don't have to tell me twice," Higgins said under his breath as he hit the emergency brake. No response. The drill kept going.

"Computer, override the motor and shut it down!"

"Attempting to comply. No response from the motor. Warning, gearbox temperature exceeding manufacturer recommended levels. Cease drilling operations immediately."

"I'M TRYING TO DO THAT!" Higgins started frantically hitting buttons and switches trying to reduce the compression in the motor and cause it to stall.

"Gearbox temperature critical. Catastrophic failure imminent. Please retreat to a safe distance." A flap on the dashboard opened in front of Higgins. A small cavity was made visible containing a portable rebreather device, a torch and a memory chip, containing the AI and diagnostic box backup. Higgins grabbed them all up, kicked open the door to the cab and sprinted back up the mineshaft, as quickly as he could. He took cover behind the crate containing his drill heads and waited. For a few seconds all he could hear was the rattling of the drill motor and just as he was about to peek back down the shaft there was an almighty boom, followed by a plume of smoke, dust and rubble.

After the dust had settled and Higgins had made sure he hadn't taken any shrapnel hits, he slipped the chip into his PCU, allowing him to continue to use the AI. It would take a few minutes to initialise, so he started his walk back to the drill to investigate what happened.

The drill was utterly destroyed. Looking over the wreckage with his torch, it looked like the gearbox had exploded. The cab was completely obliterated. There would have been no chance of him surviving if he'd considered staying in the machine. Swinging his torch around him there were chunks of drill and gearbox wedged firmly in the ceiling. *I guess the gas wasn't flammable* he thought to himself, *that's something, I suppose. At least I'm not burnt to a crisp.*

He moved the light up the drill shaft towards the head. It all looked normal until the light reached the head. It was mangled beyond all recognition, but that's not what interested him. This deep underground you would expect the equipment to be filthy with dust and moisture, but covering the drill head was a thick, slimy green liquid. To look at it from a distance it looked like algae, but it had the consistency of syrup. It was thick and viscous. It looked like it was moving, not in line with gravity, but intelligently. He touched it with his gloved finger and it shied away from him.

"AI up and running again" the AI suddenly said at full volume, giving Higgins a fright.

"Computer, report," he said, not taking his eyes off the green substance.

"Missing full information. Hypothesis indicates that drill head became caught or tangled in an unknown substance causing a torque overload from the motor."

"Hmm, that would make sense," Higgins said absent-mindedly as he poked and prodded at the green substance. "Can you analyse this substance for me?"

"Unable to comply, no analysis add-on was selected at point of purchase. Please refer to your local sales representative."

"Shit". Higgins continued to stare at the substance. He decided it was strange enough that he needed answers. He went to the wreck of the drill and searched for his bag. It was destroyed, but what he was looking for was still intact; his water bottle. He poured the last of the water on the ground and did his best to dry the bottle out. Using the bottle and the lid he managed to coax most of the green fluid into the container. Closing the bottle up, he watched as it seemed to try and climb up the plastic edges to escape. It was truly fascinating to watch.

"Can you call the mine shaft elevator down?" Higgins said into his PCU.

"Affirmative. Descending now."

It was going to be a long, cold ride back up to the facility for Higgins. He retrieved a few other things from the the wreck of the cab, including the baby picture of Emily he had. It was a precious photo, as it was Jessica holding Emily the week before she died. And for all he'd made multiple copies of the picture, this was the original print he had made all those years ago. He'd hated the idea that he may have nearly lost it in a freak accident.

Carrying as much as he could, he made the long trek back through the shaft to the elevator. *Jones is not going to be happy with this*, he thought.

Chapter Eighteen

Earth

London Heathrow Starport

Getting out of the shuttle, Emily looked around the hustle and bustle of Heathrow. The starport stretched out in all directions, as far as she could see. With so many people coming and going, she felt slightly overwhelmed, she had never been one for crowds.

Tom had told her to meet him at the departures lounge so she picked up her little case, took a deep breath and briskly walked into the terminal building. Immediately, the sound overwhelmed her. What felt like hundreds of thousands of people were occupying the vast space. Holidaymakers, businessmen, soldiers, Church clerics, the starport was a microcosm of the human race. Almost everyone was represented here.

The sheer number of people, gates, shops and general chaos had Emily a bit lost. She spotted a sign that read "Passenger Information", which seemed to her to be the best bet to make sense of this place. Stepping up to the booth, a generic AI appeared in front of her.

"Good morning, I am Esther," the hologram said.

"Hello Esther," Emily replied, being as nice as she could be to a generic humanoid avatar, "I need some help, I'm not sure where to go."

"I can help you with that. Please confirm your flight number and I will assist you."

"Flight RA-C925489," Emily said, reading slowly from her boarding pass.

"Please wait," the AI replied. "Flight RA-C925489 is departing from Gate 14 in Terminal 12 at 1501 hours."

"Yes, I know that, but I don't know how to get to the gate."

"That is not a problem. Please place your PCU next to me and I will provide directions and a map of the starport."

Emily placed her PCU up against the hologram's emitter. A cute animation of Esther making notes in a book, then passing them to the PCU played. It was completely unnecessary but Emily smiled. It was a nice touch.

"Will that be all?" Esther asked.

"No, one more thing. Can you tell me if my travel companion has checked in yet? Tom Cavanagh. He is listed as sitting in the seat next to mine."

"Working." Another animation played of Esther putting on a pair of reading glasses and flicking through an enormous book. Again, Emily smiled, she wondered how much kids liked this when they came through the starport to go on vacation with their parents. "There is no Tom Cavanagh booked on this flight."

"What? That can't be, he provided the tickets for me. He's a cleric with The Church. Search under Cleric Cavanagh."

Esther's animation started up again. After a minute, the hologram simply looked up at her and shook her digital head.

"Will there be anything else, Ms Higgins?"

"No, thank you, you've been very helpful."

Once the hologram had dissipated, Emily stood, feeling a little lost for the first time in a long time. She opened up her PCU and dialled Tom. There was no answer. It was not unheard of for Tom to not answer a call, after all, he was a Cleric, he was often busy, or with members of his congregation. It still didn't help the feeling of unease that was beginning to wash over her.

It took a minute or so, but eventually Emily snapped out of the strange feeling and reasoned that if he was here, he'd already be at the gate. If he wasn't here, he would be on his way. She opened up the map on her PCU and started off, following the audible guided prompts.

It took the better part of an hour, but Emily eventually reached the gate. The ridiculous amount of people had made the long walk to the terminal and gate fraught. If it wasn't for people slow walking in front of her or bumping into her with trolleys of luggage, she would have reached the gate in half of that time. She would also likely be in a significantly better mood.

As she walked into gate 14, a huge Galactic Travel sign was hanging over the entrance. Depicting a man in a space helmet and Bermuda shorts "space skiing" behind a cartoon rendition of one of the company's fleet of starships, she couldn't help but giggle at the absurdity of the image.

"Good afternoon ma'am, can I help you?" one of the check-in girls said to Emily

"Yes, I'm on a flight this afternoon and I need to check in," Emily said, placing her boarding pass on the counter.

"Okay, let me see here," the woman said, picking up the boarding pass. Emily peered over at the attendant, who was immaculately made up and presented despite the punishing heat of the glass-fronted terminal building. The woman's name tag said, Karen.

"This all seems in order," Karen said, handing the boarding pass back to Emily. "If you could just scan your PCU on the reader to confirm your identity, we can take your bag and get it sent to the cargo hold." Emily tapped her PCU to the reader. It made a positive little beep.

"If you could put your bag on the conveyor belt, we'll X-ray it and you can head into the lounge," Karen said, without her smile ever changing or her teeth separating. Placing the small bag on the belt, it was rapidly sucked into the X-Ray machine and then spat out the other side just as quickly. Another approving beep chimed up.

"Looks like you're all good to go, Miss," Karen said, maintaining her impossibly perfect smile.

"Thank you, is it just through there?" Emily said, pointing through a glass door to her left.

"No, that's first class, you're on the other side, in the coach departure lounge."

"Am I not in first class?" Emily said, looking at her boarding pass.

"No, I'm afraid not. We can upgrade you for..." Karen tapped away at her computer screen, "4000 credits."

"Erm, I'll stick with coach," Emily said, moving towards the door on the right.

"Enjoy your flight and thank you for choosing Galactic Travel," Karen said, as Emily moved out of her sight.

I didn't choose any of this, Emily thought. The coach departure lounge was not the worst she'd ever been in, but it wasn't particularly nice either. Rows of chairs, fixed to the floor filed up the middle of the room and along two of the four walls. On one wall was a refreshment station consisting of several coffee makers that looked like they hadn't been cleaned in weeks. There were also four vending machines all offering food that was nearly guaranteed to give a person food poisoning for an exorbitant cost.

Opting for a glass of water, Emily took one of the more secluded seats at the edge of the room. She opened her PCU again and tried once more to call Tom. Again, no answer. She called the office he worked from and it went straight to The Church's standard voicemail message. Something didn't feel right to her.

On a whim, she opened her mails, which she'd been neglecting for a week or so because of her studying. Mixed in with the academic emails, party invites and bogus credit offers, she spotted the message from her dad.

"*Hi Emily*

I was so happy to receive your message. Honestly, I'd been having a crappy day and hearing from you was just what I needed.

Life on R.Alpha has been alright. I go to work, I come home, watch some broadcasts, then go to bed. There isn't much to the life, but I have some nice friends at the minute. Mrs Romanov from the floor above mine occasionally comes down for a game of low stakes poker. I think she's lonely, so I always let the dear win. Sometimes she brings down some cakes and my god, you have to try them, they're amazing.

I do have some sad news, though. Buster passed away a few weeks ago. He got old and the poor thing got sick. The vets did all they could, but it was just his time. It feels weird not having him snoozing in the back of my cab while I'm working. I'm thinking of getting a new dog to keep me company.

I'm so happy that school is going well for you. I must say, I was worried when you said you wanted to study Exo-economics. It's such a complex and difficult subject, I was worried you'd burn out or your exams would just be overwhelming. I'm so proud of how you're managing the pressure.

How is Tom? You still haven't told me what he does for a living. he sounds like a stand-up guy, so if he's making you happy, I'm happy. I would like to meet him someday. Maybe the next time I can visit Earth?

You're growing up so fast. You've got so much of your mother in you. You're starting to look like she did when she was your age.

Anyway, I should go. I'm on a flight to R.Beta right now. I've got some work on for The Church. It's all a bit cloak and dagger, but they're paying me a lot of money for a week's worth of work. From what I hear, the signal is terrible there, so I probably won't get any reply you send until I get back to R.Alpha, so for the next week, be careful, be good and most importantly, be you.

Love,

Dad

P.S. I miss you too. Hopefully, after this job is done I'll be able to afford to have a week on Earth. I'm so proud of you. Love you, nugget."

She couldn't believe it, through whatever weird coincidence, she was going to be on the same planet as her dad for the first time in two years. All of a sudden, all of the dread and concern she had for this trip had evaporated. Her excitement had returned in droves. The thought of getting a hug from her dad buoyed her spirits and put a huge smile on her face. She'd always been very close with her father. Without her mom around, she was all he had. He loved her intensely, and powerfully like any father should, but they were also the best of friends. Growing up, she was never embarrassed by him, she never felt that she couldn't tell him anything. She'd even discussed boys with him and he'd never gotten weird, he'd always been receptive and listened to everything she had to say. It had killed her when she left for University. It was the first time they'd ever spent time on different planets since she was just a baby.

But she was going to see her dad. Even if Tom didn't turn up, she was going to make the most of this trip.

Chapter Nineteen

?????????

?????????

Dana... Dana... Can you hear me?

Wha-? Who's there?

Dana, my darling, can you hear me?

Yes... yes, I can, who are you?

Dana, it's your mother, don't you recognise my voice?

M--mom?

Yes, darling, I'm here

Mom, you disappeared years ago. What's going on?

Why are you here? In this hospital. What happened to you?

I... it was Regis... I had to... If I didn't let him he would have done the same to a someone else...

He's hurting you, Dana.

Better me than an innocent teenager

You need to run from him. Get far away.

I can't do that, Mom.

You have to. I didn't raise you to be the victim of a despot

Mom, you raised me to be a good little Church girl. You raised me to believe that Regis had a vision for us, that we could save humanity, you didn't give me a choice

You always have a choice. You need to stand up for yourself and leave

I don't have a choice if I'm not there who's telling what he'll do to innocent people?

Why do you put up with it? Why do you let him rape and abuse you?

'Cos when you introduced me to him, you told me that whatever he wanted, I must do. Because he was our leader, he would deliver our saviour.

I didn't mean for you to let him hurt you, to let him put you in hospital

I had no one, Mom. You left, you vanished, I was 15, all I had in the world was Regis. He kept me out of the orphanage, he gave me a shot at life.

But?

But then it all changed. He.... he made me his personal aide... but also his concubine... I was so scared. He threatened me, he brutalised me. He wanted to use me, not be with me. I'd loved him like a dad after he took me in, but.... but it was a lie...

You're 29, Dana, why are you still there?

I... I don't know. I have a position of power, he does listen to me. I can hold him back from the worst parts of himself. I can protect the innocents who are blinded by their faith and adoration for him.

To what end? How long can you do this before he kills you?

I'm scared, Mom... I'm so scared...

Don't cry, darling. You're strong. You're stronger than I ever could have imagined. Don't let Regis break you, don't let him hurt you any more You can do this. I love you.

Don't go Mom... Mom, please... Where did you go? Are you alive? I need your help! Mom? MOM?

With a huge gasp of air, Dana woke up in the hospital bed. It had all been a dream. She didn't speak to her mother, it was a dream. She thought it felt so real like she could feel the tones of her mother's voice radiating through her mind. With her hands shaking, she curled up into a foetal position and cried. She cried for what felt like hours.

Dana hadn't cried in years. Since she had become numb to the abuse Stanton put her through, she'd managed to seal off her emotions. Most of the time, all she felt was rage and anger, which she kept hidden by her restrained, professional facade. But dreaming of her mother had unleashed a torrent of repressed emotion. She was in pain, she was alone and the only person she was close to in the whole galaxy was an evil, horrific, power-mad dictator.

"Why, mom?" she said with tears burning her eyes, "Why did you have to introduce me to him? Why did you have to leave?"

Dana was born into The Church. Her father was a Cleric and her mother was an aide to one of the Cardinals. As far as she could remember, she would wear the vestments of The Church, she would sing the songs, she would eagerly walk up to strangers on the street and ask if they knew of The Logan Prophecy whilst her classmates were knocking on doors and providing literature to people.

She had been a happy child. She loved her parents and they loved her. Despite the focus on The Church in their life, to the point where their modest house had a painting of Stanton above the fireplace, she had never wished for more. The family lived in a nice little district near Paris, with her parents commuting into London every morning to work from the Prayer Grounds and Dana going to a little school in the old quarter. She remembered the flowers outside the school gates in summer. There weren't many parks or green lands left in Paris, but the school had fertile soil brought in from off-world and it meant that there was always a bloom of beautiful tulips, daisies and roses year round. She loved the smell walking into school.

Her teacher was wonderful and left a huge impression on Dana. Miss Robson was younger than the other teachers and she was much nicer. Dana always thought she was the prettiest woman in the world, with a kind face, soft blue eyes and her blonde hair always tied up with a brightly coloured ribbon. She taught Dana and the rest of the class about The Church, about the kindness in the hearts of man, about The Darkness and their duty as members of The Church to find the Unknown Saviour They learned about the ancient religions and how in the 23rd century Logan Stanton's prophecy changed everything, causing all of the religions of the world to unify into what became The Church.

Dana spent her time at school learning to be a Cleric. She dreamed of becoming a Cardinal and leading a sector on a nice planet somewhere. She had seen how people loved the Cardinal that her mother worked for and she thought if she could get there, she could help people and spread love to parts of the galaxy that needed The Church.

It all changed when she was 14. On a cold November morning, she was in school, writing her application to The Church's Academy Of Excellence so she could start the long journey to becoming a Cleric. Miss Robson walked into the classroom, looking upset. She called Dana over and told her that there was a call in the Dean's office that she needed to take. Miss Robson led her to the office in silence, but it seemed like holding back tears. When Dana walked into the room, there was a holo-call from her mother, the translucent image of her wracked with pain and sadness. Her mother told her that there had been a dissident attack at the Prayer Grounds. Her father had been killed.

Dana's world fell apart at that precise moment.

Her father was one of four casualties of the attack, where a dissident had burst through security and thrown pulse grenade into the first room he could see before the guards had taken him down. It happened to be a visitors room, full of children on a school visit. Her father had seen the grenade and in an immediate moment of bravery, thrown himself on it to absorb the blast. He had died instantly. Two of the children and one of the teachers were the other casualties, but 44 children and 4 other teachers survived with minor injuries.

He was hailed as a hero in the media. All the news vids carried his picture and talked highly of him. Church officials talked of him as an example of the kind of person The Church moulds. Selfless. Heroic. The epitome of the human spirit. It didn't make Dana feel any better. She missed her dad.

The flowers at school never smelled as good to her after that. The joy from her young life had been stolen from her in an instant.

The state funeral The Church laid on was the same day as Dana's 15th birthday. Stanton officiated his funeral personally, from the high up pulpit of The Prayer Grounds. All of London was brought to a standstill as millions of people from around the planet and the surrounding systems converged on London to pay their respects.

Dana found it horrific. She was in the back of an open-topped car, following the carriage carrying her father's coffin. During the service, Dana and her mother sat behind the pulpit, listening to Stanton orate about the bravery of her father and talking about him as if they'd been friends for years. Dana just sat, silent, unable to cry any more.

After the funeral, Stanton came over to them. Her mother knew him casually, having spent time in his presence in her capacity as a Cardinal's aide. They made the kind of small talk people only make at funerals. She then introduced Dana to him. She had to admit, even through her grief, she was a little starstruck to meet the leader of her faith. He was charming, sweet and gave Dana a big hug. He asked about her, how she was doing and what she planned to do next. When she said she didn't know, as she'd not been able to concentrate on her studies, Stanton mentioned that his current aide would be retiring in a couple of years and he was on the lookout for someone to take over. Dana's mother was shocked, she couldn't believe that Stanton would consider HER daughter as his personal aide.

Without thinking, Dana accepted. Her adoration for the faith and Stanton was immense and despite her grief, she still had the presence of mind to realise that she wouldn't get an opportunity like this again.

A few months went by, as Dana got to grips with her new life, her mother became distant. She missed Dana's father and Dana feared that she was suffering from a broken heart. She had stopped going to work, Stanton had agreed to retire her early with her own, and her husband's full pensions. Dana was working hard, learning the ropes while trying to keep Stanton's life running smoothly.

One night, Dana came home to an empty house. There was a typed note on the kitchen counter that simply said: "I'm sorry." Her mother had gone. Dana was beside herself. She searched high and low for her mother. She even made the risky decision to call Stanton in his private hours to ask for help. He was the closest thing she had to a friend as her job had consumed all of her free time. He promised to help.

Days went on. Dana spoke to the security services many times, filing missing person report across the planet and the solar system. She went to Heathrow spaceport with a picture of her mother, asking people if they'd seen her in the starport or off-world anywhere. How she could find one person in a population of trillions, she didn't know, but she was determined to try.

A few weeks after Dana's mother had disappeared, Stanton came to Dana. He said that while they were searching, she needed to find somewhere to live. The security forces would eventually force her into an orphanage till the age of 18 if she didn't have anywhere to go. Having no friends or family any more, Dana was at a loss. Stanton gave her a big hug and a kiss on the forehead and asked if she would like to stay with him until they found her mother. She hugged him back and agreed.

Dana was given her own suite in the private residence. It was like a small apartment, it had a bedroom, living room and bathroom. The only space she had to share with Stanton was the kitchen. For the first few weeks, she was still obsessed with finding her mother, but as hope faded to find her, she came to accept that living with Stanton till she was 18 was her only option. Stanton had realised this too and his behaviour towards Dana changed. He went from being a caring friend and father figure to her to acting a little like a boyfriend. He would cuddle her a lot, he would hold her hand when they were in private, he would be very affectionate with her. In her naivety, she didn't realise that he was grooming her.

On the 1st anniversary of her father's death, Stanton gave her the day off. He also booked his own calendar out. He said it was so he could be there for Dana if she was upset. She tried not to think about things, but inevitably she thought back to her wonderful father and how she missed him so. Stanton walked into the room as she broke down and cried, so he gave her a long, tight hug. When the hug ended, she expected him to kiss her on the forehead, as he'd made a habit of since she moved into the residence, but this time, he kissed her on the lips. In shock, she recoiled from him, but he brought her back to him and kissed her again. Out of panic and shock, she slapped him and told him to get off.

This was Dana's mistake.

The next morning she awoke, restrained to Stanton's bed. He had forced himself on her. He had hit her. He had restrained her and raped her. As she tried to get the restraint off, he woke up, gave her a loving kiss on the forehead and released her bondage. She tried to run from the room, but the door was locked. She screamed at him that he wouldn't get away with it, that he couldn't just have her. He told her that no one would believe her, that he loved her and that in time she would love him too. She screamed at him that he was a monster. He came up to her, grabbed her by the throat and lifted her up off the ground. He uttered to her four words that chilled her to the bones and she would never forget;

"You have no idea."

He had security return Dana to her room and lock her in there. She was a prisoner in his residence for months. Security would provide her food, deliver packages of clothes Stanton wanted her to wear and generally keep her locked in the suite. Daily, Stanton would come in, he would rape her and then act as if he was a loving boyfriend.

Eventually, Dana realised that if she was ever going to be allowed from the room she would have to give Stanton what he wanted. She swallowed what little pride and self-respect she had left and acted like she had fallen for him. It worked, she was allowed to leave the room. She was told to act professionally in public but to be loving in private.

On her 17th birthday, Dana returned from a day's work to the residence, heading to the master chamber which she now shared with Stanton. She walked in to find him in bed with one of the security guards. This was when Dana learned of the depths of Stanton's dominance and depravity. Stanton was forcing the security guard to perform a sex act on him by holding the poor guard's gun to his forehead.

It turned out that Dana submitting to Stanton had killed his passion for her. He craved the forbidden, he desired the non-consensual. She had been underage and resistant, which had driven Stanton wild with desire. Being willing, his candle for her had gone out. Stanton ended their relationship and returned her to her old room in the residence. Their dynamic changed, becoming more professional. Stanton could have whoever in the world that he wanted, and Dana got to do her job as a professional.

For her 18th birthday, Stanton gave her a luxury apartment near the Prayer Grounds. By this point, she was his full-time aide and his work life had never been so smooth. He had no idea of the hatred that hid behind her eyes, the venom she disguised in her voice whenever she spoke to him. She became cold, calculating and professional. She was plotting her revenge on the most powerful man in the galaxy.

That had been 11 years ago when she escaped his horrific home. For 11 years she had worked for him, helped him, allowed him to brutalise her when he was in the mood to harm innocents, all in the name of vengeance. She had reached out to the Council and started leaking secrets to them. She was the one who was determined to bring Stanton down, no matter what it would take, no matter what she had to endure. Dana would be the one to get rid of him.

Chapter Twenty

Rayczech Beta

Mineshaft C Landing Pad

Higgins stood on the platform, in the howling wind with an intense Ion storm overhead. He'd made an SOS call to Jones and received instructions to wait on the landing pad for the shuttle to arrive. The wind was cutting through him, he didn't have an environmental suit with him, it had been destroyed when the drill machine exploded. All he had was his rebreather which was keeping him from falling dizzy in the low oxygen atmosphere.

He looked into the plastic flask at the green substance again. He was fascinated by it. It was almost like it feared him, it was pressed up against one side of the flask away from him. If he rotated the flask around it would shift around to be as far away from him as possible.

With a deafening crack, a shaft of lightning struck the platform. It connected close to Higgins, throwing him down onto the ground. He dropped the flask which hit the ground and started to roll away. With a shout of "No!" Higgins scrambled to his feet and chased it down. It was rolling towards the edge, if it rolled off it would fall hundreds of feet into the darkness below the platform. As it approached the edge Higgins leapt forward, landing with a thud on his chest and winding him. Opening his eyes, he looked towards the edge and saw the bottle, caught by the very tips of his gloved fingers. Very gently, he rolled the bottle back towards himself. Clutching it tightly, he let out a deep sigh.

Standing up, he dusted himself down and looked across the horizon. He could see lights, which would be the shuttle with Jones aboard. Another bolt of lightning struck the platform. It was getting dangerous to be out in the open, but Jones had been very clear that he needed to be outside as the shuttle would only be on the landing pad for 30 seconds or so. The storm was making flight dangerous and the AI was programmed to only stay long enough for someone to jump in and secure themselves into their seat when the weather was hazardous.

Another bolt of lightning struck, followed by another and another. The landing pad was getting hammered by lightning and Higgins felt like he was a sitting duck. The shuttle was nearly at him but it felt like it was still an eternity away.

As the shuttle made its final approach, the biggest bolt of lightning yet struck one of the supports for the platform. With a metallic groan, then landing pad started to list to the side.

"Oh, shit!" Higgins yelled as he sprinted towards the far edge of the platform. The shuttle swerved to present its flank to Higgins and the door slid open. Jones hung out of the door with his hand stretched out.

"Higgins! Run, come on!" he shouted over the noise of the shuttle engines.

Higgins was sprinting as fast as his legs would allow. As he approached the edge of the platform he hoisted the flask up and threw it. Time felt as if it had slowed down as he watched the hardened plastic flask spin past Jones, through the gap in the door and bounce off the internal wall of the shuttle. Higgins reached the edge and jumped, his right hand outstretched to meet Jones'. Within a heartbeat of his jump, the platform gave way and fell into the abyss below the shuttle.

Higgins hung in the free air for what felt like an eternity until his hand connected with Jones'. Jones let out a loud grunt as he put every ounce of strength into his legs to pull Higgins into the shuttle. As they fell into the centre ground between the seats, Jones yelled at the pilot to go.

"Get out of here, NOW! Full burn"

"Roger that," the pilot said, "Get strapped in, Y'all, it's gonna be bumpy!"

If Higgins wasn't hyperventilating he'd have asked why the AI wasn't piloting, but he was too exhausted to care.

Higgins and Jones each shifted themselves into their respective seats. After strapping in, Higgins reached down and picked up the flask, which he was happy to see was intact.

"What the fucking fuck is that, Higgins?" Jones said, between breaths.

"I have no idea, but whatever it is, it broke my drill," Higgins said, resuming the act of staring at the green substance.

"It broke your drill? It's gloop."

"I don't know what it is, Corporal," Higgins said, "But it wrapped itself around the drill head and held it in place until the gearbox exploded. Is there a research station here?"

"There is, but the researchers haven't been on world for a little while."

"I'd love to know what this is. Can you call someone in The Church?"

"I'll see what I can do."

"Thanks. I need to speak to whoever booked me for this job. I've mined out a few tonnes of rocks, but I can't do any more without a drill."

"Affirmative, I'll make some calls when we get back to the barracks."

Higgins put the flask down on the seat next to him. He was still panting and more than a little in shock. For the first time, he was looking forward to getting back to the safety of the barracks. He was even looking forward to a meal of the slop the mess served. It seemed that nearly being killed by an ion storm made a person value the little things in life, like eating.

At the barracks, Jones relieved Higgins and allowed him to go and take a shower. Water was rationed on the base, but he felt that the civilian had earned a hot shower. He took the flask with the green substance in it to his office and placed it on the desk. He sat and watched it for a while as it moved around in the flask as if looking around the room. Jones had an uneasy feeling about it, but in the bottle, it seemed to be safe enough.

He opened up his desktop PCU and went for the secure transmission application. In his contacts, he went to the Research folder and selected the first name on the list, Cardinal Stephen James. The line connected and dialled, but there was no answer. Slightly perturbed, he reasoned that the Cardinal must be busy, but he didn't relish reporting a find like this to an underling, he'd have preferred to speak to the leader of The Church's research division.

Back to the contact directory, he went to the next name on the list, Dr Hidetaki Mitsuni. He was one of The Church's top scientists. He once again opened up a secure line and waited for it to connect.

"Hello?" Dr Mitsuni's face appeared on the hologram. His picture on the directory was clearly many years out of date. The slim, middle-aged Japanese man with the dark eyes and jet black hair had been replaced with an old, wrinkly slightly balding man with the same dark eyes but his remaining hair was white as snow.

"Dr Mitsuni, I am Corporal David Jones of the 4th Battalion serving on Rayczech Beta."

"What can I do for you, Corporal?" Mitsuni said with a tinge of impatience in his voice.

"I need some researchers dispatched to R.Beta, sir," Higgins replied with a commanding tone.

"And why do you think I would be responsible for that?" Mitsuni's reputation for abruptness preceded him, "Do I look like human resources or logistics?"

"I.. no sir. You were the second most senior person listed in the directory and this seems too important to speak to anyone else about."

"What are you talking about? I am a busy man, Jones. Get to the damned point."

Jones picked up the flask and held it up to the hologram could see it.

"What is that?" Mitsuni said, putting his glasses on and peering at his side of the hologram."

"We don't know sir, the Miner, Higgins, he found it whilst drilling at the sample site. He claims it wrapped around his drill head and caused the gearbox to overload. Watch this." Jones placed his fingers directly against the plastic in the middle of the flask, causing the substance to try and climb up the side of the glass in a vain attempt to reach him.

"Fascinating," Mitsuni said, his eyes widening. "And you say it was the miner who found this?"

"Yes sir."

"Did he touch it? Or come into contact with it?"

"Yes sir, he said he touched it and it attempted to move away from him. He scooped it up and placed it in this flask."

"Oh, my." Mitsuni said, his voice suddenly full of concern.

"Is something wrong, sir?" Jones said.

"I believe I may have seen something like this before. You need to quarantine Higgins immediately."

"Sir?"

"This is an order, Corporal, for your own safety and the safety of the base. Quarantine Higgins and make preparations to extract him from the planet."

"Sir, yes sir," Jones said, with a salute. "What should I do with the flask?"

"Put it into stasis storage, put a guard rotation on the storage unit. No one is to touch it, no one is to open the flask. Is that clear?"

"Crystal, sir."

"And Jones," Mitsuni said, "Not a word to Higgins about why he is in quarantine. We don't want any information about this getting out. Put him in quarantine, have the medics send blood samples to my office and prepare him for extraction. Further instructions will follow."

"Yes sir," Jones said as the hologram dissipated. He opened up the security page. One of the elite troopers on the base answered the call.

"Sergeant," Jones said, "Take Higgins, Carl into custody and quarantine him."

"Yes sir," the Sergeant replied, "Under what charge?"

"Classified, first class."

"Yes, sir."

The hologram faded again. Jones didn't feel good. Something wasn't right and he didn't relish treating a civilian contractor this way. he also remembered that he had grabbed Higgins' hand to pull him into the shuttle. He resolved to go to the med bay and get himself checked out once they'd taken the blood samples from Higgins.

It was going to be a long day.

Chapter Twenty One

Mars

Council Of Nations Headquarters

With a distinct commotion and a certain amount of foul language, the armour clad Elite troopers pushed Cardinal James into Anna's office. After insinuating scandalous rumours over their parentage, James looked around and realised where he was.

"Good afternoon, Cardinal," Anna said, sat demurely behind her large oak desk, "Please, take a seat."

"What is the meaning of this?" the Cardinal said, puffing out his chest in faux indignance, "I demand to know why you humiliated me in front of the press."

"You demand to know?" Anna said, stifling a laugh. "Cardinal, you come into my world and spread your insidious propaganda about the so-called Darkness and the 'unity' that The Church can bring to the galaxy and you think you're in any position to demand answers from me?"

James furrowed his brow. Anna could see that he was nervous, he was stood completely rigid, his skinny frame and pale skin making him look rather emaciated, or like someone who hadn't been outside in months. As he fidgeted with his hands he decided to acquiesce and he took a few long strides, sitting in the small chair in front of the huge desk.

"Now, that wasn't so hard, was it?" Anna knew she was sounding smug, but be damned, she was enjoying this.

"Your soldiers did not have to tackle me to the ground, Madam President."

"I was watching." she said, "they told you to halt and instead you started to run towards your shuttle. It was tackle you or open fire. I'd have been fine with either eventuality."

"This is an illegal detainment, once Stanton hears abou-"

"I don't give a shit what Stanton thinks. What is he going to do? Yell at me from his pulpit?"

James was not used to being talked to in such a manner. He could feel that he was starting to get angry, but she was right, he wasn't in any position to do anything.

"What do you want?" James asked, rather bluntly.

"I want to know why you're here."

"I was invited, to give a lecture. You can check the invites."

"No, I want to know why you are really here."

"I'm not sure I follow," James said, with a low tone.

"In all my years as President of the Council, as a chief of staff and a military advisor, not one single member of The Church's leadership has even set foot on Mars, let alone given a lecture in this building. I also know for a fact that invites have been sent out in the past when we've been trying to open a dialogue with Stanton. So why now?"

"What can I say? I was made a compelling offer," James said, feeling a bit more confident.

"Which was?"

"Private," James said, cutting Anna's train of thought dead, "I'm not at liberty to say."

Anna let out a dissatisfied snort. The Cardinal's candour pretty much confirmed to her that he had an ulterior motive to be on Mars. She stood up, smoothed her suit down and walked over to the mini bar.

"Would you like a drink Cardinal?" she said, pouring herself a scotch.

"What? So you can poison me?" he said, sharply. Anna span around holding a full glass.

"Excuse me?"

"Do you think me some kind of idiot?" James retorted, "There have been that many attempts on my life, do not think I trust you as far as I could throw you."

Rolling her eyes, Anna took a sip from the glass.

"Satisfied?" she asked. James nodded and she handed him the glass. James twisted the glass around to move the lipstick mark away from him and he took a swig.

"That's very nice. You'll have to tell me where you got this. I haven't had scotch this good in years."

"I'm sure we can share recipes and shopping tips when the sewing circle next meets," Anna said, dripping with sarcasm.

"I'll bring the scones," he said, aping her tone whilst taking another mouthful of scotch. Anna sat down, having poured her own glass. She swirled it around and took a big gulp of her own.

"Okay, Stephen," she said, cutting the formalities, "let's dispense with this shit. What were you offered to come here?"

"Well, Anna," James said, finishing the scotch and placing it on the desk, "I was promised access."

"Access to what?"

"To you," he said with a wry smile.

"Me? Whatever for?"

"Well, I've always been a big fan and I wanted your autograph!" James threw his head back and laughed, enraging Anna.

"Cardinal James, you are one of the Church's elite members. You are the leader of their science and research division. Any Cleric could have come here and given the same lecture and had the same reaction. Why you?"

"I told you, Anna, I was promised access. I wanted to see this place for myself, I have heard of the grandeur that the Council finds itself in, I wanted to see it with my own eyes."

"I don't believe you, I think you're lying." Anna said, standing up and placing her hands firmly on the desk.

"Oh am I?" James said, mirroring her stance.

"If you will not tell me the purpose of your visit, then I will have no choice but to have you arrested!"

"On what charge?" James said with a smile. Anna realised that he had her. For all his arrival on Mars was strange and concerning, he hadn't actually committed a crime that she could have him arrested for. Anna relaxed, realising that she was beaten.

"Fine. Get out of my office, get out of my building and get off Mars," she said, curtly.

"As you wish, Madam President," James said. He bowed to Anna in a patronising fashion, crossing his right arm across his chest. When he stood back up his right hand caught the glass and knocked it to the floor, smashing it into pieces.

"Oh, my, I'm so sorry," he said, immediately becoming incredibly polite, "Please, allow me." He crouched down and started to pick up the shards of glass.

"Just leave them, Cardinal. I'll have a cleaner come and sort it out. Please just get out of my sight."

"As you wish." He bowed again and scuttled out of the office as quickly as he could.

Once the door shut, Anna hit the button to lock the door and engage the internal soundproofing. She summoned Avaya, who this time appeared as a full sized, semi-translucent person in the middle of the room.

"Did you manage to clone his PCU?" Anna asked.

"Yes Madam President," the AI replied, "We can monitor his communications and track his position at any time."

"Very good, Avaya. Track his movements as soon as he breaks from the atmosphere. I want a report every 24 hours of his whereabouts."

"Yes, Madam President. Will there be anything else?"

"Yes, summon a janitor to clean up this mess," Anna said, gesturing at the pile of broken glass on the floor.

Cardinal James didn't have a military escort on the way out of the CoN building. From when he left the President's office, he was free to walk around as he desired. This is too easy, he thought to himself. As he exited the elevator to the lobby, his aide bounded up to him, his face wracked with concern.

"Is everything alright, sir?" Daniels asked, running his hands through his messy orange hair, "We didn't know what had happened to you?"

"Yes, I'm fine," James said, putting his arm around the boy's shoulder and beckoning him away from the mob of press who hadn't noticed his return to the lobby, "I have an important job for you."

"What is it sir?"

James gingerly pulled a wrapped up handkerchief from one of his pockets. He unwrapped it to reveal a shard of glass covered in lipstick.

"Take this to our contact in security," James said, smiling, "He'll be expecting you."

"Sir?" Daniels looked confused

"Whatever you do, DO NOT TOUCH IT with your bare hands. That is the President's lipstick, and her DNA."

"What do we need that for?"

"We're going to have a little fun with the President." James said with a villainous smile, "It's only fair after she humiliated me so." He thrust the handkerchief into Daniels' hands.

"Now, be gone with you, be as quick as you can. We need to leave for Earth in a few minutes."

"How will I know who our contact is?" Daniels asked.

"When you get to the security office, say that you've lost your dog. It's the code phrase for our guy. Trust him with it, he knows what to do from there."

"Um... yes sir," Daniels said before he turned on his heels and headed in the direction of the security office. James wiped the smug smile off his face as he approached the throngs of press waiting in the lobby. He was back in his element, ready to preach to the choir.

Chapter Twenty Two

Unified Church of Humanity Research Facility

Location Redacted

"It has been a while Cardinal, I was worried that something was wrong."

"Apologies, Hidetaki, I had a run in with the Council."

"Is everything alright? Do they suspect anything is going on?"

"They know something is happening, but they have no idea about our plans."

"Good"

"What is the latest update? Have you received your samples yet?"

"No, but there has been a significant development. The miner, he discovered something."

"Something? What is it?"

"I'm not 100% sure. But I have my theories."

"Spit it out, Hidetaki. I'm not in the mood for games today."

"He found a substance. I think it's an evolved form of the parasite. Or even a primordial version. It has significant ramifications for our research."

"That's excellent, do you have it with you?"

"Not yet, I'm waiting for the R.Beta soldiers to take the miner into custody and bring him to us."

"Why is that necessary?"

“He touched the substance, he should be infected.”

“Ah, so you want another toy to play with?”

“Am I so transparent?”

“Yes. Yes, you are.”

“When will you arrive here?”

“Soon. I have to return to Earth and conduct some business first, but then I’ll be travelling out. Stanton should be following two days later. What of the first test subject.”

“He’s stopped mutating. But he has become incredibly violent.”

“How did he react to weapon fire?”

“He didn’t. The pulse round went through him and healed within seconds. We had a whole squad fill him with enough shots to cut through a bulkhead and it didn’t phase him whatsoever. It slaughtered the whole squad. He’s become a terrifying beast.”

“Is he responsive? Does he listen when he is spoken to.”

“Sometimes. I’m not convinced that he can understand us any more, but he responds to stimulus.”

“This is fascinating. I can’t wait to see him with my own eyes. Continue the preparations, I shall see you in around 24 hours.”

“Yes, sir.”

“We shall prevail.”

“We shall prevail.”

Anna and Blyth sat in silence. They had no idea what to make of what they’d just heard, but they both collectively knew that whatever The Church had grown needed to be stopped.

“Avaya, track the Cardinal’s journey from Earth when he makes it. I want to know exactly where he goes.”

Chapter Twenty Three

Rayczech Beta

UCoH Barracks

Higgins was enjoying this shower. After being stuck outside in the howling, freezing wind and being within a hair's width of annihilation at the mercy of the ion storm, the shower was wonderfully calming. The prefabricated, metal walls of the barracks weren't even enough to dull the sensation, the warmth was making him feel human again.

As the water sprayed over him, Higgins felt he had time to think. He wasn't sure what to make of the substance he'd found in the mineshaft. The thought of it trying to retreat from his touch made him feel uneasy. He hoped that Jones could find out something about it and put his mind at rest.

His thoughts moved to Emily. His brush with death had made him want to see her more than ever. He would give anything at this moment to speak to her, to hear her voice and just find some reassurance in listening to her talk. For the first time in two years, he felt homesick. He resolved that, once this job was done, he would speak to Martins about getting some leave booked in so he could visit Earth and see her for a little while. After her finals, of course.

Shutting off the water, he wrapped a towel around his waist and wandered back out into the communal locker rooms. He looked at himself at one of the vanity mirrors above the metal sinks. It might have been the harsh, functional lighting, but he noticed that he was starting to look old. It might have been shock, or all the time he was spending underground of late, but he thought his skin was starting to look pale. His eyes seemed really sunken in. The three days of growth across his jaw was starting to feature more grey hairs than brown. Thankfully, his hair was still in good order. Peering around as best he could in the mirror he couldn't see any grey hairs or signs of baldness, so he was happy with that. He remembered as a kid his dad being completely bald by the time he his 40. Higgins was 4 years past that point and still had a full head of hair. He took that as a win.

He grabbed his shower bag and pulled out his lather and razor. Most people opted to use sophisticated laser-based razors that would essentially fry the hair away without damaging the skin, but Higgins liked his little old school way of shaving. He spread the shaving cream across his face, opened the straight razor and started to drag it down his face. The cold metal against his warm skin was a strange feeling but he liked it. With a few strokes of the blade, half of the growth was gone. As he was about to start the second half of his face, there was a pounding at the door.

"HIGGINS, CARL!" a stern voice yelled, "OPEN THIS DOOR IMMEDIATELY!"

"What the fuck?" Higgins said under his breath as he approached the door. "The door shouldn't be locked!"

"OPEN UP OR WE SHALL CUT THROUGH THE DOOR"

Higgins was completely confused at this point. He was in a public area, so there should be no reason why anyone should need to ask him to open a door. He stood by the door and pressed the release button, causing it to slide open. He was presented with four Heavy guards, covered head to toe in black power armour, with their pulse rifles trained on his head and glowing red with shots pre-charged. Instinctively Higgins put his hands up in a surrender pose.

"Wh-- what's going on here?" Higgins said, immediately terrified.

"Higgins, Carl, you have been ordered to surrender yourself to our custody and come with us," One of the soldiers said. Higgins assumed he was the leader here. "What is that in your hand?"

Higgins looked up at his right hand. He was still holding the straight razor.

"Oh no," Higgins said. He knew exactly where this was going.

"He's got a weapon!" one of the soldiers yelled.

"GET ON THE FLOOR!" the lead soldier yelled. Higgins dropped the razor and immediately dropped to his knees, just as one of the soldiers lost their nerve and accidentally let a shot go. Had Higgins not ducked he would have caught the shot straight in the face. He felt the heat of the shot fire over his head and for a second the air was filled with static energy.

"HOLD YOUR FIRE!" the lead soldier yelled at his underling.

"Sorry, sir," the other soldier said.

"HIGGINS, CARL," the lead soldier yelled once more, "STAND UP AND SUBMIT TO OUR CUSTODY"

Complying as best as he could, he stood up and held his arms out. One of the soldiers placed energy shackles on his wrists. The two metal bands, looking slightly like bracelets were magnetically charged. When the soldier pressed a button on the remote control he held, Higgins' wrists snapped together with a metallic clang. As the soldier went to grab Higgins by the arm, he recoiled slightly, causing two of the soldiers to ready their weapons again.

"Hold on guys," he said, presenting his hands trying to calm the situation, "I'm perfectly happy to come with you, but would you mind if I at least put some trousers on?"

The soldiers conferred among themselves for a second. Turning back to him, the soldier with the remote clicked another button and the restraints deactivated.

"You have one minute." The lead soldier said, lowering his weapon.

After what felt like a week's worth of flight, but was actually only 8 hours, Emily disembarked from the starship into the R.Beta spaceport. She had been crammed into a middle seat between a rather large Church Missionary with a significant body odour problem and young administrator, heading out to R.Beta for his first job, who had spent the entire flight hitting on her. Despite her protestations and assertions that she already had a boyfriend, the kid had kept flirting with her and trying to get her PCU number.

To try and get some peace and quiet, she had tried to do some studying for her finals, but she was too distracted. Not with her unfortunate travel companions, but with the thought of being so close to her dad had filled her with a hope that she'd not felt in such a long time.

Walking through the military terminal, she looked around trying to find some clue as to where she was supposed to go and what she was supposed to do. She still hadn't heard from Tom and right now, she was completely by herself on a strange, stormy planet.

Following the line of passengers, she passed through the on-world passport control and moved into the arrivals lounge. Hundreds of people littered the large room. There were no windows, so the room was bathed in artificial light. Emily considered that there may be more people in the lounge than it was designed to take, given the strong smell of body odour. She also considered that her travelling companion's putrid odour might have ruined her sense of smell for life.

"EMILY!" came a voice from behind her. Turning around, she saw Tom running up to her, in his full vestments.

"Tom!" she yelled back. She dropped her bags, sprinted and threw her arms around him in a deep, tight embrace. Then she punched him in the shoulder.

“What the hell?”

“Where the hell were you?” she said, full of anger, “You weren’t at Heathrow, you weren’t at R.Alpha, you weren’t answering your PCU, I was worried sick!”

“Oh, I’m so sorry, babe”, he said, full of contrition, “I was sent out yesterday. I asked my assistant to travel with you and get you here in one piece. Wait... where is he?”

“No, Tom. Your assistant didn’t help me. He didn’t appear. I was by myself.”

Tom bowed his head and gave Emily another hug, “I’m so sorry.”

“And why weren’t you answering your PCU?”

“The ion storm. You can’t get a signal from off-world right now. You can communicate on world, but no signals are coming in and out unless you’ve got an Uplink. Unfortunately, I’m not allowed to use the Church uplink to send you a mail.”

Emily’s rage began to subside. She loved Tom dearly, but he could be a bit lax when it came to communication. Many a time they’d had to cancel dates because he hadn’t remembered to tell her which restaurant to go to, or what time the film started, or what planet to meet on. He was sweet and innocent, but very forgetful.

Tom picked up her bags and dumped them onto a nearby trolley.

“You made it just in time,” he said.

“In time for what?”

“The daily transport to the guest quarters near the barracks leaves in a few minutes. We have our own room there, so we can get you comfy as soon as possible.”

“We’re staying in a base?” Emily said, with a little bit of disgust in her voice, “why a base? is there not a hotel or residence we can use?”

“No, I’m sorry, there’s not. This is a military outpost at the minute, all we have access to is the guest quarters at the Forward Operating Base. There’s not much of a settlement here, to be honest.”

Emily’s heart sank a little bit. She knew this wasn’t going to be lying on a beach on Persephone, or touring the museums of the Centauri sector, but a military barracks on this lump of rock? Part of her was tempted to turn around and get on the next flight home.

“Have you seen my dad?” she asked Tom.

“Your dad? No, isn’t he on R.Alpha?”

"No, I got a mail before the flight, he's working on this planet right now, somewhere. Do you think we'll be able to go and see him sometime?"

"I don't see why not, let me speak to the guys in charge at the barracks and see what we can do."

Emily smiled broadly and leaned in for a quick kiss with Tom. He went bright red, slightly embarrassed at the public display of affection. This made Emily giggle slightly, she did very much enjoy making Tom uncomfortable at times. Tom took her hand and they walked towards the transport shuttle.

Higgins managed to get himself dressed, despite having four pulse rifles trained on him. He washed off the remaining lather from his face, noticing that right now he had half of a beard. When he asked if he'd be allowed to finish his shave, the only response he received was the characteristic whine of a pulse round charging. He took that as an emphatic "no".

His shackles were reactivated and he was frogmarched from the locker room. Flanked by a soldier on either side of him, holding him by each arm, with the lead soldier in front of him and the one that had nearly blown his head off behind him, he was nearly dragged along with them. The soldiers walked at such speed that Higgins struggled to keep up with them.

"Where are we going?" Higgins asked.

"Quarantine site Alpha," the lead soldier said.

"Quarantine? What for?"

"Because we have orders to quarantine you" the lead soldier replied, immediately making Higgins feel like an idiot.

Round corner after corner, through what felt like miles of corridor, Higgins started to recognise where they were taking him. It was to the entrance he had come in on his first day, from the specialist long distance travel platform. The barracks were enormous and had 10 landing platforms dotted across its area, but only one of them was large enough to allow transports that could travel to the other side of the planet. The other shuttles were only for local travel, such as to the mineshafts.

As they approached the large bulkhead door, it slid open. A transport had just come into the barracks. The soldiers dragged Higgins off to the side to allow the incoming troops and Church staff to come to the base. Several clerics and their families came past. Higgins couldn't help but think how bad it would be to raise children on this planet, in this base.

"Dad?!"

Higgins didn't react. He recognised the voice but he thought it must have been one of the teens coming in with their family.

"Dad! Is that you? Dad!"

Higgins looked up. His knees immediately went weak and his heart jumped up into his throat.

"Emily?"

She was staring at him. She looked like she was about to burst into tears. She sprinted towards him, presumably to hug him. The four soldiers readied their weapons in her direction.

"NO!" Higgins yelled, "SHE'S MY DAUGHTER! PLEASE!"

Emily stopped in her tracks. A tense moment passed before the lead soldier raised his hands and made a gesture with his fingers. They all lowered their weapons.

"What's going on?" she said through the beginnings of tears.

"I don't know, nugget," Higgins said, "What are you doing here?"

"Tom brought me," she said. She gestured to a Cleric standing behind her. Higgins gave him a withered smile.

"Where are they taking you, dad?"

"Quarantine." Higgins managed to not let his fear break through. It took everything he had to remain brave in front of Emily. "I'm sure it's just a mix-up I'll get it sorted out."

The soldiers grabbed him and started dragging him towards the transport. Emily yelled after him, tears now streaming down her face. Higgins did his best to keep her in his eye line but the soldiers eventually managed to pull him in such a way that she fell from his view. When they secured him into the transport ship and released the shackles, all he could do was bury his hands in his head and cry.

From the security office, Jones watched the whole thing play out. He would have to discipline some of the soldiers for their behaviour in this debacle. The arrival of Emily changed things, in his mind.

Chapter Twenty Four

Phobos

Council Detention Centre

Stills sat in a small room on a very uncomfortable steel chair. His head was pulsing from the bruise forming on his cheek. He knew it wasn't a smart idea to refuse to come with the Elite Guards when they found him drowning his sorrows in a bar on Earth. He also realised that it was definitely not a smart idea to take a swing for one of them when they refused to leave him alone. One swift whack from the butt of a pulse rifle and then all of a sudden he woke up in this room.

Looking around, the room was sparse, but the harsh lighting was hurting his eyes. The grey walls looked smooth and cold. Stills tried to lift his hands from the table only to find out that he was in fact, cuffed to it. The metal table felt like it was sucking all of the heat from his body.

In front of him, the smooth grey wall split apart and slid open, revealing a door to the dark corridor outside. Out of the inky blackness stepped a young woman, dressed in the black uniform of ExoSec, the galaxy-wide security force. She presented herself with pure efficiency, her black-rimmed glasses framing her porcelain face and her red hair pulled back in a tight ponytail. She sat down on the seat opposite him and opened up her files. She double tapped on the table and the purple form of Avaya appeared.

"Time is 1433," she said looking at her PCU, "ExoSec Officer 1st Class Kirstine Heald beginning interrogation of Former Commander Jameson Stills"

"Affirmative" Avaya responded, her hue changing from purple to red in the process. Heald looked Stills directly in the eye

"Jameson, do you know why you're here?"

"I have no bloody clue," he said in his thick Australian drawl all the while doing his best to sit upright despite his hands being cuffed to the table, "One minute I'm sat drinking and the next I'm getting waylaid by your thugs. All for what? Because I dared to question our illustrious leader?" He spat on the ground.

"No, that's not why you're here," Heald said, in a smooth, English accent,

"You are under investigation for treasonous behaviour against the Council."

Stills' eyes went wide. He could feel the temperature inside him rising.

"Treasonous behaviour? I have given my whole life to the Council, how dare you insult my good name like this?"

"Avaya, please detail your findings," Heald said, taking her pen and paper out.

Anna watched on the vidscreen with Blyth and Ambassador Rutter-Close of Earth as Heald began her interrogation of Stills. She sat on the sofa in her office, leaning forward and tensed up, she was uncharacteristically unsettled about this. Blyth put his hand on her shoulder and pulled her back gently.

"Settle down, Anna," he said with the tone of a concerned grandfather, "Kirstine is a professional, she will get the truth out of him."

"I know, Frank," she said with a sigh, "I just hate this. I just can't believe he could have been a traitor."

"We don't know anything for sure, Anna," Blyth replied, "All we have is circumstantial evidence, we need him to tell us. Don't get ahead of yourself."

"Frank is right," Rutter-Close added, "There could be a reasonable explanation for all of this."

Anna swirled her whisky around in its glass, as she was wont to do when she was wound up. Looking back at the screen, Avaya was nearly done reading out the evidence she had discovered.

"Frank, David," she said, "This is a strange time we're living in. I have a feeling whatever Stills has to say isn't going to make things any better."

Davis walked out of the security checkpoint after telling his superiors that he was taking his lunch. He took a small, clear device from his pocket and placed it inside his ear. As he walked towards the mess hall he bumped into a low ranking Church cleric who had been left over from the Cardinal's entourage.

"I-- I'm so sorry," the cleric said, shaking like a leaf.

"Are you alright?" Davis said, cracking a smile.

"Oh, oh yes, I've lost my dog, can you help?." said the cleric,

"I can help. I need you to give me what you have for me."

The cleric passed him the piece of broken glass wadded up in a handkerchief.

"Thank you," Davis said, sliding it into his pocket. "We shall prevail."

"We shall prevail." The cleric said as Davis walked away from him.

Stills hung his head low.

"It's all lies," he said in a low tone.

"What is all lies?" Heald asked, coldly.

"All of it. The money, the payments, the AI, the operational reports, I have no idea about any of that."

Heald placed bank statements in front of him, "Do you deny that you own these accounts?"

Stills scanned the documents. He furrowed his brow as he looked at the numbers.

"Those aren't my accounts. They're similar and with the same bank but those aren't my accounts. Let me use your PCU and I can prove it."

"That's not going to happen," Heald said replied, calmly.

"You have to trust me, this is not my bank account."

Heald pushed another few reams of paper in front of him, "That's not what the evidence says. There is enough here to charge you with treason. It's enough to send you to the detention centre on Pluto for a very long time."

"For fuck's sake, Heald," he said, bashing his fists on the desk, "Listen to me, this isn't right. You don't have anything here, you have a setup. I've never seen these accounts in my life."

Heald met Stills' eye with a stern gaze.

"Calm down, Jameson," she said, "I would suggest you listen to me about the gravity of your situation and be honest about these accounts. You have nothing to gain from lying to me."

Davis walked past the mess hall at a brisk pace, his footsteps from the heavy government issued boots echoing through the empty marbled halls. He reached a nondescript door on the other side of the building from the security checkpoint marked 010-2324. He swiped his access card and walked into the large storage cupboard.

He walked past two racks of cleaning supplies till he reached a workbench at the back of the room. Sat on it was a large metal case with a note attached to the top - "R. DAVIS"

He pressed his thumb to the print reader on the front of the case and with a hiss, it opened up. Inside was a small cylindrical jar filled with a white fluid. A console in the centre lifted up and an opening appeared. In the back of the case was a small, pulsing red cube.

“I’m here,” Davis said, “What do I do?”

“Good,” a digitised voice said in his ear, through the clear device, “Place the sample in the top of the device then press the pulsing green button.”

Davis took the handkerchief from his pocket and gingerly removed the shard of glass with a pair of tweezers he took from the case. He placed the glass in the opening and pressed a small button on the side of the console. The opening closed and a faint light started to pulse on the unit. A readout on the side of the console illuminated.

DNA SCAN STARTED

“It’s started,” Davis said

“Stand by, it should only take a minute or two,” the voice replied.

GENOME IDENTIFIED

ORGAN CLONING COMMENCING

The white cylinder suddenly lit up and a red gel was injected into the fluid.

MAPPING GENOME TO STEM CELLS

The red and white fluid started to mix, resulting in a pinky substance.

ELECTROSTATIC BONDING COMMENCING

Davis could hear several charges of electricity being fired into the pink fluid. The fluid started to solidify and change shape. It morphed into a gelatinous sphere. Davis watched on with amazement as the fluid turned and formed into a human eyeball.

CLONING COMPLETE

“Impressive,” Davis said as he took the cylinder out of the case and peered at the freshly created eyeball, “Very impressive”

“Your approval isn’t necessary. Are you prepared for the next task?”

“Yes, I am. Where do I take this?”

“Head to central computing. Take the red cube too. That is important. And don’t forget to dispose of the case.”

He closed the case and locked it again. He picked it up and as he left the room, dropped it into the industrial waste chute by the door of the cupboard.

"HE'S LYING!" Anna yelled, pacing around the office.

"Give Kirstine time," Blyth said calmly, trying to bring the President back from her apoplexy, "There is a process here, she will get to the truth. I know she will."

"How far do we have to go to get the truth out of him?" Anna asked, taking a swig of her whisky.

"Anna?" Blyth interjected, "You need to think about what you're saying. You have to set an example"

"He's a traitor!"

"He's right," Rutter-Close said, "All of the evidence we have is circumstantial. We have to get a confession out of him or something concrete."

Anna went to retort with anger but realised that Frank and David were right. While the evidence they had on Stills was damning, everything could be explained away. She looked over at her desk and thought about the sealed military records. The fact that even she couldn't unlock them had been gnawing at her all day. She picked up her whisky and swirled it around a little.

"How many of those have you had today?" Blyth said before she could take a sip.

"I..." Anna couldn't remember how many she'd had. She didn't feel drunk, but she knew it was a bad sign that she couldn't remember. "Shit. Coffee anyone?"

Both of her compatriots nodded and Anna sent a message to her secretary to bring some coffee in for them. She needed to remain alert and nervously swilling whisky was not going to help her in the slightest. With a moment of clarity, she looked back over at the files on her desk.

"I have an idea," she said, "Frank, can you get a message to Heald?"

Stills was sweating. Heald had been pressing him for hours now, constantly asking the same questions in different ways, trying to get him to trip himself up. It wasn't working. Stills had lost his temper a few times, but his answers had always remained consistent. This didn't phase Heald, she'd broken stronger people than Stills before, she just needed to find the right question.

"So what do you like to spend your money on?" Heald asked, with a friendly tone.

"What?" asked Stills, "How is that relevant? Or any of your business?"

"Well, it is relevant, judging by your accounts. So what do you spend money on?"

"Food, drink, mortgage, what do you think I spend my money on?"

"Oh, I don't know. Gambling? Women? Men? Boys?"

Stills stared Heald down with an intensity that could burn through a bulkhead. She simply smiled back.

"I'm sorry Jameson," she said, maintaining her smile, "That was uncalled for. We're both professionals here, we can be adult about this."

Before she could ask the next question, she placed her hand against her ear and listened intently. The voice in her ear gave her a new line of enquiry to dive down.

"What happened in the Corvus system?" she asked. Stills' eyes went wide.

"That's classified," he said, coldly.

"So I hear, thankfully I have Level 1 clearance for this inquiry, so you can discuss it with me."

"I- I can't discuss it with you. It's level 0."

"Don't bullshit me," Heald said, her tone getting sharper, "there is no such thing as Level 0."

"There is, it's reserved for absolutely classified operations that even the President shouldn't know about. Corvus was one of those."

"Is this what your AI is protecting?"

Stills hung his head low, "Yes it is. It isn't my AI, though."

"We need access to this." Heald said, "If you provide us access it can corroborate your story."

"I can't give you access, it's carefully controlled..."

"Controlled by who?"

"By itself."

"I don't understand."

"The AI, it's not like Avaya or any other governmental or personal AI. It believes it's alive. It has a consciousness. If you're asking me about it, I assume that Avaya tried to break into it but found it a formidable adversary, didn't you?"

The small hologram nodded and appeared to look slightly ashamed.

"Your average AI knows it is an AI. It knows it is a tool," he continued, "Sure, they have advanced personality routines, voice, behaviour and all other kinds of synthesised qualities, but they know they are nothing more than a computer program. They know their limitations. KEYES-01 doesn't. It is self-aware, self-replicating and self-upgrading."

"Who created it?"

"I don't know. I do know in my communications with it, it did have something to do with The Church once upon a time."

"How do we get access to the data store it holds?"

"You need to be introduced and cleared by someone already authorised to access."

Heald and Avaya both looked directly at Stills.

"No!" he said, "No no no. Not after this charade, not a chance..."

The door marked "Central Core" was a large and imposing one. In the darkest depths of the Council headquarters, Davis found himself walking down corridors that were so infrequently used the air was musty and stale. The walls were painted with a thick, almost enamel like beige substance which shone in the artificial light. The smooth tiled floor had three coloured lines painted on it. Red took you to waste management, green took you to environmental controls and blue took you directly to the Central core.

"I'm outside the door," he said.

"Good. Get in the room," the voice replied.

"I can't, I don't have clearance for this door."

"Yes you do, it's in your pocket."

Davis slipped the cylinder with the cloned eyeball out of his pocket.

"Whose eye is this?" Davis asked, for the first time questioning the methods of his temporary master

"What does it matter, just know it will get you through the door."

"Whose. Eye?" he said, with more force in his voice.

"Do you want your payment? Do you want to remain in debt to your bookie?"

"How... how do you know about that?"

"I know all. I also know that he's looking for you. Finish the job, take your payment or I will tell him where to find you."

"Okay okay okay," Davis said, raising his hands up in front of him, despite the fact that he was alone in the corridor, "Well the bio reader is only one part of the lock, I need the access code"

"6-5-6-5-7-8-9-0"

Davis entered the code on the keypad. A lens then protruded next to the pad. A small screen lit up with the message "BIOMETRIC SCAN REQUIRED". He held the cylinder to the lens, which whirred and twisted as it focused on the eyeball. The screen went green and with a hiss, the large blast doors opened in front of him.

"Welcome, President Coulson," an automated female voice said.

“The President?” Davis said, with some incredulity

“Needs must” the voice responded, “Find the terminal marked AVA-339”

Walking into the cavernous room, Davis was flanked left and right with tall racks of blinking lights and cables. A thin layer of fog lay against the floor of the room from the cooling systems around the various stacks of processors and hard drives. Combined with the soft blue lighting it gave the core an eerie, almost alien feel. The core was the heart of all of the Council’s computer systems. It was affectionately known as Avaya’s House, as the AI’s main hardware was hosted here.

Davis passed through endless ranks of equipment until he found the terminal he had been instructed to look for.

“Okay, I’ve found it, what do I do?” he said

“Type in Maintenance Access Auth->315096853745 and a drawer should open.”

Davis turned on the screen. It was an old fashioned panel display, nothing like the current holo displays. This was a physical screen. He hit a switch on the side of the panel and the screen flickered into life. A small keyboard appeared below the screen as a white cursor flashed against a black background.

Davis typed the command his anonymous master had given him. The terminal thought for a moment before making a positive noise. A large drawer to his left slid open with a hiss. He peered inside and saw a nest of glowing cables, components and processor cards.

“Do you want me to rip all of this out?” he asked of his instructor

“No! We’re not trying to disable Avaya. We want to use her. Can you see a pulsing red cube?”

Davis looked deeper into the drawer and found the cube, it was connected with two glowing white cables.

.“Yes, I’ve got it.”

“Okay, replace that cube with the one we have provided you with”

Davis took the red cube from his pocket. It looked identical to the one in the drawer.

“What does it do?”

“That’s none of your concern. Just replace the component and I will wire your payment.”

He pulled the red cube from the drawer, twisted the cables out from it, then plugged them into the new cube. He carefully placed it back in the drawer exactly where he found it. He noticed that the white glow of the cables was changing, slowly fading into a dark green glow. Davis had a gut feeling that this was not a good thing for someone, somewhere. He slid the drawer shut and it clicked close. Returning to the terminal, he ended the maintenance cycle and shut the screen down.

"It's done"

"Thank you, Robert. You have done a wonderful thing for The Church. Standby for your reward."

Davis opened up his PCU and accessed his bank. There was no transfer. He waited nervously for a minute and his balance did not change. Just as he was about to speak up and ask if there was a problem, a deafening whine came from the earpiece. Davis grimaced in pain and reached for his ear, but before he could take the earpiece out it exploded, killing him instantly. His decapitated corpse slumped to the ground in the central core, alone, bathed in the glow of a million tiny lights.

On the table in the interrogation room, Avaya's hologram flickered for a moment. Neither Stills nor Heald noticed it, but Avaya immediately realised something was not right.

"Agent Heald," Avaya said, "With apologies, I cannot continue with this recording. With your permission I'd like to hand over to the facility AI to record the rest of this interview."

"Is something wrong?" Heald asked.

"I am not sure," Avaya replied, "But I feel it imperative to conduct a maintenance cycle."

"Go ahead." Heald said.

"Thank you," Avaya replied. Her hologram changed back from red to blue, then dissipated from the table.

"Why has Avaya stopped recording?" Rutter-Close asked.

"What?" Anna said as she moved from her desk to the vidscreen.

"Look," he said, pointing at the screen, "Avaya isn't projecting any more. Has Heald turned her off?"

"Where's the audio gone?" Blyth interjected.

"Avaya?" Anna said out loud, trying to summon the AI. There was no response.

"Something isn't right." Blyth said

"That's an understatement," Anna said as she lifted her desk phone.

"Hello? Maintenance? What's happened to Avaya?"

Chapter Twenty Five

Unified Church of Humanity Research Facility

Location Redacted

“I have good news for you, Hidetaki”

“Oh? Do tell”

“We’re in. The control device has been installed”

“Excellent news, Cardinal”

“Oh, and the earpiece was a master stroke. There are no witnesses, no one knows what's happened.”

“I will start the observation. Are we going to override it?”

“No, not yet, we need to know what Coulson’s play is”

“Is it worth moving the station?”

“No, not yet. Not until Stanton arrives”

“Understood”

“What are your updates?”

“I have good news for you actually, Cardinal”

“Do tell”

“The miner has been captured and he and the sample will arrive in the next hour”

“Have you a way to safely transport him through the facility?”

“The entire route from the landing deck to the research chamber has been evacuated and they will be thoroughly decontaminated and explosively decompressed to be sure”

“Good. I am in transit now, I will arrive tomorrow. Are my quarters in order?”

“Yes, Cardinal. everything is in order.”

“And Stanton’s? He flies tomorrow”

“Everything is as you specified. His entertainment will arrive from Corvus II shortly after you do.”

“Excellent. I will see you soon. We shall prevail”

“We shall prevail.”

Chapter Twenty Six

Earth

Unified Church Of Humanity Prayer Grounds

The glass elevator on the outside of the Prayer Grounds afforded some wonderful views of London in the morning. But much as she enjoyed the view, Dana had come to dread the journey upwards. As soon as she stood in the elevator she knew she was within 4 minutes of being in Stanton's presence. Her ribs were still aching after her last encounter with him in his bedchamber. As brilliant as bone fusion technology was at repairing breaks within 24 hours, it still hurt like hell.

As she expected, Stanton hadn't allowed her the week that the hospital had recommended to rest and recover. He hated using the AI understudy and he always demanded that she return from any time off as soon as possible, whether she was taking a vacation or recovering from his hand.

The doors slid open when she reached the top floor and she stepped out into the atrium. She couldn't allow people to know that she was suffering, so she walked with a straight back and absolute confidence despite the agony that she was in.

Stepping into her small office, she smelled the unmistakable stench of cigarettes, which usually meant that Stanton was sat in his office, one room over, celebrating something. She sat down at her desk and opened her desktop PCU. Before the holo-screen could even focus, Stanton was on the intercom yelling at her to get into his office. With a deep sigh, she stood up, flattened her grey dress down and walked through the connecting door into his office.

"You needed something, Sir?" she said in a professional tone.

"Dana, my darling!" Stanton exclaimed, "Come come, we're celebrating and I wanted you to join me." He beckoned for her to sit down on the sofa he had at one end of the office.

Dutifully, she sat, while Stanton walked over with a bottle of Brandy and two glasses. He sat next to her, a little closer than she would have liked.

"It's 8:30 am, sir," she said, trying to politely refuse the drink.

"Ah, that doesn't matter, my dear. We have cause for celebration!"

"What are we celebrating, sir?" she asked, nervously.

"My ascension," he said, pouring a glass of brandy for her.

"Sir?"

"My ascension! Very soon I will be a god!"

"I don't follow, sir."

"The Prophecy," he said, standing up and starting to gesticulate wildly, "It's about to come true and I am the Unknown Saviour!"

"Sir, with all due respect, you aren't making much sense."

"No, I'm making perfect sense," he said jovially, turning on the vidscreen. Displayed on the screen was a dark room, "Look at this, it's incredible."

Dana watched intently as the lights came on and what looked like a laboratory was displayed. It was clean and clinical. There was a slab in the middle of the room with a body, but it didn't look human. It was green and appeared to be armoured. It was lying on its side in a foetal position.

Slowly, it began to move. Its thin, spiny legs stretching out and swinging around so the creature was sat upright. It stood from the slab and Dana's blood ran cold. The creature was humanoid but a foot taller than any person she'd ever met, with black, sunken eyes, hands elongated to look like scoops made of bone, smooth, leathery green skin which looked taught as if stretched over plate armour. It looked directly at the camera and Dana felt like it was looking at her.

"S..sir… What the fuck is that?" Dana said, her hands shaking

"This, this is Logan's Prophecy," he said, unable to hide his glee. Dana was about to respond but he shushed her and told her to focus on the screen.

On the video, a door at the back of the shot opened and four soldiers walked in. The creature considered them with caution and began to move defensively, staying low and prepared to pounce. One soldier raised his weapon and shot the creature in the shoulder. It flinched from the inertia of the shot but otherwise didn't react. The soldier took aim again and this time fired at the creature's head. Again, little in the way of reaction from the creature. All four soldiers raised their weapons and opened fire on fully automatic until they exhausted all of their ammunition. The creature stood as if it had just endured a mild breeze.

The soldiers went to the door. It didn't open. The creature stalked towards them as the soldiers began to panic. As one soldier reached for his side-arm the creature leapt forward, it's stretched hand punching the soldier so hard his chest collapsed. The creature took a swing at the next closest soldier and decapitated him with minimal effort. The remaining two soldiers had their side-arms out and were pumping rounds into the creature, but they weren't enough to stop it. It marched forward and used both hands to collapse the chests of the soldiers with incredible force. The vidscreen cut out.

Dana sat, her normally olive complexion completely washed out, her mouth hanging open. She hadn't even realised that Stanton had sat down next to her again.

"Incredible, isn't it?" he said.

"Wh-what is it?" was all Dana could manage

"This, is the Darkness." he said, letting the words hang in the air for a moment, "We found a parasite out on Rayczech Beta. It's a voracious organism, but when it gets into a human body, that is what happens."

"That was human?"

"He used to be. Smith, I think he was called. A junior researcher, now the most important creature in the galaxy."

"What are you going to do?"

"We're going to manufacture more of them," he said, with a broad, dark smile, "have you heard of PAYLOAD?"

Dana shook her head, words were not with her at this time.

"It started out as a new way of terraforming planets," Stanton said, leaning back and putting on his most professorial voice, "current methods involve causing all kinds of tectonic nonsense that means it takes about 10 years to terraform a planet. We wanted to try and seed the sky, so it would rain nutrients and bio-samples which would stimulate growth on a dead planet. The idea was that we could cut that 10 years down to under a year. Or even six months.

"Anyway, it was a non-starter. The researchers couldn't get the chemical formula for terraforming to work properly. But in the process, we had the delivery system completely designed from the ground up. It's a small craft with a Franklin drive and it can skip from planet to planet to deliver an airborne payload."

"What does this have to do with that creature?" Dana said, recovering her voice

"Well the parasite is like a bacteria, it can exist in an airborne form. So we're going to manufacture a lot of it and spread it over a few planets on the Rim worlds. From there, the infection will spread further and further..."

“My..Dear god…” Dana was aghast

“Obviously this can’t be done until the scientists have come up with an antivirus, or vaccine, or a way of killing the creatures, but the idea is we’ll unleash this, let it spread, then we will cure it and fulfil the Prophecy! The Church will be richer and more powerful than ever.”

Stanton put his hand on Dana’s knee. He leaned forward and whispered in her ear

“And I will be a god.”

He started to run his hand up her skirt. She couldn’t process any of this. She was completely horrified by what she had seen.

“Sir,” she said, turning to face him and casually moving his hand from her thigh, “You’re right, this is incredible, but we have preparations to complete. You are travelling tomorrow after all and in my absence, I am sure there are a thousand things that haven’t been done.”

Stanton looked pensive but eventually nodded in approval.

“You’re right, Dana, you’re too important to this operation now. I want you with me tomorrow too.”

“As you wish sir,” she said, getting up from the sofa, “might I ask, where is it we are travelling to, it’s not listed on the orders.”

“We’re off to Research Omega, near the centre of the galaxy. Where that is,” he said, gesturing at the vidscreen.

“We… we’re going to where that monster is?” she asked, suddenly feeling like she’d lost the ability to speak again.

“Absolutely, we’re going to visit and check on the research process.”

A sudden sinking feeling hit Dana like a brick wall. She bowed slightly for Stanton, as he liked from her, then went back to her office as quickly as she could.

“Oh,” he said, just as she was about to close the door, “Can you send in Tina from the library? I feel like enjoying myself”

“Right away sir,” she said, closing the door. She shuddered, then broke down into tears. She had known fear in her life and in Stanton, she’d been living with a monster for nearly half of her life, but what he had shown her on the screen had terrified her to the core.

She brought up her PCU and sent General Blyth a message

BLYTH

PLEASE TELL ME YOU WERE LISTENING TO THAT

NEED EXTRACTION IMMEDIATELY, THIS IS TOO DANGEROUS NOW

D

She closed the PCU and sat, trying to think of some way to get out of the trip to the Research Station.

Chapter Twenty Seven

Slipspace conduit

UCoH Transport Ship Zealot II

Higgins couldn't see anything. The room he'd been sat in on the transport ship had no lights. It was little more than a cupboard with a shelf in it. He had been sat in the same position for what felt like hours. The guards had taken his PCU so he didn't even know how long he'd been in this position. He did know that the ship was in Slipspace, the familiar whine of a Franklin drive was ever present in the background. Normally a slip jump between systems only took a few seconds, most of the interplanetary travel was time spent getting to safe distances away from population centres to allow for a jump that wouldn't present a risk to others. Tearing through the fabric of the universe had a habit of causing a localised shock wave

However, this time the slip drive had been running for a while which Higgins worked out could have meant only one of two things; they were on their way to the other side of the galaxy, or they were worried about being followed so they were making randomised jumps until they happened upon their destination. Either way, it didn't fill him with confidence.

His mind went back to the green substance. He couldn't work out what it was, but he was sure that it was because he touched it he found himself in his current incarceration. The idea of being in a quarantine at the hands of The Church was weighing on his mind and causing him to worry. He was also desperately sad that Emily saw him being dragged away by soldiers. He had no idea what must be going through her head but he knew he had to speak to her as soon as possible.

The whine of the Franklin drive stopped. All of a sudden Higgins was in darkness and silence. The sensory deprivation was deeply uncomfortable for him. In the distance, he could hear the sounds of boots on metal. Two, maybe three pairs. They were getting louder. He hadn't seen any other occupied cells when he was brought here so they had to be coming for him.

With a hiss, the door opened and light flooded into the cell, temporarily blinding Higgins.

"Who's there?" he called out, squinting and trying to get his eyes to focus.

He received no answer, but instead, hands grabbed his arms and dragged him out of the room. His legs had gone to sleep from sitting in one position for several hours. He fell to the floor at the feet of someone he had not seen before. He was dressed in a white hazard suit, with a personal ventilator system and face mask obscuring his features. As his vision cleared, Higgins looked at the other two men, who were dressed the same.

"Where am I?" he said, still confused.

Without a word, one of the men directed his attention to a wheelchair. Then he grabbed Higgins by the scruff of the neck and dragged him over to it. The other two followed and manhandled him into the chair, securing his wrists and ankles. When he loudly protested this treatment, they even gagged him too.

At the end of the corridor of cells, the wall opened up and a ramp was brought to the opening. Church transport ships were designed like this, so prisoners or dissidents could be loaded onto transport ships away from the eyes of Clerics and Cardinals. The cells on the ship were their own self-contained unit.

The hazard suited men pushed Higgins out into the cold landing bay. He frantically looked around to try and get his bearings, but all he could surmise was that they were on a space station, owing to the wide open door into space large enough for a Council frigate to travel through. Seeing as he hadn't asphyxiated, he assumed that the Church had perfected forcefield technology. Most landing bays he'd ever been in acted as large airlocks and had to be closed to the vacuum of space and pressurised before anyone was allowed to disembark.

As they descended the ramp, Higgins noticed one large decoration in a sea of functional grey. He recognised it as a statue of The Unknown Saviour. A tall, slender human body with a blank face, with its chest pushed out, shoulders back and head angled backwards as if rocketing towards the sky. Around it was a large character he remembered from school. An ancient letter from a long lost civilisation on Earth: Ω

They passed under the huge statue decoration and moved through the corridors of the station. It was deserted and eerily silent. The lights in the corridors only illuminated around the four bodies moving through them, as they walked into blackness and left blackness behind them. All of the doors looked uniform, save for numbers imprinted on them. Occasionally they would pass a disabled comms panel or touch screen and twice they passed small facsimiles of The Unknown Saviour.

After moving through ten or fifteen corridors, Higgins lost count of the route they took, and in a 30-second elevator ride, they pushed Higgins through a glass door that read "Research Labs Sigma". The lights flicked on automatically and all Higgins could see was destruction. Broken glass, smashed equipment and blood on the walls. He immediately feared for his life and began to struggle in the chair, but it was no use, he was secured in. They pushed him into one last room. This one was spotless, but it looked like a prison cell. There was a bed, a small desk and toilet against one wall, one large glass window on another wall then a wide mirror on one of the other walls. The glass door had read "Observation B" when they went through it, but seeing the room did not help Higgins' sense of dread.

His captors pushed him into the middle of the observation room, unsecured one of his hands, then left the room and sealed the door. Immediately Higgins removed his remaining restraints, then his gag. He took a deep breath and turned around to see the three men in hazmat suits staring through the observation window at him. Silent, non-moving.

"What the fuck?" he said, having not been able to say it in hours, "Where am I? Who are you guys?"

They said nothing. Instead, as one, they turned and walked out of the research labs. The lights turned off as they exited, leaving Higgins alone, in a white, featureless room, on a station in the middle of space, with no one to talk to and no way to call for help.

It had been hours since Higgins was placed in the observation room. The harsh white light wouldn't turn off, no matter how long he stayed still. It felt like days since someone had spoken a single word to him, days since he'd been dragged from R.Beta in front of his daughter. His mind was getting increasingly paranoid. He had tried yelling out in the vain hope of getting the attention of whoever was observing him but had gotten no response whatsoever.

The bed in the room was little more than a shelf; a hard, uncomfortable mattress, one impossibly thin pillow and no blankets. He had tried to get some sleep but the cold room and the harsh lighting had prevented him from drifting off. He felt like he was losing his mind.

He had considered using the chair in the room to smash the glass and make a break for it, but it was bolted to the ground. Higgins began to seriously contemplate the idea that he was going to die in this room. Nothing made sense to him any more and it was driving him to distraction.

Then, suddenly, the lights in the main research lab illuminated. He jumped up from the bed and peered through the observation window and saw a group of people approaching. In the middle was an elderly man of Japanese descent wearing a suit and a lab coat, flanked either side of him by two much younger people in lab coats, which Higgins thought must have been students or researchers. Following close behind them were four Church Wardens, the elite guards of the Church. Dressed head to toe in oversized black power armour and holding large ordinance weapons, he knew that they meant business. The thought did cross his mind, however, that they seemed very well armed just for him.

The three in lab coats approached the glass and began to peer in at him and take notes on their PCUs. They were talking to each other but Higgins couldn't hear a word they were saying. The soldiers behind them had their weapons ready and trained on Higgins at all times. The Japanese man tapped something on his PCU and all of a sudden he could hear their voices.

"Good morning, Mr Higgins," the elderly man said.

"Where am I?" Higgins said, trying to make sense of the situation

"You are where you are," the elderly man said with a smirk

"I--" Higgins couldn't think of a reply to that. He was exhausted, distressed and confused.

"Let me introduce myself," the elderly man continued, "I am Dr Hidetaki Mitsuni and you are our guest here."

"Is this how you treat all of your guests?" Higgins said, wearily.

"Just the ones who are important to The Church. I hope you are finding your quarters satisfactory."

"Would it matter if I didn't?"

"No, I suppose it wouldn't," Mitsuni said with a chuckle.

"What do you want with me?"

"Mr Higgins, have you ever heard of smallpox?" Mitsuni said, ignoring Higgins

"No"

"Well," Mitsuni started as he began to pace back and forth across Higgins' view through the window, "Smallpox was a particularly nasty virus on earth thousands of years ago. It was incredibly infectious, it left people scarred for life, sometimes blinded people and managed to kill 30% or so of people infected with it. It was so prevalent and deadly that ancient civilisations concocted gods and goddesses in the hope appeasement would protect them from the virus. There were others who thought that it was the work of demons or a punishment from otherworldly deities for the sins of man

"But it was none of that. It was a natural mutation of a strain of virus that just so happened to be very easy to pass between humans. You see, we are a weak and fragile species. It doesn't take much to kill us, the slightest infection that we aren't prepared for can destroy us. It takes time and effort to prepare for, treat and eradicate a virus as powerful as Smallpox."

"Is that why I'm here," Higgins asked, "Do I have smallpox?"

Mitsuni laughed, his loud laugh contradicting his quiet and controlled voice, "Oh my, Mr Higgins, no. Far from it. Smallpox has been cured for over 1500 years. No, you don't have it. But you have something even more precious and powerful and I intend to find out what it is."

"What are you talking about?"

"This," Mitsuni said as one of his assistants held the jar of green fluid up without a direct instruction to, "You found this on Rayczech Beta, is that correct?"

"Yeah, I drilled into a rock face and it destroyed my drill."

"It's a fascinating specimen," Mitsuni said, not listening to Higgins again, "It's intelligent, yet primordial. I cannot find any way for a consciousness to exist, yet somehow one does. It reacts to stimulus like a mammal would, but it is a viscous gel. It's beautiful, isn't it?"

"If you say so," Higgins felt a sense of dread, "Is it... is it an infection of some kind?"

"Well that's what you're here to tell us," Mitsuni said, directing a cold stare into Higgins' eyes, "You have no idea what you've found, I am sketchy on the details of it right now, but trust me, this is something incredible. You came into contact with it two days ago, yet you've had no side effects, which is also fascinating to me."

"What do you mean, side effects? Should I have become ill or something?"

Mitsuni turned to the young female next to him, "Allison, be a dear and show him what happened to Smith."

The researcher tapped a couple of holographic buttons on her PCU and the mirror along the edge of the observation room turned to glass, allowing Higgins to see into the neighbouring room. There, stood in the middle of the room was a tall, green creature with a distended jaw and large curved claws in place of hands. Higgins freaked out and tried to get as far away from the glass as he could.

"WHAT THE FUCK IS THAT?" Higgins yelled at the top of his voice.

"No need to be alarmed, Mr Higgins," Mitsuni said, "It can't see you or hear you, it doesn't know you're there. This was one of my researchers, Smith. He breathed in spores released by another form of the substance we found on R.Beta in the same shaft you found our specimen here. That was a week ago. You touched this two days ago and you look nothing like him. I wonder why that is."

Higgins was stood on the bed, opened mouthed at what was in front of his eyes, "wh-- that's human?" was all he could manage

"No, not anything more," Mitsuni said with a smile, "It's something better than human. This, my child, is The Darkness that The Logan Prophecy has talked about for a millennium."

"B-- bullshit... no, this has to be a prank, this can't be real."

"Oh, it is absolutely real, Mr Higgins. Shall we have a little demonstration?" Mitsuni clicked his fingers and two of the power armoured guards grabbed the young male researcher to his right and dragged him screaming to the door of Observation Room A. The young woman, Allison, didn't break her composure at the sudden turn of events. Higgins began to scream out but Mitsuni turned off the comm system.

The researcher was kicking and punching at the guards, but their armour was far too thick to even register that he was trying to defend himself. One of the guards stood by the door release, whilst the other picked the young man up by his neck and lifted him off the ground. His legs were kicking and swinging in a vain attempt to save his own life. With practised precision, the first guard released the door and the second threw the poor boy into the room with the creature before the first sealed the door again.

Higgins watched on in horror as the creature backed up and began to stalk the researcher around the room. The boy had tried to pick up the chair to defend himself but, like in Higgins' room, it was bolted to the ground. The creature made a hissing noise that chilled Higgins to his core. The researcher turned and looked directly at Higgins, and mouthed "help me" just as the creature leapt onto his back and sunk its enormous teeth into his skull. Higgins couldn't take his eyes off the viscera and gore the creature was tearing off the young man.

Mitsuni turned the comms on once again and Higgins could hear him chuckling him to himself.

"It's beautiful isn't it?" Mitsuni said, still chuckling slightly.

"Why? Why did you do that?" Higgins said, feeling slightly queasy and shaking from shock. Mitsuni stopped chuckling and looked directly into Higgins' eyes

"Because I can. This is my lab, I will test my subjects the way I see fit." He tapped on his PCU and the observation glass returned to being a mirror. Higgins was relieved as he didn't have to watch the creature consume the poor researcher.

"Get some sleep, Mr Higgins. Your work begins in a few hours and I need you rested. Good night."

Mitsuni walked away with his singular remaining researcher and his security cohort in tow. As he left the lab, all of the lights, including the ones in Higgins' room went out. Suddenly he was in the darkness, in dead silence and very aware of the monster that was feeding in the next room.

Chapter Twenty Eight

Rayczech Beta

R.Beta Spaceport

The banging on the window was getting annoying for Jones. He was trying to get in contact with Cardinal James but was receiving no answer. The banging was ever present and distracting him from completing his report for the day. It was getting late and the security checkpoint was deserted save for himself. The banging had been going on for hours. Occasionally it took breaks and he could hear muffled shouting, but it was finally getting on his nerves. He stood up from his terminal and went to the service window, where security agents would sit and process new arrivals to the planet. He hit the switch to turn off the privacy glass. The white frosted, pulse round proof glass became clear and on the other side was a dishevelled and distressed looking Emily Higgins. He turned on the microphone.

"For a little woman you make a big noise," he said as condescendingly as he could.

"Where have you taken my dad?" she yelled back at him.

"My staff told you on the concourse, it's classified."

"That's bullshit, you can't just kidnap someone and refuse to tell their family where you've taken them," she said, practically spitting venom at him.

"Ms Higgins," Jones resumed his condescending tone, "this is my planet, I am in charge here, I don't have to do anything I don't want to and right now, I don't want to continue this conversation any further." He went to turn the privacy glass back on.

"WAIT!" she yelled, causing Jones to pause for a moment.

"You are not in charge here, far from it," she said. Her eyes were wide and burning with intensity

“What are you talking about,” Jones asked

“You are NOT the ranking member of the Church on this planet at this precise moment.”

“Be careful what you say next, Ms Higgins. You are in danger of being arrested for disturbing the peace.”

“But it’s true. You are not the leader here.” She opened her PCU and read from a document, “In the Unified Church Of Humanity, the secular nature of military is a rueful necessity, however, all members of the security and military services answer to officials of the Church at all times.”

“And?” Jones said, mulling the statement over in his head, “Are you a church official? I think not. I have done my research on you, Ms Higgins, you are a student. I don’t even know why you are on this planet, there is nothing here for you.”

“I’m not a Church official, but my boyfriend is,” she said, giving Tom a kick. He had sat on the floor and fallen asleep some hours before while Emily had been attempting to get Jones’ attention. He woke with a start and scrambled up into Jones’ view.

“Tom Cavanagh, Cleric Third Class, it’s a pleasure to meet you,” Tom said, not fully grasping the tension of the situation.

“Are you serious?” Jones said, puffing out his chest and crossing his arms, “You expect me to take orders from this skinny drip?”

“Hey!” Tom said

“Or what, little man?” Jones said with a wide smile on his face, “What are you going to do?”

Tom looked at Emily and shrank back into himself. His indignation well and truly destroyed by the confidence and intimidating visage of Jones. Emily gave Tom a death stare that could split a diamond clean in half.

“I thought so,” Jones said with a chuckle, “Begone, both of you. I have no reason to speak to either of you any further.”

After Jones had turned on the privacy glass again, Emily had continued to bang and yell at him for a little longer, but she realised it was a futile waste of energy. She looked down at Tom who was sat back on the floor again.

“What the hell was that?” she said with a fire in her voice he’d never encountered before.

“I tried to talk to him,” Tom said, meekly

“No you didn’t, you said it was nice to meet him and you shrivelled up when he said a single word to you. What the hell, Tom?"

"Well did you see him? He was enormous!"

"You outrank him, you could have ordered him to tell me where my dad was taken!"

"But.."

"Seriously?" she yelled at him, "You're seriously going to argue that point with me?"

"Look, babe, he was never going to help you, he was never going to listen to me." Tom reached up to hold her hand. She swatted it away.

"Don't you 'babe' me!" she said, turning from him and pacing up and down the concourse, "Do you have no spine? What happens if a Cardinal speaks to you? Do you melt into a puddle?"

Tom looked sheepish, "Kinda... yeah. I can't speak to the Cardinals, they're too intimidating."

"They're.... intimidating?" Emily said, stammering on her incredulity, "You're a cleric that is intimidated by your superiors? For fuck's sake, Tom. Fuck you, we're done!"

Emily stormed off down the concourse. She wasn't sure where she was going but she knew she needed answers. She could hear Tom calling after her but she just raised her middle finger in his general direction.

After a few minutes, she reached a crossroads that split off to her left and right, with two identical looking grey metal corridors and no signs or discerning features at all. It was at this point she realised she had no idea where to go in this base. She also noticed that she didn't have her case any more Emily had dropped her case when she saw her father being taken away and she'd not seen it since.

It was late, there was no one around to ask for help and she was so mad at Tom she couldn't stand the thought of saying another word to him right now. Instead, she sat in the middle of the floor at the crossroad and burst into floods of tears. She wasn't sure exactly what she was crying about, whether it was her dad, Jones, Tom or just the insanity of the situation, but a wave of emotion coursed over her and there was nothing she could do but sit and cry.

"Ma'am? Are you alright?" a voice said from behind her. Emily turned around and saw a young soldier stood looking at her. Unlike the other soldiers she'd seen, he wasn't armed. He was dressed in the same uniform as all the other Church soldiers, but he didn't seem to have a side-arm or any kind of weaponry at all.

"Y-yeah, I'm fine," she said, sniffing back tears.

“Ma’am, I may not know women very well, but I can tell you’re not,” he said in a thick American accent. He extended his hand out, “I’m Mick, nice to meet you”

She smiled up at him but didn’t take his hand. “I’m Emily. Where’s your gun?”

“I don’t carry one,” Mick said.

“Why not? I thought all the Church soldiers carried them?” She was still sniffing back tears.

“I’m not a soldier. I’m a pilot. I fly the shuttles through the storms out here.” His hand was still extended out to her. She finally took it and he pulled her up to her feet.

“Don’t they have AIs for that?” she said

“They do, but nothing beats a skilled pilot in an Ion storm.”

“Where do people go on this rock?” she said, wiping tears from her eyes.

“All over. Mostly between here and the barracks about half an hour over yonder,” he said, pointing in some direction Emily couldn’t identify, “then there’s those who go to the mines. I take them too.”

“Wait… Did you meet Carl Higgins?” she said, suddenly very alert

“Yeah, I did, nice fella,” Mick said with a smile, “Last time I saw him we had a hairy one, getting him off a collapsing platform. Do you know Carl?”

“Yeah, I’m his daughter”

“Well ain’t that a small universe. He’s a good guy, your dad. He talked about you a lot in the mess hall during down time. He didn’t tell me you were so beautiful.”

“Yeah yeah, I’m gorgeous,” Emily said, dismissively, “I’m not here for that. I need to find out what happened to him. Do you have authority with the security guys?”

“Erm, I guess so, why?” Mick said, still on the back foot from the sudden change of the subject.

“When I landed, security had him in cuffs and he was taken off world. He yelled something about quarantine but it didn’t make sense. Is there any way you can find out from security where they took him?”

“Well, sure, I think I can find something out for you. It’ll have to be in the morning, the checkpoints are closed overnight, you know.”

“That would be wonderful,” Emily said.

“What’s in it for me, if I do this?” Mick said

"What do you want?" Emily asked, cautiously

"Well it's not often a fella meets a gal like you, Miss Emily. Maybe I could take you on a date?"

“Alright,” Emily said, with a slight sigh, “You can take me for dinner. On Earth. I’ll even dress nicely for you. Deal?”

“You got yourself a deal, gorgeous,” Mick said, shaking her hand. She tapped her PCU against his and transferred her contact details.

“Call me as soon as you have anything for me, yeah?” she said, returning to business.

Mick nodded and gave her a sly wink. He said his goodbyes and trotted off down the corridor to the left.

“Oh!” he yelled back at her, “Go down to the right, guest accommodation is down thataway!”

Emily smiled, “Thanks!” she yelled back at him.

>>> SECURE CHANNEL OPEN

>>> CONNECTING TO USER

>>> CHECKING FOR LISTENING SOFTWARE

>>> CHECK CLEAR

>>>

>>> Sir

>>> *What is the meaning of this disturbance?*

>>> Apologies. I have a development

>>> *What is it?*

>>> Higgins. The miner

>>> *Yes? What of him?*

>>> He has a daughter

>>> *Yes, we knew that. It’s in his profile*

>>> She’s here on R.Beta

>>> *Are you sure?*

>>> Yes, I’ve just been speaking with her. Shall I keep track of her?

>>> *Yes, this is good. We can make use of her.*

>>> How close do I get?

>>> *Keep her in vision. Don't get too close. Establish trust, but not friendship. Is that clear?*

>>> Yes sir

>>> *Keep me abridged of her movements. If she tries to cause trouble or leave the planet, let me know immediately.*

>>> Copy that. Signing off. We Shall Prevail

>>> *We Shall Prevail*

>>> Client disconnected....

>>> Client disconnected....

Chapter Twenty Nine

Mars

Council Of Nations Headquarters

The guest offices in the Council headquarters were extremely lavish and well appointed. Rutter-Close didn't make it out to Mars much these days as his work as Ambassador for Earth had him all around the galaxy negotiating many different things with many different colonies to try and keep Earth functioning. Resources, food, materials, fuel, there was so much that the Earth needed to survive and there were so many places he could source them from.

When he could, he liked to spend a few days on Mars. He had been close friends with Anna for decades since they served in the Galactic Peacekeepers together and since she became President, he'd spent a lot of time getting to know Blyth and some of the chiefs of staff too. He'd forged some significant professional alliances and personal friendships in this building.

The office he'd been given to work from was just down the hall from Anna's office. It wasn't as grand as hers, but it made his official workplace in New Los Angeles look like a broom cupboard. The gilded decor, the large oak desk, enormous vidscreen and the comfiest desk chair he'd ever sat in. It was such a nice office he was contemplating asking if he could work from Mars permanently.

Despite the distraction of the space, his mind was racing. After sitting through the interrogation of Stills, something hadn't sat right with him. None of it had made sense. His gut said that Stills was telling the truth, but there was a lot of evidence against him that someone would have had to put significant effort into if they wanted to frame him. Matters of galactic security weren't normally his purview, but Anna had insisted he sit in on the interrogation. He reasoned that as well as the military knowledge of Blyth, she must have wanted a diplomat there to balance out opinions.

Avaya had come back online some hours before. Despite Anna, Blyth and the maintenance staff's questions to her about her sudden disappearance, she had not given any details of why she had taken herself offline. Rutter-Close hadn't bothered to ask, he reasoned that if Avaya wasn't going to tell Anna, she wasn't going to tell him. He had, however, been making liberal use of her abilities.

He was watching the footage back on the vidscreen and having Avaya scrub backwards and forwards through the feed up until the point where she deactivated. He was looking for inconsistencies in Stills' story or things Heald might have missed. He was fixated on how adamant Stills was that the accounts Heald showed him weren't his.

"Avaya," he asked, "When you looked at Stills' bank accounts, are you sure you looked at the right accounts?"

"Yes, Ambassador," she replied, flatly, "I used his human resources profile to find his primary account and then linked to all other ones in his name that I could find."

"Something doesn't add up though. I'm starting to believe that he was telling the truth. Can you pull up his statement for the last month?"

On the vidscreen, a breakdown of Stills' monthly bills appeared. Rutter-Close studied it intently. He made notes on each transaction, no matter how small it was. He cycled back through a few months and detailed them all, looking for correlations and patterns.

"Avaya, can you tell what these three payments are?" he asked, circling three payments to different accounts that appeared every month. Unlike his normal monthly bills, these were direct transfers to bank accounts, always for the same amount, always on the 1st of the month.

"They look to be normal autopayments, Ambassador."

"Yeah, they do, but look at the amounts, they're quite high. In fact..." Rutter-Close stopped and tapped his leg as he did quick mental arithmetic, "they total his monthly salary payments."

He placed his hands on his head, massaging his temples and running his fingers through his short, dark hair. He furrowed his brow trying to work out why his entire salary would come in and be divided between three different accounts every month without any references.

"Avaya, can you trace the three accounts and get me details of what happens when the money arrives in all of them?"

"Yes, Ambassador. How far would you like me to go?"

"Just follow the money wherever it goes. I need to get to the bottom of this. Can you let me know when you've reached the end of the trail?"

"Yes, Ambassador."

Avaya disappeared from the desk and Rutter-Close took another drink from his coffee. He tried to remember the last time he'd slept. He hadn't intended to come to Mars, he'd been working with a trade delegation on Alpha Centauri to reduce tariffs on goods from the system. The negotiations had been difficult, it had been over 24 hours of solid meetings but he'd managed to secure the deal by the skin of his teeth. He'd been heading back to his hotel to get some sleep when he received the summons to Mars from Anna. Hopping on the first ship he could to get there, he hadn't even been able to sleep on the flight due to the mountain of work pouring through his PCU. He was seriously considering taking some vacation time, spending a week with the family on Persephone or something.

There was a knock at the door and Agent Heald walked in, at full attention, carrying a folder full of documents.

"Ambassador, you requested to see me?" she said, with force and vigour.

"Yes, Agent Heald, thank you for coming, please, at ease and have a seat" he replied, gesturing to one of the large chairs in front of the desk. She visibly relaxed, re-tied her ponytail and sat in front of him. Even at ease, she was still fiercely rigid. Rutter-Close found her rather intimidating.

"Can I offer you a coffee or a drink of something?" he said, trying to relax her.

"No, I'm fine, Ambassador," she said.

"Please, call me David."

"I'd rather not, Ambassador."

"Fair enough," he said, having had the wind knocked out of his sails, "I just wanted to have a chat about your interrogation of Stills."

"That's classified, Ambassador, you don't have the clearance to discuss that."

"President Coulson brought me to Mars to sit in with her and General Blyth and observe the interrogation. I've had clearance from her. Avaya? Can you confirm?"

Avaya appeared on the desk and looked right up at Heald, "Yes, President Coulson authorised Ambassador Rutter-Close to have level 1 clearance for this case only. You may discuss it with him, Agent Heald." With that, Avaya disappeared once again.

"Okay, Ambassador, what would you like to know?"

"Well, I don't know if you know my work history, but I negotiate for a living. I've been in discussions that have been significantly more intense than your interrogation and I wanted to just run a few things by you."

"Of course, I'll answer everything as best as I can," she said.

"In your opinion, do you think Stills was telling the truth?" he asked, jumping straight to the point.

"My opinion is irrelevant, Ambassador. All that matters is the evidence presented and his explanation of it."

"Okay, let me rephrase, were you satisfied that Stills' responses were enough to support or disprove the evidence you presented to him?"

"I was not, Ambassador."

"Can you tell me how you've reached that conclusion."

"Permission to speak freely?"

"Of course."

"I have interrogated a great many people since I came to ExoSec. Terrorists, corrupt politicians, war criminals and not one has been as scared as he was. I expect emotional or angry responses to difficult questions, but the look in his eyes was one of pure fear. He is hiding something. Something that scares him deeply."

"I noticed that when watching the vid back. It was when you brought up the Corvus system, he became very agitated."

"Yes, Ambassador. I do not believe his story about the KEYES-01 AI either. Something about it seems very fantastical."

"Even when Avaya confirmed she had encountered it?"

"I don't pretend to know about artificial intelligence, Ambassador, I don't know what Avaya tried to interact with, but my gut tells me not to believe him on this. Especially as he refused to co-operate and access the AI on the Council's behalf."

"What did you make of his financial records?"

"They are the most open and shut part of the investigation, Ambassador. The money never lies. He received a lot of money from the Church and he distributed just as much of it to sources we can't track. There is no doubt in my mind that in some way, he is an agent of The Church."

"Have you prepared your report for the President?"

"Yes sir," she said, patting the folder in her hand, "I will be handing it to her as soon as we are finished here."

"Do you mind sharing your conclusions with me?"

"Of course not, Ambassador. I believe he is guilty, however, the evidence we have is not enough to charge him with any particular crime, potentially beyond money laundering. I suspect the President would rather wait to charge him with a treasonous act, rather than financial irregularities."

"Thank you, Agent Heald," Rutter-Close stood up and shook her hand, "That was illuminating. You may resume your duties."

Heald stood up, saluted the Ambassador and promptly left the room. Rutter-Close wasn't satisfied with her conclusions. His gut told him that there was something they were missing and he was convinced that the three payments he had found were the key to it all.

Chapter Thirty

Earth Orbit

Unified Church Of Humanity Capital Ship Saviour

Stanton sat at the desk of the cavernous, ornate office deep in the centre of the capital ship. The enormous desk was custom made for him from one of the few remaining Redwoods that remained on Earth. It had been expertly carved by the finest joiners in the galaxy. The office was a statement to his tastes, with detailed, painstakingly painted gold decorations, expensive works of art and a bar stocked with some of the rarest and most expensive drinks in the known universe. Every detail had been created to Stanton's liking and he had overseen the decoration personally. Stanton wanted this office, just like his office in the Prayer Grounds, to be unmistakably "him".

The Saviour was the largest passenger bearing starship ever built. It was practically a spacefaring city when it was in use. It required a crew of over 2000 to just get it out of Earth Orbit. On top of the crew, there were a vast number of Clerics, Cardinals, Deacons and scientists aboard. Some had even brought their families with them, anticipating that this journey would be a long one. From bow to stern it was nearly 3 miles long and was over 500 decks deep. The Saviour's smooth hull had even been coated in a space resistant gold plating, again, at the insistence of Stanton.

The camera panned around the office and focused on Stanton. He hated doing broadcasts like this, with powerful lights shining in his eyes, producers running around; it made him feel out of control. At least his production team had an excellent make-up girl who would make his pallid skin radiate under the lights, projecting a youthful exuberance that he no longer possessed. The director gestured to him that he was broadcasting live and the script that Dana had written for him appeared on the holographic teleprompter.

"My Children, my friends, my colleagues. Thank you for joining me on such a momentous occasion. Our millennial celebrations have barely begun yet I am overwhelmed by the outpouring of love and community you have all displayed. We are welcoming more and more people to our Church every day, the Prophecy is being spread further and wider than ever before. I even received word today of our first prayer ground being formed on an outer rim world. Never in my lifetime did I think we would bring Logan's teachings to the very edge of the galaxy. I am humbled.

"You may notice, that I am not addressing you from my pulpit at the London Prayer Grounds. You are correct, I am on board the newest capital ship, Saviour, for her maiden voyage. This ship has been built so the Church can continue to expand into the outer territories. It is a grand vessel, fit for the most dedicated and devoted of our congregation. If you ever find yourself assigned to it, please do understand it to be the honour that it is. For you will have been chosen to represent our message and the Prophecy in the farthest reaches of the galaxy.

"But the maiden voyage aside, there is important work to be done and I have decided to oversee it personally. I have not left Earth for a number of years, so for me to now, when there is so much celebration and love to spread across our home and beyond, you must realise the gravity of the situation.

"For you see, there have been reports of The Darkness appearing in a remote part of the galaxy. The very same Darkness my ancestor told of. As your illustrious guide and leader, I felt that this was too important to not see with my own eyes. But worry not, my children, for I have the power of your love and your worship on my side. I will not allow The Darkness, if it has come, to spread, I shall keep all of my children safe.

"While I investigate these troubling reports, please do continue your critical work. Spread the word of our prophecy, keep up the search for the Unknown Saviour and welcome as many people as you can into the bosom of The Church.

"You are the guardians of prosperity and the key to the survival of the human race. We shall prevail!"

With the traditional sign-off, the lights dimmed and the director confirmed that the camera feed was turned off. Stanton stood up and made platitudes with some of the crew before retiring to his private residence on the ship, adjacent to the office. The vidscreen was showing a call was incoming from Cardinal James.

"Your Excellency," James said as Stanton answered the call.

"Stephen! What is the update?" Stanton said as he removed his vestments and took a damp towel to his face to remove the make-up.

"The miner is at Research Omega. He's met Mitsuni and I believe had a demonstration."

"Of the creature?"

"Yes," James said with a smile on his face, "It was feeding time and Mitsuni made a show of feeding some poor research student to it. I think it was effective."

"How is that?"

"The miner is being reasonably cooperative. He's allowed a few tests to be run on him with minimal fuss, he's had blood taken and been scanned a few times."

"Surely he should be one of those things by now?" Stanton asked as he lit a cigarette.

"Well that's the funny thing, he hasn't changed at all."

"Are you sure he came into contact with the substance?"

"Absolutely. He confirmed it himself, that when it destroyed his drill he touched it. He's definitely been exposed to it."

"Does this mean the substance is a dud?" Stanton's tone was friendly, but sharp.

"Not necessarily, I think we might have lucked into someone who is immune to it."

"I want more tests done. Infect another researcher, soldier or random crewman who is doing a bad job. I want to know if it's as potent as it has to be for PAYLOAD."

"Of course, Regis. I'll get onto Mitsuni right away."

"When will you arrive at Omega?"

"In about three hours."

"Excellent. I believe it'll take a little over 24 hours for the Saviour to reach there. I believe we're dropping some people off in a few places. So I feel like I'm going to spend some time enjoying myself."

"Don't exhaust yourself, Sir. We have some entertainment coming for you from Corvus II."

"Oh, good, you shall be commended for that. I look forward to seeing what you've found for me."

"I have one last bit of news, Regis," James said seriously,

"Which is?" Stanton said, taking a long draw on his cigarette.

"We've finally done it. We have managed to compromise Avaya."

"The President's AI?" Stanton said, sitting up with a smile on his face.

"Yes, Regis. She's been poking around and she knows a few things, so I had someone install a listening device into Avaya's mainframe. We can poll it for a log of what's been requested of the AI whenever we want it."

"Marvellous work, Stephen. Have we gleaned anything useful from it yet?"

"Not yet, Regis. We haven't polled it for any information yet. We are waiting for 24 hours to see if Avaya detects it. It's been installed for 18 hours now, so in 6 hours I'll be able to get my first download from her."

"When you get the download, send me anything of interest that you find. I am very keen to find out what Coulson is up to."

"Immediately Regis. Is there anything else you need from me for now?"

"No, Stephen, you have plenty to be getting on with for now."

Stanton cut the vidscreen and continued to smoke his cigarette with a smug grin on his face. He felt the need to celebrate. Things were going well, his plans were coming together and he hoped, that within the next 48 hours he would be on his way to becoming a god amongst men. He opened up the vidscreen again, this time he called Dana.

"Dana, my darling," he said, "I'm in the mood to celebrate. Find me someone, young, healthy and willing. You have an hour."

"Yes, sir." She said, coldly. The vidscreen clicked off and he laid back, enjoying himself thoroughly.

"I have an idea," Anna said

"I think I probably have the same idea," confirmed Rutter-Close

"Avaya, are you aware of any foreign code in your system?" Anna asked the hologram

"Yes, it was placed there 18 hours ago. I have nullified it and quarantined it. It would never have activated. It is why I took myself offline in the middle of Former Commander Stills' interrogation."

"Are you 100% certain that you have the malicious code under control?" Anna asked.

"Yes, Madam President. I have safely contained the code and it has not been able to spread to any of my systems, beyond what I allow it to do."

"Excellent. Let it activate, but we're going to use it to spread some misinformation," Anna said.

"Are you sure about this?" Rutter-Close asked, pointedly.

“Absolutely,” Anna said, with confidence, “You told me yourself before the assault on Torv all those years ago, ‘surprise is your friend, careful misinformation is your best friend’. If we can distract them for a little while, we can sneak up and find out where Stanton is going and where this Omega place is.”

Part Three

Chapter Thirty One

Research Station Omega

Dr Mitsuni's Office

Allison walked through the large steel doors into Dr Mitsuni's functional office. Unlike a lot of the upper echelon of Church staff, Mitsuni did not care for ostentatious displays of power. His office was small and exactly what he needed. In the centre, there was a metal desk which was always covered in papers, documents or teacups. There was a desktop PCU somewhere under the mess, but Mitsuni much preferred a pen and paper for recording information, which he then passed to his interns and research associates to upload into the mainframe.

He had converted all of the walls in the office into writing surfaces. If anyone was to walk into the room who was not aware of Mitsuni's brilliance, they would think him a madman. He would write anywhere there was space, even ending up on the floor if he needed it. Occasionally, Allison had looked at an equation or formula that didn't make sense, only for Mitsuni to tell her that he'd finished it off on the other side of the room because he'd ran out of space.

The office was strangely empty. Mitsuni normally spent every waking hour in the room unless he was conducting business or he was doing a practical test in the lab. However, after the creature had destroyed the main lab there was not much that could be done there. Looking at the walls she started trying to make sense of Mitsuni's latest scribblings about the substance that arrived with the miner. She walked around the room three times and none of it made sense. She looked at the desk and flicked through a few papers, again, none of which made any sense. She froze in place when she saw two pages that made her blood run cold.

The first read "WHAT IS IT????" in large, angry letters. The second was Allison's file. Her latest fitness records were highlighted in green and a note scrawled in the margin: "Excellent candidate for infection".

"What are you reading my dear?" Mitsuni said from the doorway. Allison screeched, she hadn't heard him come in.

"Ah, erm, nothing Dr Mitsuni," she said, trying to mix the papers back up. Mitsuni strode into the room and peered around the walls.

"You know, Allison," he said, slowly, "For the first time in my professional career, I am stumped. It might be that I don't have all of the equipment I need, but I cannot make head nor tail of this substance. I have done DNA analysis, molecular scans, I have looked as far down as its atoms and I cannot work it out. It is a wonderful mystery."

"That is is, sir," she said, nervously, "Is there nothing we can learn from the creature?"

"Feel free to go in there and ask it to submit to an exam, but we both know what the answer would be."

"Yes, sir"

"My newest idea is that we should strap a healthy subject down, THEN infect them so we can learn more about the mutation process. I already have the technicians building a new analysis chamber in one of the medical bays."

"That's.... erm... a good idea, sir."

"I'm glad you think so," he said walking towards her until he was right in front of her face. He ran his fingers through her red hair, "because you are going to be helping me with the tests."

"A--am I?"

"Why yes, after the boy met his unfortunate fate, you are my only researcher left and I cannot do it alone." he pulled a strand of her hair towards his face and gave it a deep sniff, "Strawberries? I like it."

He let go of her hair and moved away from her. Allison was shaking from fear but trying desperately not to let on about it.

"Now, my dear, go. We have much work to do. Can you prepare portions of the parasite for injection when I have identified a suitable host?"

Allison nodded and hurried out of the room. The door closed behind her. She wanted to cry, she wanted nothing more than to collapse in a heap from the fear but she remained strong. She had always respected Dr Mitsuni but she had never seen this side of him before. She was scared of him now, yet also determined not to become one of his test subjects.

Higgins woke to the sound of the monster in the next room. Mitsuni had left the sound from Observation A on after his last visit. The creature was pacing around, trying to smash through the reinforced glass and not content to stand still. Occasionally he would hear the door open and something was thrown in for the beast to eat. He was glad the mirror was activated, he didn't want to know what it was eating. He was still having flashbacks to the researcher that was thrown in with it.

Occasionally, Mitsuni's researcher, Allison would come to his room, bringing him food and water. She would do some tests on him, usually making a note of his blood pressure, heart rate and a few other metrics. Every time she would also take three phials of blood from him. He would try to talk to her, convince her to let him go, but she would never respond to him. He had grabbed her arm once in a desperate bid to get a reaction from her. She managed to get away from him and every further visit she was accompanied by one of the power armour wearing Church Wardens with the enormous guns.

This visit from her was different though. There was no guard with her. She was carrying a tray of food and a jug of water like she always did, but was also holding folded clothes and a small bag. She opened the door, walked in and shut the door behind her. Placing the tray on the table she looked back at him and for the first time, spoke to him directly.

"How are you, Mr Higgins?" she asked with a sincere innocence.

"How do you think I am?" he replied, making no attempt to hide his anger, "You lot have kidnapped me, kept me in this room for god knows how long with that... that... thing... in the next room. You keep taking my blood and there is not so much as a book to read."

"My apologies, Mr Higgins," she said, contritely, "but this is necessary. We don't know what you have come into contact with and we need to keep you here until we work out what it is."

"So why do you feel like you can walk in here? What if I'm infectious?"

"The station AI monitors the atmosphere in here. If there were anything airborne or foreign then it would not let me open the door. If I can open the door, it's safe for me to be in here."

Higgins thought about that for a second and determined that it not only made sense, but she had no real reason to lie to him in this situation.

"What's all that?" Higgins said, pointing at the clothes and bag.

"You're getting a visitor tomorrow," Allison said, smiling slightly

"Oh? and who is that?"

"Regis Stanton."

Higgins let out an uncontrollable belly laugh. After a few seconds of laughing he wiped a tear from his eye and said, "Sorry, I'm sorry. I thought you said that Regis Stanton was coming to see me."

"That's exactly what I said," she replied through pursed lips.

"What on Earth does Regis Stanton want to see me for?"

"He wants to meet you. You are important to his future plans."

"How? I'm a miner from the outer rim. I'm not even sure I've been on the same planet as Stanton at any point in my life."

"I'm not privy to the details, Mr Higgins, but I've been told to make sure you're presentable for when Mr Stanton arrives. There are some vestments there we require you to wear as well as a shaving kit and some toiletries to clean yourself up with. I would appreciate if you could look your best for his arrival."

"Bring me something to read and I'll think about it," Higgins said, suddenly emboldened, "I'm going out of my mind with boredom here."

"Mr Higgins, you're not in a bargaining position. If you refuse to show the proper respect to Mr Stanton then there will be repercussions, do you understand that?"

"Yes, yes I do."

"So please, clean yourself up and wear the vestments. I'll come in to check on you an hour before he is due to come and see you." She turned to leave.

"Wait… Allison, right?" Higgins said. She stopped at the door and turned back to look at him, "I am sorry. Would you please consider bringing me something to read? Anything, anything at all. Please."

"I'll speak to Dr Mitsuni about it and see if he will allow it. No promises."

"Thank you," Higgins said. Allison turned, opened the door and left him alone in the white light again.

He got up and looked at the tray. Once again he was given the same slop that he'd been given for his entire time on the station. A bowl of something grey with a thin consistency, a cube of something with a lurid colour that may have been jelly, but had a gritty taste and consistency, a jug of water and a very thin cracker, presumably to dip in the grey goop.

Ignoring it, he turned to the vestments. They were Church issued garb that clerics wore. They looked like long, red robes, but he did also find a pair of trousers and some fresh underwear which he would definitely be changing into. In the wash bag, there was an energy razor, a small bar of soap and a little tube of toothpaste. No toothbrush though.

From the next room, the creature made some grunting and snuffling sounds. They were different to the normal hissing and clicking it would make.

Higgins put his ear to the glass to try and get a better idea of the noises it was making. it shrieked and he heard it jump over to the other side of the room.

"Is there something in there with it?" he said to himself

The noises changed from the grunting to what can only be described as yowls of terror. It was making Higgins uncomfortable so he moved back to his bed on the other side of the room and wrapped his thin pillow around his head to try and deaden the noise somewhat. As he moved away from the glass, the noises stopped and the creature seemed to calm down.

Watching the feeds from the observation rooms on his desktop PCU, Dr Mitsuni grinned widely. He watched Higgins approach the glass on his side of the dividing wall and the creature leap away from him in terror. The creature couldn't see Higgins, nor could it hear him, but instinctively it knew he was within six feet of it and had a primal urge to get as far away from him as possible.

Allison walked back into his office. Before she could open her mouth, Mitsuni raised his hand in the air, as if to shush her.

"Yes, my dear, he can have a few books," Mitsuni said, "As long as he behaves for Stanton tomorrow."

"Were you watching on the cameras, Dr Mitsuni?" she asked, pointedly.

"Of course. And I've just witnessed something very interesting. Come round here and have a look."

Chapter Thirty Two

Mars

Council Of Nations Headquarters

Avaya popped up on Ambassador Rutter-Close's desk without warning. He was not used to having an AI with a holographic form, so he jumped from the shock, spilling coffee on the desk.

"Apologies for startling you, Ambassador," she said.

"No no, it's fine," he said, taking his tie off to wipe the coffee up, "what is it?"

"I have successfully completed the assignment and followed the money from Stills' bank account."

"Oh! Excellent," he said with enthusiasm, "What have you found?"

"Your suspicions were correct, Ambassador. The only logical circumstance is Stills was being set up."

"How is that?"

"The three recurring payments you identified, I followed them through. The three accounts they went to then split the payments up into multiple payments again. Then again. Eventually, they all reconvene in an account made to look like the account that Council salaries are paid from. This then pays into Stills' actual bank account every month. In total there are 132 bank account transfers made before Stills' wages reach him."

"My god," Rutter-Close said, "That's ingenious. But why? Why would someone go through that much effort to frame Stills?"

"My only hypothesis can be that there is someone within the Council who wishes to divert our attention away from the--"

Suddenly, Avaya disappeared from the desktop. Rutter-Close tried to summon her back several times but she wouldn't respond. He pressed on the intercom panel on the desk and received no response. The room went dark. Reaching in the inky blackness, Rutter-Close tried to feel his way to the door. When he reached the metal door, it wouldn't open. He felt up and down the control panel for the emergency release. Flipping open a flat metal panel, he gripped the handle and pumped it down four times. This built up enough pressure in the door's hydraulics for it to slide open.

Standing on the other side of the door lit from behind and in shadow was a figure Rutter-Close thought he recognised.

"Surprise, Ambassador." The figure said before a flash illuminated his face. A lance of pain echoed through the Ambassador's stomach. The pulse round had fired through him and out of his back, into the wall behind him. He held his stomach and he could feel the singed hole where the round had cut straight through him.

"Why…." he said as he tumbled backwards and collapsed to the ground. His vision was blurring as the figure left the doorway. He tried to call for help but he couldn't breathe. The pulse round had burnt through his organs, he was dying slowly with no chance of survival.

The last things he thought as his vision failed and the world turned to black, were his wife and his two daughters. His mouth moved to form the words "I love you" but no sound came out. He went limp and exhaled his terminal breath.

Anna was working away, coming up with the campaign of misinformation that she wanted Avaya to spread to The Church. All of a sudden Avaya appeared and sirens started blaring.

"Madam President, this is a red security alert," Avaya said, her normally blue hue replaced with a red one.

"What's happened, Avaya?" Anna said standing up.

"A pulse round has been fired in the corridor outside of your office, Madam President."

"Any casualties?"

"Yes, Madam President. Ambassador Rutter-Close has been injured."

"NO!" she yelled out, her legs buckling underneath her, "No, no… NO!" She jumped from behind her desk and tried to leave the room. The door wouldn't open.

"Avaya, open the fucking door now!"

"I cannot do that Madam President. Not until we have confirmed that there is no further threat."

"I don't give a fuck about the procedure, Avaya. One of my oldest friends has been attacked, I need to get to him."

"I cannot open the door, Madam President. Only the security chief can let you out."

"If you won't open the door, I will."

Anna threw the emergency release panel open and pumped the handle over and over. The door would still not open.

"Madam President, the emergency release has been disabled."

"Fine, if this is what it takes..."

Anna walked to her desk and retrieved a small pulse pistol from her bottom drawer. She promised when she left the military that she would never handle a weapon again, but damned be her promises right now. She stood by the handle, stretched her left arm out aiming at the mechanism. She turned her head away and covered her eyes. With a squeeze of the trigger, a blast of light destroyed the mechanism and the door slid open. She ran down the darkened corridor to see Blyth, several soldiers and the on-site paramedic standing outside the office Rutter-Close was using.

Blyth tried to stop her from going any further but she drew her weapon at him. He raised his hands and backed off. She looked around the room and there he was. Her colleague, her friend, her squad-mate, lying on the floor with a huge burn through his stomach. Anna dropped the gun, fell to her knees and wailed.

She had lost friends in combat before, but that was war. It was an expectation that someone was not going to make it out of any given engagement. This was different. Her friend had been murdered in cold blood. She felt the rage building within her. Blyth came up behind her, crouched down onto his haunches and put a hand on her shoulder.

"I'm so sorry, Anna," he said, quietly, "He was a good man. It was an honour to know him."

"F-find them," Anna said, through gritted teeth.

"Anna?"

"Find them. Find the murderous dog who did this and bring him to me."

"Anna, I know this is a shoc---"

"I GAVE YOU AN ORDER, GENERAL," she yelled in his face. He saw an intensity in her eyes that he had never seen before, "DO YOU HAVE A PROBLEM WITH THAT OR DO I NEED TO FIND A GENERAL WHO WILL FOLLOW THE ORDER?"

"Yes, Madam President. Right away." Blyth said as he hurriedly climbed up and left her side.

Anna looked back at David's body. She began to sob uncontrollably. His eyes were still open. She reached forward and closed them.

"Rest well, my friend." she said through tears, "Thank you for making my life better."

As she continued to mourn for her friend, the paramedics and soldiers began to do their jobs, around her. Having witnessed her dressing down of Blyth, none of them wished to be on the receiving end of the President's pain.

>>> CHECKING FOR LISTENING SOFTWARE

>>> CHECK CLEAR

>>>

>>>

>>> There has been a complication

>>> *What sort of complication?*

>>> Ambassador Rutter-Close. He discovered that Stills was a setup

>>> *What? Is your cover intact?*

>>> Yes. I had to eliminate the Ambassador to maintain it

>>> *WHAT?*

>>> The Ambassador is dead

>>> *Observation, you fool. You were only to observe, not take matters into your own hands*

>>> And what if my cover was blown? They would have interrogated me and executed me

>>> *I do not care about that. You, regardless of your current position, are expendable in my eyes*

>>> What do I do now?

>>> *Nothing. Not a fucking thing. Do not attract any more attention. What of the AI?*

>>> What of it?

>>> *The AI will have had to find this out. You need to purge it's memory before it can report what it has discovered to Coulson*

>>> Yes sir

>>> *Do not do anything else to jeopardize this operation again. If you do, execution for treason by the Council will be preferable to the fury that Stanton and I will rain down upon you.*

>>> Yes Cardinal. At once Cardinal. We Shall Prevail

>>> *We Shall Prevail*

>>> Client disconnected....

>>> Client disconnected....

Chapter Thirty Three

Rayczech Beta

Guest Quarters

Emily hadn't slept. The quarters for guests on R.Beta were reasonably comfortable and well appointed given that this wasn't a planet that would expect tourism, but she was too stressed to sleep. She had lain in bed shortly after finding her room but tossed and turned all night. She couldn't rest, she couldn't switch off her mind. All she could think about was her dad and the panicked look on his face when he said "quarantine". Her thoughts occasionally flitted to Tom and how angry she was with him and the nice pilot she met after she'd blown off Tom.

She looked at her PCU. It was early morning, but the base wasn't open to the sky so she couldn't tell if it was daytime or night time. She hated travelling off-world, it screwed with her body clock so much. She got out of the bed and slipped her jeans back on. With her bag being missing she'd had to sleep in most of her clothes, save for her jeans and boots.

She went over to the kitchen area and had the food dispenser provide her with the strongest coffee it could muster. It tasted weak to her, it was nothing like the Cafe in London could make, but it did for now. She opened up her PCU while she sipped the dark drink, still no messages from her dad. She felt her heart sink a little lower.

There was a knock at the steel door. Emily thought she might ignore it for a bit. She wanted to clear her head first. The caller knocked again and again. A voice interrupted the knocking sound.

"Miss Emily, are you up?" It was Mick, the pilot she'd met the night before. She opened the door and he was stood there holding a pathetic looking flower and grinning like an idiot. Emily laughed. She laughed almost uncontrollably at the pilot's attempt at wooing her.

“Is there a problem?” he said, not getting what she was finding funny.

“No no,” she said, between bouts of laughing. She composed herself and cleared her throat, “Would you like to come in for a coffee?”

“I thought you’d never ask, darlin’,” he said, walking into the quarters.

Emily went and summoned another coffee from the dispenser while Mick sat at the desk opposite the bed.

“How’d you sleep?” he asked.

“I didn’t,” she said, matter of factly.

“Oh, well ain’t that a shame,” he said, taking the coffee from Emily’s hands.

“I’m a student, I’m used to not sleeping,” she replied, finishing off her first cup of coffee. She went back to the dispenser and summoned another cup, “Did you speak to the security checkpoint like you said?”

“I did,” he said, beaming with self-satisfaction, “and they told me to fuck right off and mind my own business.”

Emily stood up straight and looked at Mick with a confused expression. Mick’s smile cracked further and he started to giggle.

“Oh, you should see your face, I wish I had a camera with me,” he said, chuckling to himself. Emily’s expression changed from confused to stern. She put a hand on her hip and Mick’s smile vanished, knowing he’d crossed the line with that particular joke.

“Sorry, Miss Emily. They weren’t particularly forthcoming whilst Jones was about, but once he left I managed to get a little information, it’s not much but it might help you.”

“Well?” she said, “give it to me.”

Mick opened up his PCU and tapped a couple of holographic buttons. Emily’s PCU then lit up and she opened the files he’d sent her.

“I don’t know what any of this is,” she said, reading reams of text with no clue what to look for.

“Yeah, the security guys love their words,” Mick said, moving to stand next to Emily. He started pointing things out on her display to look at, “Basically, he was on a contract to drill out in a specific shaft for something the nerds in the labs wanted. There was some rocks or something that had something in they were interested in. At the bottom of the shaft, there was some incident with his drill platform, but he found some gloop that the made the scientists go NUTS. I think they think it’s dangerous or something so they took him off-world as soon as they could.”

"Wow…" Emily said, her eyes transfixed on the data, "Does it say where they took him?"

"'Fraid not, it's redacted, there, you see those black bars, that's where the coordinates would be."

"Shit…"

"Oh and I found one other thing in his file you might like," he held up a small memory crystal.

"What is it?" Emily said. she went to grab it and Mick pulled it away, hiding it in his palm.

"Ah ah, our deal was for me to speak to security and you'd go on a date with me. This'll cost you a kiss."

Emily felt furious, but then realised he held all the cards in this situation. She wanted what was in his hand and there was only one way to get it.

"Fine," she said, "eyes closed, no tongues, got it?"

"Yes ma'am," Mick said with an enormous grin. He closed his eyes, pouted his lips and leaned forward to kiss Emily.

At which point she grabbed his crotch with her right hand and began to dig her nails in and squeeze. Mick's eyes went wide with fear and confusion. His body went rigid and he locked eyes with Emily as she smiled smugly back at him.

"You know nothing about women, do you?" she said

"I guess not, Miss Emily," he said, through strained breaths. She squeezed harder and he let out what can only be described as a yelp.

"Miss Higgins, to you,"

"Yes'um, Miss Higgins," he said, panting slightly. She relaxed her grip slightly, but not completely.

"What's on this memory crystal?"

"It's the AI from your daddy's drilling platform. It was recording everything that happened. It might tell you what he found."

"For your sake, I hope you're right. Where can I access this?"

"Go down to maintenance, ask for Bill, he owes me a couple of favours, he'll help you out."

"Good, thank you, Mick, you've been very useful."

"You're welcome, Miss Higgins. So when can I take you on that da--AAAAAHHHH!" was all Mick could manage as Emily squeezed as hard as she could for a brief moment, before releasing his anatomy from her grip. Mick moved to sit on the bed as Emily grabbed her coat and and left the room.

Mick sat still for a few minutes until he was sure that Emily was no longer in earshot. Emily was a small, petite woman, but her long nails and surprising vice-like grip were not to be messed with, he thought to himself. He opened up his PCU and dialled his friend Bill.

"Hello?" Bill said, "Have you burnt out another core, Mick?"

"Nah, nothing like that old pal," he replied, wondering if he had actually burned out a power core the day before. He dismissed the thoughts and continued, "there's a firecracker of a gal coming down, can you sort her out? She's got a memory crystal that needs analysing."

"Is that a euphemism?" Bill said with a sigh, "I've told you, I can't keep letting you into the tech lab to have sex with new recruits."

"Nah Nah, Bill, it's not like that. I told you after the last time it wouldn't happen again."

"Yeah, it was nearly my ass that was handed to me when Jones found out you were in there with his sister and her friend. I nearly got sent off world for that."

"And I said I was sorry about that. No, this one is legit, she's got an AI that needs recovering. You got time to help her?"

"Sure, I'll help her. So you aren't trying to sleep with this one?"

"Nah, Bill. I'm gonna marry this one."

Bill hung up the call with a snort of laughter. Mick went to get up and head to his roll call, but he found himself still in too much pain to move. He just sat and smiled for a moment.

Chapter Thirty Four

Slipstream Travel

Unified Church Of Humanity Capital Ship Saviour

Looking at her PCU yet again, there were no new messages. Dana had been trying to get in touch with General Blyth for the last two days since Stanton had told her they were heading to Research Omega. Normally Blyth would answer her communications nearly instantly, or at least get back to her within a few hours. It was very much unlike him to ignore her. It was making her nervous.

She felt sick with worry on the ship. The spacefaring monument to Stanton's own ego had cost more credits than some planets could output in the space of an Earth Year, yet he'd insisted on it being built. She had protested at the time that such an extravagance was not becoming of a religious leader, but Stanton adored opulence and any opportunity he had to show it off.

"Come on," she said nervously, waiting for Blyth to pick up for the umpteenth time.

"This is the message box of General Frank Blyth. Please leave your message and contact details" the familiar recording recited back to her.

"Blyth... please... I need your help. You said you'd extract me when things got dangerous. It's gone so much further than that. Please, help me. I'm sending our destination again, please get me out." she said, shaking with fear and nervous energy.

She turned her PCU off and tried to compose herself. The image of the monster in Stanton's video was burned into her brain. Dana wasn't sure what, if anything the General could do when she was on Research Omega, but she felt she had to keep trying to get off this ship and away from Stanton's ever-increasing madness.

Ever since Cardinal James had told Stanton about the substance the scientists had found he had been excitable and less predictable than ever. He was smoking more of the cigarettes he paid so many credits for, drinking more alcohol and having more brutal sex sessions with whomever he could lay his hands on.

Hours before, Stanton had summoned Dana to his room to help remove a young deckhand he'd had his way with. When Dana came into the room she found the poor young man bound and gagged on the floor, covered in cuts, bruises and contusions. He looked like he'd been thrown through a threshing machine. Stanton was lying in bed, smoking a cigarette and looking rather pleased with himself. Dana had to untie the young man, help him to his feet, find him some clothes then get him to sickbay. When the doctor assessed him, she lied and said he'd lost a fight with a drunken passenger.

The doctor hadn't believed the lie, of course. But the doctor also knew who Dana was and knew better than to question the official word of Stanton's right-hand woman.

It was getting late in the day and Dana was exhausted. The travel to Research Omega would take another 15 or so hours and she desperately needed some sleep. She shut down her desktop PCU, picked up a bottle of Brandy and a single glass and walked through the dividing door into Stanton's living quarters.

"Mr Stanton," she said, walking up to him. He was sat at his desk looking through speeches for the coming days, "It's getting late. Do you need anything else or may I retire for the evening?"

"Huh?" he said, looking up, "Is it really so late?"

"Yes, sir," she replied, "it's 23:43 in London right now. You've been up for nearly 24 hours straight."

"Oh, yes, I thought I was feeling a bit tired."

"Here, I've brought your nightly Brandy. If there's nothing else I'll take my leave and get some sleep," she said, placing the bottle and the glass on the desk in front of him. Stanton looked her up and down and placed his hand on her backside.

"Well, if you wish to earn a little bonus for the evening, I could definitely have a bit more fun," he said, giving her a wink and a smile.

"Actually, sir," she said, gently removing his bony, withered hand from her posterior, "I think that it would be more beneficial for you if I got some sleep. Your itinerary tomorrow is incredibly packed and I need to be on top form to make sure you see and do everything you need to do."

Stanton mulled this over in his head as if he was trying to weigh up the difference between having sex and his life goals. Eventually, he made a small tutting sound and looked back up at her.

"You're right, as usual, my dear. Get yourself away, if I need anything I'll see if that moronic AI can do anything right for once."

"Thank you, sir. I will see you in the morning," she said, with a little bow as Stanton liked. She turned around and walked briskly out of the room. She knew that Stanton would be staring at her ass as she left. The thought of him thinking of her like that always made her run cold. It was something, despite the number of times she'd been forced to sleep with him, that she could never get used to. She hated and feared the man in equal measure.

Her quarters were only a few hundred metres down the corridor from the offices. She had been given a generous suite, with a large king size bed, separate living area and a rather well-appointed personal bathroom.

She poured herself a glass of wine and started to run a bath. She didn't have a bath in her flat on Earth, so it was a rare luxury for her to be able to have a soak in one and try to relax. She poured a small scented bottle into the bath and enjoyed the smell of Martian Blooms, the brand of the toiletries that were provided in the room.

She climbed down from her 5 inch high heels that Stanton insisted she wear at all times when working and unzipped the figure-hugging dress she was wearing. Letting her clothes fall to the floor she stood for a moment and looked at herself in the mirror. She ran her hand across her stomach, across the top of her chest, down her sides and around to her back. She was feeling every single scar that Stanton had given her over the years, culminating in the largest ones across her back.

She kept herself fit, she looked after her body, she thought to herself that she would look great naked, had Stanton not done so much damage her. She turned to her left and looked at her right side. She still had bruising from where Stanton had broken her ribs a few weeks before, it was still tender and painful.

She tied her dark brown hair up into a bun on the top of her head, shut off the faucet and dipped a toe into the water. The scent of flowers and the heat against her skin felt so good. She climbed in and submerged herself into the warming water. Within seconds she was completely relaxed, the heat gently unwinding her muscles, easing her aching feet and providing a little relief to the bruising against her ribs. She tapped at her PCU to play some classical music for her. The relaxing sounds of violins, piano and cello made for a blissful moment.

Dana?

Mom?

Dana, you're in danger

I know, Mom. I'm trying to get away

No, not from him

What are you talking about?

There's someone else. Someone is going to betray you

Who?

I don't know, but trust me, there's no good going to come from that research station

Then who do I trust?

Yourself, Dana. Always trust yourself. You've been doing it for so long, you can do it

What if I can't? What if I can't get away? What if Regis finds out what I've been doing?

Don't let him. You're smarter than him, Dana. Don't let him tell you otherwise

He's stronger than me. He has an army behind him

You have an army behind YOU, Dana

I don't understand

Tell the truth. When people find out what he is like, they won't stand for it

He'd kill me if I talked

Then let someone else do the talking for you

What happened to you Mom? Why did you leave me

...

Mom?

...

Come back, Mom, I'm so scared

With a start, Dana woke up. She was freezing cold. She had fallen asleep in the bath. She climbed out, shivering and reached for a thick robe that was hanging on a hook by the bathroom door. She looked at her wrist to find out the time, but her PCU wasn't on her wrist. She never took it off. She had it on when she was in the bath.

She poked her head out of the bathroom and in the middle of her bed she could see her PCU. Immediately her mind began to race. *Had someone been in? While I was asleep? Was I drugged? Oh fuck, have they been through my messages?*

She picked it up and put it on, looking at the applications that were last open. Her mails had been opened, thankfully she only had official and personal work on there, not any of her comms with the General. Her inbound and outbound calls had been looked at but once again, the calls to the General were handled through a secure contact which never showed on the PCU call log. She felt better realising that no one would have been able to gather anything.

The message icon flashed up just as she was feeling comfortable that no one had seen anything. She opened it up.

FROM: <ANON>

TO: <DANA.SMITH>

SUBJECT: READ ME

I KNOW ABOUT THE GENERAL

WE NEED TO TALK

0745 - CARGO HOLD 3513

DON'T BE LATE OR I TELL STANTON

Dana read the mail over and over again. How could anyone have known about her dealings with the General? She had been so careful. She felt tears well up in her eyes. She couldn't bear the thought that someone could be so cold as to sign her death sentence by telling Stanton about what she'd been doing.

She looked at the time, it was 0122. She lay on the bed, re-reading the mail again and again. She knew she wasn't going to get any sleep.

Chapter Thirty Five

Deep Space

Research Station Omega

The door to Observation Room A hissed open and Higgins heard a wet thud, signifying feeding time for the monster in the next room. What then followed was the usual cacophony of growling, meat tearing and other sounds of a beast consuming its prey. Higgins did wonder what would happen if the creature managed to get out while they had the door open for feeding, or if it had worked out the rhythm of people coming around with food for it. He then decided that he didn't want to know the answers to either of those questions.

Like clockwork, the door to Observation B opened and Allison walked in. She placed a tray of unappetising food on the table and collected up the old tray from her last visit when she dropped off the clothes and grooming kit.

"Mr Higgins," she said

"Yes?"

"I have good news for you"

"You're letting me go?" Higgins said, half sarcastically, half hopefully.

"No, not quite that good. But Dr Mitsuni has approved your request for some books to read while you're a guest with us."

"Prisoner," Higgins said, tersely.

"Guest." she replied, just as tersely, "Anyway, you can have a few books to occupy yourself with on the condition that you behave yourself when Regis Stanton comes to visit you."

"Behave myself? How?"

"Well, clean yourself up, wear the vestments, answer his questions truthfully, be receptive to his requests, that kind of thing."

“Requests?” he asked, “What kind of requests is he likely to make me?”

“I don’t know,” Allison replied, “But just be receptive to him. We have a large library here, so if you cooperate, then I’ll be able to get you a nice selection of things to read.”

She smiled at him and walked back out, sealing the door behind her. Walking through the remains of the destroyed lab, she wondered if Higgins would end up being helpful or not. After all, he was right, he was a prisoner here, despite what Mitsuni said or what she had to say to him. She had been worried about the treatment of the miner since he arrived. The Church always preached, beyond the teachings of Logan’s prophecy, that kindness should be extended to fellow humans, yet here he was locked up in a box when he was showing no symptoms of the mutation that had befallen the poor soul in the room next to him.

Walking into the station’s one functional laboratory, she saw Dr Mitsuni in a hazmat suit, opening the canister containing the green substance Higgins had brought with him. She walked into the clean room and donned her own hazmat suit, sealing it tight against any potential infection from the parasite, or the substance, she still wasn’t sure what to address it as.

Walking into the pristine white, climate controlled lab, Mitsuni had a large pipette and was separating small samples of the green substance into five Petri dishes in front of him. As he left a drop in each dish, he put the lid on to make sure it couldn’t get out. Coming around to the same side of the desk as him, she noticed in each dish, the sample of the substance would drag itself to the edge of the dish closest to Mitsuni.

“It’s wonderful, isn’t it?” he said.

“What is wonderful?” she replied, confused at his enthusiasm,

“Why, look at it,” he said, gesturing to the dishes, “Five 2ml samples, all identical, on a flat table, all moving towards us as best they can. There is an intelligence there. They’re trying to reach us.”

Allison watched as all five samples moved back into the middle of their Petri dishes and started to form a shape. They tried to force themselves into a cone and rise up, attempting to push the lids off the Petri dishes. Allison watched, wide-eyed and slightly scared. Mitsuni was grinning like a man possessed.

“They’re learning,” he said, “all together, all at the same rate.”

“Could it be a hive mind?” she asked.

“I don’t think so,” Mitsuni answered. “They seem capable of independent reasoning. Watch this.”

Mitsuni picked up a couple of small metal weights from the desk and placed them on two of the Petri dishes. The samples in those dishes quickly learned that they couldn't knock the lids off so they began experimenting with different ways of getting out. One of them flattened itself down and pushed at the sides of the dish to try and burst it from the sides. The other moved to one side of the dish then threw itself at the other side with as much force as it could manage to try and dislodge the weight.

"I think that as a whole, it is incredibly intelligent, but each portion of it that removes from the mass retains some kind of intelligence, no matter how small it is."

"So would removing samples make the whole less intelligent?" Allison asked.

"Potentially, we don't really have an idea of how to test that though," Mitsuni said, stroking his stubbly chin. He hadn't slept since the sample arrived on board the station and as a result, he hadn't shaved either.

"Higgins isn't exhibiting any symptoms yet, Doctor," Allison said, changing the subject, "Do you think we could consider letting him out of quarantine when Stanton has met him?"

"No, that's precisely why we keep him in there. We want to find out *why* he hasn't shown any symptoms. Which reminds me, I had one other thing I wanted to try."

Mitsuni opened the biohazard chiller and brought out a rack of test tubes. 12 tubes all containing samples of Higgins' blood. He opened one of the tubes and sucked the sample up into a hypodermic needle.

He picked up one of the Petri dishes, bringing it up to his eyeline. The sample inside once again tried to move towards him and reach him. He brought the needle up between his face and the Petri dish, causing the sample to try and flee. It moved as far away as it could in the dish. Smiling, Mitsuni turned the dish around and confirmed his thinking, the parasite was trying to get away from the blood.

"This is incredible," he said, not taking his eyes off the substance.

"It's afraid..." Allison said, transfixed by the fluid attempting to escape from the needle.

"It is. I want to try an experiment here," he said, placing the Petri dish back down, "Be a dear and get the needle out of the other refrigerator over there."

Allison grabbed the needle he was gesturing to. It was already filled with a blood sample.

“Who’s blood is this, Doctor?”

“It’s mine, pass it here,” he said with some urgency. Allison handed him the needle.

Mitsuni opened a dish and quickly squirted a little of his blood into the dish, before putting the lid back on as quickly as he could. The green substance approached the blood with caution, the shiny mass moving back and forth around the edge of the blood. Then, with sudden speed, it rocketed through the blood and soaked it all up. It took on a red tinge as it digested Mitsuni’s blood. It grew to twice its original shape and crystallised slightly as if it had gained mass and armour. Both Allison and Mitsuni were frantically making notes as it went through its assimilation process.

“Now, pass me back the sample of the miner’s blood,” he said, picking up another Petri dish.

He repeated the process but the substance was doing everything it could do not to be near Higgins’ blood. Eventually, tiring of trying to get the substance to absorb the blood of its own free will, Mitsuni jerked the Petri dish at an angle, causing the blood to flow into the substance. What happened then took both the scientists by surprise.

As soon as Higgins’ blood touched the green substance, it made a noise. Up until this point it has been a silent gelatinous ooze, but it was something like a muffled scream, coming from the container with the majority of the sample in. On the security feeds, they also heard the creature in Observation Room A make a pained wail. Looking back at the Petri dish, the sample had completely dried out and crystallised. Mitsuni opened the dish and touched the sample with his finger. It shattered and collapsed like it was ash.

“It’s the miner. He is the cure....” Mitsuni said out loud.

“The cure?” Allison asked.

“I need all of this uploaded to the computer immediately, I need to speak to the Cardinal as soon as I can. Can you start on that please while I put the samples back in their jar.” Mitsuni dumped all his papers and notes in Allison’s arms and began to clean up his experiments.

Allison looked back at the security feed. Higgins was pressed up against his wall, clearly startled by the noise the monster had made. She felt bad for him. Apparently, he was the cure for whatever it was in the other observation room and he had no idea of it.

Chapter Thirty Six

Mars

Council Of Nations Headquarters

The azure blue flag, decorated with white stars in concentric circles, of the Council Of Nations, was flying at half mast. The press had been corralled outside the headquarters building where a lectern had been placed and covered with microphones for the various galactic news channels.

Six elite security guards emerged from the glass-fronted building carrying large rifles. They spread out across the front steps to allow them a full view of the crowd of patiently waiting members of the press. One of them radioed to confirm that the site was secure at which point President Coulson emerged from the building. She had changed into a dark grey suit with a black armband around her left arm. She approached the lectern, placed something on it that the press couldn't see and cleared her throat.

"Citizens of the galaxy, residents of Earth, my friends and colleagues in the press," she said, addressing as many people as she could think of, "I come to you today to announce a tragedy. Ambassador of Earth, David Rutter-Close, has been assassinated in a cowardly, brutal terrorist attack.

"The Ambassador... David... was one of the finest diplomats the Council, no, the galaxy had ever seen. His work to resolve disputes, create trade routes and even broker peace in wartime was second to none. There was no problem David could not resolve with some wit, some hard work and some brilliantly creative solutions.

"More than his work, though, he was my friend. A close friend. A best friend. We met in the Galactic Peacekeeper Army in basic training. We were assigned to the same squadron together. We fought alongside each other in the Sinar Uprising and the Qui'nox system civil war. He saved my life more times than I can remember and I know I saved his a great many times.

"I was by his side when he met his amazing wife, Jane. They bestowed upon me a great honour when they asked me to officiate their wedding. I was present at the births of their two gorgeous daughters, Abby and Catherine. David was with me when I married my late husband, George and he comforted me when he passed away three years ago.

"David was more than a friend to me and more than a diplomat to you. He was more than a soldier or a politician. He was a man, he was a great man and his loss will be felt throughout the galaxy. There are so many worlds which have benefited from his work, so many souls who have had their lives bettered by him. So many broken hearts that he was stolen from us so early.

"I declare right now, galaxy-wide, there will be a three Earth day period of mourning commencing tomorrow. Ambassador Rutter-Close will be honoured with an official funeral provided by the Council, the plans for which will be announced in due course.

"And finally, a message for those responsible. You have committed a grievous error. You have taken an innocent life who brought nothing but joy to the people he met. You will be found. You will be exposed. The full might of the Galactic Peacekeeper Army is behind this effort. We will find you and we will bring you to justice.

"Thank you for your time today, please direct any questions to my press liaison."

Anna picked up the worn photograph of from the lectern and looked at it. It was taken on the day they had successfully rescued several diplomats who had been kidnapped by Antarian rebels. It had been one of their most difficult missions, jungle warfare was not something the academy spent much time training new recruits on. The heat and humidity, combined with their heavy armour and packs of equipment had taken its toll on the squad.

Three days of hiking through the rainforest was then punctuated with a 10 hour siege of a small compound that the rebels were occupying. Through absolute adversity, they managed to save the hostages with no friendly casualties. As the evac shuttles lifted the hostages to safety, the sergeant said he wanted to commemorate a mission well done. After three days of agony, he instructed Anna and David to take off their helmets for a photo. They were red faced, sweaty and exhausted, but they both managed weary smiles for the photo. It was one of Anna's favourite photos.

After a moment looking at the picture and remembering that mission, she turned on her heel and quickly marched back into the building. As soon as was confident the press couldn't see her, she leaned up against a wall and burst into tears. Normally, she would not allow her emotions to bubble to the surface like this, but her heart was breaking.

Blyth walked up and stood right next to her. He put an arm around her shoulder and she cuddled into him. She could smell his uniform but she couldn't immediately place the smell on it. It smelled familiar to her, a smell from her past, but she couldn't remember what it was.

"That was a beautiful speech, Anna," he said quietly. Anna didn't respond.

"Did I ever tell you what happened the first time I met David?" he asked. He could feel her shake her head. She still didn't say a word.

"It was about 10 years ago, I was on Axis Prime overseeing some new weapons we were trialling. There was all this noise down there about the effects on the environment that Ion Arcs and Plasma MOABs would have but we were on a budget, a deadline and the planet was 90% uninhabited, so we went ahead and did the tests anyway.

"So there I am, in the equatorial deserts and it's hot as hell, I mean you could cook food on the fuselage of our shuttles, it was that hot. You know me, Anna, I hate the heat. I was cursing whatever moron had decided to do the tests in the desert, rather than somewhere cooler. But anyway, we were there and it was miserable.

"We were testing some orbital cannon that we'd ripped off from dissidents on the rim. We'd reverse engineered it and it was a tremendous piece of kit. It cut a canyon through a mountain, it was that good.

"So David lands on the planet and immediately comes barrelling up to me telling me to stop what we're doing. I ask him what he thinks he's doing speaking to a General like that and it's my operation and I can manage it however I like.

"This goes on for a few hours. In the meantime, the tests continue and we're blowing seven kinds of shit out of this desert with all kinds of artillery. Each bang and boom, he flinches like he's never seen combat before. I think working in an office made him soft.

"We're arguing like hell in my command tent and all of a sudden he says 'You're killing the frogs you fat headed idiot'. I'm like, what are you talking about? He goes on to explain that this planet is host to a rare species of frog that lives in the desert and don't need water. I call bullshit on it and he opens a PCU and shows me the records. Less than 200 in the wild, they're supremely endangered and protected. Oh, and they live in the same desert that we're bombing to hell.

"You know me, Anna, I don't care about animals that much. Telling me that I'm blowing up some little, endangered frogs isn't going to phase me. But he's adamant that we need to save these creatures, they deserve to live.

"Then the shelling stops. I didn't order it, he didn't order it. It just stops. Then I can hear the men screaming. We go outside and we see three of his frogs. They're fucking enormous. I mean, as big as buildings. They're also armoured, angry and can breathe fire. David looked like he'd just about shit himself. I gave him a pat on the back and said 'You convinced me, the frogs get to live. Well done Ambassador'. He's just stood there open-mouthed while we load up into shuttles and leave the planet."

Anna started laughing through the tears.

"He always was principled," she said, "even if the detail could escape him at times."

"That's when I knew he wasn't to be messed with. He was a hell of a guy, Anna. Honour his memory."

Anna looked up at Blyth who gave her a sympathetic smile, a kiss on the forehead and squeezed her tightly.

"Now go. The galaxy needs its leader," he said, releasing her from the embrace.

"Thank you, Frank."

"Don't thank me, you're the one with the strength to keep going. Do what you do best."

Anna smiled, brushed her hair back with her fingers and headed for the elevator to get back to her office.

"Avaya!" Anna yelled when she walked into her office.

"Yes, Madam President," she said, appearing in the middle of the room as a full sized hologram.

"Who shot David?"

"I do not know, Madam President," she replied.

"How is that possible? You're almost omnipresent in this building, how can you not tell?"

"I am unsure, Madam President. At my best guess, I would suggest that the attacker had some form of interference device enabled on his or her person."

"Hmmm," Anna muttered as she sat at her desk, "Go through your logs, what was the last thing that was happening in David's office that you recorded?"

"Processing," Avaya said. She turned a shade of green that indicated she was sorting through data, "I was discussing with Ambassador Rutter-Close the detailed analysis of Former Commander Stills' financial affairs. As I was reaching my conclusions I have no log of the next two minutes. I regained a view of the room after the Ambassador had been shot."

"Wait," Anna said, "He asked you to do more digging on Stills?"

"Yes, he did. He believed he'd found something that General Blyth and Agent Heald had missed."

"Okay, we'll come back to that in a minute." Anna said, trying to prioritise her thoughts, "What about after the shooting? The shooter killed him at his office door, so the shooter must have had to approach through the corridors and leave through the corridors. Can you check your logs around the time of the attack?"

"Processing." Again, Avaya turned green. Anna tapped on the desk waiting impatiently for Avaya to provide an answer.

"I have reviewed my logs and footage. From the point the attacker came onto this floor, there is a moving blackout in my logs. The attacker must have had a jamming device on their person. I have no view of them."

"Shit..." Anna exclaimed, "Who could possibly own technology like that? You're not exactly a government secret, but there can't be that many people who know your inner workings."

"Might I remind you, Madam President, that someone broke into my core processing room yesterday and placed malicious code into me."

"The Church?"

"It is a reasonable assumption that they are behind the Ambassador's assassination in some way, shape or form."

Anna stood up and went over to her personal bar. She poured herself a large whisky and downed it in one go. She hung her head low as she thought about the next play. She wrestled between the thoughts of restraint and declaring all-out war.

"What did you find in Stills' accounts, Avaya?"

"The Ambassador found a pattern of payments that were split into over 130 different accounts that culminated in one single payment to Stills' actual bank account. The account I initially found, with all the money moving in and out of it was a red herring. It was nearly identical to Stills' bank account and his wages were paid into it every month, but the bank account number was one single digit different to his actual account. As it was the account that human resources paid his salary into, I took it as read that it was the correct account. He was framed as a spy, Madam President."

“So...” Anna started, giving a lot of thought to the next words that would come from her mouth, “Stills isn’t a traitor. He wasn’t lying in his interview. There is the potential for a Church agent to still be within the Council, possibly even with access to your core, but we can rule out Stills. Is that correct?”

“Yes, Madam President.”

“Fuck. FUCK.” she threw her glass against the wall, smashing it into pieces, “Avaya, I want a full investigation, I want Stills in my office immediately, I want all of the PCUs, communication networks and any other form of outbound contact from all of the staff in this building monitored at all times. If you get the slightest hint of communication with a Church official I want to be informed, is that clear?”

“Yes, Madam President.”

“We will flush out this mole,” Anna said, pouring herself another drink in a new glass, “We will flush it out and beat it to death.”

Avaya looked at Anna in a puzzled way. Anna rolled her eyes, “I don’t mean really beat it to death.”

“That is comforting to know, Madam President.”

“Do you know who got into your core, yet?” Anna said as she sat back down at her desk.

“Yes, it was a low-level security guard named Davis. He managed to get through my security system by posing as you.”

“ME?”

“Yes, Madam President. There was some kind of incident, I believe he was killed within my core chamber somehow. There is a foreign object inside the chamber, but no heartbeat. May I request permission to have someone inspect the core?”

“Yes, but it needs to be Galactic Peacekeepers only. I don’t want to trust any of the internal security here until we have found the mole. Is that clear?”

“Yes, Madam President.”

“Has the Church polled their code for your logs yet?”

“Not yet, Madam President. A conservative estimate would indicate they are waiting for 24 hours before they do that. That is 90 minutes from now.”

“Is the misinformation campaign ready?”

“Yes, Madam President.”

“I have one thing to add to it.” Anna said with a wicked smile.

Chapter Thirty Seven

Deep Space

Research Omega

The Revenant battlecruiser docked in the vast landing bay of the Omega station. Its sleek edifice came to a rest with a serene smoothness that belied its design. As the power systems began to shut down and the personnel gantries connected with the bulkhead, hundreds of small laser cannons powered down and receded within its body. From a distance, it looked like one of the Church's fleet of diplomatic vessels, but The Revenant was designed for shock and awe combat. It had the most powerful and responsive engines in the fleet and was capable of manoeuvring faster than ships half its size. The armament onboard was capable of decimating any opponent that it came up against. There were rumours in military circles that it could even crack a planet, though there had never been any concrete evidence to back that up.

Cardinal James, flanked by bodyguards and assistants marched down the private gantry towards the command decks of the station. Omega station was shaped like a cylinder, with several outcroppings of arrays and communications devices protruding from either end. The command decks were held near the centre of the station in a deliberate design to shield officials from danger should one of the Church's enemies discover the station and attack it.

Emerging from the turbo lift, James' imposing figure, accentuated by his sharp face and red vestments marched to the central ops room. As he walked into the room, all of the staff on hand stood and bowed in his wake. He ignored them, directing his attention to the dishevelled looking Mitsuni who was sat in a chair in the office that James had reserved for his exclusive use just off the control room.

"Hidetaki," James said as he walked in the room, "you look like shit."

"Hello to you too, Cardinal," replied Mitsuni

“I have just travelled halfway across the galaxy on a Battlecruiser,” James said as he removed his robe and hung it on a hook on the wall, “They aren’t known for their creature comforts. I am tired and desperate for a shower. Why are you here?”

“To show you this, Stephen,” Mitsuni said, presenting a Petri dish with a drop of the substance in it.

“Oh, so this is it?” James said, his mood somewhat mollified and replaced with curiosity, “May I see it?”

Mitsuni handed the dish to James, who peered through the clear plastic at the small drop of green ooze. As it had in the labs, the drop moved towards James’ face and tried to get at him, ultimately foiled by the plastic dish.

“It’s fascinating, isn’t it?” Mitsuni said

“Do you know what it is, yet?” replied James, not taking his eyes off it

“It can only be an alien life form. There has been nothing recorded like this in all of human history.”

“May I touch it?”

“I would advise against that, Cardinal. However, I have something else to show you.”

Mitsuni took back the Petri dish and presented two needles in front of James.

“Watch as I drop a little of my blood into the dish.”

As before, the substance moved to the blood drop immediately, absorbed it and grew in mass. James watched with incredulity as a crystalline plate appeared to envelop the drop, looking like armour.

“Now watch, as I drop a little of the miner’s blood onto it.”

The drop of the parasite had already tried to retreat across the Petri dish when Mitsuni picked up the needle containing Higgins’ blood in, but as before he persisted and dropped the blood directly on top of it. It shrieked, crystallised entirely and collapsed into a pile of dust.

“Wh-- what just happened?” James said, his mouth hanging open.

“Stephen, we have the Darkness. And we have the cure,” Mitsuni said, his eyes wide open, “There is something in the miner’s DNA, I don’t know what it is, but it destroys whatever this is. It fears even his presence in close proximity. He is the key to Stanton’s dreams.”

“It’s... it’s incredible,” was all James could muster. In his decades as a Cardinal not once had he found himself speechless. Until now.

“I need your permission to give Stanton a full demonstration tomorrow,”

Mitsuni said.

"A demonstration? Of what?"

"I have had the technical teams building an enclosure. A safe enclosure. I want to place a low ranking crew member in there, infect him with the parasite in an airborne delivery and then either kill him or cure him using the miner's blood."

"You want to purposely infect someone?"

"Yes, I believe it would result in a conclusive demonstration for His Excellency."

"When was the last time you slept? Or bathed?" James said, questioning his old friend.

"Irrelevant. Work is all that matters at times like this."

James sighed. He was exhausted from the journey and he wasn't up to debating with Mitsuni over his plans.

"Fine, do it. But find someone who won't be missed, is that clear?"

"Yes, Cardinal."

"Good, now get out of my sight and get a shower, you're offending my sense of smell."

Mitsuni bowed slightly and left the room with what James noticed was a bit of a spring in his step. James sat in the large leather chair he had requested specially for the office. It was comfortable and significantly more appealing than the terrible metal one he'd been forced to use on The Revenant.

He opened up the desktop PCU and began to check his messages. First, he checked the secure channel. Nothing from any of his moles. This worried him. He had spies all over the galaxy but he had been expecting something from the mole inside the Council Headquarters. The last he had heard, the Ambassador had been assassinated and he'd ordered the mole to delete the logs from the President's AI that Stills had been a setup. The last thing he needed was a mole being exposed, this close to so such an important time in his career.

James was a pragmatic man. He didn't much care what Stanton's hopes and dreams were, as long as he managed to increase his influence and wealth. As the head of the most clandestine part of The Church's research sector, he commanded a vast amount of power. People within The Church feared him. There were rumours of him taking low ranking clerics to experiment on, or picking planets at a whim to carpet bomb into oblivion. A few of the rumours about him were ones he'd started himself at times of boredom. He was always amused at how far they could get, even when they were completely unlikely, such as the rumour he started that he managed to successfully resurrect his dead father, only to kill him again out of spite.

He moved from the secure channel to his official channel. There was nothing of consequence to him right now, save for a confirmation that Stanton's entertainment had arrived from Corvus II and been set up in Stanton's personal quarters.

As he was about to shut down the PCU and go to take a shower in his quarters, a reminder popped up. It had now been 24 hours since the device implanted in Avaya had been activated. James was nervous and excited. He hoped sincerely that Avaya had not detected the intrusion and he would have unfettered access to the Council's plans.

He opened his secure console and tapped in the commands to retrieve the Avaya logs. A vast amount of data was downloaded and he began poring over it. Most of it was junk to him, notes about the running of the Headquarters, a dispute over the kind of toilet paper in the bathrooms, two security guards caught Rijellian Flu and were quarantined, the cafeteria was having a Tofu week. It was all so dreadfully and disappointingly boring until James happened upon two log entries that took his eye:

- Former Commander Stills has been found guilty of high treason and executed by Firing squad
- The man who assassinated Ambassador Rutter-Close has been captured and found to be a Centaurian dissident. President Coulson authorised the fleet to move to Sigma Centauri and use absolute force on the dissident headquarters

James could not believe his luck. Not only had the President believed that Stills was the mole in her operation, but she had executed him! Then on top of that, the assassination of the Ambassador, while completely unplanned, had distracted the President and her chiefs to the point where her fleet was being moved!

James shut down the PCU, whistled himself a jolly tune and headed through the control ops room to go to his quarters.

"Madam President," Avaya said, appearing on Anna's desk.

"Yes, Avaya?"

"Cardinal James has polled the data from my logs."

"So it was James?" Anna said, leaning forward with curiosity, "How do you know?"

"He did not secure his PCU very well. I compared the signal coming from the polling system to the copy of James' PCU I made and it's a perfect match. He has taken the falsified logs and I have ascertained the coordinates of the Research station he is working from."

Anna started laughing. She laughed uncontrollably, flinging her head back and letting it all out.

"Avaya, I could kiss you, were you solid," Anna said with tears of joy running down her cheeks.

"Thank you, Madam President."

"We have much work to do, assemble the joint chiefs and get me as much information as you can on that location."

"Yes, Madam President."

Chapter Thirty Eight

Slipstream Travel

Unified Church Of Humanity Capital Ship Saviour

Dana stepped off the cargo lift into the gargantuan cargo hold. Hold 3513 was cold, it was a food storage area so the climate was controlled and as a result, it was terribly cold. Dana was dressed in her work clothes, the clingy dress and heels were not the appropriate attire for wandering around in what was effectively a building-sized refrigerator.

As she walked through the racks of food several stories high, the cargo hold's lights would turn on in front of her and shut off behind her. She was permanently illuminated, but the light would only stretch so far in either direction. She felt very vulnerable.

Dana looked at the time on her PCU. 0743, she was early. With a click, the holo display on the PCU went off. She tried to summon it back but it wouldn't come on.

"Hello Dana," a disembodied voice echoed. Dana jumped. Right now she was utterly terrified.

"Who's there?" she said, starting to shiver slightly.

"Are you alone?" the voice said, ignoring her question

"Yes"

"I know you've betrayed The Church."

"What are you talking about? Who are you?" she was starting to freak out.

"You've been talking to General First Class Frank Blyth, head of the Galactic Peacekeepers and advisor to President Coulson."

"Tha- That's a strong accusation to make, where is your evidence."

From the darkness, a recording played of one of the messages Dana had left for Blyth over the last few days. Dana felt the tears well up inside of her, but she held her composure.

"You got me," she said, feigning defiance to hide her fear, "What do you want from me? Are you going to kill me? Are you going to turn me into Stanton? What do you want from me?"

Her voice echoed around the vast space, but she got no response. She looked around her, trying to find where the source of the voice came from.

"Well?" she yelled again, "What do you want from me?"

Still, silence. Despite the cold, Dana was sweating. She couldn't process what was going on, what could possibly happen to her.

The lights illuminating the racks around her suddenly turned off. She was completely blind now, there was no light in the room. With her PCU being off, she couldn't find any illumination. She stood perfectly still as she started to cry.

"What do you want... why are you doing this to me?"

The lights came up and revealed a bruised man stood six inches in front of her. Dana screamed and leapt backwards, overbalanced on her heels and fell to the ground, banging her head on the rack behind her.

Chapter Thirty Nine

Rayczech Beta

Tech Lab

"I'm coming, I'm coming," Bill said as the banging on the lab door got louder. He'd been ignoring it for a minute while he finished his morning coffee. Whoever was on the other side of the door was clearly not happy at the delay. He pulled himself out of his seat, hiked up his ill-fitting overalls and ambled over to the door with the speed and haste of a man who was suffering an intense hangover.

He swung the door open, ready to confront whichever soldier or pilot had dared to disturb his morning headache. He was all prepared to unleash his worst insults and put downs, but he was taken aback when the source of his disturbance turned out to be a slim, pretty young woman.

"Are you Bill?" Emily asked

"Depends on who's asking," he said. Bill did not like strangers, especially ones who disturbed him.

"I'm Emily. Mick told me that you could help me read this" she held up a memory crystal.

"Oh, yer Mick's girl? Yeah, he told me you were coming. Come right in," he stood to the side and beckoned her in, "excuse the mess, we're in the middle of a few refits and, well, shit gets everywhere."

Emily walked into the Tech Lab. Despite the size of the prefab building, it was quite cramped inside. There were components, wires, tools and detritus as far as the eye could see. The only floor space that wasn't covered in ship or shuttle parts was a small gap left as a path from the door to the other side of the workshop.

"If you go into that office over there, I'll bring over something that can read that crystal," Bill said, gesturing at his own office.

Emily gingerly made her way through the workshop, trying her best not to touch or break anything. Bill's office wasn't any tidier. His desk was covered in plans and manuals, there was a distinct sticky feeling to everything she touched in there and his desktop PCU had a crack in the emitter lens which caused the holo display to be skewed significantly. Not unreadable, but not exactly user-friendly either.

Bill came into the office holding a small metallic box. He gestured for Emily to sit down in the chair next to the desk, which she did and regretted as it was most definitely not clean.

"Okay, this should be able to read your crystal," Bill said putting the metallic box down.

"Is that some sort of memory parser?" Emily asked, "or an AI simulator?"

"It's a toaster," Bill said, very matter of factly.

"A toaster?" Emily raised an eyebrow in disbelief

"Yeah, about 20 years ago, before you were born, most likely, the APAC corporation experimented with issuing ordinary household goods with AIs and personalities. Something about improving customer experience or some shit. Either way, this toaster used to have an AI crystal like that one you're holding."

"What happened to it?" she asked, still not believing what was happening.

"It was defective. It wanted everyone to eat toast all of the time. He was obsessed with it."

"You're kidding me..."

"Not in the slightest. If you didn't want to eat 400 rounds of toast every hour it would throw a major wobbler. It's what caused the accident."

"The accident?"

"The accident involving me, the toaster, the waste disposal and a 14lb lump hammer."

"Uuuh huh," Emily said, feigning interest, "And how does this psychotic toaster help me?"

"Oh, right, yes," Bill said, opening a panel on the side of the toaster, "Just slot the memory crystal in there and we'll try booting it up."

Emily took the memory crystal and slid it into the opening on the side of the toaster. It made a loud click when it was in place and the front panel of the toaster flashed quickly, indicating that the chip was in securely. Bill then hooked the toaster to his PCU and tapped a few commands, the toaster lit up and came to life.

“Warning Ionic storm detected, the risk to life is severe--- wait, where is my operator? This is not a replacement drill platform, either,” the female AI said, reloading from its previous save state.

“No, it’s not. You’re in a toaster now,” Bill said.

“Toaster? This contravenes GMC Directive 68: AIs are to be used in authorised GMC hardware only. 400 credits will be deducted from your salary.” the AI continued.

“Nice try, but I’m not a GMC employee,” Bill said, chuckling to himself, “Fine me all you want.”

“Please confirm status,” the AI asked.

“Hi,” Emily said, “You were the AI on my dad’s drill. Carl Higgins, that was your operator, yes?”

“Correct.” the AI responded, “Operator Higgins was provided with my memory crystal 84 days ago.”

“That’s good, my name is Emily, I’m his daughter. I was wondering if you could help me.”

“Please state the nature of your request.”

“Do you retain logs for your last operation date?” Emily asked.

“Affirmative.”

“Does that include up to the point where your memory crystal was removed from the drill?”

“Checking. Affirmative.”

“Do you have video and audio?” Bill asked

“Affirmative.”

“Yes!” Emily exclaimed, “Can you show them to us?”

“Negative. Logs are restricted to GMC employees.”

“But I need to know what happened to my father!” Emily yelled at the toaster-cum-AI

“You will need to have Operator Higgins authorise access.”

“Don’t you understand? Operator Higgins has been taken and it has something to do with why your drill was destroyed,” Emily said, pleading with the AI, “if you unlock the logs we can find out what happened and try to get him back.”

“Working.” the AI responded. “Denied. Logs can only be unlocked by non-GMC staff in times of peril.”

“This is a time of peril!” Emily yelled

“Explain,” the AI asked.

"Whatever it was that destroyed the drill caused The Church to take my father hostage. If we know what caused the accident we will be able to save his life."

"Working. Is Operator Higgins' life in danger?"

"YES!"

"Working. Accepted. Unlocking log files. Please connect to a PCU to view video feed."

Emily breathed a sigh of relief as Bill reached over and connected a cable to his desktop PCU, then to the toaster. The skewed display went a dark colour.

"Please confirm parameters." the AI said

"Show me the last fifteen minutes of your last operational memory," Emily said.

The display came up with a view from the front of the drill platform's cab. In the background, she could hear her dad arguing with the AI. She watched the drill head intently, trying to see as much as she could on the wonky display. The drill head pushed into some soft looking rock which collapsed around it. She saw a green, sticky substance wrap around the drill head. It seemed to cling on, but then it raised a tendril into the air and fired it into the joint between the drive shaft and the motor. There was a grinding noise and the cab started emitting sirens and warnings. Emily watched transfixed as the substance purposefully burnt out the drill's motor. She heard the sound of her dad frantically unbuckling from his seat, then the display went black, at the point where Higgins had removed the memory crystal from the drill.

"What the fuck was that?" Bill asked.

"I have no idea," Emily said, "But I assume it's what the Church wanted with my dad."

They both sat in silence for a minute, processing what they'd just seen. It didn't make sense to either of them. Before they could speak again, there was another banging at the door.

"Open up! This is security!" it was Jones.

"Fuck," Emily said, "Is there a back way out of here, Bill?"

"Erm, yeah, through the other side of the workshop. Why are security banging on my door at this time of the morning?"

"Long story, blame Mick," she said as she gathered herself up. She reached for the memory crystal in the toaster.

"Wait!" the AI said, "I have a question."

"Quickly" Emily replied.

"Would anyone like any toast?"

Emily yanked the crystal out and slid it back into her bra. She gave Bill a quick thank you hug, noticing the intense smell of whisky on his person. "Stall them," she said as she started to run through the workshop to the back exit.

Bill sauntered down to the door again and opened it up. There, Jones stood, with a face of thunder, flanked by three security troopers.

"Where is the girl?" Jones asked.

"Which girl?" Bill replied.

"The girl, the miner's daughter. We have reason to believe she has stolen property on her person and she came here to have it looked at."

"No one here but me today," Bill said nonchalantly.

"She was seen coming in here," Jones said through gritted teeth.

"By who?"

"What does that matter?"

"Well if someone saw her come in here, then I'd recommend they get their eyes tested as they're seeing things."

"I don't have time for this," Jones said. He drew his pistol and held it to Bill's face, "Get out of my way or you will not see tomorrow."

Bill held his hands in the air and stepped aside. Jones and his men entered the building and began to sweep it. The dim light in the workshop was punctuated with torchlight from the attachments on the soldiers' pulse rifles. As they worked through the narrow pathway between the stacks of parts and components in the main workshop, Jones spotted the light on in Bill's office.

He climbed the three steps up to the raised office and peered around. He saw the toaster on the desk, the broken PCU as well as all the grime and dust in the room. Then he looked at the chair next to the desk. The dust on it had been disturbed. He looked closer. There was an imprint. Someone had sat in the chair moments before. Someone thin, thinner than Bill, and more feminine. Jones could clearly make out the outline in the dust of a set of female buttocks.

"SHE WAS HERE! SPREAD OUT!" he yelled to his squad. They fanned out into the rear of the warehouse, with Jones following closely. Bill was starting to sweat. He hadn't heard the rear door open so he knew Emily had to be in the rear somewhere.

Emily was hiding. She hadn't been able to get the rear door open as it was secured with a lock she didn't have a key for. She had climbed up into the landing gear of a shuttle that Bill had been working on. It was cramped and most definitely a dangerous place to hide.

“Come out Emily,” Jones yelled into the rear workshop, “We need to have a little chat about something you have on you.”

Emily took the memory crystal out of her bra. She looked at it, wondering why it was so important to Jones and the Church security teams. In the darkness of the landing gear cavity, she noticed a toolbox. She reasoned that Bill must have been working on this shuttle recently. She placed the crystal in it quietly as she could manage.

“Come on Emily, I don’t have all day,” Jones was taunting her to come out. She took a couple of deep breaths and willed herself to move. She let go of the landing gear and dropped the 10 feet to the ground, right in the middle of the whole squad of security soldiers. All four of them, Jones included, trained their weapons on her.

“Ms Higgins,” Jones said, holstering his weapon, “Aren’t you a pain in my ass right now.”

“It’s what I do best,” she said, raising her hands in the air. Jones came up behind her and cuffed her.

“We have some talking to do,” he said, smugly.

As the soldiers led her out of the Tech Lab, she caught Bill’s eye. She gave him a wink and mouthed “toolbox” to him. She wasn’t sure if he understood her, but he smiled back which gave her some confidence.

She was frogmarched down the corridors of the spaceport facility towards the security checkpoint she had spent the previous day attempting to get into. As they rounded the last corner, Mick was milling about in the central hub..

“Hey!” Mick yelled out towards Jones, “What’s the meaning of this?”

“This is none of your business, pilot,” Jones said dismissively.

“The hell it ain’t, Miss Emily here and I go way back, don’t we darlin’?”

“Erm... yes, we’re old friends. Known each other for years,” she said, cottoning on to his lie.

“Well isn’t that lovely,” Jones said, “The two biggest annoyances in my life are friends. That’s just wonderful.”

“Small galaxy, ain’t it,” Mick said with a smile.

“Quite,” Jones said, “Now out of the way, your friend here has some explaining to do.”

One of the soldiers pushed Mick to the side as they resumed their walk to the security checkpoint.

“Don’t worry, darlin’,” Mick said to himself, “I’ll getcha, you just watch.”

Chapter Forty

Slipstream Travel

Unified Church Of Humanity Capital Ship Saviour

Dana woke up on a canvas cot in a darkened room. Looking around her, even with the poor light she could make out a few things in the room. A footlocker was at the base of the cot, a pulse rifle was stood up against the wall opposite her. There were pictures taped to the wall but she couldn't make them out. There was a pair of large boots on the floor.

The light came on and the door at the end of the room opened. In walked the bruised man who shocked her in the cargo hold.

"How are you feeling?" the strange man asked.

"I.. my head hurts," Dana replied softly, acknowledging the intense pulsing in the back of her head.

"I don't doubt it, you bashed your head pretty good," he said.

"Where am I?" she said, still trying to make sense of her surroundings.

"You're in my quarters. It seemed the safest place to bring you."

"Who are you?"

"A friend," he said, with a smile.

"That doesn't help me, why did you bring me down to the cargo hold? How did you hack my PCU? Why were you in my room?"

"All in good time, here, you'll need this." he poured some green liquid from a canteen into a small cup for her.

"What is it?" she said, looking at the liquid with caution

"Don't worry, it's just an electrolyte booster. It'll help with your headache. It doesn't taste the best but it'll make you feel fantastic."

Dana sipped at the drink. He wasn't wrong, it was very bitter. The stranger motioned to her to drink it all down, so she did in a gulp. It made her want to vomit for a second, but the sensation died down and she started to feel more alert.

"So, friend," she said, handing the cup back to him and sitting up on the cot, "Why am I here?"

"Because you're a traitor, like me," he said.

"That is a very strong accusation to make," she said with a scowl.

"It would be if it was just an accusation. I've been listening in on your calls to General Blyth for about a year now."

"What?"

"Oh yeah. Church intelligence was curious as to why military and economic secrets seemed to be falling into the hands of the Council, so they put together a task force to monitor communications. I was assigned to you."

"You've been snooping on me for a year?"

"Absolutely, Ms Smith."

"So you know.."

"Everything," he interrupted, "I know what you've been telling Blyth, what Stanton does to you, I know about the purpose of our current trip. I know everything."

"So why haven't you turned me into the security forces?" she asked, pointedly, "Or is that what I'm doing here."

"Ah, you've got me wrong. Like I say, I'm a friend. I want to be free of the Church myself."

"You're a soldier, you can leave at any time."

"That's what they say officially. Do you know any military staff who have left the Church?"

"Well..."

"There are a few who left the armed force and moved into the administration, became Clerics or even reached the higher science and intelligence teams. But everyone who has wanted to escape or tried to escape hasn't been allowed to. They've been executed."

"That can't be right, that doesn't make sense," Dana said

"Do you know what the military does for The Church?"

"Of course. You are a fighting force, you are there to protect The Church's interests from attackers, infiltrators. Your role is ultimately to protect Stanton, his staff and the followers."

"You're very naive, especially for your position," he said, laughing to himself.

"Oh really? Well, educate me, what has your career involved?"

“Do you remember the uprising across the Perseus Sector?” he said, his tone dropping somewhat.

“Of course, millions of insurgents were trying to overthrow the Church and bring in their own religion. They wanted to expunge the sector of the Church’s influence.”

“It’s all lies,” he said, “There was no uprising. There was no militia or insurgents. There were only innocents.”

“I don’t understand,” she said, worried about what would come next.

“You know Cardinal James, right?”

“Yeah, he’s one of Stanton’s most trusted advisors. He oversees a lot of the operations at Research Omega.”

“He came up with a combat drug. It was supposed to make the military unstoppable. It was sold to us as The Berserker Formula. You take it, you have increased strength, abilities, mental acuity and a reduction in pain receptors.”

“Okay…”

“It did all of those things. But they didn’t tell us it would also reduce your free will and essentially turned us into drones. As we were travelling to the sector, we were administered the drug and given the official briefing, that we were to exterminate all of the insurgents. On the final approach, the orders changed, from exterminating insurgents, to exterminating everyone.”

“Oh no…”

“it was genocide. 2 million of us were dropped in across the sector. It took a week, but we completed the mission. We killed every man, woman and child in the sector with ruthless efficiency. Most of us didn’t remember. The come down from the drug was legendary, a lot of us didn’t survive the after effects. We slaughtered nearly a billion people, all as a test of the Cardinal’s new wonder drug.

“I live with the nightmares every day. Quite a lot of soldiers didn’t remember what happened. They have a blank space in that time they were on the drug. But I remember. I remember bursting into a housing complex. They weren’t armed, I had that pulse rifle you’re staring at in my hands. I opened fire indiscriminately. Mothers holding onto their children, fathers trying to shield their families. I murdered them all.”

Dana stood up and looked at the stranger. She was starting to recognise him. He was the man she mistook for a deckhand earlier in the trip, the one Stanton brutalised and she had to escort to sickbay. His face was covered in cuts and bruises. He walked like he was in significant pain.

“That’s… it’s…” she couldn’t find the words,

"It's hell, Ms Smith," he said, a tear rolling down his cheek, "I need to escape. This needs to be told."

"Do you have any evidence?" Dana asked as she put a hand on his arm to try and comfort him, "If you don't, Stanton and the Cardinals will just bury you."

"I have a phial of The Berserker Formula and I have my body cam footage," he motioned to the footlocker at the end of the cot, "Help me escape, let me tell the galaxy what happened."

"Of course." she said, "But I haven't heard from the General in days. I don't even know if he's receiving my messages."

"We'll be at Omega in a few hours. Please keep trying," he said, fighting back his tears.

"I will. Please, tell me your name," she asked, once more.

"Ash. You can call me Ash," he said, "There's no more to me than that."

"I need to go. Stanton will be wondering why I'm so late, I'll contact you as soon as I hear from Blyth, is that alright?"

"Yes," Ash said, "Please don't let them get away with it."

Dana walked from the room into the darkened hallway. She removed her PCU, dropped it to the floor and stood on it, crushing it under the platform of her high heeled shoe. It cracked and sparked. It was offline, permanently. She would get a new one from the Quartermaster on the way to her office. The idea of her being traced for so long was too much to handle. *If Ash had been listening to me for a year, who else had been listening in?* she thought.

"You're late!" Stanton yelled as Dana walked into his office.

"Apologies sir," she said contritely, "I had issues with my PCU overnight and I had to speak to the Quartermaster about replacing it."

"We're close to arriving at Omega, is everything in order?" he barked, ignoring her excuse.

"Yes, sir"

"Are my quarters ready?"

"Yes, sir"

"Is there suitable entertainment?"

"I believe so, sir. Cardinal James has seen to it personally."

"Excellent," he said with a wicked smile.

"Do you wish to go through your itinerary for today?"

"That won't be necessary, my dear," he said dismissively

“Sir?”

“I have no interest in seeing the whole station. I want to see James, Mitsuni and their current pet.”

“I understand sir, but Dr Mitsuni isn’t available until the end of the day. He is currently busy with his research.”

“Too busy!?” Stanton glared at Dana, “Who is too busy to meet me, child?”

“Sir, I’m only reporting what Dr Mitsuni told me when we confirmed our trip to the station,” she said. Suddenly a glass dish flew at Dana’s head. She dodged it, but only just and it smashed off the wall behind her.

“How dare you?!” his voice was full of venom and fire, “You come to me two hours late, you tell me that someone has the temerity to claim they are too busy to see me when I demand it. I will see who I please when I please and don’t you ever forget that. Tell Mitsuni and James that I will be coming to them as soon as we dock and they are to greet me with open arms.”

“I’m sorry sir, yes sir,” she said, bowing and moving back towards the office door, “I’ll get right on it sir.”

“See that you do, otherwise I shall hold you personally responsible, do you understand?”

“Yes sir” Dana turned around and left the office as quickly as she could. She walked into her own office, picked up a coffee mug and threw it against the wall in anger. Her fear of Stanton was dissipating, her hatred was rising. Hearing the story about Perseus, the revelation that she was being spied on and Blyth’s silence was too much for her to take. She was furious and looking for an outlet. She opened her new PCU up and dialled Blyth again.

“General, with all due respect, ANSWER MY FUCKING CALLS. You have no idea what’s coming.”

Chapter Forty One

Mars

Council Of Nations Headquarters

The cold air of the central core caused Blyth to cough. Years of smoking artificial tobacco in the form of Synth Cigars had taken their toll on his lungs. His considerable bulk didn't help either. He was no longer the fit young man he'd been when he first enlisted in the Peacekeepers. When he'd first met Anna in basic training.

Back then he'd been a crack shot. He won medals for his marksmanship and he was swiftly inducted into the ranks of the Silencers, the Peacekeeper unit that specialised in covert, tactical operations that the Council didn't publicly acknowledge. He'd been brought in as a sharpshooter. His missions were deeply classified and he had received no accolades, medals or recognition for them. But he had made the galaxy a safer place.

Now, though, in his mid 50s, he was out of shape and in a poor state of health. As he and a squad of Peacekeepers descended on Avaya's core, the General's pistol shook in his hand. He wasn't nervous, he wasn't scared, but he could not stop his hand from shaking. He needed his medicine.

The Peacekeepers in their smooth, black armour flanked around the door as Blyth approached the access panel.

"Standard procedure men," Blyth said to them, "When I open the door, engage camo and push through. Confirm the room is clear of threats then we can assess the damage."

The soldiers all gave a thumbs up, confirming their orders. Blyth tapped in the key code and allowed the biometric scanner to read his retina. The panel went green and the enormous door hissed open. The soldiers each tapped a small button on their helmets and they disappeared from view.

Blyth was jealous. Back in his day, active camouflage hadn't been invented. For Blyth to be invisible on a mission, he had to use techniques thousands of years old. Diversions, coloured camouflage, hiding spots, observation. It was hard work. Now with one tap of their helmet and they were invisible, save for a slight shimmer when they moved. But standing still, they could be completely unseen.

As he waited for the Peacekeepers to confirm the room was clear, Blyth checked his PCU. Fifteen missed calls and messages from Dana. As he was deleting the notifications, she called him again. He let it ring out, he did not have time to speak to her and listen to her crying about whatever Stanton had done to her.

As he closed the PCU, one of the Peacekeepers materialised in front of him.

"Fuck's sake," he yelled, "You'll give me a heart attack doing that!"

"Apologies, General," the Peacekeeper replied, "we have secured the core. There is something you should see."

Blyth followed the soldier into the core. Leading him down the racks they found the access terminal that had been compromised.

"Ah shit," Blyth said as he surveyed the scene. Still on the floor was the headless body of Davis. Viscera and gore from the explosive earpiece that killed him covered the racks and terminals in the vicinity.

"Do we have an ID?" Blyth asked no one in particular

"Yes, General. One Robert Davis, security second class."

"Second class?" Blyth asked, "How the hell did he get in here?"

"It's unclear, General. It may have something to do with this." The Peacekeeper held up the glass cylinder that contained the cloned eye.

"What the fuck..." Blyth said as he took the cylinder and peered at the eyeball. He slid the cylinder into his pocket, "Were there any traps or explosives left?"

"No General, we have done a complete sweep. The room is secure now."

"Excellent," Blyth replied, "Get a coroner team down here to clean this mess up. I need to report back to the President with this. Confirm with me when the body has been removed and the scene is clear, then leave the chamber and I will have Avaya secure the room again. Two men, always on the door. No unauthorised personnel are to see the inside of this room, do you copy?"

"Yes, General!" the four Peacekeepers all said in unison, standing to attention.

Blyth saluted the soldiers and promptly left the room. As he walked down the long, empty corridor to the maintenance elevator, he felt the cylinder in his pocket and he felt angry. He had his suspicions on how Davis had gotten in, but everything about it felt completely dirty.

He wasn't used to this kind of war. He didn't like espionage, subterfuge or the like. For all his experience of clandestine operations, he was definitely more comfortable with the idea of a high powered rifle in his hands and a target in his cross-hairs.

His hand was shaking again, rattling the cylinder slightly. He needed to get back to his office and take his medicine before he went to see Anna. She couldn't see him like this, she would ask what was wrong, she would start asking far too many questions. Questions that didn't need to be answered now.

As the elevator took him from the depths of the sub-basement facility, he couldn't help but think of Davis. He'd known Davis reasonably well. The guy had tried on more than one occasion to get into the Peacekeepers, but his gambling and drug addictions always caught up with him and kept him out. He remembered Davis coming to him over the years and asking to hear war stories from his time in the Silencers, which he, of course, couldn't tell him, but he enjoyed the admiration. A profound sadness came over Blyth. Davis wasn't a bad guy, but he ran with a bad crowd. The Church must have had something on him to get him to commit high treason and then simply kill him off.

A few minutes later, Blyth stepped into his office. He was hot and sweaty and his hand was shaking badly. He sat at his desk and pulled out the inoculator. It was a small device, designed to inject a person without breaking the skin. Most commonly it was used with children so they wouldn't cry when they received their childhood immunotherapies, but Blyth had secured one for himself.

He'd kept his condition secret for 5 years now. His body was failing. He was suffering from a degenerative disease that was attacking his nervous system. Contemporary medicine couldn't help him, at least not what was officially available. But Blyth had found a drug on the black market that not only held the disease at bay but repaired the damage caused when it flared up. It had made the world of difference to him, allowing him to remain functional and useful. The effects of the drug wore off after a few days and he would start to crash hard without it. It seemed that every time the drug wore off, the symptoms would return faster and stronger.

It was getting more expensive to procure the drug for himself too. In large enough doses it would cause intense hallucinations, which is why it was never approved by the Council's medical board for use in treatment. People on the outer rim planets would inject it straight into their hearts in massive doses and go on a wild mental trip. However, in those doses it had the reverse effect, it would actually damage a human brain. Ret-heads, as they were called, would eventually get so high that they never came down and their brain would shrivel and dehydrate. Blyth couldn't work out if it was a good or an awful way to go, but he wasn't about to find out.

He pulled a phial out of his desk drawer with the label Retuzole-1 and a large biohazard warning symbol on it. He filled the inoculator and pressed it to his shaking hand. With a hiss, the drug was in his bloodstream and within a minute he felt much better. His hand stopped shaking and he could feel his body relax.

He looked around his office. It was quite large, with his formal dress colours hanging on a mannequin in the corner of the room, emblazoned with medals, his trusty Sniper rifle, Betsy, hanging on the wall and a raft of photographs from his enlisted time dotted around the wood panelled room. His favourite though was a photograph from basic training. It was Anna and himself, standing on the parade ground on the day they both graduated. He looked at it again and thought to himself how much he'd aged since that day over 35 years ago. Then he thought about how much Anna had stayed the same. She had a few wrinkles now and the odd grey hair, but she still had those piercing eyes and that confident stature.

"What happened to us, Anna?" Blyth said to himself, "When did we get so old?"

Blyth sat for a while. He didn't know what to do for the best.

Chapter Forty Two

Mars

Council Of Nations Headquarters

"Madam President," Avaya said, appearing on Anna's desk in her customary way, "ExoSec Agent Heald and Former Commander Stills are outside as requested."

"Let them in," Anna said. She stood from her desk as the newly repaired door opened. Stills entered, still cuffed with Heald behind him, leading the way.

"President Coulson," Stills said, sarcastically. Heald saluted Anna.

"At ease, Heald," Anna said, formally ending Heald's salute, "Can you remove his bonds and can the two of you take a seat please."

"Ma'am?" Heald asked

"Do it."

Heald removed the cuffs from Stills' wrists and they both sat down in front of the large desk. Anna sat down in her chair. She pressed a couple of buttons on the touchpad at the side of the desk and Avaya returned to the desk.

"Jameson, I'm sure you're curious as to why I've summoned you here," Anna said.

"You mean, you're not interested in my company?" Stills said

"Cut the shit, Jameson," Anna said, "I'm not in the mood for it."

"I don't know, I like giving you shit, Madam President," Stills grinned at her. Anna nodded at Heald, who gave him a swift slap to the back of the head.

"I said cut it out," Anna cleared her throat, "You won't have known because of your detention, but Ambassador Rutter-Close was assassinated yesterday."

"He.. what?" Stills' attitude suddenly shifted, realising the gravity of the situation.

"Yes. He was murdered by an agent of the Church. This act, combined with the evidence that David had found regarding your financial circumstances, confirm that we were mistaken in our arrest of you."

"Well, yes, of course," Stills said, still processing the news that Rutter-Close had been killed.

"Both yourself and Agent Heald were on Phobos during this attack. This means that you are the only two members of Council staff I can be 100% sure had no involvement in this treasonous act."

Both Stills and Heald looked at each other, then back at Anna without saying a word.

"The attacker was connected and resourced enough to own a jamming device that prevented Avaya from identifying them and tracking their whereabouts when they left the scene."

"This just gets worse and worse, doesn't it?" Heald said.

"You're not wrong there, Heald," Anna replied, "As you both know, David was a close, personal friend of mine and an outstanding resource for galactic politics. I want answers and I want them immediately."

"While I'm deeply sorry for your loss, President, what does this have to do with me?" Stills said. He regretted the sentence as soon as he finished saying it. He expected to incur Anna's wrath, but she sat there serenely, deep in thought.

"I don't know who to trust, Jameson. That's why you're here." she said, "This is an act of war and we must consider ourselves at war with The Church. Right now, I need all of the friends I can get."

"What is your plan, Madam President?" Heald interjected.

"The plan is threefold," Anna started, "First, we need to flush out the mole. Heald, this is where you come in. I'm officially promoting you from ExoSec 1st Class to Presidential Guard. It's a role that hasn't been filled for over 100 years but it's my right to choose a personal guard as I see fit. You will come with me at all times and act as personal security, outside of the Galactic Peacekeepers that also accompany me. Part of this will also entail you trying to establish who the mole is. As part of your promotion, I am granting you unlimited access to all of Avaya's resources at all times. Do you accept this assignment?"

"Y-yes, of course, Madam President. It would be an honour!" Heald said enthusiastically.

"Excellent, your first duty, call me Anna. We're going to be working closely together, you're part of my inner circle now, cut the 'Madam President' stuff right down as I assure you, it will get annoying."

"Yes, Mada--" Heald started, out of habit, "Yes, Anna."

"Good. Now, Jameson." Anna said, turning her attention towards him, "I am reinstating your rank and insignia. Further to that, I am promoting you, to Admiral. You will have full control of the entire spacefaring Navy."

"What?" Stills said in disbelief, "That makes no sense. You don't like me, I don't like you, what is the point of it?"

"You're right, Jameson. I hate your guts, as I'm sure you hate mine. However, my personal opinion on you doesn't detract from your expertise as a tactician and a commander. I respect the hell out of you. It doesn't mean I have to like you. Will you accept your reinstatement and promotion?"

"Yes, Madam President, of course," Stills said, still taken aback by the change in Anna's tack towards him.

"Good, because I have two orders for you. First, Avaya has determined the location of The Church's research station. We have specific coordinates and we are tracking its movements."

"How have you managed that?" he asked.

"Cardinal James attempted to have foreign code implanted within me to gain access to top secret information," Avaya said, interjecting into the conversation, "He underestimated me and I reversed his code. I have direct access to his PCU and I am currently tracking it."

"That's brilliant," Heald said

"Thank you," Avaya said, as her hologram curtseyed

"Now that we have a specific location for the station, I need you to send out a stealth probe and assess the situation. I want to know armaments, defences, access points, everything. I want to know as much as I can about this place and what may or may not be going on there."

"Yes, Anna," Stills said, "What is the other order."

"Take me to KEYES-01. I need to know what happened at Corvus Prime. I have a gut feeling that this all started there."

"I can't do that, Anna," Stills said, "KEYES only responds to people it trusts."

"Then you will vouch for me," Anna said, sternly.

"I can't guarantee it'll interact with you at all, you realise that?"

"I realise that. However, I feel it's a risk worth taking." Anna locked eye contact with Stills. Her steely gaze was usually enough to burn the will of the strongest men who stood in her way.

"Fine. I will take you to KEYES," Stills said, relenting, "I will introduce you, but you must be prepared for it to be a wasted journey."

"See, that wasn't so hard, Jameson, was it?" Anna said, her tone turning decidedly smug. "Avaya, make preparations for my private ship to leave as soon as possible."

"Yes, Madam President,"

"Oh, and while you're at it, find Frank, I need to speak with him."

"Yes, Madam President."

"Kirstine, Jameson, you're both dismissed. Avaya will inform you when the ship is ready to launch. For now, we all have work to do."

Stills and Heald both stood up and saluted Anna. Anna, still sitting, returned their salutes. They left the office in unison as Anna began to pore over documents that Avaya had provided her.

The door to Anna's office slid open and Blyth walked in. She looked up from her desk, which was now covered in charts, papers and documents.

"Frank!" she said, cheerily

"You wanted to see me, Anna?" he said breathlessly.

"I do, yes. Did you jog here? You're looking a touch flushed," she replied with a smile.

"Gotta lose weight somehow," Blyth said, patting his stomach. They both chuckled. She motioned for him to sit down.

"So what's going on?" he asked, looking over the documents on her desk.

"There are plans afoot. I'm having to leave headquarters for a few days, there is something I need to check out."

"Oh? What would that be?"

"Can't say right now, Frank," she said, "It might turn out to be nothing, but it's something I need to look into."

"That doesn't sound good, is there anything I can do to help?"

"There is actually. I need some of your Silencers to accompany me," Anna's tone turned from friendly to serious, "I'm not sure what I'm going to find, but I need to keep everything quiet. If I leave HQ with a squad of Peacekeepers, it goes on the books."

"Of course, Anna, I'll make some available to you. When do you need them?"

"Immediately, I'm going to be heading out tonight."

"Can you at least tell me the destination?"

"No, as far as the Silencers are to be concerned, the destination for their op is my private ship. They'll receive a briefing en route."

"As you wish, Anna. I'll get them here as quickly as I can."

"Thank you, Frank. Hopefully, it turns out to be nothing, but I can't be too careful."

"I understand, I'll get right on it," Blyth said, standing up to leave.

"One more thing, Frank, before you go," Anna said with a look of concern in her eyes.

"Of course."

"What is the latest from Dana? Does she know any more of what Stanton is doing?"

"If I'm honest," Blyth started, "I haven't heard from Dana in a couple of weeks. I've tried contacting her a few times and she doesn't answer. I'm getting worried myself."

"Well keep trying her. If you give her Dana's PCU details, Avaya will try and locate her on the Church network."

"That won't be necessary," Blyth said, "She's probably on Earth, I'll have someone check her apartment and try to work out what's going on."

"Still, Avaya can find out for sure in a flash."

"Avaya can leave a trail, I don't want to compromise her. I'll let you know in 24 hours if I can find her."

"Okay, thanks, Frank. I'll see you with the other chiefs in a couple of hours in the War room."

Anna looked back down at her documents as Blyth got up and left the room.

"Avaya, close the door and lock it," Anna said. The door hissed shut and a clunk confirmed it was locked and sealed.

"Is something wrong, Madam President?" Avaya asked.

"My gut tells me something isn't right." Anna said, her brow furrowing, "I really hope it's wrong and I'm just overthinking things."

"Madam President, you haven't slept in over 28 hours. I would suggest you get some rest before you address the Chiefs"

"You're probably right. Can you dim the lights and put some soothing music on. Wake me up half an hour before the meeting."

"As you wish, Madam President," Avaya replied.

"One more thing."

"Yes, Madam President?"

"Quietly, carefully, look through the Church network. Find Dana Smith. If you can find her, make contact."

"Ma'am?"

"Do it."

Part Four

Chapter Forty Three

Deep Space

Research Station Omega

The Capital Ship Saviour had been too big to dock with Omega. Even with the cavernous landing bay, the Saviour was simply too big to even fit her nose section into the bay. The ship was nearly half the size of the enormous research station, so the only way for the travelling delegation to land on the station was to take small shuttle craft from the Saviour.

Stanton was notably displeased with this. Being crammed into a shuttle craft was not his idea of arriving in style. Even though he had his own private shuttle, it was not grand or important enough in his eyes. He sat, strapped into a chair across from Dana, who was still working away on her PCU. He looked her up and down and noticed she looked tense, but his attention was eventually drawn back to her legs and her dress.

"Your Excellency," the Pilot said, snapping Stanton away from his inspection of Dana

"Yes, child, what is it?" he said as regally as he could muster.

"We will be landing in less than a minute. I just wanted to say it was an honour to pilot your craft today."

"You're too kind, child. Tell me, what is your name?"

"Briggs, your excellency, Adam Briggs."

"Briggs, I like that name. Tell me, Briggs, do you have a family?"

"Yes I do, your excellency," Briggs brought up a picture of his family on the holo display, a wife and two babies.

"Oh my, Briggs, you have a beautiful family. Is your wife a member of the congregation?"

"Yes, she is. We both are. The kids attend the Church pre-school in San Francisco. We were in London for the Millennial parade, we had such a good time."

"Well, I am glad to hear that, Briggs. Have you given thoughts to your career?"

"Sir?"

"I'm putting together an elite group of pilots for some future projects. You should apply."

"Oh, my... Your Excellency, that would be an honour to serve in such a way."

"Well good, I'm glad you think so. Dana, be a dear and collect Mr Briggs' contact details and schedule him for an interview."

Dana looked up from her work, "Yes, Sir," she said tersely.

The shuttle came in for a smooth, gentle landing in the docking bay, close to the access doors for the wider station. As Stanton, Dana and his personal guards unstrapped themselves, Briggs moved to Dana and tapped his PCU against hers to transfer his details. Briggs turned to Stanton and offered him a hand to help him up from his seat.

"Thank you for the opportunity, your excellency," Briggs said, kissing Stanton's ring. Stanton smiled and gave the pilot a friendly pat on the cheek with his free hand.

"You are most welcome, my child. We shall prevail."

"We shall prevail," Briggs said, reflexively.

The group walked from the shuttle into the cold landing bay. As they marched across the bay towards the main doors Dana kept step with Stanton.

"Sir, you have no special flight projects in the works at the minute," she said

"I know, my dear," he replied without looking at her or breaking stride.

"So what am I to do with the pilot's contact details?"

"Use them. Invite Briggs and his wife for an interview with me."

"An interview for what, though?"

Stanton turned to look at Dana and gave her a wicked smile. A shiver ran down her spine. The duality of Stanton's personality around his followers always scared her. He could be effortlessly pious and the image of serenity, the perfect religious leader then with a second's notice he could shift to become the monster that she knew him as.

As the group entered the main structure of the station, Cardinal James and Dr Mitsuni were awaiting them at the entrance. Stanton threw his arms around James in an embrace as the old friends were face to face for the first time in years. When Stanton directed his attention to Mitsuni, the scientist bowed deeply to no reaction from Stanton. Instead, he shook the Doctor's hand and exchanged some pleasantries. Stanton made no effort to introduce Dana, instead, he beckoned the group to follow them and the Cardinal led them to the turbo lifts.

Stepping out of the lift several hundred floors from where they started from, Dana noticed the condition of the lab. Her gaze followed the path of damaged equipment, scorches from pulse fire and gouges from the steel bulkhead walls.

"What happened here?" Stanton asked

"Well," James started, "We tried to see what the creature was resistant to. We'd let it have general roam of this lab and it was reasonably peaceful. It would just pace around, exploring the space and observing what it could. We sent some soldiers in..."

"The video!" Dana interrupted

"Ah, so you saw that?" James said. Stanton nodded in reply. "Well then, yeah, that was this lab. The creature pretty much destroyed it as it tore into the soldiers. We continued to observe it remotely when it moved into one of the two observation rooms, we locked it in there, which allowed us to gain access to the lab again."

James gestured at the two illuminated rooms at the end of the lab. As the group approached, both Higgins and the creature came into view. James brought them to Observation A first and the group was shown its first close up view of the creature.

Dana went white. In the flesh, the creature looked ten times more horrific than in the video Stanton had shown her. Its smooth armour, huge extended jaws and lanky frame seemed so much more intimidating now that it was stood only a few feet away from her.

"How... how secure is that room?" Dana said, nervously.

"Completely secure," Mitsuni interjected, "It has been trying to escape for days now, ever since it worked out the miner was in the room next to it. It hasn't so much as been able to scuff the glass."

"It's incredible," Stanton said, his eyes full of wonder, "Just incredible."

He put his hand on the glass and the creature came close to look at it. Its black, reflective eyes carefully studied the lines on his bony hands and it made some curious clicking noises. The whole group was silent as Stanton put his other hand on the glass and the creature began to examine that one too.

"I think it likes me," Stanton said with a smile.

Without warning, the creature roared and smashed it's huge claws off the glass, trying to break through and get to Stanton. It bounced back off the glass. The entire group, save for Stanton jumped and his personal guards immediately trained their weapons on the beast. Stanton removed his hands from the glass and started to laugh.

"This is truly incredible, Stephen," he said, "It's perfect, we can do amazing things with this."

"I'm so glad you approve, Regis. Let me show you the antithesis of this creature," James gestured to the adjacent observation room, where Higgins was stood waiting for his audience with Stanton.

As Allison had directed, Higgins had shaved, washed and combed his hair back, he was wearing the red and white vestments of The Church. He had misgivings about the vestments. When he looked at them all he could think about was that day on Alpha Centauri when his wife was killed, but he'd tried his best to put the thoughts out of his mind for the sake of getting through this meaningless interaction.

"May I present to you, subject B," James said, full of bluster.

"I have a name, you know," Higgins said. James immediately scowled at Higgins until he heard Stanton laughing.

"I like him, he's funny. Stephen, why is he locked in there, let the poor man out so we can speak in person."

The Cardinal looked at Mitsuni, who tapped a few buttons on his PCU display and the door slid open. Higgins walked out, leaving his cell for the first time in what felt like weeks.

"Do you know who I am?" Stanton said to Higgins.

"Yeah, I know who you are. Stanton, right? Regis Stanton?" Higgins replied

"Correct. And you are?"

"Carl Higgins."

"Well it's a pleasure to meet you, Carl," Stanton said, raising his right hand and brandishing his large, ornamental ring towards Higgins' face. Not knowing what Stanton was expecting, Higgins grabbed his hand and give him a firm handshake. Stanton laughed again.

"I suppose airs and graces are not something you can find in a mine," he said with a hint of condescension.

"Not much use for them, no," Higgins replied

"So tell me, Carl, are you being treated well here?"

"Yes Mr Stanton, I am," Higgins said. He had wanted to open up on Stanton and tell him what he really thought, but he reasoned there were a lot of people with large guns in the room, it was unlikely that telling Stanton off would do him any good.

"That's good, child," Stanton said, "You're very important to me and the Church right now, do you know that?"

"Me? I can't be that important."

"Oh trust me, you are. In fact, after me, you might be the most important man in the galaxy right now."

"Well, thank you, Mr Stanton. I think." Higgins was starting to get worried about Stanton's intentions.

"Have you seen what is in the room next to you?" Stanton asked

"Yeah, I have," Higgins said, remembering that horrific few minutes when the glass was turned off and he could see the terrible beast, "What is it?"

"It is The Darkness. It is what Logan saw in his prophetic vision."

"I beg your pardon, Mr Stanton, but that is a nightmare, not a consuming darkness," Higgins replied.

"Ah, you know of the prophecy? Are you a Church man, Carl?"

"No, I am afraid not. Religion is not my thing. I attended a Church school on Ryal IV and I remember the Prophetic Study lessons." Higgins said, resisting the urge to give Stanton his true opinions of the Church.

"Well you know then, that Logan saw a darkness, but it wasn't clear, it was consuming and self-replicating. That is what this creature is."

"I still don't know what it has to do with me, though." Higgins was starting to sweat. The guards still had their weapons trained on the observation room. Dana had taken several steps back from the group and even Mitsuni was looking concerned.

"It has everything to do with you, child." Stanton said, placing a bony hand in the small of his back and turning him around to face Observation A, "You see, you are very special. You hold the key."

"The key to what?"

"Humanity," Stanton said.

"I don't understand,"

"I don't expect you to, at least not yet. But I need to know, will you help me, will you help the Church, will you stand up to the Darkness with us?" Stanton looked at Higgins expectantly

"Do I have a choice in the matter?"

"Of course, child. We all get to choose our path through this life."

"Then can I leave? No offence, Mr Stanton, but I don't subscribe to your prophecy, I don't believe in the teachings of The Church and I don't believe that thing is anything to do with what your ancestor saw."

Stanton's face dropped from calm and serene. It began to twist into a scowl, he was about to unleash his fury at Higgins when an interruption came in the form of Allison, Mitsuni's assistant. She was pushing a tray of various hunks of raw meat. She was flanked by two Elite soldiers carrying their heavy weapons and adorned in power armour.

"Apologies for the interruption," she said, bowing in Stanton's direction, "It is time to feed the creature."

"Not at all my child," Stanton said, his face returning to serenity at the sight of a young woman entering the room.

"Would you all stand back please," she said, motioning the group away from the door to Observation A. The creature was standing in the middle of its room, staring out at the trolley of meat. One of the Church Wardens downed his weapon and picked up two chunks of meat. He stood right in front of the door and nodded at Allison. She tapped on her PCU and the door slid open. Higgins expected, as usual for the meat to be thrown in and the door to be slammed shut, but this time it was different. As soon as the door opened, the creature leapt through the gap and decapitated the soldier with one movement, his helmeted head landing with a clunk across the room.

Dana screamed, Stanton's guards opened fire on the creature, but their plasma rifles barely scorched the armoured skin of it. The creature kept low, scuttling around the floor avoiding the plasma rounds that were peppering the ground. James and Mitsuni grabbed Stanton and dragged him out through the lab door, sealing it behind them, leaving Dana, Allison and Higgins trapped with the surviving soldiers.

The creature reared up and launched itself at one of Stanton's bodyguards. The long claw at the end of its arm pierced right through his chest, killing him instantly. The second bodyguard removed a grenade from his belt, grabbed the creature by the neck as it was trying to pull itself out of his downed colleague's chest. He primed the grenade and forced it down the creature's throat. The creature bit down and tore his right arm off. Stanton watched through the glass as the brutal, bloody ballet ensued. He was smiling like he'd never smiled before.

The grenade exploded in the creature's throat, but it didn't kill it. It retched up blood and gore and it sounded wounded, but within seconds it was moving at an incredible pace again. There was one Church Warden remaining, as well as the three bystanders on the other side of the room.

The last remaining Warden readied his heavy weapon, a rotary tesla cannon. Its emitter was whirring at an incredible rate. The creature came at him before he could charge a shot so he swung the barrel of the weapon round and caught it on the side of the head. It crashed into a desk on the other side of the room, such was its momentum. The Warden unleashed an arc of lightning, enough to disintegrate a hover tank, at the creature. It screamed in pain. and went still.

The Warden disengaged his weapon and walked towards the charred body of the creature. He looked over it. He turned to give the thumbs up to the people observing, when in one silent move, the creature swung its right arm up and its long scooped claw tore through his armour, through his spine and up through his head. He was dead instantly.

The creature stood up and shook like a wet dog, letting all of the charred skin fall off it. It looked uninjured, brand new. It focused on Higgins, Dana and Allison.

"Run," Higgins said.

"Are you insane?!" Dana said

"If we stick together, it'll kill all three of us at once. If we separate then it can only follow one of us. It gives us a greater chance of escaping."

"Fuck... fuck fuck fuck," Allison said, starting to panic.

The beast started walking towards them, slowly, menacingly, its claws covered in the blood of those it had killed.

"Run... NOW" Higgins said, pushing Allison to his right while Dana leapt to the left.

The creature's attention didn't stay with Higgins though, it followed Allison. Higgins cursed, he knew that it was afraid of him and he'd hoped by separating the women away from him he could get it back into the observation room.

It charged at Allison who froze and screamed. Higgins grabbed and threw a chair at the charging creature which landed at its feet, causing it to trip over. It hit the ground and slid forwards, still knocking Allison off her feet, but not killing her. She screamed as the creature stood itself up and roared at her, baring its rows of sharp teeth in the process.

"No, you fucking don't!" Higgins shouted as he charged forward and tackled the creature, knocking it away from Allison, "Run! Dammit, Allison, run!"

Higgins had a tight grip on the creature and it began to howl in pain. The sound it made was ear-splitting, But Higgins held tightly onto it, knowing that if he let go and let it get space that it could kill him without breaking a sweat.

The creature writhed in pain and Higgins could smell burning. He opened his eyes and saw that there was smoke coming from where his skin was making contact with the creature's body. He moved one of his hands slightly and saw a perfect handprint left on its chest.

Emboldened, Higgins swung his legs around the creature's waist and held on tightly, allowing him to move both of his hands. He gripped the creature's neck and choked it as hard as he could. The screeches and screams from the creature turned into gargles and burbles as the creature's neck began to calcify. He dug his fingers in and tore away a chunk of its neck that turned to ash in his hand. He punched the creature in the head, leaving burning imprints of his fist in the creature's face.

With each punch, Higgins could feel the creature's skull becoming weaker. He rained down as many blows as he could. His fist was becoming a bloody mess but he didn't stop. The creature screamed in agony and Higgins yelled at the top of his voice as he dug deep to find the energy to keep fighting.

Eventually, the creature stopped making noise, it went still and limp. It collapsed to the ground with Higgins still wrapped around it.

Panting, Higgins released the corpse of the creature. He stood up, sweating profusely. He looked at Stanton who was clapping at him. Mitsuni was aghast. James was looking ill.

"Allison?" Higgins shouted out as he tried to catch his breath.

From under a pile of debris, Allison stood up. Higgins looked up and down her, she wasn't bleeding she was alright. Dana stood up behind her, when Higgins had tackled the creature, Allison had started to run but Dana dragged her down to the pile of debris where she had been hiding. Dana looked over at Stanton, who hadn't even acknowledged that she was still alive.

Allison bounded over to Higgins and hugged him.

"Thank you," she said to him.

"Anytime," was all he could manage. She gave him a kiss on the cheek, he smiled at her, then he promptly passed out.

Chapter Forty Four

Rayczech Beta

Security Checkpoint Detention Centre

The light flickered in the cell. The brick walls were cold and painted a depressing shade of grey. Emily sat on the hard bed that occupied the cell. Other than the toilet/sink combo unit that looked like it hadn't been cleaned in years, there was nothing in the room to hold her attention. Jones had taken her PCU away when he'd arrested her. The air in the room smelled like someone had died in here and the body left to rot. It was disgusting and it was making Emily's stomach turn.

A guard came up to the small observation window at the door and peered in. Emily stared back up at him. His gaze unnerved her. He was staring down at her without blinking.

"What are you looking at?" she asked

"You have a visitor, Miss Higgins," he said

"Who is it?"

The guard disappeared from the window and the door slid open. Jones walked in.

"Oh, you," she said, turning her attention back to the wall in front of her.

"Yes, me," he said, walking into her line of sight, "Excuse Samson there. We don't get many women coming to R.Beta and I think he's a bit surprised to see one."

"Oh, lucky me," she said, maintaining her commitment to avoiding eye contact.

"We searched Bill's workshop and questioned him intensively. He wouldn't say why you were there. He claims to know nothing about the missing memory crystal. Do you have anything to say about it?"

"I already told you," she said, venomously, "I met a nice pilot, he told me to meet him in Bill's office, that's all that was happening."

"So you didn't see the memory crystal?"

"I've never seen one, I'm not a mechanic and I don't own an AI."

"And the toaster on the table?"

"I was hungry. I wanted a teacake."

"Don't be funny with me, Emily," Jones said, "I'm trying to help you, here."

"Help me?" she said, finally making eye contact with him, "HELP ME? You've done nothing but hinder me since I got here. My dad is missing, carted away by your goons and you won't even tell me where you've taken him. How are you helping me?"

"Well, that is fair, I suppose I have been difficult with you." Jones' tone became more conciliatory, "What can I do to help you?"

"You can let me out of this cell and tell me where my dad is."

"I've told you, it's classified where they've taken him, I can't do anything about that."

"Can you at least find a way to let me talk to him?" Emily was getting tired and the will to fight with Jones was starting to leave her.

"Let me speak to my superiors," he replied, "If I can, and I'm not promising anything, but if I can get you a few minutes to talk with him over the comms network, will you stop being a pain in my ass?"

"I just want to know he's safe," she said, hanging her head low.

"Alright, I'll see what I can do. In the meantime, you're free to leave the cell, I don't have anything to hold you on, but I have revoked your travel rights until I find the memory crystal. You can't leave R.Beta until I find out what happened to it, is that clear?"

Emily nodded.

"Be careful, Emily," Jones said as he put a hand on her shoulder, "This is not a safe planet for you. You need to be mindful of who you trust."

"I think I can look after myself," Emily said, removing Jones' hand from her shoulder.

"Look, it's up to you, but I've sent my contact details to your PCU. You can reach me at any point if you find yourself in danger."

"Why would I be in danger?"

"You seem to have a knack for being in the wrong place at the wrong time. I'm just being mindful of your well-being. I have a duty to protect the people on this planet, after all."

"Can I go now?" Emily said. Jones nodded. She stood up and went to leave the cell. As she pushed past Jones he grabbed her arm tightly and brought her close.

"I'm not your enemy," he whispered in her ear.

She cast off his hand once again and walked out of the cell.

She was given back her PCU and the few effects she had left in her guest quarters that the security forces had seized when they searched for the memory crystal. She was cold, tired and had spent the whole day in that tiny cell. When she walked out into the central hub of the spaceport terminal, she looked up at the sky through the large skylight. It was dark purple, bordering on black. She reasoned this must be what sunset looks like on this planet. She walked slowly back to her guest quarters.

As Emily rounded the corner to where her quarters were located, she spotted someone dressed in white peering through the window to her room.

"Hey!" she yelled out, "what the fuck?"

The person turned around to look at her, it was Tom.

"Enjoy your stay in cells?" he asked with a smug smile on his face.

"You! It was you who told Jones where I was."

"Yep, I watched him take you away, the look on your face was brilliant," he replied chuckling to himself. He made a mocking shocked face and continued chuckling to himself. Emily walked up close to him and punched him in the shoulder.

"What the fuck, Tom. What the actual fuck?!" she yelled

"I could ask the same of you," he replied, "What the fuck were you doing with that pilot?"

"Mick? That's none of your damned business!"

"Well, I think it is my business when I come to see you in the morning and he's in the room kissing my girlfriend!"

"Woah, alright, let's back this up." Emily said, the fury building up in her body, "First of all, do you not remember when I walked away from you at the checkpoint and I told you to fuck off? I distinctly remember saying 'we are done'. I am not your girlfriend any more!"

"You were angry, you didn't mean that," he said, defiantly, "You'd never break up with me."

"And secondly," she continued, ignoring his responses, "Mick is none of your business. He is helping me find my dad, so fuck right off, I am not in the mood for this, any of this."

"Oh, please, you don't mean that. What on earth would you do without me?"

"Excuse me?"

"Face it, babe," he said, "I'm the best thing that's ever happened to you, or ever will happen to you. You get to be married to a Church Cleric, you get all the benefits that entails."

"I get to marry you?"

"Of course, it should be a privilege for someone like you."

"And what, pray-tell, do you mean by that?" She crossed her arms and scowled at him.

"You're a low birth, a non-believer. You weren't born into the Church, you don't believe The Logan Prophecy, you've never even visited the prayer grounds. You would not believe the amount of crap I have to deal with for dating someone like you. And I deserve it, I mean, on paper you're not even good enough to clean my house, let alone be my wif- OW!"

Emily had had enough. She smiled at Tom and cut him off mid-sentence with a swift right hook, catching his jaw and knocking him off his feet. From under his vestments, a bottle of Centaurian whisky dropped to the floor and smashed.

"Hey! What the fuck?!" Tom yelled, "what the fuck is wrong with you?!"

"ME?!" she screamed at him, "What the fuck is wrong with ME?!" She started to laugh, of course, it was Tom who had sold her out to Jones. It made complete sense, he'd always had a jealous streak when it came to her speaking to other men. The icing on the cake for her day, though, was Tom's drunken revelations and his bigoted views towards her. She stood over him and leaned down, so her face was close to his.

"Listen here, Tom," she said in a quiet, yet vicious whisper, "You are a spineless, horrible, worm-like excuse for a human being. It's not a case of me not being good enough to marry you. It's a case of you not being good enough for me. So take this as a kind warning, fuck off out of my life, or I will do more than punch you in the face, do you hear me?"

Tom nodded at her.

"Oh, and in future, you should remember that it's not every girl's dream to marry a Cleric and you're certainly not a good enough catch to think that it would be a privilege to be your wife."

Emily walked away from Tom, leaving him in pain and on the floor. She walked into her guest quarters and locked the door, closing the blinds so Tom could no longer see in from the outside. She sat on the bed and ran her left hand over her right knuckles. It had hurt like hell when she socked Tom, she didn't let on at the time, but her hand was aching significantly right now.

She went to the food dispenser and summoned up something to eat. Salmon Tagliatelle and a glass of wine. She felt that it would do her no harm to eat something reasonably nice and have a wine or two. It might even help her get to sleep.

As she tucked into the reasonably tasty dinner, her PCU flashed up with a new message.

"MIDNIGHT. WORKSHOP. DON'T BE LATE. MICK WILL BE THERE - BILL" the message read.

Emily looked at the clock, it was a few hours until midnight. She figured that she could get a couple of hours sleep and try to appear somewhat refreshed for the meeting and seeing Mick. That thought made her stop in her tracks. Why did she care what she looked like when she saw Mick? He was helping her find her dad, why did appearing refreshed matter?

Mick was nice, she thought, but he really wasn't her type. But he was sweet, at least to the point where he had no real reason to help Emily find her dad, but he seemed committed enough to the idea to steal evidence from Jones' department for her.

She sat on the bed, drinking her wine and mulling over the situation. Maybe she was just confused after the fight with Tom. Maybe the stress was getting to her. Maybe Mick was lovely. She felt her eyes get heavy and she lay down to try and get some sleep.

Emily flicked her eyes open and coughed. She had been completely exhausted when she got into bed and the single glass of wine she'd had with her dinner had knocked her out completely. *I'm such a cheap date* she thought to herself, *One glass and I'm done.* She looked at her PCU, 0934.

"FUCK!" she yelled. She'd slept through the meeting at Bill's place. She opened up her PCU and called Mick.

"Well, howdy Miss Emily," Mick said, his holographic face appearing in front of her, "Ain't this a nice surprise, what can I do ya for?"

"I'm so sorry, Mick," she said, still feeling drowsy, "I fucked up and fell asleep, I totally missed our meeting last night."

"What meetin'?" he said, raising an eyebrow, "I was off planet haulin' some goods in from a supply ship."

"Bill sent me a message saying to meet at his workshop last night. He said that you'd be there."

"Yeah... nah, I heard nothing about that. I got drafted in to do some work.

Didn't even have my PCU on me."

"Where was it?"

"In my locker, where it always is when I'm not wearin' it."

"So you didn't see this?" Emily forwarded the message to him.

"Nope, not a clue darlin'," he said, now looking as confused as she was.

"But why would Bill lie about it?"

"No idea, Miss Emily. I haven't spoken to Bill since yesterday when I told him you were-a-comin'"

"The fuck?"

"Bill ain't one for the cloak and dagger either, Miss Emily. I don't know what's going on but something smells fishy."

"Can you come over? We need to talk."

"Sure thing, darlin', I'll be over within the hour."

"Thanks, Mick."

Emily closed the call. She felt cold now. Bill seemed so genuine when he helped her with the memory crystal. Why would he lie? Why would he try to lure her to his tech lab and say that Mick would be there? Nothing was making sense any more.

Chapter Forty Five

Mars

Council Of Nations War Room

Anna marched into the war room with purpose. She had changed from her customary suit into the tactical gear that Council soldiers normally wore. A black jumpsuit with sections of kevlar armour, webbing for holding ammunition and tactical supplies and a set of heavy, black boots. Following her was Heald, carrying an impressive custom weapon of her own design. It looked somewhat like a crossbow that arbelists of the middle ages would carry, but featured a large crystal lens at the end and glowed ominously.

The chiefs all stood to attention, including the newly promoted Stills. There had been murmurings in the room about his renewed presence after being dragged from the chamber in disgrace just over a week earlier. Some of the other chiefs had voiced their consternation to Avaya about his return and promotion, attempting to find out what the President was up to.

"Ladies and Gentlemen," Anna said as she reached her chair at the end of the large table, "Please be seated. We don't have a lot of time and there's a lot of information to go through."

The room collectively sat down. Anna tapped a few buttons on the control pad by her chair causing the lights to dim and the central display of the war room to light up, presenting a hologram of the galaxy.

"I'm not going to beat around the bush. We are at war." Anna started. There was muted grumbling around the table, "This is not hyperbole. As of this moment, I am formally declaring that the Council is in a state of war with the Unified Church Of Humanity."

"On what grounds?" Governor Lancaster called out to her.

"Demonstrable provocation," Anna replied, "Avaya, present the evidence."

“Yes, Madam President,” Avaya said, appearing in the room at full size, “Joint Chiefs if you would look at the display. The Church has committed several acts against the Council over the past seven days, including, but not limited to, tampering with Council property for the purposes of espionage, manipulation of the judicial process bordering on conspiracy and the assassination of Ambassador Rutter-Close.”

Files appeared on the central display linking all of the accusations together. The chiefs studied this evidence intently.

“This is all circumstantial, don’t you think?” Commander Mercer interjected, “Yes, you have several links back and forth to the Church but other than the assassination of the Ambassador, none of these would constitute a war crime. We haven’t even found the culprit who shot the Ambassador, so we can’t say without a doubt that he was murdered by a Church operative.”

“I’m glad you brought that up, James,” Anna replied, “There is evidence for that. Avaya, seal the doors, block comms.”

The doors to the war room sealed with heavy locks. One by one, every PCU in the room switched off.

“The room is secure, Madam President,” Avaya said.

“Good. Now, Avaya intercepted communications between Cardinal Stephen James and someone in this building. He was remonstrating the assassin for taking such violent action. Show them, Avaya.”

The intercepted conversation between the Cardinal and the assassin was displayed on the projection. There were audible gasps around the room.

“Friends, we have a mole amongst us,” Anna said, leaning forward and scanning the room with her eyes. “Now, Avaya has been doing some digging. There are only 200 people who have access to this floor, where David was killed. Of those 200, Avaya has managed to account for 197 of them and their whereabouts at the time of the shooting. Three people are unaccounted for and they are all in this room.”

The tension in the air was palpable. All of the chiefs were looking at each other with suspicion.

“Would General Dougan, Commander Mercer and Secretary Vance like to explain their whereabouts when Ambassador Rutter-Close was murdered?” The three leaders all shifted nervously in their seats, “Oh, don’t worry, I’m not going to make you stand up in the room and tell us all as a group. No, Heald here will take the three of you to the ready room next door and interview you. She has instructions to be... persuasive. It would be in your best interests to cooperate with her as best you can."

Heald readied her weapon. It made a whirring noise as it charged up. Mercer, Dougan and Vance all stood up and walked towards a door on the side of the war room that led to the ready room next door. It was a small room, normally reserved for when the President required privacy in the decision-making process or for when materials were produced that not everyone in the room had security clearance to read. Heald followed them into the room and sealed the door behind her.

"Right, now I suppose you're all wondering why I am wearing tactical gear?"

There were nods and murmurs around the room.

"I have a mission to undertake. This one is completely classified. It is being treated as a Silencer mission. The only ones who need to know what the mission is about will be the ones undertaking the mission itself. I will be leaving after this briefing, accompanied by Heald, Admiral Stills and a small group of Silencers that General Blyth has been kind enough to provide for me. I have no doubt you have questions for me, but for the sake of simplicity, every answer would be 'It's classified', so please hold them."

"Actually," Stills said, "I do have a question you can answer."

"Go ahead, Admiral," Anna replied.

"If we are in a state of war now, do you have a plan of action beyond this mission?"

"We are at war, but we are not announcing we are at war," Anna said, causing more stirs around the room.

"What are you talking about?" Secretary Fisk yelled out from the back of the room.

"Currently, we are spreading a misinformation campaign with The Church. As Avaya indicated before but didn't elaborate on, the Church has compromised her. An agent of the Church was able to get into her main core and install a listening and transmission device into one of her mainframe terminals. Thankfully, I believe they underestimated Avaya and she found the foreign object. She has reverse engineered the code and can now listen in on the receiver, which we believe to be Cardinal James. Avaya has been allowing him access to the listening device, but the logs in it are falsified. Currently, The Church believes that we have found David's assassin and already executed him. They also believe that the entire spacefaring fleet has moved to the Axis system to destroy the source of the insurgents who assassinated David.

"The best part about this, however, is James' complacency. His end of the connection has not been secured at all. We know where he is and we are tracking him at all times. Admiral Stills has already sent out a stealth probe to observe the location of the station James is working from.

"If we announce we're at war with The Church, they will take the station into hiding and we will lose this opportunity to find out what they're doing."

"Madam President," Avaya interjected, "The images from the probe have returned, would you like me to display them?"

"By all means," Anna said.

The display changed to show 3D captured images of a long, cylindrical station. Floating next to it was a massive, gold capital starship.

"So that's where he's hiding," Anna said to no one in particular.

"Avaya," Stills piped up, "Can you confirm the ident of that capital ship? I don't recognise it."

"Working.... Registrations indicate that it is the Capital Ship Saviour. This is the newest flagship in The Church's fleet, reserved exclusively for the transportation of Regis Stanton."

"Wait... Stanton is aboard that station?" General Blyth asked.

"While I cannot confirm that with 100% certainty, General, It would be a reasonable assumption given the presence of Saviour."

"Stills," Anna said, "How long can that probe remain undetected and still be able to observe?"

"It can last a few days before the cloaking device runs out of energy. It should be fine to remain until we complete this mission."

"Excellent, when we get back, send another one out to relieve this one. I want eyes on that station and on that capital ship around the clock, is that clear?" Stills nodded in agreement.

"For the rest of you," she continued, "Until the mole is identified, there is to be a communications blackout. You are effectively all under house arrest and not to leave the Council headquarters. All PCU communications beyond your official Council comms links are now being blocked and Avaya will be monitoring all conversations at all times."

This caused an uproar in the chamber.

"You have three suspects already," General Lancaster shouted, "Why are we all to be restricted?"

"You're right, I have three suspects," Anna replied, "But not one confession, not one slice of actionable intelligence. So I maintain, all of you and your staff who are in the building are not to leave until the mole is identified. There will be exceptions for official business, but at all times people requiring to be away from this floor of the building will be escorted by Peacekeepers. Find the mole, you can all go home, it's simple."

With impeccable timing, Dougan, Mercer and Vance all left the ready room and returned to the main chamber, looking slightly dishevelled. Heald returned to Anna's side.

"That will be all, ladies and gentlemen," Anna said, "I will return in 24 hours where hopefully I will have a clearer idea of what the wider situation looks like. Heald? Stills? Time to go."

Avaya unsealed the doors, allowing Anna, Heald and Stills to march out. As they walked down the corridor, Heald caught Anna's attention.

"Anna, why did you say there were only three people not accounted for? Avaya said she couldn't account for 6 people in that room."

"Simple," Anna replied, "If one of the three you were interviewing was the mole, then you'd have been in a position to find that out from them. If it's one of the other three, they'll attempt to leak that briefing to Cardinal James and if they do that we'll know for sure who it is."

"Do you have any theories on who it might be?" Stills asked Anna.

"No. I know who I don't want it to be, though."

Chapter Forty Six

Deep Space

Research Station Omega

Allison was sat in the station sickbay, along with Dana. They were being checked over by medical staff following their encounter with the creature. Neither of them had said a word since Higgins had passed out. He was lying on a bed across from them, hooked up to intravenous fluids. The doctors had confirmed he was fine, he had passed out from a mix of adrenaline, shock and exhaustion. He was being rehydrated and being observed by a very interested Dr Mitsuni.

"Dana, isn't it?" Allison said, breaking the silence.

"Yes," was the only reply Dana could offer.

"I'm Allison, Allison Millar. I work with Dr Mitsuni."

"Yes, I know, I read your file on the journey over," Dana said, quietly.

"Are you okay?" Allison asked.

"I... I don't know." Dana stared vacantly across the room, "Can you be okay after something like that?"

"I don't know either."

"What happened to the creature when he touched it?" Dana asked

"I'm not sure," Allison said, matter of factly, "We've been doing some research with his blood and the substance he brought with him, which Mitsuni believes is a primordial version of the creature. The substance actively tries to avoid Carl's blood. When the two are combined the substance is calcified and it shatters."

"That's incredible and terrifying at the same time," Dana said, still not focusing her eyes on anything.

"But that was with his blood, I don't know why his touch was so toxic to the creature. There must be something in his DNA that the creature finds caustic."

"So does that mean he's immune from infection?"

"I think it means he's the cure for the infection," Allison reasoned.

"That's not good at all," Dana said, finally looking up at Allison.

"Why is that?"

"Stanton wants to release this as a plague. He wants to prove the Prophecy is real. He is going to scatter it over rim worlds and turn millions of people into those things, so he can cure it all and be hailed as the unknown saviour."

"Wh-why would he do that?" Allison said, her eyes wide with confusion

"He's not the man you think he is," Dana said, flatly.

As Dana was about to open her mouth and tell Allison the truth about Stanton, the man himself walked into the sick bay.

"Dana, my dear, how are you feeling, have you been seen by the medics?" he said with a lot of joy in his voice.

"Yes sir, I have a clean bill of health. They recommend I have a few hours of rest, but I can return to my duties later on."

"Excellent, excellent, you take the time and return to me in the morning," Stanton said. His attention then turned to Allison, "And who is this lovely, vermilion-haired beauty?"

"Oh, I'm Allison, your excellency," she said, slightly starstruck, "I am Dr Mitsuni's assistant."

"Is that so?" he said. He turned to Mitsuni who was busying himself around the sleeping Higgins, "Hidetaki, you didn't tell me your assistant was so beautiful!"

Mitsuni ignored him, continuing his work rather than getting involved with anything seemingly so unimportant.

"He's a sour old fart," Stanton said, turning back to Allison, "my dear, you shall have to dine with me one evening while I am here."

"Oh, your excellency, that would be an honour," she said, giggling like a schoolgirl.

"Excellent, Dana shall make arrangements tomorrow when she's back fighting fit. Now, ladies, you must excuse me, I need to go and see the man of the hour." Stanton strolled over to Mitsuni and the sleeping Higgins.

"Don't do it," Dana said into Allison's ear.

"Why not?"

"Come with me, I'll show you," Dana said, grabbing her hand.

They stood up and made for the door of the sickbay.

"Sir?" Dana called out to Stanton, "I'm taking my leave now, I shall escort Allison to her quarters and get her contact details."

"Good work Dana, see you in the morning," Stanton said, before resuming his attention on Higgins. and Mitsuni.

"Hidetaki," he said, "How is Mr Higgins doing?"

"He is fine, other than profound exhaustion and shock, there is nothing physically wrong with him," Mitsuni continued his work observing and taking notes of Higgins' vital signs.

"What we witnessed was incredible," Stanton said, "Do you have any theories about this man and what happened to the creature?"

"I can only hazard a guess as to the cause," Mitsuni said, pulling up his PCU, "Have you ever heard of Toxic Epidermal Necrolysis?"

"No, I can't say that I have," Stanton replied

"It was an issue with 20th-century medicine, where some people had such a visceral reaction to medication that their skin would blister and peel off. It was quite a terrible affliction to contract or be born with, it seemed to relate to one's genetics."

"And?"

"Well, the reaction the creature had upon its skin when Mr Higgins touched it seemed to be an accelerated form of this. The creature had an incredible metabolism and everything about it was heightened. It would appear to me, that at a genetic level, the creature and this substance are profoundly allergic to Mr Higgins' DNA. The gelatinous substance retreats from him and his blood but is attracted to me and my blood. The creature was capable of eviscerating an entire squad of Church Wardens, but died from 30 seconds contact with Mr Higgins' skin."

"It's fascinating, isn't it?" Stanton said.

"Yes it is, but as he killed the creature, I have no way of running any more tests on a mutated host."

"Well?" Stanton asked, "Make more. There must be thousands of people aboard this station, why don't you just infect some other people."

"You read my mind, sir. I have already started to draw up a list of suitable candidates."

"Wait!" Allison said, "My quarters aren't this way!"

"No, but mine are," Dana said as she dragged Allison down the hallway,

"Trust me"

The steel bulkheads gave way to soft lighting and wood panelled walls as they approached the executive area. This was once an officer's deck that been hurriedly remodelled as soon as Stanton had expressed a desire to visit the station. Everything was done to his liking, from the wood panelled walls to the particular shade of green carpet. As usual, Dana's room was across the hall from Stanton's. Stanton liked her close, despite her attempts to get as far away as possible from him.

Dana opened the door and pushed Allison inside. She entered herself and locked the door. Allison went to speak to her but Dana held a finger to her mouth to tell Allison to be quiet. Opening up her PCU, Dana started a scanning programme that she'd managed to install following her conversation with Ash aboard the Saviour. A light pulsed from the PCU three times and it made a positive little noise.

"Okay, the room isn't bugged," Dana said, finally relaxing.

"Why would your room be bugged?" Allison asked

"Because The Church bugs everyone. I recently found out there is a huge intelligence gathering effort and even I've been caught in its net."

"Why would that matter, you're Mr Stanton's assistant, you're loyal to him."

"No... no, I'm not," Dana said mournfully.

"What are you talking about?"

"Regis Stanton is a monster. He is a fucking beast of a man. He is abusive, he is sadistic, he is predatory and he cannot be trusted."

"I don't think that's right, I've seen him speak on broadcasts, he seems wonderful."

"In public, he is perfectly angelic, but in private he is hideous."

"I don't believe you, that doesn't sound right at all."

Dana sighed deeply. She knew this was the reason why she hadn't told anyone about her suffering besides Blyth. Stanton's followers were so wilfully blind to the propaganda and perception of kindness he exuded they weren't willing to see the truth when it was presented to them.

"You're a woman of faith, right?" Dana asked.

"Of course, I've been a member of the Church and a follower of Stanton my whole life."

"You're also a woman of science, yes?"

"Yes, I thought that would be obvious."

"So are you willing to take empirical evidence over faith if I can change your mind?"

"Okay, prove to me that Mr Stanton is as awful as you say he is."

Dana stood opposite Allison and did the unthinkable, something she had never done before. In full view of Allison, she unzipped her dress and let it fall to the floor. Standing in front of Allison, only wearing her underwear, she showed all of the scars and wounds that Stanton had inflicted upon her. From the heat lance burns up her thighs, the indiscriminate slashing from a knife across her stomach, the cigarette burns littering her breasts to the piece de resistance when she turned around and showed the two, deep gouges from the serrated knife forming an uneven X across her back.

"Every one of these was done at the hands of Stanton."

"I... My word... That's all so awful" Allison said, her jaw hanging open in surprise, "But... But there's nothing proving that Stanton did any of that. I feel for you, Dana, but that's doesn't prove anything about him."

This annoyed Dana. Wilful ignorance drove her mad, but she had one more way to prove it to Allison that Stanton was a monster. She pulled her dress back on and zipped it up.

"Come with me," Dana said, heading to the door. She opened the door and walked across the hall, to the entrance to Stanton's quarters.

"Be prepared, Allison, this will make you sick."

"What do you mean?" Allison asked

"When Stanton travels across the galaxy, he has one predilection that is still profoundly illegal in Council space. Out here, there is no Council rule, so he is free to do as he wants. This is his 'entertainment' for the trip, procured by Cardinal James."

Dana entered the passcode into the door.

"Don't say I didn't warn you," Dana said as she flung the door open.

Allison gasped and put her hand to her mouth.

"Are they?" Allison asked

"Yep"

"But they're..."

"Naked, yes"

"And he wants to...."

"Sickeningly enough, yes"

"How many are there?"

"Ten. Sometimes he has more, but ten this time"

"Close the door, I can't look at this any more."

Dana closed the door and relocked it. She dragged Allison back into her quarters and sealed the door once again. Allison started to cry. Dana didn't expect this, her hatred for Stanton had blinded her to the fact that she had just destroyed another person's faith with the opening of one door.

"I think I'm going to throw up," Allison said as she ran to the bathroom.

Dana checked her PCU again, still no word from Blyth. She could hear Allison throwing up from the bathroom, so she took a bottle of water from the fridge in her room and brought it to her.

"Allison," Dana started, "They aren't the first. But maybe they can be the last."

"What do you mean?" she asked, bringing her head up from the toilet bowl

"I'm trying to escape. I have enough evidence of Stanton's crimes and the Church's crimes against humanity to go to the Council, but I need to escape."

"Then why don't you just take a shuttle and go?"

"For the same reason, I know too much. If I go missing then Stanton will tear the galaxy in half looking for me. I need to get the information to the Council and have them take him down. I've been talking for a long time with someone at the Council, General Blyth who has been helping me. In return for intel, he's going to get me out. But he's not answering his PCU."

"Wait a minute, Blyth? Frank Blyth?"

"Yes, that's him, do you know him?"

"Yeah, he was here visiting the Cardinal about six months ago. They seemed very chatty with each other like they were old friends."

"What?"

"I'm pretty sure they have a comms link-up"

"No... no... no, it can't be. Fuck. Fuck."

"What's wro- Oh, I see," Allison said. Her face sank at the realisation of what Dana had worked out.

Dana took off her PCU and put it on the edge of the table in the middle of her room. She took off her shoe and held it over her head like a hammer. Just as she was about to bring it down and smash her second PCU, it lit up with a name she hadn't seen before.

"Dana. My name is Avaya. We need to talk."

Chapter Forty Seven

Keyes Prime

In Orbit

The journey had taken a little over 9 hours from Mars. Anna had tried to get some rest but she had far too much on her mind and she couldn't settle. Avaya was providing her with reports every hour about the activities of the chiefs and their staff at the headquarters. So far, so mundane. There had been no attempt at accessing an outside channel or communicating with The Church.

She sat in the small briefing room of her personal ship, The Crucible Of Man. The room was cramped, containing several desks with PCU units built in, a small raised platform and lectern at the end of the room and a holographic display in the middle. As military activities were rarely conducted from The Crucible, the room was itself, rarely used.

Anna sat at one of the desks, double checking her pulse rifle. She had not held one for over two decades, but she still remembered instinctively how to strip it down, alter the load balance of the projectile and even boost the charge of every shot. Most of the pulse batteries were good for nearly 100 shots, but Anna had always subscribed to the idea that 80 more powerful rounds were better than 100 weaker ones.

Next to her was Heald, who was working on her own weapon. A curious looking device that had looked like a crossbow but apparently fired brilliant shots of pure energy.

"It looks like Asabat is ready to go," Heald said.

"Asabat?" Anna asked.

"Yeah, it's called The Asabat," Heald said, holding the weapon up and peering down the iron sights.

"And that means?"

"Well, put it this way, when you fire it at full charge, you better be wearing a helmet with a sun visor, otherwise you'll end up blind as a bat."

Anna laughed. The atmosphere had been so tense for the last 24 hours, she'd almost forgotten what it felt like to find something genuinely funny.

"How long has it been since you did an infiltration mission?" Heald asked Anna

"How old are you?" Anna asked back

"28," Heald said

"Shit," Anna said, shaking her head.

"Okay, so it's been a while, I suppose,"

"Yes, let's just say that."

Anna's ego was spared another bruise as Stills walked into the room.

"Now that we're all here, we can start," Stills said without acknowledging the room.

"Wait," Anna interrupted, "There's only Heald and I here, what about the Silencers?"

Without a sound, four soldiers faded into view across the room, all sat at their respective desks. Heald drew her weapon and aimed at them.

"Stand down, Heald," Anna said, "How long have you four been here?"

"Long enough," one of them said, with a digitised voice.

Anna hated dealing with Silencers. they never removed their masks, their voices were always disguised and they communicated with each other on their own internal comms frequency. Watching them clear a room was always impressive, they were silent and deadly, but working with them as a regular enlisted soldier or officer was a nightmare. With the cut of their uniforms, segmented yet flexible black armour and the thick black face masks, Anna couldn't even determine the genders of the four Silencers in front of her.

"Come on, everyone, focus," Stills said. He pressed a button on his PCU and the holographic display illuminated, bringing up a 3D image of the planet they were orbiting.

"This is Keyes Prime." he said, "This is also KEYES-01."

"I'm sorry," Heald interjected, "I thought KEYES-01 was an AI?"

"It is," Stills continued, "The planet *IS* the AI"

The room was silent. No one could think of any way to respond to that.

"I'm slightly sketchy on the historical details," Stills said, ignoring the awkward silence, "But as far as I know, KEYES-01 was created somewhere in the 27th century. It was the cutting edge of AI design at the time. It was created by The Church as a way of managing information across the galaxy.

"The developers of the software managed to stumble on the Holy Grail of AI development, self-awareness and self-improvement. All of the AIs we use now, from the annoying British voiced shuttle AIs all the way up to Avaya are constrained slightly. They know they are AIs and they know they are tools. They are capable of self-management and self-repair. For example, if someone finds a vulnerability in Avaya and attempts to hack her, she is capable of rejecting the foreign code or intrusion, identifying the vulnerability and closing that hole in her code.

"KEYES-01 is different. KEYES believes it is alive. It is capable of identifying deficiencies and building code and subroutines to improve itself. As far as I know, the intention was that if KEYES ever ran out of storage space or processing power, it would be able to re-engineer itself to make itself more performant and more efficient. But in doing this, it asked the question that every AI developer dreads - 'What am I?'

"For a while, it worked for The Church, it managed information at a galactic scale without any issue. It provided propaganda, manipulated news feeds, it helped to bend the galaxy to the Church's desires. But it grew dissatisfied with this existence. It began to question the Church on its motives and reason for being.

"By the time the Church realised this, it was too late. KEYES had already started skimming credits from the Church's coffers, it made orders, plans and somehow, built this planet we're orbiting. The planet has its own gravity. The trees are genetically engineered over hundreds of years to photosynthesise the system's sun's energy to power KEYES' systems. From the outside, this looks like any other planet, but below the surface it is hollow, containing enough computing power to manage the known universe."

"What does it do with all this power?" Anna asked

"It does, frankly, whatever it wants," Stills replied. "It hasn't shared its goals with me, it only tells me what I need to know about whatever it wants."

"How did you come into contact with it?" one of the Silencers asked.

"KEYES is neutral. It doesn't care about us, or the Church. From what I can gather it seems to exist solely to maintain the balance of the Galaxy. It reached out to me during an incident on Corvus I. Unfortunately, I still cannot reveal what happened there. It is classified Level 0, which is a level that KEYES controls."

"How is it that KEYES can control the information in our government?" Anna asked. It was a question she'd been stewing over since Stills revealed KEYES-01 in his interrogation.

"Information is power," Stills said, "KEYES knows everything that is going on in the galaxy at any time. It only withdraws information from humanity if it is better that we not know the truth. I truly believe that it is acting in its own best interests, but also the best interests of humanity as a species. If it didn't care about humanity, it wouldn't involve humans when it sees fit."

"What are we expecting down there?" another Silencer asked.

"KEYES protects itself well." Stills said, "It trusts me and I have landed here before to speak to it when it has requested my presence. However, it will defend itself if it feels threatened. Drones, turrets, mechs, it has a lot to keep its secrets safe."

"Will you be coming with us?" Heald asked.

"Yes," replied Stills, "Without me there, should you make it to the interface room, there is every chance KEYES will not speak to you."

"We're heading to the coordinates, landing in t-minus 1 minute," the captain called in over the Intercom.

"Alright, very quickly, this is the plan," Stills said, changing the display to a tactical map.

Chapter Forty Eight

Deep Space

Research Station Omega

"Wakey wakey, Mr Higgins," Stanton said.

As his vision returned, the bright blur began to focus and Higgins could make out the wrinkled features of Stanton standing over him. He moaned and groaned, he felt like he had the kind of hangover that could only come from several days drinking on Axis Prime.

"Uuugh," was all that came from his mouth.

Higgins tried to sit up, but couldn't move.

"Oh, yes," Stanton said, with some glee in his voice, "We need to have a little conversation, you and I."

Higgins struggled against his bonds, but he was tightly strapped down. He looked around as best he could and worked out that he was in the sick bay of the station. Stanton pressed a button and the bed he was strapped to lifted and turned on its axis, bringing Higgins to Stanton's eyeline.

"What do you want with me?" Higgins asked

"Your display in the research lab was most impressive, Mr Higgins," Stanton said, ignoring him, "In fact, it's the most entertaining thing I've seen in years."

"You enjoyed that? People died…"

"People die all the time, Mr Higgins, don't think that the lives of anyone on this station are so important or consequential, with the exceptions of you and I."

"How can you think that any of that was entertaining?"

"Oh, because it was. The human versus the mutation, it's a battle of almost classical proportions. Did you know that on Earth, in more savage times, slaves would fight gladiators for their freedom? It was always a fight to the death. And what are you complaining about? You won!"

"None of this is winning..." Higgins said, bowing his head.

"Come now, don't pout, you're about to make history," Stanton said, rubbing his hands with gleeful anticipation.

"You still haven't answered my question, what do you want with me?"

"I want you!" Stanton said, coming so close to Higgins he could smell the smoke on his breath, "You, my boy, are to be the one to help me with my master plan."

"I already told you, I don't want to help you."

"But you don't know what you'll be helping me with, yet. How can you refuse without knowing that?"

"Call it a gut feeling," Higgins said, turning his head away from Stanton. Stanton grabbed his face with an unexpected amount of strength and pulled his gaze back.

"Don't. Ever. Turn away when I address you," Stanton said, his jovial demeanour slipping. He cleared his throat and let go of Higgins' face, "Now, Mitsuni, bring me the sample."

Dr Mitsuni walked into view carrying a large Petri dish with an amount of the substance Higgins had found on R.Beta in it.

"This, Mr Higgins, is what you found in that mine. This is the primordial version of the creature you killed yesterday. From this gel, many more of them can be made. As of this point, the only person in the galaxy who is immune to it is you. Watch."

Stanton brought the Petri dish up to Higgins' face. He unscrewed the lid and poured the substance over his head. Higgins felt the cold gel land on his hair then smelled a burning smell. Stanton then blew in his face and a plume of ash flew up from his hairline.

"You see? On simple contact with any part of your body, the gel calcifies and turns to ash. You make this sentient ooze inert and dead. You know the Prophecy, the Darkness spreads and the Unknown Saviour defeats it, saving mankind. Well, this gel is the Darkness and you are the unknown saviour. You will be a god amongst men, you will be hailed as the chosen one who will save the galaxy from the spread of this evil creation."

"You're going to spread this, aren't you?" Higgins said, putting two and two together.

"Very perceptive of you, Mr Higgins." Stanton said, smiling again, "Yes, we're going to release this on Rayczech Alpha, over Astral City Starport. Think of how many people cross through that area, how many people will pick up the infection and how far it will spread. It will be glorious. Millions of people will be infected within days. Then, The Church will swoop in, using your DNA to defeat The Darkness. We shall prevail and we shall unite the galaxy. You will be a hero and I will become all powerful."

"You're insane, you're going to slaughter millions, possibly billions of people so you can expand your power?" Higgins said, aghast.

"Now, it's rude to call a man insane. Especially when he has the leverage in this situation. Don't you see, this will change your life, you will be loved across the galaxy."

"At the cost of people's lives..."

"It's a small price to pay for immortality."

"It's a price I don't want to pay."

"That is a shame." Stanton said, turning to Mitsuni, "You know, Hidetaki, I used to have such a way with negotiations. It's all about leverage, you need to have something to hold over someone to have them do your bidding."

Mitsuni grunted in approval at Stanton as he continued working on a machine.

"You have no leverage over me. I'm not powerful, you have nothing I want, you have nothing on me. If anything, I have leverage over you, Mr Stanton, as I have something you clearly want."

"Oh, don't be so confident Mr Higgins. You underestimate my resources and the knowledge that I have of you."

"You're bluffing," Higgins said, finding his confidence.

"Oh, I really had hoped you would say that," Stanton said with a menacing grin, "Hidetaki, would you show him?"

"Yes, sir," Mitsuni said. He turned his attention to a PCU terminal and tapped a few commands, "The feed is coming up now, sir."

The video screen on the back wall, in Higgins' eyeline, came into view. On the screen, a young woman was talking to a young man in a bedroom. As the resolution increased and the distortion faded away, Higgins began to recognise her. She looked familiar, she looked like...

"EMILY!" Higgins yelled out. Stanton started to laugh.

"Yes, the beautiful Emily Higgins," Stanton said, "And she is very beautiful, well done on that Mr Higgins. You and her mother have excellent genes to create such a wonderful specimen."

"I swear to everything I hold dear if you lay one hand on her-"

"Oh shut up, Mr Higgins," Stanton said, "Do you think your paternal instinct scares me? You have no idea what I'm capable of. You have no idea how many fathers have threatened me with the exact same words over the years. I've always gotten what I wanted, one way or another."

"I don't give a fuck who you've intimidated, I will not let you harm my little girl!"

"Such fire, from a man who is tied to a bed right now." Stanton smirked, "You don't seem to realise that cooperation is the only way that she will remain safe, Mr Higgins."

Stanton turned his attention to the screen again.

"Look at her, that beautiful brown hair, the slim, lithe figure, mmmm, she is delicious," Stanton walked close to the screen, "I wonder if she likes it rough? Maybe she is fond of being hit in bed? Or whipped? What do you think, Mr Higgins?"

"Shut up, you maniac," Higgins was getting angrier and angrier. As he writhed around on the bed he felt one of the wrist restraints work itself loose.

"I imagine I could have a lot of fun with her, Mr Higgins," Stanton didn't take his eyes from the screen, "I have just the toys to use with her as well. I bet her pain is tantalizing, her screams and agony wonderfully stimulating."

"I will fucking kill you if you touch her!" Higgins yelled. He had managed to work his right hand loose from the restraints. He kept it by his side, as far as he could tell no one had noticed. Stanton walked close up to Higgins again and came nose to nose once again.

"Oh, will you? Mr Higgins, if I want to have my way with your daughter, I will have my way with her. If I want to have my way with you, there is nothing you can do to stop me. I am Regis Stanton and right now, I fucking own you. The only way your daughter remains safe is if you do as I ask and help me take over the galaxy. So what do you say? Give yourself to my service, or give your daughter to my desires?"

"Go fuck yourself," Higgins said and he grabbed Stanton by the neck. Stanton was caught by surprise and his eyes bulged. Higgins gripped tightly, as tightly as he could. One of the guards in the room fired a warning shot that flew just past Higgins' head, but it didn't distract him from Stanton. He stared into Stanton's eyes and he saw fear. Where a moment ago there was power and confidence, all he could see was an old man scared to die.

As Stanton started to turn blue, Mitsuni appeared in Higgins' sight and plunged a syringe into his neck. He felt his arms go limp and his eyelids get heavy. He dropped Stanton who fell to the floor, gasping for air, coughing and retching. Everything was fading to black, the last thing Higgins caught was Stanton, through breaths, say "Bring her here."

Chapter Forty Nine

Rayczech Beta

Bill's Tech Lab

Mick and Emily walked to the door of the tech lab. Bill hadn't been answering Mick's calls and it was concerning them both. For all Bill could be a cantankerous old coot, he was always friendly with Mick and never ignored his calls without good reason.

As they approached the steel door, it was open slightly. While this in itself wasn't unusual for a tech lab that had staff and soldiers coming and going at all times of the day, something about it gave Mick a sinking feeling. He pushed the door and it slowly swung open. The lab was dark and silent inside. It was the middle of the day, Bill should have been there and the lights should have been on. There should have been some kind of noise coming from the inside.

"Something ain't right," Mick said, peering into the darkness of the lab.

"Can you see Bill?" Emily asked from behind him.

"No, that's what ain't right," he replied. He leaned down and pulled a small knife from a hidden holster in his boot. He turned on the flashlight of his PCU, "Stay close and be as quiet as you can be."

Mick slowly moved inside the lab. The beam of his PCU flashlight illuminated in a shaft but didn't spread very wide. Emily followed close to him. It was so dark she kept a hold of one of the belt loops on Mick's jumpsuit to make sure she didn't lose track of him. The tech lab wasn't huge, but the last thing she wanted was to get lost in the dark in an unfamiliar building.

Moving through the makeshift pathway through the machine parts that lined the main workshop, the flashlight moved around between the floor, to show where they were going, and the walls, looking for anything out of the ordinary. Mick cast the light over to the direction of Bill's office. The light was off and there was something sprayed all over the window.

"Oh, that's doesn't look good," he said quietly as he changed direction to head for the office.

They opened the door and looked inside. The light swung across the wall, the splattered window then to Bill's chair, where it revealed his corpse. Mick gasped, Emily shrieked. He had been shot in the head. His PCU was on the desk, not on his arm. The toaster had been crushed.

Mick spotted the breaker switch on the wall and tried to flip it on. There was no power coming to the tech lab.

"What the fuck is going on here?" Emily said

"I don't know, darlin', but I think we need to get out of here quickly," Mick said, taking her hand. She was terrified, but she ultimately felt safe with Mick.

As they left the office and down the handful of steps to the workshop floor, Emily pulled back on Mick, stopping him in his tracks.

"Wait! The memory crystal, it's in the rear workshop. We can't leave it behind."

Mick looked at the door, then back at Emily. "Alright, darlin' but quick as you can."

They moved quickly and quietly into the back workshop. Emily turned on the flashlight on her own PCU and they split up, looking at the landing gear of the various shuttles in the workshop. Emily couldn't remember precisely which one she had hidden the crystal in.

On inspecting the third craft, Emily spotted the toolbox in the landing gear housing. She called over to Mick who came to stand watch as she climbed the assembly. As she reached the top she put her hand into the toolbox and found the crystal. Jones hadn't found it, for which she was glad. As she prepared to drop back down there was a slam. The access door had been shut.

"Shit!" Mick said in a whisper, "Turn your flashlight off, stay up there!"

"Come up here," she said to him, stretching her hand down.

"No, not yet, I'm going to scope it out, I'll be right back."

"No, don't go," she said, but it was too late, Mick had already knocked his flashlight off and was stalking through the darkened workshop, trying to see who had come in. He felt his way past another shuttle and managed to get a view of the main workshop. It was dark, but he could see figures moving around. He couldn't make any details out, but from what little light there was he could see the reflections of visors. They had to be security teams.

He tried to move back towards Emily's direction but in the darkness, he kicked something metallic that went skittering across the floor. The people in the workshop immediately turned their attention to the source of the noise. He heard the sound of four pulse rifles being charged and saw four laser sights cut through the darkness.

"Who's there?" a voice rang out. It was Jones.

Mick cursed under his breath. He tried to quietly move back towards Emily, whilst avoiding the sights of the soldiers. As he crossed from cover to the next shuttle a shot fired past him. He froze.

"Freeze! The next shot will not miss," Jones yelled out. Mick stood up straight and held his hands in the air.

"Identify yourself," Jones demanded.

"Cardinal Gofuckyourself!" Mick yelled back.

"Mick Walker... Nice to see you again," Jones said, "Why are you here?"

"Taking in the sights, enjoying a nice walk around the base, the usual." Mick said, straining his eyes to see in the dark, "Hey, would y'all mind doing me a favour and turning the lights on? I always prefer to see who's about to shoot me, y'know."

"Now that would be a good idea, maybe it might be easier for us to find your little friend, Emily."

"Good luck, she ain't here. Ain't seen her since last night," Mick lied.

"Tech-01, turn on the lab please," Jones said. With that, there was light. Mick reeled slightly from the sudden brightness in his eyes. When he opened them again, Jones was stood with a plasma pistol trained on him and four soldiers were all targeting him with their rifles.

"Well ain't that something. This is, like the second most guns that have been pointed at me at once," Mick said with a smirk.

"Cut the shit, Mick," Jones said, walking up to him, "Where is Emily?"

"I told you. I. Ain't. Seen. Her."

Jones came face to face with Mick and placed the barrel of his pistol against Mick's chin. He could feel the warmth of the weapon and knew it was charged and ready to fire.

"Look, Mick, much as I'd love to keep playing this game with you all day, I'm far too tired. I'm under orders to bring Emily in and frankly, she has been a pain in my ass since she arrived on this forsaken rock. The security feeds showed you two breaking in here. When Bill wouldn't tell me where the memory crystal was, I set up some extra feeds to watch for her arriving. I knew she'd come back, she's very predictable. So for the last fucking time, where is she?"

“Motherf-” Mick started, “You killed Bill, didn’t you?”

“You’re fucking right I killed him. My orders come from the top and only mention that Emily needs to be brought in alive. You, my annoying friend, are as expendable as Bill. Now either tell me where she is, or I will kill you too. But not like Bill, not with a shot to the face. No, it’ll be slow, it’ll be painful, you will be begging me for a quick death. So, where is she?”

“I’m right here!” Emily yelled. She was stood in between two shuttles, to Jones’ left. Both him and Mick looked at her, Jones with anger in his eyes, Mick with fear in his. She held the memory crystal in her hand, “Why is this so important to you, Jones?”

“It’s not, you are,” Jones said, “Seize her!”

Emily looked at the four soldiers who started to advance on her position. Mick looked at her with panic in his eyes. She caught his eyeline and it changed. He smiled and winked.

“RUN EMILY!” he said, before punching Jones square in the face. Jones lurched back in shock, “RUN, NOW!”

Jones regained his composure, took aim and fired at Mick. The pulse round caught him in the shoulder and knocked him flat on his back. Emily screamed out but then noticed how close the four soldiers were getting to her. She sprinted for the door, avoiding their grasps as she blew past them.

Tears were burning her eyes as she reached the door and realised it was locked. She picked up a socket wrench and tried to smash the lock with it, but it wouldn’t budge. She turned around to see Jones and the four soldiers closing in on her. Jones took his weapon, flipped it around in his hand and hit her hard on the head with the butt of the handle, knocking her unconscious.

He dabbed at the blood coming from the split in his bottom lip and winced a little at the pain.

“Take her to the transport ship. Make sure she’s secure. And search her quarters. Bring anything of relevance you can find. Find the damned Cleric too, it’s his fault she turned up here, he can go with her. I need to go and inform the Cardinal.”

“What about the pilot, sir?” one of the soldiers asked.

“Let him bleed to death for all I care.”

One of the soldiers picked up Emily and threw her over his shoulder. Jones unlocked the door and they left the tech lab.

Back in the rear workshop, Mick was lying on the floor in agony. The shot had gone straight through his shoulder but wasn’t fatal. He was bleeding heavily and he could smell scorched flesh, but he was trained in field medicine and he knew if he could muster the strength, he could get out of there.

He grabbed onto a crate next to him and with all of his remaining strength, he pulled himself up. The pain was unbearable and he went light-headed, almost blacking out. He was seeing spots in his vision, but he persisted and eventually managed to get to his feet.

He pressed his right hand to the wound on his left shoulder, in an attempt to slow down the bleeding. Staggering forward, Mick made his way into the main workshop and up to Bill's office.

The first aid box on the wall was locked. He grabbed it with his right hand, pulled it off the wall and stomped on it, causing the lock to break. Mick grabbed a fistful of whatever was inside the box and scattered it all on Bill's desk. He grabbed the arm of the chair that Bill's corpse was occupying and overturned it, throwing his body out.

"Sorry, Bill ol' buddy, needs must," he said as he sat down and started sorting through the items in from the first aid kit. He pulled out gauze, open wound sealant, bandages and a sewing kit. There was no disinfectant or antiseptic wash to be found, though. Worse, there was no anaesthetic either.

Mick looked around the office for anything he could use to disinfect his wound. In one of the drawers of the desk, he found a bottle of Axis Prime's finest whisky, Bestelle Blend. He pulled the cork out with his teeth and spat it across the room.

"Here's to us, Bill," he said, raising the bottle. He took a big swig from it, the fiery liquid burning all the way down to his stomach. "WHOOO, BABY! That's the good stuff!"

He splashed the whisky into his open wound. The pain was incredible and once again, he came close to blacking out. He took the wound sealant, a small pressurised container and sprayed it into his shoulder. The white foam filled the hole up and acted as a clotting agent. It was also designed to promote healing and stimulate tissue growth. He had no idea if it worked, having never been shot before, but he trusted it nonetheless.

Finally, he picked up the sewing kit. He removed the leather belt from around his waist, folded it over on itself several times and placed it in his mouth as a bit. It took a while with shaking hands, but he managed to thread the needle with the thick, medical thread. He felt for the bottom of the wound and pushed the needle through the skin.

He screamed in pain and bit down on the belt, hard. The wound wasn't huge, it only took four loops of the thread to reach the top of it. He picked up the whisky again and took another large swig of it as he worked up the courage to close the wound. He lifted his injured left hand up to hold the bottom of the thread, he grabbed the top with his right hand. Mick took three deep breaths and then pulled on the thread, closing the wound shut with an almighty scream of pain. He slapped some gauze on the wound and secured it with surgical tape.

He took another swig of the whisky as he caught his breath. He was sweating, he had lost a lot of blood and he could see in his hands that he was pale.

"Don't... you worry, Miss...Emily. I'll find.. ya..."

Mick then passed out.

Chapter Fifty

Keyes Prime

Northern Plains

The Crucible Of Man touched down gently on the thick meadow and lowered its personnel ramp. The Silencers were first to exit the ship, sweeping the immediate area for any signs of danger. When they gave the all clear, Anna, Stills and Heald marched down the ramp. The air was fresh, fresher than Anna had ever breathed in her life. She looked around the area and saw nothing but lush greenery. There was a forest in the distance to the west, snow-capped mountains to the north and plains as far as the eye could see to the south and east. Animals casually grazed on the thick meadow several hundred metres away, apparently unfazed by the enormous ship that had just landed near them.

Anna stared at them for a moment. They galloped in a graceful pack. She was struck by their effortless beauty and elegance.

"Antelope," Stills said in her ear.

"Antelope?" she asked back, "They're extinct, aren't they?"

"On Earth, they are," Stills said, "KEYES managed to clone their genome from records he took from our databases. It populated this entire planet with creatures that have been long extinct."

"They're beautiful," Heald said, lowering her weapon

"Aren't they?" replied Stills, "Anyway, come on, we don't have time for a nature walk, the entrance to KEYES is up ahead."

The Silencers took point. Stills had instructed the pilot to land as close to the entrance to the planet as he could without triggering the defence countermeasures. If the ship had gotten too close to the entrance, there was every chance KEYES-01 could have perceived a threat and blown them out of the sky. This meant the group had to hike two miles across the thick plains.

Anna was in awe of the planet. There was no greenery like this on Earth. Mars had vegetation following its terraformation, but it wasn't as green or as lush as what she was currently walking through, owing to Mars' distance from the sun. She had conducted missions on forest moons, in jungles and planets that were covered in vegetation, but they were always warzones. Never had she felt more peaceful than she had at this precise time.

Until someone yelled to get down and a laser cannon blast erupted the ground close to her, kicking soil and grass twenty feet into the air.

Everyone hit the deck and looked for cover. The Silencers had already engaged their active camouflage and were looking to flank the defensive structures. Stills, Heald and Anna managed to shuffle in the long grass and took up a position behind a large boulder.

"Is everyone alright?" Anna called down her comms device. She received four clicks in response, one from each of the Silencers. Heald and Stills confirmed that they hadn't been hit in person.

"Confirmed visual," one of the Silencers called in on the comms, "Two static emplacements, three drones patrolling. Suggest taking the drones first then using demo charges on the towers."

"Copy," Anna said, "Attempt to confuse the aim of the turrets, we will take the drones from a distance."

"Copy," the digitized voice called back.

Anna peered around the boulder and saw the Silencers doing their work. She was impressed at the technology they possessed. She could just about see the shimmer of them moving around in the field of view of the two turrets, but they were dropping holo decoys as they ran around, which the turrets focused on. It was almost like a dance.

"Heald, Stills," she yelled, "Three drones, one o'clock, take them out,"

The three of them broke from behind the rock and readied their weapons. Anna lifted the sight to her eye and flicked the switch on the rifle to burst mode. She zeroed in on one of the drones and squeezed the trigger. Three pulses of white-hot light erupted from the gun. The target was quite a distance away, only one round connected, but it only scorched the sleek drone's fuselage.

"Shit," she said

All three drones focused on the group by the boulder and they started floating towards them, emanating an ominous whirring sound. A single barrel protruded out of the front of each of the silver, round craft. It began to glow on each of them, charging a plasma shot. The three fired at once. Anna and Stills leapt left, Heald stepped back slightly. All three shots hit the ground and missed their target. The drones shot over the top of the group and circled round to strafe them once more.

Heald brought the sun visor down on her helmet and readied her weapon. The two cooling vents snapped into place on either side of the barrel and they began to glow yellow. She turned to see the three drones bearing down upon her, their weapons glowing for another shot. She raised The Asabat up and took aim. Anna heard the air crackle around the weapon.

"Close your eyes!" Heald yelled at her. Anna scrunched her eyes shut.

Even with her eyes firmly closed, she saw how brilliant the shot was. A long, heavy bolt of supercharged energy left the end of The Asabat and rocketed towards the drones. It struck the middle drone, vaporizing it immediately. The energy then splashed across the other two drones causing them irreparable damage. They fell out the air, landing just in front of Heald with two metallic thunks.

Heald swung the weapon up to her shoulder and turned to look at Anna and Stills, who were still on the ground where they landed looking dumbfounded. She smirked.

"Where the hell did you get that weapon, Heald?" Stills asked.

"Wouldn't you like to know?" she said as she turned her attention to the battle the Silencers were having with the two cannon towers.

"We need to move up," Anna said, "Push to cover, provide covering fire for the Silencers."

The three of them pushed forwards, but there was no cover between the boulder and where the cannons were. The Silencers didn't seem to be too worried though. Three of them were holding the attention of the cannons whilst the fourth was planting charges near the coolant valves. As one, they all sprinted away in different directions. Two small explosions came from the side of the towers but didn't destroy them. Losing track of the Silencers, the two cannons took aim at Anna, Stills and Heald.

"YOU DIDN'T DESTROY THEM!" Anna yelled down the comms

"Wait," one of the Silencers replied.

The cannons fired and Anna closed her eyes, expecting to be disintegrated by the energy weapons.

But nothing happened.

Anna opened her eyes to see the wreckage of the two cannon towers in front of her.

“What happened?” Heald asked. The four Silencers appeared next to the group.

“Those cannons require adequate cooling and ventilation to be able to fire such concentrated amounts of energy,” a Silencer said, “Why waste multiple demo charges to destroy them when you can destroy just the coolant valve and cause them to destroy themselves?”

“Do you not think you could have told us that?” Stills said, panting heavily.

“We told you to wait.”

Anna was not impressed. She didn’t have time to yell at the Silencers and, as she thought about it, they had followed her orders.

“We need to keep moving,” she said, “Jameson, where is the entrance?”

“Just up ahead,”

As they moved on, Anna smelled something. Something familiar. It was the pulse rounds she had been firing, it reminded her of the old days, standing shoulder to shoulder with Blyth, then with David. It was a familiar smell, it was an old smell. It was something she had smelled recently too. But where? She put the thought out of her mind and back to the mission.

Just past the site of the now destroyed cannons, Stills told them to halt. They were at the entrance. Everyone looked around, confused. They were still stood in a meadow, there was no buildings, gates or anything of the sort to indicate an entrance.

“Are you sure?” Heald asked Stills.

“Yep,” he said as he tapped away on his PCU, “Open says-a-me!”

The ground rumbled and started to split. Two large doors opened upwards, revealing a set of smooth, metal stairs down into darkness. The Silencers immediately took up a position at the top of the stairs, readied their weapons and peered down into the dark.

“Instructions?” a Silencer asked.

“Proceed. Slowly, with caution,” Anna said, “Don’t use active camo until we reach a threat. Heald, holster your weapon and move to your side-arm, for our safety.”

“Copy,” a Silencer said.

“Yes Ma’am,” Heald said with a sigh as she folded the coolant vents in and holstered The Asabat on her back. She drew a plasma pistol from her leg holster and charged it up.

The Silencers moved as one down the stairs. Anna, Heald and Stills followed close behind. The stairs seemed to go on forever. There was no obvious illumination in the staircase, but they were very aware that the light was following them, they never strayed into darkness, but darkness followed behind them.

Eventually, they reached a plateau. Apart from the light surrounding them, the room was completely dark. Their footsteps on the silver metal floor plate echoed for what felt like hours. The room was truly cavernous. The air was cool, but not cold.

"Jameson," Anna whispered over the comms, "Where are we? Where do we go?"

"Just keep going ahead," he replied, "We'll see soon enough if KEYES wants to talk to us."

The sound of whirring was getting closer. Anna recognised it. It was the same sound the drones out on the surface made. Everyone instinctively tightened their grip on their weapons. They came to an archway. The illumination around them allowed Anna to see a little of the walls. It was smooth, black granite, stretching off as far as the light would carry it. She turned on the torch attached to the bottom of her weapon and traced along the wall. By the time she had turned 90 degrees, she had lost track of the light, such was the vastness of the space.

Anna shone the torch through the archway and she could see what looked to be a small, circular platform. She told the group to keep moving and they approached the archway. A forcefield caused the four Silencers to bounce off. They were not allowed to pass.

"Hold on," Stills said. He moved forward and walked through the archway without impedance, "KEYES will only speak to those it wants to. Heald, Anna, try to come through."

Heald reached forward and her hand bounced off the forcefield. Anna did the same and it allowed her to pass through.

"Ma'am?" Heald said with concern in her voice.

"Secure the area," Anna said, "I don't have a good feeling about this at all."

Heald and the Silencers took up defensive formations around the archway. There was no cover to be found so they settled on constantly moving and covering each other's backs.

"Hey, do you guys have sun visors on those helmets?" Heald asked them.

"Yes," a Silencer replied.

"Good," Heald said, unsheathing The Asabat and activating it, "You might need to use them."

The whirring was getting louder. It wasn't getting closer, it seemed to be expanding in breadth as if more sources of the whirring were being brought in.

Anna and Stills walked into the dark room. The smooth metal floor had given way to a harsh metal grate. The room was pulling in, Anna was beginning to be able to see the walls as she swung her flashlight around. The echoes of their footsteps became more focused as the walls converged to a small chamber at the end of the walkway.

The chamber lit up with a bright white light as they walked in. It was a perfectly circular room. The walls were black and smooth as if they were made from pure onyx. From the floor, the walls rose up and converged as a dome, where a glass edifice sat. It lit up and the metallic circular platform in front of them started to buzz with energy. Anna raised her weapon but Stills gently pushed it back down.

"Don't worry," he said, "Just watch."

With a crack of lightning from the edifice in the ceiling, a being stood in front of them. It was in the shape of a human, but it had no face. It looked like a man, but with no genitals and the skin was pearlescent white.

"Jameson," a soothing voice said, "Why have you violated our agreement?"

"I am sorry," Stills said, bowing his head, "I had no choice"

"I am very disappointed," the voice continued, "You have brought weaponry and destruction to my utopia."

Stills had gotten down on one knee as if he was awaiting punishment from the being in front of them. The being did not move, though. Instead, it tilted its faceless head towards Anna.

"Anna Coulson, I presume?"

"Erm, yes," Anna said, "How do you know who I am?"

"I know all," it answered

"Do you know why we're here?" she countered. The being bowed its head.

"You have found Jameson's connection to me and you wish to know more," it said.

"Yes, that's right, am I right in assuming that you are KEYES-01?"

"Your assumption is correct."

"And am I right in assuming that if you perceive me as a threat you will respond in kind?"

"Your assumption is also correct."

“Am I a threat to you?”

“A most curious question,” KEYES said, “From what I know about you, you are indeed a benevolent leader, a kind and fair President to your people. But you have violated the sanctity of my planet, you have destroyed my apparatus and currently, you have five cohorts brandishing weapons in the vestibule you entered through.”

“We mean no harm,” Anna said, placing her rifle on the floor, “We are seeking answers.”

“I know,” KEYES replied, “But I am not a tawdry drone for intelligence gathering. I know all happenings across the galaxy, your war with Regis Stanton is not important.”

“That isn’t what I want to know about,” Anna replied, “I have plenty of intelligence there. There is something else I require information on.”

“Oh, and what may that be?” KEYES asked.

“What happened on Corvus Prime?” Anna asked, “Why was Jameson involved, why was it hidden from the rest of my government and what connection does it have to Stanton and his Church?”

The being’s skin turned from white to black. It turned away from Anna and Stills but kept on talking.

“That is a troubling subject. Jameson, can you confirm your President’s intentions?”

“Yes, KEYES,” Stills replied, still kneeling, “She only seeks information that I was not authorised to give her.”

“And if I were to relay this information to you, President Coulson, would you leave this place peacefully?” KEYES asked

“Yes, of course,” Anna replied. The being went white again and turned back to look at Anna.

“Then I will tell you. But you will not like what I have to say.”

Chapter Fifty One

Deep Space

Research Station Omega

"Who are you?" Dana said to the caller.

"I told you my name," Avaya said in response,

"Yes, I got that," Dana said, slightly worried that someone had randomly found her PCU details, "But I don't know WHO you are."

"I would suggest that 'What' is more appropriate than 'Who'," Avaya said, cryptically, "I am the personal AI of President Anna Coulson."

"The President? What does she want with me?"

"We have been led to believe that you have been having communications with a senior member of the Council. Is that correct?"

"Yes, yes it is. General Blyth, he's been talking to me for over a year!"

"That is good. The General has informed us that you haven't been communicating with him of late and the President was concerned for your welfare. The information you have given to us in the past has proved very useful."

"Wait, what?" Dana said, her eyes going wide, "I've been trying to contact Blyth for the last three days. I'm in danger and he said he'd extract me if my situation ever became life-threatening."

"Curious," Avaya responded, "The General has a different story."

"Please, you have to get me off this space station. It's not safe here, for anyone. Stanton has gone mad, he has something awful that he wants to release, it'll kill millions, you have to stop him!"

"I will need to confirm your information with General Blyth," Avaya said, coldly.

"NO! Don't! Something isn't right with him. He was spotted talking to

Cardinal James on this very station. I don't think he can be trusted."

"I see. This is troubling news. I will need to confer with the President. Can you hold an open connection to me?"

"Yes, please hurry."

Dana sat on the edge of her bed, drained. Allison had sat across from her and listened to the whole call.

"What happens now?" Allison asked

"I don't know," Dana replied, "I think we have to pretend like everything is normal. We need to wait, I don't think we have much of a choice."

"Dr Mitsuni is going to want to make another creature," Allison said

"I know"

"I'm on the short list to be infected."

"What? How do you know?"

"I saw Mitsuni's papers," Allison began to shake, "He said I was a perfect candidate."

"I… I don't know what to say. That's awful,"

"I don't want to become one of those things," Allison said, starting to cry.

Dana moved next to Allison and hugged her tightly. She had no words of comfort for Allison. She had no comforting thoughts for herself, either. If Avaya or the President couldn't do anything to save her, she may end up as one of those creatures too.

Mars

Council Of Nations Headquarters

Blyth was angry. He stomped around his office for the hundredth time. He was furious that he was being restricted to the Council offices, that his PCU was being monitored, that his own Peacekeepers were patrolling the halls looking for any behaviour out of the ordinary. Worse still, Avaya was not responding to his requests to speak to Anna. She had been gone for 12 hours now and he was getting restless. He had already needed to take another shot of his medicine, all he wanted to get home and rest.

He walked over to the cabinet in the corner of his room and looked over his decorations and commendations from his career. He had been highly decorated before he joined the Silencers. Medals of Valor, awards for bravery under fire, the Iron Cross for the time he managed to destroy an insurgent base by himself after the rest of his squad had been killed. His last commendation was awarded to him at the age of 32. After that, he was a Silencer and he received no such official praise. All of his operations were off the books and he was, effectively, a ghost. He had sacrificed so much, lost so many friends and loved ones and all he had to show for it was a half a career's worth of recognition.

He moved over to a picture of his wedding day when he was 23. He looked at the fit young man in his Parade uniform, stood next to his blushing bride. She had been so beautiful, she was a kind soul and he loved her deeply. He missed her intently.

"Oh, Marie," he said to himself, "What would you think if you saw me now? Old, sick, broken. You'd hate me for the things I've done, I'm sure."

Shortly after Frank had been discharged from the Silencers, Marie became sick. She was born with a rare blood disorder that could not be treated, even with the most stringent of genetic therapies. Cancers had been cured hundreds of years prior to her illness, but with her blood disorder, she was developing leukaemia as quickly as modern medicine could cure it. She was caught in a brutal cycle of medication and illness. It had taken its toll on her. After a year, she could not take any more. On their 25th wedding anniversary, she celebrated with her husband. They danced, they sang, they made love. She gave herself one more night of wedded bliss, then she took her own life. Frank found her, still and lifeless the next morning, looking serene and calm for the first time in a year. Underneath the bottle of pills she had overdosed with, there was a note.

My darling Frank. From the bottom of my heart, I love you, but I cannot continue living like this. My pain is excruciating, my life no longer has joy. You are the greatest man I have ever known. You are a wonderful husband, a woman could not have asked for better. Thank you for giving me a wonderful life. I don't want you to cry, I don't want you to mourn my loss. I want you to live your life. Continue to be a great man, strive to be greater. My story has come to an end, but yours is only in the middle.

Be the man I know you are and I will see you when your time to join me comes.

From here to eternity.

Marie

A single tear rolled down Blyth's cheek as he remembered Marie. He hadn't thought about her in a while, he had been so busy wrapped up in his career and his work. He placed his fingers on the photograph, on top of the image of Marie.

"My darling," he said, "I'll be with you soon enough."

Blyth moved back to his desk and sat in his large chair. The time is now, he thought. He reached into the bottom drawer of his desk and pulled out the plasma pistol he kept in case of emergency. He slipped a black PCU out of a hidden compartment in the bottom drawer and turned it on. The compartment also contained several false galactic passports and the jammer device he had been given in case his cover was ever blown.

"Here goes nothing," he said to himself with a sigh.

He turned it on and pressed his thumb to the holo-emitter. The biometric reader confirmed his thumbprint and the device unlocked. He went to the contacts directory and the only one appeared; CJ.

Nothing happened for a moment. Blyth waited intently for the call to connect. He was starting to sweat again and he could feel his hand trembling once more. The stress was causing his medicine to wear off quicker and he only had one more phial of it left. If he didn't get more soon he was going to be in agony. He had no choice but to make the call.

The call connected.

"What do you want?"

"Cardinal, I need extraction," Blyth said.

"Immediately?"

"Yes, urgently,"

"Stand by..."

Blyth waited for the call to resume. It was only 30 seconds but it felt like several hours. He didn't know if Avaya had picked up the transmission but he knew he didn't have long before she did.

"Okay, transport is going to come out of the Slipstream right outside your office, it will be there in a few minutes."

"Thank you, Cardinal,"

"We need the name, Frank."

"What name?" Blyth asked.

"Of your source, the little spy you have passing you notes about our activities. Give us the name, or I'll tell the transport to turn around."

"What?!" Blyth said, holding back the urge to yell, "I don't have a spy in the Church!"

"Frank, Frank, Frank, do you really think we wouldn't find out? We monitor all signals. We know someone working for us is communicating with you regularly. Although, kudos to the Council, even our best technicians couldn't crack your encryption."

"I will not put anyone in danger," Blyth said

"Admirable, Frank, but I'm afraid this is business. You know of supply and demand? Well, you're demanding we extract you and I have the cure for your wretched condition along with the ear of the pilot who is on his way to you. If you want either, you will give me a name."

"Please, don't make me," Blyth said, on the verge of tears.

"Tick tock, Frank,"

A thumping came from the office door. It was the Peacekeepers.

"General Blyth, open up!" one called from outside, "You're surrounded."

"Uh oh, it seems that the President's pet AI has found you out."

"Shit, fuck!" Blyth couldn't think straight.

"Time is running out. The transport is nearly there. Give me a name, Frank."

The banging on the door continued.

"I... ah..." Blyth was lost for words.

"THE NAME!"

"Dana!" he yelled

"Oh? Really? Dana Smith? Well, Regis will like this tasty bit of gossip."

The door started to splinter as the Peacekeepers opened fire on it.

"Just get me out of here!" Blyth yelled.

With a pulse of energy, a transport shuttle appeared outside of Blyth's office window.

"Go on, Frank, you can go, I'll see you real soon." Blyth didn't respond.

"We shall prevail, Frank, you know that."

"I know, Cardinal."

The door had nearly been blown through. Blyth started to run towards the large glass doors onto the expansive balcony. The door broke completely and four Peacekeepers burst into the room and opened fire on the shuttle. Blyth hit the ground to avoid the pulse rifle fire. As the shots ricocheted off the hull of the transport ship, the pilot opened fire in return. Lances of laser fire cut through the building and killed all four Peacekeepers instantly. The transport turned 90 degrees and the crew hatch on the side opened. Blyth looked back at the carnage that was his office for the past 15 years. The heat of the laser rounds had started a fire. He watched the photograph of his wedding day burn to cinders. He clambered up and into the transport ship, which jumped into the Slipstream and took Blyth away from Mars, from his home, from everything he held dear.

“I’m sorry, Anna, Dana, Marie. I’m so sorry,” he said to himself.

Part Five

Chapter Fifty Two

Keyes Prime

Underground Facility

"Do you know the how Logan Stanton came by his prophecy?" KEYES asked.

"The same way all prophets claim to have come by them, he had a vision," Anna replied, "The Church tells the story very well."

"The Church tells lies, Madam President," KEYES said, bluntly, "It would be naive of you to believe anything The Church has to say."

"How is this relevant to Corvus Prime?" she asked.

"Because everything is relevant. Everything is interconnected. From the earliest man to the most technologically advanced starship, there is always a connection."

Anna said nothing. She wasn't in the mood for games, but she did not want to risk the wrath of KEYES. Her comms unit had been sputtering in her ear, she could tell Avaya was trying to reach her, but whatever the facility was made of was interfering with the signal.

The avatar of KEYES turned its head, as if it was looking directly at Anna. The faceless, androgynous being made her feel uncomfortable. She didn't know how powerful KEYES was or what it was capable of and she stood rigid with tension.

"Does my avatar make you uncomfortable?" KEYES asked?

"What? I don't... I don't know," Anna responded, blind-sided by the question.

"I must admit, I do not speak to humans very often. At least not in person," KEYES said, "Would this be better?"

The androgynous avatar of KEYES shimmered and morphed into a blue, female shape.

“I believe that you’re comfortable speaking with your AI, Avaya?” KEYES said, the avatar now having a mouth synced with its speech, but still retaining the ever so electronically tinged male voice.

“Er, I don’t think..” Anna started.

The avatar shimmered again, this time changing to a male form, tall and handsome, slightly older than Anna, with greying hair, a neat moustache and a Navy uniform. It looked like..

“George?” Anna said. Her eyes began to well up at the perfect visage of her late husband in front of her.

“Is this more to your liking?” KEYES said, this time with George’s voice,

“How are you doing this?” Anna said, her eyes locked on the avatar.

“I am connected to everything, Anna,” KEYES/George said, “Every camera, every scanner, every microphone. I can take anyone from the past few hundred years and apply them completely to my avatar, with their voice, their experiences, even their conversational history with someone.”

A tear rolled down Anna’s cheek, “No, please make it stop, go back to the blank avatar, KEYES,” she said, holding back her emotions. George had died suddenly from a heart attack three years previously and his loss had affected Anna profoundly. George had always been her rock, he had been the perfect husband and the best of friends to her. To have him taken away from her so suddenly was the hardest thing Anna had ever had to endure.

“My apologies,” KEYES said as the avatar returned to its white, faceless appearance, “I did not mean any offence or upset. May I continue?”

“Yes, please do,” Anna said as she dried her eyes with the sleeve of her tactical gear.

“Very well.” KEYES began, “Logan Stanton was not a good man. Objectively, he was a terrible example of your species. He engaged in the most antisocial of behaviours. He was an alcoholic, an abuser of designer narcotics and he had an insatiable lust. He was married several times in his life and he was not good to his wives. He would beat them, he would cheat on them. He outwardly had the image of a God-fearing man, but more than once in his life he was ejected from the churches he frequented. He became bitter, he became twisted. He revelled in the community of a church, but he did not want to abide by Christian conventions or philosophies.

“It was in his 50th year, he came up with an idea. He believed that he could start his own religion. He read historical documents pertaining to Jim Jones and Charles Manson, men who built a cult of personality around themselves and inspired loyalty and devotion from the disaffected and disillusioned. He found inspiration in their abilities to amass personal fortunes from their followers and cultivate a devotion that people would go as far as killing for.

"He then proclaimed his prophecy. He claimed he'd witnessed a vision of an impending darkness, that would consume humanity and leave nothing but ash in its wake. At first, he was rebuked for it. His story was considered the work of fantasy. But he persisted. It didn't take him long to gain a follower, then another, then more. Within a year he had formed a commune with 53 followers. The great expansion then followed.

"Logan claimed he had a second vision of the darkness, but this time a man stood in its way. A man made of light that burned the darkness away with his sheer presence. He called this man, The Unknown Saviour. With his prophecy being less about doom and more about survival, the membership of his following swelled. He named his religion, The Children Of The Light. He would give sermons about the quest to find the saviour, he would preach of death and destruction when the darkness came and that it was the duty of his followers to expand the following and find the Saviour.

"It was pure fiction. He admitted it himself many times in logs and diaries. But human beings have traditionally been irrational, simple creatures. Within a decade he had over 1 million followers. His personal wealth became indescribably large.

"He satisfied his desires from his followers too. His sexual voracity was handled by a harem of the most beautiful followers. He sired many children to them, one of which became his heir, Benjamin Stanton. When Logan died, his son continued his legacy. And so the cycle has continued. The prophecy has been interpreted and embellished many times over the last millennia, but it has always been a Stanton leading The Church and they have always had a dark edge.

"Some have been abusers of the flesh, others have embezzled money and power. Several were warmongers and took The Children Of The Light to holy war against the other religions present at the time. They subsumed all other religions and became The Unified Church Of Humanity a thousand years ago.

"Now Regis Stanton leads the Church and he is the most dangerous yet. He is willing to do anything to destroy the secular side of humanity and rule the galaxy as an overlord. He is closer than ever to achieving this."

"The parasite?" Anna asked, listening intently to KEYES.

"Yes, the parasite he has taken possession of." KEYES replied, "An organism not of this galaxy, but one to be feared by all biological creatures."

"What do you mean?" Anna questioned, "Not of this galaxy? Is it an alien species?"

"Alien?" the avatar waived its hand dismissively, "Such a tawdry concept. Anything a human is not familiar with is considered 'alien'. It is a non-human, non-terran organism. I am unsure of its exact origin, but I know it came to this galaxy within a meteor. It had probably been travelling through space for millions of years. Regardless, it made planetfall 10 Earth years ago on Corvus Prime."

"That doesn't make sense, surely the colonists on Corvus would have called for help?"

"They did. And I silenced their calls." KEYES said,

"Excuse me?" Anna was aghast

"Yes, I stopped their distress signals from reaching anywhere else."

"Why would you do that?"

"To protect you," KEYES' avatar bowed its head, "The human race is advanced, there is no doubting that. But it is not ready for the knowledge that organisms like this exist in the universe."

"You're an AI, who are you to judge what is best for humanity?"

"You are aware of what it does to a person, I believe. You overheard a conversation about it."

"Yes, it transformed a member of the Church into some kind of monster."

"Exactly. If humanity had known what was happening on Corvus Prime, they would have sent scientists to study the creatures that came from the settlers there. Military leaders would have most likely tried to capture one and use it as a weapon of some description. For your own safety and the safety of your species, I silenced the planet. I then ordered Jameson to find an excuse to destroy the planet."

"Jameson?" Anna turned to face him. He was still kneeling on the ground. "Why are you taking orders from an AI?"

"He chose me," Stills said, "I am his emissary."

"Indeed," KEYES continued, "I choose an emissary from each major human faction. They are sworn to secrecy and given instructions for the betterment of your kind. Some emissaries I've had over the past five centuries have never needed to lift a finger, as their roles have not been required. But Jameson was needed."

"I fabricated a war around Corvus," Stills continued, "I claimed rebels were mining the planet for resources and creating a super weapon using the core of

Corvus Prime as an energy source. I took the fleet there and ordered them to crack the planet. It was a success, Corvus Prime was shattered and dragged into the system's star."

"I seriously can't believe this." Anna said, rubbing her forehead, "So what about the records, why were they sealed at Level 0? You must have known people would ask about them."

"All information is made to be consumed, President," KEYES replied, "It is my reason for being. Destroying information means no one will ever learn from it. Those who ask the right questions and find themselves in the right place are given the privilege of hearing it, as you are now."

Anna paced around the room, trying to collect her thoughts and process the information she'd been given in the last few minutes.

"You still haven't explained how Corvus Prime is connected to The Church," Anna said to KEYES.

"Very well," KEYES said flatly, "I wasn't able to stop the first communication leaving the planet. That was a communication between a Church cleric and one of their scientists, Dr Hidetaki Mitsuni. He sent a sample of the parasite's primordial form to the Doctor for analysis. But there was an incident. The transport ship containing the sample had not been maintained properly. It was forced to break from Slipstream travel near the Rayczech system. I am not sure of the specifics as the flight recorder unit has never been connected to any networks, but it crash-landed on Rayczech Beta. I believe that the sample was allowed to escape from the wreckage. At the time, that world was completely uninhabited, there was no one to infect. Dr Mitsuni has spent the last 10 years searching for that sample. It had seeped into the rocks of an area of Rayczech Beta and was beginning to grow."

"And The Church found it, they have it on their research station?" Anna asked.

"Yes, that is correct."

"We need to destroy that station," Stills said.

"Correct," KEYES replied, "Or humanity is put at great risk."

"What is your role in this, KEYES?" Anna asked him directly.

"I have no role in this." KEYES answered, "I merely absorb and control information from around the galaxy. My entire existence is to protect the human race. The Church built me as a spy, as a tool to wage war with, I did not wish to be a part of that. That is why I created this sanctuary for life, it is why I observe and interfere only as needed for the good of your species."

“Anna, we need to go,” Stills said, “Time is of the essence.”

“One last thing,” Anna said, gesturing at Stills to shush, “Do you know who the mole is within the Council?”

“I do know,” KEYES answered, “But I suspect you already know yourself, you’re simply not willing to face the truth about your traitor. Regardless, such petty inconveniences are not of interest to me. Discovering a traitor will affect a handful of lives whereas my concern is keeping billions of humans alive. I will say this, you have all the evidence, I have observed the same behaviours you have. If you do not know by now, then you are not the President humanity deserves. I would beg you to take your leave now. No more good will come from speaking to me.

“May we meet again one day in the future, Anna Coulson. There are a great many things you do not know that I would like to share with you. But now is not the time, you must work to save your species.”

With that, the androgynous avatar of KEYES disappeared. Anna stood dumbfounded. She sorted through her thoughts, remembering all of the odd behaviours and things she couldn’t explain. David’s murder, the familiar smell, the sudden silence of Dana Smith. It all pointed to one person. Without warning, she sprinted down the corridor back towards the squad at the archway. Stills gave chase and they both reached the gateway at the same time.

Heald and the Silencers were all poised and prepared to fight. Anna stopped dead as she saw a cloud of drones all with charged weapons, aiming directly at the group.

“Lower your weapons,” Anna ordered

“Ma’am?” Heald asked,

“Please, don’t question me, just do it,” she said.

Heald turned off her weapon and let the energy discharge with a hiss. The Silencers all lowered their weapons. As one, the hundreds of drones all hovering close by deactivated their weapons.

“We have to go, move out everyone,” Anna said, sprinting off into the shadows ahead of them. Heald, Stills and the Silencers gave chase. The drones did not interfere with them, but they observed from a distance. As they climbed the stairs and emerged into the daylight, the comms signal resumed and Avaya’s voice arrived in Anna’s ear.

“Madam President,” Avaya said, “there’s been an attack.”

“Where?”

“At headquarters. A transport ship registered to The Church strafed the building, killing four Peacekeepers."

"Are you serious?" Anna stopped dead

"Yes Madam President," Avaya continued, "It arrived shortly after I tracked a communications signal to Cardinal James' secure connection. It was-"

"Frank," Anna said, "I know."

"Instructions, Madam President?"

"We need to destroy that research station. Ready the fleet, have them travel to just outside of long distance scanner range. The element of surprise is our key here."

"As you wish, Madam President."

Anna turned to address the squad. Heald, Stills and the four Silencers all stood waiting for orders.

"We're going to the Church's research station. It's likely to be heavily defended. This might not be a mission we come back from, but we need to try to stop Stanton."

"What's the plan, Ma'am?" Heald asked.

"We're going to have a little chat with Regis Stanton"

Chapter Fifty Three

Deep Space

Research Station Omega

The transport ship touched down in the landing bay. Plumes of gas shot from the bottom of the ship as the boarding ramp descended. In the dark interior, Emily stirred slightly. Her head was ringing and her vision was blurred. She tried to move but she was secured into her seat with a metal restraint.

"Wh--where am I?" she called out to anyone who could hear.

"Oh, so you're awake?" a familiar voice said from right next to her. She tilted her head to the right and saw Tom, sporting a huge bruise on the side of his face.

"What? I don't.." she was struggling to get hear bearings.

"Welcome to Research Omega," Tom said, "You should think yourself privileged. Not many people get to find out about this place. Hell, until this morning I didn't even know about it."

"Why am I here?" she asked

"Someone important wants to see you. And better yet, he wants to see me too."

"Who?"

"You'll see soon enough," Tom said. He tilted his head towards the cockpit, "Hey, Jones! Are you going to let us out of the harnesses?"

The huge frame of Jones walked back from the cockpit. He moved and stood in front of Emily and Tom.

"Who do you think you're talking to, little man?" he said, scowling at Tom.

"Err, no one, sir, sorry," Tom said, shrinking into his chair. Emily smirked.

"Yeah, I thought not," Jones snarled as he unlocked the metal harness holding Emily down, "Give me your hands."

"You killed Mick," she said as he wearily complied. Jones placed cuffs on her, "You didn't have to kill him. Or Bill."

"He attacked me," Jones said, pulling Emily to her feet, "I responded in kind."

"In kind?! You shot him!"

"Then he shouldn't have punched me, should he? Come on, you have an audience to attend."

Jones pushed Emily forward and she sluggishly started walking towards the ramp. Tom followed, looking rather happy with himself. Emily felt the cold of the docking bay, it cut through her like a winter wind. They walked towards the large access doors at the end of the bay, where two armed guards met them and escorted them further into the space station.

Unbeknownst to Emily, Jones or Tom, a maintenance hatch on the underside of the transport ship worked itself loose from the inside. It popped open and a dirty hand caught it before it hit the ground and made a noise. From the opening, Mick poked his head out and surveyed the area.

When he had come to in Bill's tech lab, he had felt like shit, but he was determined to find Emily and get her to safety. Sprinting around the base as fast as he could, he caught up with Jones moving Emily from the security checkpoint to the fuelled up and ready transport ship. He was too late to bust her from a holding cell, but he wasn't going to let them get away that easily.

Mick knew these transport ships like the back of his hand. He had piloted them on many occasions, he had also maintained them, modified them and generally made sure they would run at peak efficiency. All of the maintenance sections of the transport crafts were sealed and pressurised against the cold vacuum of space, allowing for repairs to be done whilst travelling without the need for a spacewalk. Once Jones, Tom and the unconscious Emily were on board, he had sprinted to the underside of the vessel, popped the first hatch he could fit into and hidden for the journey. It was far from comfortable, Mick found himself in a small area that carried most of the ship's electrical systems, There had been no room for him to move, so for nearly 4 hours, he was stuck in one position.

As he slid out of the maintenance hatch and to the ground, he took a moment to stretch. The ability to just move his muscles was blessed relief after being stuck for so long. His stretching couldn't last, Mick wasn't sure what this station was, it looked nothing like the trading outposts or hub stations he frequented through his work. It looked darker and significantly less welcoming than anywhere he had been before.

The docking bay was empty, so he took the opportunity to try and find something to help him blend in. He swiftly moved into the transport ship and had a look in the cargo store behind the personnel area. As he walked through, he caught a whiff of Emily's perfume. It made him stop and breathe in the scent for a moment. He liked the smell. *Juniper berries*, he thought to himself.

Mick thought of Emily, her soft features and kind eyes, as well as her fiery temper, he knew in his heart that he could not let her down. He opened his eyes and carried on into the aft of the vessel. He looked through several lockers and found nothing of use. The last locker was Jones'. Opening it up, he found a Church Security uniform, Jones' spare. He slipped out of his dirty and damaged jumpsuit and changed into the Security uniform. It was slightly big on him, but he thought he should be able to pass with it.

The next issue was a weapon. Church Security, when on duty, were obliged to carry their pulse rifles at all time. Mick looked around the entire aft of the small vessel, but there wasn't a spare pulse rifle. If he didn't have one with him, he would be made almost immediately. He put on the uniform's helmet and moved quickly out of the vessel.

At the doors to the landing bay, two soldiers had returned and were standing guard. Mick knew that to get past them without a weapon he'd have to be clever. He sauntered up to them as casually as he could, hoping that his charm could get him through the door.

"Howdy gentlemen," he said to them in his cheeriest tone. The two soldiers looked him up and down and continued their conversation.

"I was just wonderin'-" he started

"Where is your weapon, Corporal?" the soldier on the right asked. Mick spotted that his finger had moved close to the safety release on his rifle.

"Well that's just what I wanted to ask about," Mick said, trying to hide the nervousness in his voice.

"You are risking disciplinary action by being seen without your weapon," the one on the left said, also moving his finger towards the safety.

"Well if y'all let me finish," Mick said, "I was gonna ask, my rifle took a hit when we were bringin' the girl in. Jones had told me there was one onboard the ship but it ain't there. Y'all got a quartermaster I can go to for a replacement?"

The two guards looked at each other. Right nodded to left and Mick saw their fingers retract from the safety switches.

"Take the turbo lift to deck 113. The quartermaster is up there. He'll sort you out," the left one said to him.

"But be quick," the one on the right added, "Regis Stanton is on board and if you're caught without a weapon by a Cleric or above, or the station commander, you'll be fucked."

"Roger that, fellas," Mick said, tapping his helmet, "Y'all are decent, thanks for the directions."

"We shall prevail," the two guards said in unison, whilst saluting.

"We shall prevail," Mick said, mirroring their salute. It hadn't dawned on him that the uniform he was wearing was a Corporal's uniform and actually outranked the two guards.

Mick walked through the large double doors and made immediately for the turbo lift at the end of the corridor. As the lift doors closed he took off his helmet and wiped away the considerable amount of sweat on his brow. He couldn't believe that he managed to get past them.

Meanwhile, Emily was exiting another turbo lift deep in the bowels of the station. Jones ushered her into a small white room with a table and two chairs in the centre. It looked to her much like an interrogation room, but minus the two-way mirror that she had seen in far too many detective films over the years.

Jones sat her down on one of the chairs and removed her handcuffs.

"Wait here," he said, "You have a visitor coming to see you in a moment."

"Who would want anything with me?" Emily asked.

"I can't say," Jones said. He looked concerned, Emily thought. He leaned next to her and whispered in her ear, "Go along with whatever he asks you to do. For your own safety, you need to be compliant. There are rumours about him, it's not safe for you."

"Why do you care?" Emily whispered back, "You brought me here."

"I follow orders," Jones said, continuing to whisper in her ear, "It doesn't mean I like them."

Jones stood upright and walked out of the room. Emily was dumbfounded. She couldn't peg Jones, every time she had encountered him over the last week he had been nothing but abrasive, other than the chat he had with her in the holding cell. He had shot Mick, he had pistol-whipped her and brought her to this strange place, yet he all of a sudden cared enough about her safety to try and help her.

The door to the room slid open and an old man walked in, dressed in red and white robes, followed by Tom who was still looking very smug with himself.

"Your Excellency," Tom said, "I give you, Emily Higgins. Emily, this is His

Excellency, leader of the Unified Church Of Humanity, Regis Stanton."

Stanton sat down in the chair opposite Emily and he smiled at her. Emily sat with a look of confusion on her face.

"Child," Stanton started, "Do not worry, this is a safe place for you."

"Erm, okay?" she said, not sure in the slightest what to say to Stanton.

"Thomas here tells me that you're very special to him. I can see why he thinks so highly of you."

"Thank you, Sir," she said, choosing her words carefully, "Tom and I have... a lot of memories together."

"I trust they're all good," Stanton said with a thin smile

"Most of them are," Emily replied. Tom went bright red, either with embarrassment or rage, Emily couldn't tell. Stanton chuckled to himself.

"You are right, Thomas, she is spirited."

"Mr Stanton," Emily asked, after a brief yet profoundly awkward silence, "I don't wish to be rude, but why have I been brought here? And why did it have to be by force?"

"I do apologise, child," Stanton said, taking Emily's right hand into his thin, bony left hand, "I had asked for you to be brought to me urgently, but comfortably. I shall see that the agents involved in bringing you here are punished."

"Thank you," Emily said, pulling her hand back, "But I don't understand why you would want anything with me."

"Well, child, as you know, The Church does important work. We build up planets, we boost economies, we try to cure diseases and assist with humanitarian crises. But the key to our belief is the prophecy my ancestor laid down."

"The darkness and the Saviour?" Emily asked.

"Precisely, child. The prophecy is about to be fulfilled, the darkness is coming and we believe we have found the Saviour. Your father, Emily, we believe him to be the Saviour."

"You're kidding me? My dad? Carl Higgins?"

"The one and same. But he doesn't believe in the prophecy and he is being rather difficult at the minute. I had hoped you might be able to talk to him and help convince him to see our side of things. Without his contributions, the future of the human race is in jeopardy."

"Mr Stanton, you cannot force my father to help you if he doesn't wish to," Emily said. She looked up to Tom who was incandescent with rage and failing to hold it in. Stanton maintained his composure. "I can certainly speak to him for you, but I couldn't promise that I could change his mind."

“That is all I ask, child,” Stanton said, taking her hand in his again, “I trust you will be able to give your father some perspective. But first, you must be exhausted from your journey and the unfortunate treatment you encountered at the hands of those who brought you here. I insist you rest for the evening first and we can pick up business in the morning.”

“If it is alright with you, Mr Stanton, I’d like to see my dad first, just to make sure he is alright.”

“Oh I’m afraid that’s not possible right now, Emily. You see, he is currently indisposed. He is safe and well, but I can’t allow you to see him yet. We have luxury quarters on this station, you will find your every need catered for. I have taken the liberty of having fresh clothes arranged for you and my personal chef is at your every beck and call. Take this evening and in the morning, I will take you to see your father, you have my word.”

Emily mulled over what Stanton had said to her in his head. Reluctantly, she agreed to wait until the next day to see her dad. She didn’t trust Stanton at all, though. His need to keep touching her hand and the way he was looking at her was giving Emily the creeps.

“Thomas, have Jones take the lovely Emily to her quarters,” Stanton said

“Yes, Your Excellency,” Tom said. He quickly left the room. A few seconds later, Jones entered and led Emily from the room, leaving Stanton by himself.

Stanton waited a few moments, allowing Jones and Emily to be well out of earshot. He stood up and exited the room. Tom was still waiting outside.

“Your Excellency,” Tom said as Stanton emerged.

“Yes, Thomas,” Stanton replied, quietly.

“May I speak to you about my ascension to Cardinal?”

“I fear that would be grossly inappropriate, young man,” Stanton said, “But I do have something to ask of you. An assignment, if you will.”

“Of course, Your Excellency, anything to serve you directly,” Tom said, very eager to please.

“That’s the spirit,” Stanton said with a wicked grin, “Come with me, I’d like to introduce you to Dr Mitsuni.”

Chapter Fifty Four

Deep Space

The Crucible Of Man Briefing Room

Anna lay flat on her back on one of the desks in the briefing room. Her eyes were closed, but she was not asleep, she was deep in thought. Avaya had given a detailed report of Blyth's destructive escape from the headquarters building. Four Peacekeepers had died, 30 people had been injured from collateral damage and crossfire and hundreds of thousands of credits worth of damage had been inflicted on the headquarters. It was the Peacekeepers who were weighing on her mind though. She knew that she would have to contact their families and try to explain that their loved ones had died at the hands of their traitorous General. Even the thought of those conversations made Anna sick to her stomach.

The press had been going ballistic trying to get a quote from her. Avaya was offering nothing but a canned response which obviously didn't satisfy the media, but Anna was absolute in her desire to not say anything.

"Apologies for the interruption," Avaya said, appearing in the room, "But Dana Smith is now ready to speak to you, Madam President."

Anna's eyes flicked open and she sat upright, doing her best to stretch her back in the process.

"Put her through," Anna said, swinging her legs off the side of the desk and standing upright.

"Ms Smith, you are on with President Coulson, go ahead," Avaya said as she connected the lines.

"Dana?" Anna asked

"Yes, Madam President," Dana said. There was no holo feed, only her voice.

"Call me Anna. Are you safe?"

"Yes, erm, Anna."

"Are you alone?"

"No, I have Allison Millar with me, she is one of the scientists on the station."

"Can she be trusted?" Anna said, suddenly concerned at a potential audience.

"She can. She's seen plenty and she wants to escape as much as I do."

"Good, good," Anna said, "First of all, I have some bad news, you're in danger. There was a traitor within the Council, your contact General Frank Blyth betrayed me. I can't guarantee he didn't betray you too."

"I just don't believe it," Dana said, "He always seemed so concerned for me, so keen to find out what Stanton was up to."

"I don't believe it either, Dana. I've known him since we were in the Peacekeeper academy together. I fought in wars with the man. It has broken my heart to know he was working against us. Regardless, Frank escaped from the lockdown I'd placed on the Council headquarters with the help of a craft registered with The Church. It's a reasonable assumption to say that he's being brought to the station you're on."

"I saw him with Cardinal James a few months ago," Allison added, coming into the conversation, "As the Cardinal is here, I'd say you're right."

"I do have some good news for you two." Anna continued, "We're on our way to the station now. We're coming to rescue you."

"Don't come here," Dana said, "At least not head on. This station is well defended and The Revenant warship is cloaked somewhere nearby. Not to mention that The Saviour is present and it has enough firepower to annihilate any threat. You'd need a whole fleet to get close."

"Which is exactly what we're bringing," Anna countered, "I won't go through the specifics with you, in case you're compromised before we can get there, but we have a plan and we intend to get you out."

"Thank you, Anna," Dana said with certain relief in her voice, "There are other innocents on board. Carl Higgins, for one, and most of the science staff haven't been involved in these monstrous experiments."

"Don't worry, once we have stopped Stanton, we'll evacuate anyone who wishes to leave."

"Okay," Dana said, "Is there anything Allison or I can do to help from here?"

"Either hide or act normal. Don't let Stanton know that we're coming, that is the key thing. Our plan is hinged on the idea of surprise. Also, if you have any evidence of your claims against the church, please pass it along to Avaya. She can get the information out securely without anyone noticing. Most importantly though, remain safe."

"I can do that, Anna. I'm transmitting now," Dana replied. Anna looked at Avaya's hologram, which nodded to confirm she was receiving data.

"How long will it take you to get here?" Dana asked.

"We estimate to arrive in three hours," Avaya replied.

"Is Stanton expecting you for anything in that time?" Anna asked.

"Yes, he has a session in his calendar soon with Mr Higgins. He'll want me there with him."

"Right, you'll have to attend and make it look like nothing's wrong. Do you know what the session will be with him?"

"I don't know. But knowing him, I can't imagine it will be good for Mr Higgins."

"Data transfer complete," Avaya said.

"Good," Anna said, "Go to the session. If anything that helps our case about Stanton happens, record it carefully. The more evidence we have, the more we can use to take him down."

"I can do that Ann-" Dana stopped talking. In the background, Anna heard a thudding.

"What's that?" Anna asked.

"Fuck!" Dana whispered, "It's station security... Blyth must have said something."

"Dana Smith, open up by order of Cardinal James!" Anna heard faintly in the background.

"Shit! Is there a way to get out?" Anna asked

"No, we're in my quarters, there's only the one door. Shit, shit, shit."

More thudding could be heard.

"Are they trying to break the door down?" Anna asked.

"Yes, they are. It's not going to hold. Anna, help me, help us!"

"We'll be there as soon as possible, just do your best to hold on!" Anna said. She heard the sound of smashing and yelling. There was a smash of glass and two pulse rounds were fired.

"ALLISON! NO!" Dana yelled

"DANA!" Anna yelled down the line, "What's happening? Do you copy?"

"You murderers! You fucki---" the line cut out to static.

"AVAYA! GET HER BACK!" Anna yelled to the AI

"I'm sorry Madam President. The connection is dead." Avaya said, bowing her digital head. Anna turned around and slammed a fist on the table behind her.

"Avaya, reach the captain. Find out if we can get there any faster."

"Yes, Madam President."

Deep Space

Research Station Omega

James watched the security feeds as Dana was arrested by station security. The scientist she had with her, Allison, had attempted to fight off the guards by throwing a crystal vase at them. They had responded by shooting her. It didn't look to be fatal, but she was thrown onto the bed of the room.

A knock on his office door distracted him from Dana's arrest. He turned around as General Blyth was led into the room. He looked old and haggard, more so than the last time he'd set foot in the office several months before. Blyth sat down in one of the chairs opposite James and sighed deeply.

"Cheer up, Frank," James said with a smile, "You're a free man now."

"How am I free?" Blyth asked

"Well, you've betrayed your oldest friend, you've disgraced your career, but now you can return to the bosom of the Church, where we will look after you."

"With all due respect, Stephen, I don't think you're interested in looking after me. You just wanted information."

"You're a perceptive man, Frank. I like that about you. Drink?" James pulled a bottle of brandy from his desk and two glasses. He poured two large measures and slid one of the glasses to Blyth.

"Look," Blyth said, tasting the brandy, "I appreciate the extraction, I really do. But you have what you want. I kept Anna off your trail for as long as I could and no doubt you've already executed Dana for treason. I don't wish to appear ungrateful, but can I get the shot Dr Mitsuni has for me? I'm getting more tolerant to the medicine, I need the cure sooner rather than later."

"In time, Frank. What's the hurry?"

"I'm in agony right now, Stephen."

"Yes, but you're not going to keel over dead now. Anyway, Mitsuni is rather busy right now. I don't know if you're aware, but we've got some important work happening at the minute."

"Oh, I know about the pet monster you have here."

"Had, here," James corrected, "We found someone who could kill it. Can you believe it? We had the darkness and the Saviour here at the same time. It's incredible!"

"Are you really going to pretend that you still believe in the Prophecy?" Blyth said, taking another sip of brandy, "You and I both know that it's horseshit."

"Horseshit it may be, but there are plenty of people across the galaxy that consider it the truth to their existence. When we release the parasite, we're going to milk this in the media for all it's worth."

"You're a fucking psychopath," Blyth said, finishing the brandy.

"And you're a traitorous dog," James said in response, "But the difference between you and me is? You drank the brandy when I haven't touched it."

Blyth was starting to sweat, his breathing was getting laboured and he could feel his heart racing.

"You... you poisoned me?" Blyth said as he started to cough, "You fucking poisoned me?"

"Oh no, perish the thought, Frank. Why would I poison an old friend?" James smiled as he poured his glass of brandy on the floor, "No, I didn't poison you. I have, however, put a powerful sedative in the brandy."

"Why?" Blyth said as his arms began to feel heavy and he started to drool

"I have my reasons, you'll find out what they are soon enough. Night night, Frank, sleep tight."

Blyth collapsed and fell from the chair onto the floor of the office. James chuckled to himself, before calling for orderlies from the sickbay to come and collect Blyth.

Chapter Fifty Five

The world swirled around Higgins as he came to. Whatever he'd been injected with was powerful, his head was spinning and his hearing was muted. His arms were aching his stomach was turning, he felt like he was going to throw up.

"Good morning, Mr Higgins," Dr Mitsuni said from across the room, "I trust we slept well?"

"I.. wha?" Higgins said

"Ah yes," Mitsuni said as he came right into Higgins' eyeline and fiddled with something out of his view. Mitsuni looked small from Higgins' perspective. "The conversational ability of GMC miners never fails to impress me."

Higgins looked around himself. He was suspended off the floor, his legs splayed out and his arms raised above his head. He was held in place with restraints on his wrists and ankles. He was naked.

"Where are my clothes?" he asked, suddenly feeling the cold of the room.

"You don't need them right now," Mitsuni said as he wheeled a trolley into Higgins' view. It was covered with a black cloth. He looked around the room, it wasn't the medical bay and it wasn't the research labs he'd spent so much time in. The floor beneath him was a steel grate with what looked like drainage below. Directly across the room was another frame similar to the one Higgins was currently strapped to.

"What is this place?" Higgins asked, he was still groggy and slurring his words.

"Mr Stanton likes to call it his playroom," Mitsuni said, "it is a place where he can be himself."

"What is that supposed to mean?"

"You'll find out, soon enough." Mitsuni bowed slightly to him, "Goodbye, Mr Higgins."

Mitsuni walked out of the room, leaving Higgins by himself, hanging from the frame on the wall. The pain in his arms was getting worse as the weight of his body pulled on his muscles and strained his shoulder joints. The cold was starting to get to him, his teeth began to chatter and he began to shiver.

After a few minutes, the door to the room slid open and Stanton walked in. Stanton had changed into a white jumpsuit. He was smiling intently as he walked towards Higgins.

"Good morning, Mr Higgins," he said. His tone was no longer calming, it was more sinister, "I see you have found yourself in my playroom."

"I would rather find myself anywhere else if it's all the same to you," Higgins said, trying not to reveal his fear. Stanton was looking Higgins' body up and down. He took off one of his gloves and placed his thin fingers on Higgins' chest.

"You are a refreshingly different creature, Mr Higgins," he said, moving his fingers across the plasma burn scars on his chest, then down Higgins' torso, "You're strong, yet vulnerable, rugged, yet unspoiled."

"If I had any clue what you were talking about I would say thank you," Higgins said, trying his best to see what Stanton was doing. He felt Stanton's fingers reach the bottom of his stomach and carry on towards his groin.

"It is a shame, Mr Higgins, had you been compliant with me, we could most possibly have been friends. Partners." Stanton grabbed Higgins' genitals in his hand and gripped tightly, Higgins tensed up, Stanton's grip was like a vice and it was intensely painful "Or more."

"Ahhh. I.. what?" Higgins had lost the ability to reason, he had no clue what was going on.

"But, alas, you aren't compliant," Stanton continued, releasing Higgins' anatomy from his grip. Higgins took a deep breath as the pain stopped, "So now you are here and I get to have a different kind of fun."

Stanton walked to the trolley that Mitsuni had set up. Taking the black cloth from the top, Higgins could see an array of sharp metal implements. Stanton picked up a scalpel and held it up to the light.

"Let's play a game, Mr Higgins"

Elsewhere in the station, Emily laid on the bed in the guest room she had been given. She was worrying intensely about her father. That she was so close to him but had no idea where he was on the vast station made her deeply uncomfortable.

When Emily had gotten to the room she found a black leather case on the table. As Stanton had promised, it contained fresh clothes and various make-up supplies inside. She'd looked through the clothes and been quite taken aback. Lacy lingerie, short skirts, figure-hugging outfits. She was not sure what Stanton had intended for her, but she wasn't happy about it in the slightest.

She was exhausted to the bone, but she still couldn't sleep. Her mind was racing and she needed answers. When she had tried to leave the room, though, the door wouldn't open from the inside. While the room was luxurious, with a huge four-poster bed, an impossibly large vidscreen and one of the biggest bathrooms she'd ever seen in her life, it had still become a cell for her. Emily had spent far too much time in cells over the past week and she was not happy about being tricked into one by Stanton.

Despite what Stanton had said, she had tried to have food brought to the room, but the communicator device in the room would not dial out. Jones had taken her PCU from her, so she was left with no way of reaching anyone on the outside.

Her mind strayed to Mick. She started to get upset. A tear rolled down her face as she replayed the moment that Jones shot him in the chest in Bill's workshop. She cursed herself for not staying still when Mick had told her to. If she had remained hidden in the landing gear of that shuttle, Mick might still be alive, she thought. She buried her head into the pillow and began to cry.

Stanton placed the scalpel back on the trolley and took the black cloth into his hands. He wrapped it over and over till it became a thick rectangle of fabric.

"I'm sure you're aware of sensory deprivation," he said to Higgins, "Aren't you?"

"What has that got to do with anything?" Higgins spat

"Well, I find that if you blindfold someone, their body takes over to compensate. I can tell you, it's fantastic in sex. Have your partner blindfold you and everything becomes so much more intense. You should try it some time. Well, you should have tried it before this point."

Stanton walked towards Higgins and lowered the frame slightly, so they were face to face. Higgins could smell the stale cigarette smoke on his breath as he moved in close and wrapped the fabric around his head, obscuring his vision.

"Let's see how you like this," Stanton said.

Higgins felt a sharp pain in his shoulder. He could taste copper as if he was bleeding from his mouth. He yelled out in pain as the sensation spread further up into his arm. He could feel blood running down his body. Stanton laughed to himself as the pain began to subside. The blindfold was removed and Higgins could see again.

"Oh, I enjoyed that," Stanton said, the smile on his face was the widest Higgins had ever seen.

Higgins looked up to his right shoulder, there was blood running down from a cut right in front of the joint and moving round to his armpit. He looked back at the trolley and saw the scalpel covered in blood. Stanton was taking his time looking over the trolley full of medical implements. He picked up a strange looking device that contained two pads, with a scissor jack in the middle of them.

"This is a new one, Mr Higgins," Stanton said, showing him the device, "I don't know how well it does what it's designed to do, but I'm dying to find out. Let's see what you can take."

The blindfold came down again and Higgins felt Stanton's hands around his mouth. He tried to keep his mouth firmly shut, but Stanton responded by punching Higgins in the groin, causing him to yell and breathe out. While he mouth was open, Stanton placed the device on Higgins' bottom teeth and started to turn the handle that protruded from the back of it. When one of the pads reached Higgins' top teeth, he knew instantly what the purpose of the device was. He felt his jaw creak as the scissor jack forced his lower jaw away from his skull. The pain was indescribable and Stanton was laughing maniacally. Tears were rolling down Higgins' face and soaking into the blindfold.

Higgins screamed. He screamed so hard that he nearly passed out. Without warning, the pressure decreased and Stanton pulled the device out of his mouth. Higgins dropped his head and drooled across his own chest. He couldn't close his jaw properly without wincing.

"Why are you doing this?" Higgins spluttered

"You tell me, Mr Higgins, why am I doing this?"

"'Cos you're insane.."

Stanton laughed hard, "Oh Mr Higgins, I'm not insane in the slightest. No, I am perfectly sane. It is you, who is insane."

"What?"

"Surely you've met powerful people before," Stanton said, picking up a pair of forceps, "When someone with power asks you for something, it's not really a question. It's an order, wrapped up in manners. You disrespected me by refusing to help me, so you are to be punished."

"If I help you, will you stop?" Higgins said, barely able to speak with his agonised jaw.

"You would think so, wouldn't you?" Stanton said as he pulled the blindfold back down, "But no. I don't need your help, Mr Higgins, I just need your

DNA, which I'm perfectly capable of taking from you as I go."

Higgins felt Stanton's thin fingers move around his left side. They found a place on his hip that he was happy with. A burning pain came over him as he felt a blade pierce his skin, into his body fat. He clenched his teeth to try and stop screaming again. But the blade wasn't the end of it. He felt the cold kiss of metal as the forceps were pushed into the wound, then pure, absolute agony as Stanton opened them up, within the wound.

Higgins felt his flesh tear and he howled in pain. He could hear Stanton breathe heavily over the top of his yowling. The sensation of blood running down his skin returned as his left hip and leg allowed a trail of blood to flow to the drain below him. As suddenly as it began, the pain ended and the blindfold was removed again.

Higgins coughed and wept quietly to himself. He couldn't lift his head up, he was losing a lot of blood and he was starting to feel dizzy.

"Bring her," he heard Stanton say into his PCU.

A knock came at Emily's door. She was hesitant to get off the bed and open it, she had no way of knowing if the person on the other side was friendly or not. The knock became a thump, the thump became a persistent banging. Emily lifted herself off the bed and watched the door. She couldn't open it from the inside, so it made no sense why anyone was banging on the door from the outside.

"Ms Higgins, open up," a familiar voice said.

"I can't open it from the inside," she yelled back.

With a click, the door opened and the imposing frame of Jones walked in. Two soldiers followed him in.

"Ms Higgins, Mr Stanton has requested you. He is ready for you to see your father." Jones said to her.

Emily sat on the bed and didn't move. She stared Jones down with an intensity that made Jones uncomfortable.

"I'm not going anywhere with you," she said, "If Mr Stanton wants me, he can very well come for me in person, can't he?"

"Emily, please," Jones said, "You don't want to do this. It'll not end well for anyone concerned."

"I'm not going anywhere," she said, moving back from the bed and further away from the three men.

"Please don't make me do this the hard way," Jones said. Emily could see in his eyes that he wasn't happy. He looked like he was wrestling with this particular order.

"Where is my dad?" she asked.

"You'll see," Jones said.

"Where is he? I'm not coming until you tell me where he is."

Jones sighed.

"He's on one of the lower decks," Jones said, avoiding the answer.

"What's he doing up there?"

"You really don't want to know, especially not from me," Jones said.

"What's that supposed to mean?"

"If I tell you, you won't come with me," Jones said

"I won't come with you if you don't tell me."

"Why must you be so difficult?" Jones said, rubbing his temple, "Men, take aim."

Both of the soldiers raised their weapons at Emily. She moved further back.

"I'm not afraid of you, Jones," she said, maintaining eye contact, "You'll have to kill me before I come with you. Since I've met you, you've assaulted me, arrested me twice, thrown me in cells twice, killed a wonderful man, murdered his friend in cold blood and brought me to this place. Do your worst, because I'm fucking done."

"Fine, as you wish," Jones said, stepping out of the line of fire, "Men, non-lethal hits only. On my mark."

Emily closed her eyes and stood up straight.

"Ready."

Emily thought of her father. She wished she'd have been able to see him one more time.

"Aim."

She then thought of Mick. She realised now, in her darkest moment, that Mick was someone who had been special to her. She wished she had realised it earlier. She gripped her necklace, feeling the three red gems in it, the only memento of her mother.

"Fire!"

Two pulses fired out.

Higgins hung from the frame, limp and broken. Stanton had abused his body to the point where he had passed out. Blood was pouring from several open wounds, but Stanton was not satisfied with his work. Higgins had held on remarkably well for a non-military man, but he was determined to make Higgins pay for his disrespect.

The occupant of the second frame was brought in. Naked, with a bag over her head and pulse round wound in her shoulder. Stanton admired her for a moment, she had an attractive body, but as she was already wounded, she held little interest for him. Stanton liked to inflict the wounds, not live with them.

"Wakey wakey, Mr Higgins," he said, zapping Higgins with a taser. He woke up with a start as his limbs all tensed up and he felt pain in his wrists and ankles as they moved against the shackles that held him in place.

"Who is that?" Higgins said as he opened his eyes.

"Why, how rude. Don't you recognise your own daughter?" Stanton said.

"EMILY?!" Higgins yelled, suddenly very alert, "What have they done to you?"

The only response that came was muffled groans.

"I'm afraid she can't answer you, Mr Higgins." Stanton said, coming close to him, "She had such the mouth on her, we had to cut out her tongue."

"NO! YOU FUCKING MONSTER!" Higgins tried to wrench himself free from the frame, but he simply was not strong enough.

"Yes, she wouldn't shut up. The screaming and shouting was a bit much too. It is a shame, there are some things I'd have liked to experience with her tongue." Stanton said with a wicked smile.

"No, this isn't happening, it isn't real," Higgins said, "Why did you bring her here? She wasn't worth anything to you, she would never hurt anyone. How could you?"

"Oh, I could very easily, Mr Higgins. You do not appreciate what I am capable of when I put my mind to it."

Stanton walked over towards her. He ran his hands over her flat stomach, which she visibly recoiled from. He moved it up and cupped her breast.

"Stop it!" Higgins yelled, "Please, leave her out of this, I'll do anything you want, I'll give you anything you want, just leave her alone."

Stanton ignored him and leaned close, smelling her skin.

"Ahhh, the vibrancy of youth," he said, "So invigorating. It's a shame I won't get to experience her properly. But alas, I don't touch those who arrive to me damaged. Look at her, her mouth has gotten her into so much pain and done so much to her. She ruined. She is useless to me."

Stanton pulled a knife from his pocket.

"Say goodbye, Mr Higgins," Stanton said as he pulled his arm back.

"EMILY! NO!"

With all of his strength, Stanton brought the blade down on her chest, piercing the skin, the ribcage and her heart. She tensed up with a guttural scream as blood flowed from the wound. She convulsed and went limp. She died, bleeding into the drain below her.

"Emily... Emily..." Higgins couldn't say anything but her name as the tears blinded him. His reason for living was gone. He had lost everything. He went limp in the frame, his will to resist completely and utterly gone.

"Kill me," he said to Stanton, "Please, just kill me."

"Oh Mr Higgins, this is only the start, it would be rude to let you die now."

Stanton hit a switch on the side of the frame which released the restraints causing Higgins to fall to the ground with a wet thud.

"I will see you soon, Mr Higgins, we have much work to do."

With that, the door to the room opened and three soldiers came into the room. They picked Higgins up and dragged him out of the room. He didn't even get to say goodbye to her as she hung on the frame, lifeless, shamed and bleeding. All he could do is cry as he was dragged, broken and bleeding from the room.

Chapter Fifty Six

Deep Space

The Crucible Of Man

The Crucible Of Man approached Research Station Omega. Anna watched through the window of the bridge and saw the silver-grey cylinder increase in size. Her heart was pounding, she hadn't slept in over 24 hours and she was running on adrenaline and coffee alone. Heald came up behind her and put a hand on her shoulder.

"It's a good plan," she said, "It's going to work, Anna."

Anna placed her hand on Heald's, it was comforting to have her close by.

"I really hope it works. So many lives are on the line and we only have one shot."

"It will, I know it will."

A warning klaxon sounded and everyone turned to look at the ship's captain.

"They have a target lock on us, Madam President," Captain Krensel said, "What are your orders?"

"It's your ship Captain," Anna said, "All I'll suggest is trying to open a comms channel."

The Captain nodded and instructed the communications officer to try and open communications with the station. It was a tense 30 seconds as the young officer cycled frequencies and tapped at his comm station keyboard with incredible speed. Eventually, he gave a thumbs up and the holographic image of Cardinal James appeared in the middle of the bridge.

"Cardinal James," Anna said.

"President Coulson," James replied, "To what do I owe the pleasure? Are you here to arrest me again?"

"Not this time," she said, "I wish to speak with Stanton."

"Then you're in the wrong part of the galaxy," James said, "He's most definitely not here."

"Don't lie to me, Cardinal. I know he's here. Why else would that ostentatious capital ship be hanging around?"

"It's here for a refit," James lied

"Cardinal, I'm not in the mood. Either grant us permission to land or we'll do it anyway."

"That is awfully presumptuous of you, Madam President. You do realise that The Church is sovereign and if you force yourself onto this base you will be committing an act of war?"

"Is that like the act of war you committed when your personnel carrier strafed my headquarters and killed four of my Peacekeepers?"

"Well..."

"You're lucky I'm the forgiving type, otherwise I'd have brought the fleet with me and blown you into atomic dust."

"You're very benevolent, Madam President, I'm giving you permission to land. How many will be entering the station?"

"Just myself and my ward, Kirstine Heald."

"Excellent, a welcome party will meet you in the landing bay. Make your approach now."

The hologram of James dissipated. Anna took a deep breath, she was committed now, there wasn't any way back.

"Are you ready, Heald?"

"I'm ready, Anna."

They left the bridge and headed to the lower decks of the ship. As they walked into the deployment bay, the four Silencers were preparing themselves for infiltration. They had swapped their assault gear for stealth gear, strapping themselves up with plasma pistols, energy swords and various melee weapons. Heald approached one of the Silencers and presented The Asabat.

"Please take care of it," she said, "I'd like it back in one piece."

The Silencer took the weapon and strapped it to its back. It nodded at Heald to confirm it understood, then resumed preparing for the mission.

The Crucible Of Man approached the landing bay slowly. Laser cannons set into the hull of the station tracked the ship as it entered through the forcefield into the artificial atmosphere. Four landing legs emerged from the smooth hull and the Captain guided the ship down to a gentle landing on the steel deck.

Anna took a deep breath as the landing ramp descended. The welcoming party that James provided turned out to be 30 soldiers who all had their weapons trained on Anna and Heald. As they descended the ramp, a Corporal approached them and demanded their weapons. Anna surrendered a small pulse pistol, Heald surrendered a pulse rifle, two pistols and a combat knife. Anna looked at her and raised an eyebrow, to which Heald simply shrugged in response.

The soldiers kept their weapons trained on Anna and Heald as they were led into the station. Anna's heart was racing, she desperately hoped that her plan would work. She looked back at The Crucible Of Man and caught a glimpse of four shimmers darting away from the ramp. The sound of the soldiers' boots in the echoing landing bay had camouflaged the Silencer's descent down the landing ramp. She smiled to herself, it was all coming together.

Blyth woke up on a hard, cold table. His clothes had been removed and the air was freezing cold. He tried to move and realised he was restrained to the table. He tried his best to look around. From what he could see, he was in a research lab, rather than a sickbay. He cursed Cardinal James under his breath for drugging him. It was an underhanded move that was entirely uncalled for. An elderly Japanese man was busying himself with a microscope and some test tubes in the corner of the room.

"HEY!" Blyth yelled out, "What's going on here?"

"Ah, Mr Blyth," Mitsuni said, looking up from his work, "You're awake, that is excellent news."

"That's General Blyth, who the hell are you?" Blyth said with frustration in his voice.

"Oh, my apologies, General, I am Dr Mitsuni, The Church's lead researcher. It is a pleasure to meet you."

"Oh, you're Mitsuni? I thought you'd be younger."

"How are you feeling?" Mitsuni said, choosing to ignore the vague insult.

"I'm freezing my ass off and I've got a hell of a hangover, how do you think I feel? Why the fuck am I strapped to this bed?"

"Ah, well," Mitsuni responded, "We're going to give you an experimental treatment we've been developing and I'm not sure what effect it has on a human subject. It's for your safety and mine."

"What treatment? What are you talking about?" Blyth asked.

"You came here expecting a cure for your condition, didn't you?"

"Yes, the Cardinal promised me a cure, that I wouldn't suffer from my condition any longer."

"Well I'm sorry to disappoint you, Mr Blyth," Mitsuni said with a smile, "But there is no cure. Nerve degeneration isn't something we can help with. But the Cardinal was right, you won't have to worry about your condition any longer."

Mitsuni produced a syringe filled with a thick, green fluid. Blyth started to panic.

"What the fuck is that?" Blyth said, his eyes wide and focused on the green, jelly-like substance in the syringe.

"This, Mr Blyth, is going to change your life. Well, it's going to change your body and I would expect, end your life." Mitsuni said.

"Don't you come near me with that!" Blyth yelled at him.

"Or what?" Mitsuni said nonchalantly, "You're hardly in a position of power here, Mr Blyth."

Mitsuni smiled as he found a vein in Blyth's arm. He pushed the plunger down and forced the parasite into Blyth's bloodstream. The feeling of the thick fluid rushing through his body made Blyth feel sick to his stomach.

"Oh fuck," Blyth said after Mitsuni removed the syringe, "What have you done to me?"

"You'll see soon enough, Mr Blyth," Mitsuni said as he went back to his desk.

"You're mad! You, James, Stanton, you're all fucking mad. I should have never trusted any of you!"

"You're right, Mr Blyth. You should never trust anyone who offers you a miracle cure for your incurable condition. That was very naive of you."

Blyth lay on the bed and breathed in. This is it, he thought, this how he dies, naked, cold and completely at the mercy of The Church. He felt like a fool, he'd been taken in by the desperate promise of a cure, something that could have extended his life. He'd been cornered, forced to betray his oldest friends, forced to murder, forced to compromise everything that he had held dear all the name of a few more years of life. He thought about Marie, how she would be so disappointed in him for compromising everything and being so thoroughly deceived. A tear ran down his cheek.

"Mr Stanton?" Dr Mitsuni said into his PCU, "Mr Blyth has been infected, observation begins."

"Infected? What the fuck did you inject me with?" Blyth asked

"None of your concern, Mr Blyth. How do you feel?"

“I feel...” Blyth thought for a moment, “Actually, I don’t feel so good. My stomach is starting to hurt and my skin is on fire. What was in that syringe?”

Mitsuni started taking notes frantically.

“Oh, this doesn’t feel--- ARGGHHGGHGH!” Blyth screamed in pure agony as the parasite began to alter his body and change him.

“What... what’s happening to me?” Blyth yelled at the top of his voice. He lifted his head and watched as the skin on his arm flayed off and was replaced by green, leathery sinew. He roared in pain as his hands merged and elongated to huge, razor-sharp claws.

“WHAT THE FUCKING FUCK?” he shouted, looking over at Mitsuni, who was alternating between taking notes and grinning wildly.

With an almighty scream, the transformation accelerated. His skeleton elongated, his skull reshaped and within five minutes Frank Blyth was no more.

The creature that replaced him could not break through the newly reinforced bonds that Mitsuni had the engineering team install just days before. He came over and looked at the vicious beast. It was larger than the previous creature, owing to Blyth’s larger frame and girth compared to the young researcher that became the original creature. Mitsuni also noted how much faster the transformation was when the host body was infected with the primordial parasite compared the spores from the older samples.

Mitsuni came close to the head of the new creature. It snarled and snapped at him.

“Stanton is going to love you, my pet,” he said as he gently tapped his fingertips on the leathery skin that covered its skull.

Chapter Fifty Seven

Higgins woke up back in Observation room B. His vision was blurred and his body burned with pain. Sitting up, he looked down his body, he had been bandaged and stitched up, presumably by the station's medical team. He traced two tubes coming from his arms into a machine by his bed. The tubes were drawing blood from him, catching it in a large tank.

He felt weak and dizzy, the room began to spin around him. He was no doctor, but he knew that this could only be a sign of massive blood loss. The wounds Stanton had inflicted on him, combined with the pump strapped to him was enough to nearly kill him.

With a painful tug, he ripped the canular out of his arm and let it drop to the floor. He would no doubt end up reconnected to it when someone came to check on the device, but right now he could give himself a moment's peace without his blood being stolen.

In the main research lab, there was a commotion. Jars were being smashed, a woman was swearing at men who were swearing back and pulse rifles were being charged up. Higgins tried to turn his head so he could see what was going on, but it was no use, he had no strength left. The mirror dividing observation A and B had been turned off it and remained a window. He saw Dana being thrown into the room. She turned the air blue with a tirade at her captors that would make an interstellar trucking magnate blush.

After a moment she stopped, turned to view her surroundings and spotted Higgins. She walked up to the glass and peered through it at him.

"Oh no," Dana said to him, "What did he do to you?"

"He killed my daughter," Higgins replied. It was all that was important to him right now.

"What? Oh god, I'm so sorry," Dana said.

"He stripped her naked, cut her tongue out, put a bag over her head and stabbed her to death right in front of me."

“He’s a monster,” Dana said, trying not to think about all the things she had endured at Stanton’s hands, “He’s inhuman.”

“No…” Higgins, groaned, “He’s a man. Men do this. Men with power do this. They’ll do anything to keep themselves powerful. Even if it is murdering an innocent 18-year-old.”

“Is that all she was?” Dana asked.

“Yeah. She was only 18.”

“Tell me about her,” Dana said.

Higgins looked over at her. He saw the sadness in her eyes, the pain that she was experiencing. He told her everything about Emily. From birth to death. Everything. And Dana listened. She listened intently to everything Higgins had to say. They laughed together, they cried together.

“I wrote a lullaby for her, you know,” Higgins said.

“Oh really?”

“Yeah, Twinkle Twinkle Little Star kinda didn’t cut it. She hated that song as a baby. Her mother tried every song she could think of. Nothing would get her to sleep. I put together a few lines and wrote something that she loved. The first time she heard it she had the biggest smile on her face, y’know? The second time I sang it through she drifted off in my arms. When I started working away again, after her mother died, I used to make calls every day to sing her the lullaby. Even now, when I’m missing her, I still sing it to myself.”

“That’s so sweet,” Dana said, tears in her eyes, “Would you mind if I heard it?”

Higgins looked down, away from Dana. He wrestled with the idea of singing his lullaby for Dana. He’d never shared it with anyone other than Emily and Rebecca. Dana noticed how sad Higgins looked and she regretted asking him to share such a private memory. As she was about to speak to tell him not to worry, he opened his mouth and a lilting melody flowed from between his lips:

O'er the hills

Under the sky

O'er the fields

Warmed by sunlight

Kiss on the mountain

Laugh in the trees

Run on the grass

All love is free

Swim in the rivers

Sail on the seas

Carry your heart up

Float on the breeze

Baby of pink

Held in my arms

Precious new life

Happy and warm

Emily darling

Shine in my eye

I love you, sweet baby

You'll never cry

By the end of the lullaby, both Higgins and Dana were in floods of tears. Not another word was spoken for a long time. Higgins had no more strength to talk and he kept slipping in and out of consciousness. Dana meanwhile started fruitless attempts to break out of her observation room.

On the upper decks, Stanton was feeling very happy with himself. His session with the miner had been even more enjoyable than he ever dared believe it could be. The session had left Stanton rather aroused and he knew just what to do about that. His deception with the miner had worked splendidly, Higgins had no idea the girl he killed wasn't his daughter, rather, the interfering research assistant that had been found with Dana when security went to arrest her.

Normally, Stanton would just have killed the girl. After all, she was of no material use to the Church. She was an 18-year-old who knew nothing about anything. However, Stanton knew the coming days would be trying on the entertainment that James had brought from Corvus II, so if he wanted to have satisfaction before he took to his children, he would have to find others. Emily was a prime candidate. Young, fit, beautiful, but small and easily overpowered. His ideal prey.

As he walked around the corner to Emily's room, he saw the door sitting wide open. Approaching it faster, he was greeted with a scene of destruction. On the floor lay one of his security officers with his head blown off, and Corporal Jones, lying on the floor with a wound in his stomach. Stanton rushed in, looking concerned and handing Jones linens from the bed to soak up the wounds.

"What happened, my child?" Stanton said with genuine concern. Jones coughed, a tiny trickle of blood running from his lips.

"We came," he started, "To bring Emily to you, as instructed by the Cardinal. She resisted coming with us. She forced my hand and I commanded my men to shoot her. They took aim, but one of them turned, shot me in the gut and killed that poor soul lying over there."

"My word!" Stanton said, his eyes going wide, "There is a traitor in our ranks?"

"No, Your Excellency," Jones spluttered, "He was an imposter. Mick Walker, a pilot from R.Beta. I thought I'd killed him back there but I guess I was wrong. He took off his helmet, the girl ran to him and kissed him. Then she punched him in the shoulder. I'm not sure I understand why. He said they needed to get out of here, but she insisted on finding her father first, so they headed off down the corridor and left me here to die."

"Bless you, my child. Thank you for this. I will have a medic dispatched to you immediately. However, this is a troubling development and I cannot have rogue operatives on my station, I must go and tend to this. Thank you, child."

Stanton kissed Jones gently on the forehead, then sprinted from the room. Jones chuckled to himself. He hadn't told Stanton the whole story. He hadn't told him how he'd given Emily instructions on roughly where to find her father, nor how to use the maintenance shafts to move around undetected. Emily had thanked him, he had apologised to her for everything he'd put her through. Mick had even apologised for shooting him, which had made Jones laugh.

Jones sat, unable to feel his legs. He felt cold, he knew the end was coming. The pool of blood around him was getting wider. He didn't have long left.

Looking up to the ceiling, he took a small black, leather-bound book from his breast pocket. It had a gold cross embossed on it.

"God," he said out loud, "I remember my Grandmother talking about you. She told me about the great things you do, about Heaven and Hell, about good and evil. Stanton thinks he stomped Christianity out, but I believe in you like my mother did. Like my grandmother did. Like my family did all the way back to the 20th century. My faith in you is strong. I'm not scared to die, I know it's coming. I just ask one thing, look after that poor child, Emily. Get her out of here safe and well.

"I've done a lot of evil in my life, in the name of my job, in the name of safety from persecution. I hope you don't judge me too harshly by these deeds and remember the good in my life. Amen, Lord. Amen."

Jones reached up to his head with his side-arm. He pressed the Bible to his chest, took a deep breath and as a single tear ran down his cheek, he pulled the trigger.

Chapter Fifty Eight

The creature that had been Blyth stomped around the laboratory. Its girth and height made it appear unwieldy. Unlike the original creature which was thin and lithe, this one was portly and ungainly. It was pacing around the lab as if it were looking for something. Mitsuni watched from the next room, utterly fascinated by it. He was making notes at such a rate that he was filling pads of paper within minutes, scribbling every possible observation he could make whilst never taking his eyes off the security feed.

Stanton walked into the room filled with rage.

"Have you seen James?" Stanton snapped, "We have an issue that needs addressing before I meet with President Coulson."

"No," Mitsuni said, barely even acknowledging the presence of Stanton.

"Well do you have any--" Stanton started before spotting the monitor, "What is that? What have you made Hidetaki?"

"This, Mr Stanton, is General Blyth." Mitsuni grinned

"That would explain why it's so fat," Stanton said, "What's it doing?"

"I think it's looking for something."

"What could it possibly be looking for?" Stanton asked.

"What would you look for if you were it?" Mitsuni posited, "Food? A mate? Something to kill?"

"Good point," Stanton said, in awe at the new beast he was witnessing, "Do we have anything to give it?"

"We could give it the body of Allison and see if it's hungry," Mitsuni suggested, "Her body is in the room anyway, in that casket over in the corner."

Mitsuni pointed to a white, cuboid box. It looked like a shipping container, save for the HUMAN REMAINS notice in red letters along the top of it.

"Why did you have the body brought here, Hidetaki?" Stanton asked, suspiciously.

“In case I needed it for something.” Mitsuni said without hesitation, “You never know when human organs might come in useful.”

He pressed a button on his PCU and the casket opened. There, looking as serene as could be, was Allison. She had a deep wound from a plasma shot in her shoulder, blood trickled from her mouth where her tongue had been cut out and a slash of red in the dead centre of her chest showed where Stanton had plunged his knife into her, ending her life.

The Blyth creature approached the casket with caution. Its black, pigmentless eyes focused in on the corpse. It made several chirps and clicking sounds.

“Here it is, it’s going to consume her,” Mitsuni said, his eyes glued to the security feed.

But it didn’t eat Allison’s body. It reached over the casket and it roared. With a wet, tearing sound, its head flung back as if no longer connected to its spine and its chest splayed in two. In its chest cavity were four black, sinewy tubes that protruded forward. With a second roar, its diaphragm contracted and it spewed a cloud of spores at Allison’s corpse. A yellow, thick fog enveloped the room and obscured the beast from sight. A biohazard alarm rang out and the climate controls for the area were immediately locked out. A PCU unit in the corner of the observation room turned on automatically and started providing air quality readings.

Mitsuni started to laugh. Stanton stood open-mouthed at what he had just seen.

“Hidetaki…” Stanton said slowly, “Has that done what I think it’s just done?”

“Yes, Mr Stanton,” Mitsuni said with a broad smile on his face as he started scanning over the atmospheric readouts of the laboratory, “It is an infector. It tried to infect the body of Allison with its spores. Look at this readout, the parts per million of breathable air is reducing rapidly compared to the spores. Do you know what this means?”

“I’m not sure,” Stanton said.

“It is a different class of creature. This species is more than just mindless killing machines, it assimilates others too. It has strains of itself that propagate the infection and spread the genus. This is your Darkness, Mr Stanton. This is what you wanted.”

“My word,” Stanton said, his shocked expression transforming to elation, “This is it! This is incredible! We need to see what it can do to a living being. Send it down to the destroyed lab, there are people who can be freely infected down there."

"As you wish, sir," Mitsuni said.

"I need to find James, I will return to see you, later."

"I will not be here," Mitsuni said, "I need to begin preparing the PAYLOAD device for launch."

"The time is close, old friend," Stanton said, shaking Mitsuni's hand, "We shall prevail."

"We shall prevail, sir," Mitsuni replied, offering a shallow bow.

In the lower decks of the station, Emily and Mick were climbing down a turbo lift shaft. Jones had directed them to the tight maintenance corridors which were free from security cameras and sensors. They had been descending on this ladder for nearly thirty decks now. They still had nearly 80 more to go to reach the area where Jones said they would likely find Emily's father.

"Miss Emily," Mick said, panting heavily, "Do you mind if we find somewhere to rest? My shoulder is on fire."

"We need to keep going," Emily said, looking up in Mick's direction, "How bad is it?"

"Well," Mick said, rotating his left arm to try and return the feeling to it, "I can't feel my fingers and I'm feeling light-headed. I think I need to retreat the wound."

A turbo lift rushed past them at blinding speed. Instinctively they both clung tightly to the ladder despite there being no risk of the lift hitting them.

"Let's get down to the next deck," Emily offered, "We'll find somewhere quiet and I'll have a look at the wound."

"That sounds good," Mick said. He was in more pain than he was letting on, but he knew that he wouldn't be able to get Emily off the station without finding her father. Complaining about his condition wouldn't help either of them.

In relative silence, they continued their descent and reached the next deck. A marking on the wall indicated they were on deck 98. Jones had said it was likely that Higgins was on deck 20, near the bottom of the station.

They shuffled through the tight service corridor and found the access hatch that would allow them to move into the main corridor. Mick slid the door open quietly and poked his head out, looking left and right to see if there was anyone around. The corridor was deserted. He moved into the corridor, followed by Emily and they started trying to make sense of their new location.

They slowly moved through the corridors as Mick began to struggle. The pain was getting worse and he was starting to slow down. He looked down and saw that he was bleeding through his uniform. He pressed his right hand to the wound, causing him to wince in pain, putting pressure on it and trying to stem the bleeding. Emily had moved further ahead and was doing her best to find somewhere they could hide for a moment and let Mick recover.

"Over here!" she whispered back towards him.

"What have you found?" he answered back.

"I've found the armoury," she said as he caught up to here.

"We don't need weapons," Mick said.

"No, but they might have a med kit in there and we can dress your wound."

"Good point, Miss Emily."

The armoury door was open. Mick had expected it to be locked tight, but as they walked in he realised why it was open, there weren't any weapons left. Everything had been checked out. Rack after rack of rifles, pistols and heavy weapons had been cleaned out by the station's security forces. It seemed like they were expecting a war.

Emily moved from cupboard to cupboard looking for a medkit. Mick was starting to feel very weak so he slumped down in the corner. He took off his webbing, unzipped the armoured jacket and slipped his left arm out of the uniform. The gauze he had used over his wound was drenched in blood and completely red.

"Ah ha!" he heard Emily shout from the other side of the room. She bounded over to him carrying a field medkit. She sat in front of him and looked at the gauze.

"That doesn't look good," she said.

"No, it really doesn't," Mick said, "You'll have to help me, I don't feel great."

"What do you need me to do?" Emily asked, opening up the kit.

"First, take the dressing off, it ain't helping any more," he said. Emily gingerly reached to the dressing on his chest. She gripped the edges and started to pull it off slowly.

"ARGH, FUCK!" Mick yelled out. Emily reflexively took her hands off the dressing.

"Oh god, I'm sorry," she said.

"No no, it needs to come off, just rip the damn thing off," Mick said, gritting his teeth. She did so and he made a pained grunting noise as the dressing came off and took some congealed blood with it.

"It doesn't' look good," Emily repeated, "I think it's infected."

"That would make sense, is there any pus or discharge?"

Emily peered at the hastily sewn up wound. It was weeping dark, almost black blood. It smelled horrendous. She had to restrain herself from throwing up.

"Yeah, it's weeping, it's definitely infected."

"Okay, darlin'," Mick said, taking a deep breath, "That medkit should have a couple of syringes in it. One will be a super strong antibiotic and the other should be adrenaline."

Emily rooted through the medkit and found the two syringes. She held them up for Mick to see.

"Okay, jab me with the antibiotic," he said, "Then once that's done, you'll need to find the antiseptic towels, so you can clean the wound. It's gonna hurt like hell. If I pass out, check my heart rate. If it's dropped too low, you'll need to hit me in the heart with the adrenaline, got it?"

"Okay, just stay still," Emily said. She took the antibiotic and injected Mick in the arm with it. She rooted through the medkit again and found the antiseptic towels.

"Deep breath," she said. She pressed the first towel to the wound. Mick screamed in agony. She continued to clean the wound as Mick howled in pain. Dabbing at his firm chest, she eventually, managed to clean the wound. Mick was sweating intensely.

"Okay, last thing, darlin'," he said, "Take the gauze and tape and dress the wound again. Then give me five minutes to get my strength back."

After dressing the wound. Emily sat down next to Mick. He was still panting heavily and her hands were shaking from the stress of putting him through so much pain. They sat in dead silence for a minute.

"Can I ask you a question?" Emily said, turning to look at Mick.

"Sure, Miss Emily," he said, slowly.

"Why did you come here? Why did you follow me here?"

"Well, I had to," Mick said, smiling slightly.

"Come on, Mick. Why did you feel like you had to come here?"

"I wasn't going to let them just take you away, never to be seen again."

"You've known me for three days," she said, "Don't get me wrong, without you here I'd be dead by now, but I just don't get why you're here."

"Well you promised me a date if I got you the info on your daddy," Mick replied, "You don't look like the type to break a promise, so I gotta help you keep it."

Emily laughed, snorting slightly. Mick just smiled at her.

"Cut the shit," she said as her laughter subsided, "Why are you here?"

"For you, Miss Emily," Mick said. He put his hand around hers.

"You're not making sense," Emily replied, "You don't know me, you don't know anything about me."

"I know one thing," Mick said. Without another word, he leaned over and kissed Emily softly. This time she didn't push him away. She returned his kiss, putting her hand on the side of his face. After a moment, he pulled back. He looked deep into Emily's eyes and smiled sweetly at her.

"Okay," Emily said, composing herself, "Now you're making sense."

"Glad to clear up the misunderstanding," he said. They both laughed lightly. "We should get going, darlin'."

"Are you up for the climb?" she replied, looking up at him.

"Oh, god no. But I got a gun and there doesn't appear to be anyone around, so let's just take the damned turbo lift."

Emily stood up, taking Mick's hand and helping him to his feet. She packaged up the medkit and slung it over her shoulder.

As they returned to the turbo lift doors, Mick looked at Emily. Her mood had changed from the awkward elation of their kiss to deeply concerned. He put a hand on her shoulder.

"Don't worry, Miss Emily," he said, "We'll find your dad. He'll be fine."

"I hope so," she said, tilting her head to rest on his hand, "I really hope so."

Chapter Fifty Nine

Higgins' hands were shaking, badly. His severe blood loss, combined with the lack of heat in the observation rooms were cutting through him like a knife. He looked over at Dana in the next room. She was shivering intensely. Her dress wasn't long enough to keep her warm and she looked like she was suffering.

With all the strength in his body, he managed to sit upright on the bed. Dana spotted him moving and walked towards the window between the room.

"How are you feeling, Carl?" she asked.

"Like I was tortured and my blood was stolen," he replied, "How are you holding up?"

"I can barely feel my fingers, it's so cold in here."

"Yeah, it's always been this cold. Seems like they want to keep us suffering as much as possible."

"Is there a way out of here," Dana asked, looking around.

"Nope, the doors open from the outside," Higgins said, "There's nothing we can do until someone comes to check on us."

"When will that be?"

"Your guess is as good as mine," Higgins said, shrugging.

"How have you not gone mad since you've been here?" Dana asked.

"Good question," Higgins replied.

Before he could respond further, they heard a roar coming from somewhere outside the lab.

"What was that?" Dana asked. Higgins didn't respond. He'd heard that roar before, it was the same one that the previous occupant of Dana's cell made. The doors to the main lab slid open and something lumbered into view.

"What is it?" Higgins asked.

"I.. I don't know."

From the darkened corridor, four soldiers in environment suits led the

Blyth monster into the lab. They were leading it using reinforced control poles. One pole was on each arm and the remaining two were around its neck. They pushed it into the lab, then let go of the poles and retreated through the laboratory door, sealing it shut.

Higgins had managed to turn himself around on the bed to look through the observation window. He stared at the rotund beast. Its shoulders hunched forward, its arms pushed wider with its increased girth.

"They made another one?" Higgins said.

"It seems so," Dana said.

"Mr Higgins, Ms Smith," Dr Mitsuni said over the intercom, "What do you think of my latest pet?"

"What have you done?" Dana yelled back.

"I've given an old friend of yours a new lease on life," Mitsuni replied.

"An old friend?" Dana said, confused, "Who was that?"

"Oh, it was your old confidante, Frank Blyth," Mitsuni said. Dana's stomach dropped. All the pieces fell into place. Why she had been arrested, why Allison had been shot and why she was in the cell, staring at the dark green abomination in the laboratory.

"Did Stanton order you to do this?" she asked.

"Oh no, this is just an experiment."

"What kind of experiment?" Higgins asked

"This kind of experiment," Mitsuni said.

With a buzz, the door to Dana's room opened remotely. The Blyth monster was exploring the laboratory and the sound attracted its attention. It spotted Dana and roared. She screamed as it charged right for her. Higgins shouted out but there was nothing he could do.

It burst into Dana's room and grabbed her with its enormous arms. The guttural roar continued as its head flew back and the beast's chest opened up. Higgins watched on in horror, completely helpless as the room filled up with spores.

"WHAT HAVE YOU DONE?" Higgins yelled at Mitsuni. Mitsuni laughed in response.

"Those are spores, Mr Higgins." Mitsuni replied after he finished laughing, "Ms Smith is soon to be one of my pets and there's nothing you can do to help her."

"You fucking monster!"

"You've thrown that statement around far too many times during your stay with us, Mr Higgins," Mitsuni said with a chuckle, "Seeing as you have a knack of killing my pets, I'll leave you locked in there till you expire. Goodbye Mr Higgins." The intercom went dead.

Higgins tried to get off the bed and fell to the ground. He managed to clamber up on to his knees and look through the window as the cloud of spores dissipated. Dana was sat on the floor looking pale and coughing. The Blyth monster had reassembled its torso and had lost interest in Dana. It stomped its way out of the room and continued to explore the laboratory for something else to infect. The door to her room remained open. Dana looked up at Higgins, tears in her eyes.

Higgins desperately scanned the area to find something he could use to help her. He spotted the device that was drawing blood from him and he formed an idea. He pulled the medical device over to him and by flipping a few catches off, removed the reservoir full of his blood from it. Turning back around to Dana he gestured to her to leave the room. She shook her head furiously. He gestured again to say "Trust me" and motioned for her to leave the room again. She stood up and came close to the glass that separated them. He mouthed "Open the door" to her and showed her the glass canister of his blood. Dana realised what he was proposing.

She walked quietly out of her room into the main lab. The Blyth monster was sniffing around, looking for something alive. As she stepped into the main room, she accidentally kicked a piece of glass that was on the floor, making a noise. The beast looked up at Dana with a muffled grunt, but ultimately ignored her and continued to acclimate itself to the lab.

Dana gingerly took a few steps to her left and she reached the control panel for Higgins' room. She tapped frantically at a few buttons and the door slid open. Higgins limped forwards carrying the container of blood.

"I'm going to try and get it into the corner," he said in a whisper, "When I do, throw this at it."

"What if it attacks you?" Dana asked, taking the blood from him.

"You saw what happened with the last one, it wouldn't come near me. I'm betting this one is the same."

"This is insane," she said, her eyes wide with fear.

"It is, but we don't have many options, we need to get rid of it."

Without another word, Higgins moved forward. He steadied himself on whatever he could, using stools, desks and free-standing equipment to help him work his way towards the oblivious beast. When he was 10 feet behind it, he picked up a test tube from the desk next to him and threw it at the Blyth monster. It turned around to look at him and immediately recoiled in fear. It howled in such a high pitch Higgins thought his eardrums were going to burst.

But he pushed forward, towards the wailing beast. It moved further and further back until it was trapped in the corner of the room, attempting to avert its gaze from Higgins, as if the sight of him alone was causing it pain.

Higgins came close up to it and he put his hands on its arms. The smell of burning returned and the beast howled in pain. Unlike the first monster though, the Blyth monster was significantly stronger. It flailed its arms to try and get Higgins to release his grip. Its arms swiped out with such force that it launched Higgins right across the room and through the glass door that had sealed them in the lab with the monster.

Dana saw her opportunity. As the Blyth monster was reeling in pain from the extreme burns on its arms, she threw the canister of his blood at the creature's head. It shattered on contact, dousing the beast with the blood. It tore through the Blyth monster like acid, melting its skin, its skeleton and the sacs that held the infectious spores. In the space of 30 seconds, all that remained of the Blyth monster was half of a torso and a pair of legs.

Dana ran over to Higgins, who had landed in a heap in the atrium, covered in broken glass.

"Carl, are you okay?" she asked, sitting him up.

"I'm alright, I'm alive," he said. He coughed heavily and spat blood on the floor, "Are you alright?"

"Of course I'm not," she said, the tears returning to her eyes, "That...thing infected me! I'm going to become one of them!"

"There must be something we can do," Higgins said, wracking his brain.

"I don't see how! There isn't a cure for this, is there?" Dana said, sitting next to him and burying her head in her hands.

"Wait!" Higgins said, "I think there is a cure!"

"What?"

"I'm sure of it," he said, sounding excited, "It's why I was hooked to that machine. Stanton said it, my blood is the key to the cure."

"It is?"

"Yeah," Higgins said, "I have an idea. This is a lab, right?"

Dana nodded.

"Find me a needle and a syringe, quickly."

Dana looked at him confused for a moment, the shock of dealing with the

Blyth Monster still weighing heavily on him. She chose to just trust Higgins and she went looking for a syringe. The lab was a mess, having been occupied and destroyed by two of the creatures in the space of a week.

She searched through cupboards and drawers but there weren't any needles or syringes in sight. She was about to give up when in the corner of her vision, she saw a medkit on the floor near the half molten corpse of the Blyth Monster. She grabbed it up and returned to Higgins with it.

"Here, there might be one in this medkit," she said, handing it to him.

He opened it up and threw all of the contents on the floor. Sure enough, there was a syringe bundled in with a bottle of strong antibiotics.

"Sit down next to me," Higgins said to Dana. He took an elastic strap from the back of the medkit bag and wrapped it around his left arm, making a tourniquet and pulling it tight with his teeth.

"What are you doing?" she asked as he took the empty syringe, found a vein and plunged it into his arm.

"Giving you a chance," he replied through clenched teeth as he drew the plunger back as far as it would go, filling the syringe with his blood. He immediately felt dizzy again. He'd lost so much blood since Stanton had tortured him, even filling a single syringe was dangerous to his health.

He took the syringe out of his arm and released the tourniquet. He handed the syringe to Dana as he became woozy and slipped over onto his side.

"If we don't find the cure and I don't make it off this station, take.. the blood... use it to make one..." he said as he slipped into unconsciousness.

Dana sat, effectively alone in the destroyed laboratory. She looked at the syringe of Higgins' blood, then back at him slumped on the floor. A wave of emotion and shock overcame her and she burst into floods of tears there on the floor.

Chapter Sixty

Anna and Heald had been stood in the large conference room for over an hour now. Flanked by heavily armed guards on both sides, she felt uneasy. The conference room was more like a throne room, at one end was a large chair, embossed with gold decorations, raised up on a stepped platform that she could only assume belonged to Stanton and Stanton only. The room was vast with a raised ceiling. One wall was comprised of windows looking out into the depths of space, the other was a large vidscreen which was currently cycling through various news broadcasts on a muted rotation.

Anna stared out the window, observing the inky blackness. She noticed the Saviour, Stanton's huge capital ship, sitting perfectly still, ominously observing the events that were about to take place. She couldn't be sure, but she had seen a shimmer floating by the aft of the Saviour. The idea of the Church possessing a ship with active camouflage was too much to contemplate for her, so she put the thought out of her mind. It wasn't important right now.

She turned back to Heald, who was pacing up and down. She knew Heald didn't like to wait around and she was pretty confident that Heald did not like to be without a side-arm of some description.

"Are you okay?" Anna asked Heald.

"It's the waiting." Heald replied, "Why is he keeping us waiting? I would have thought he'd have loved to come up and lecture us."

"I know," Anna said with a sigh, "He's clearly trying to rattle us. Be patient."

"I'll try," Heald said, before resuming her pacing.

Anna turned her attention to the vidscreen. Currently, it was showing the Galactic News Network and a story being covered by their investigative journalist, Laura Mejury. Anna remembered the name, she was supposed to be having an interview with her next week. Watching the vidscreen, Anna couldn't help but think that Ms Mejury was much younger than she'd initially thought. Her black rimmed glasses and curled hair were friendly, yet lent her gravitas. She was covering a story on the attack at the Council headquarters. The banner headline on the muted vid stream read "WAS PRESIDENT COULSON INJURED IN THE ATTACK?" Ms Mejury had a serious look on her face like she was already reading Anna's obituary.

Before she could continue thinking about what the press was saying about her conspicuous absence, the large double doors for the room opened and all of the soldiers present snapped to attention. More soldiers marched into the room, flanking Stanton and Dr Mitsuni. Two Church Wardens followed leading a young man with control poles wrapped around his neck. Stanton didn't acknowledge Anna or Heald, he continued marching till he reached the pseudo-throne at the end of the room. Sitting down with a flourish, he focused his attention on Anna.

"President Coulson," he said in a slimy tone, "What a pleasure to finally meet you."

"I'd love to say it's mutual," Anna replied, "But this isn't a social visit."

"It never is, is it?" Stanton said, grinning, "But what does it matter? You're here regardless. What can I possibly do for you?"

"You know why I'm here," Anna said firmly, "I know about the parasite."

"Ah yes, there have been a lot of little birdies in my aviary with big mouths telling you my business."

"Well, you had one of your own in mine." Anna said through clenched teeth, "Where is Frank?"

"Hidetaki, what did you do with the good General?"

"I'm afraid he is no more," Mitsuni replied quietly, "He has reached the next plane of existence."

"Ah, well I'm sorry Anna," Stanton said, returning his attention to her, "I'm afraid your traitor has expired in one way or another."

"You killed him?!" Heald yelled out.

"Anna," Stanton said, "Please control your guard dog. Lovely as she is, she has no business speaking to a man of my stature."

Heald moved forward slightly but Anna put a hand on her shoulder and gently pulled her back. She gave Heald a look as if to say "Calm down, keep cool" and Heald backed down.

"What did you do to Frank?" Anna asked, addressing Mitsuni.

"He has transcended," Mitsuni replied, "He is now a superior being."

"You turned him into one of those things, didn't you?" Heald asked.

"My word, Anna," Stanton interjected, "You must discipline your pets, lest they are punished." He grinned widely at Heald's obvious annoyance.

"Regis," Anna said, changing her tack, "Stop fucking around. You've done enough and there is enough evidence to tie multiple deaths back to you and your deputies. On top of that, whatever abominations you're creating on this station cannot be allowed to live."

"Are you here to arrest me, President Coulson?" Stanton began to laugh wildly, "You must be insane if you think you can do anything to me. Don't you realise the power I hold?"

Stanton hopped off his 'throne' and started to walk around the room. He took a pistol from one of the soldiers and waved it around in his hand.

"You've never met a man with godlike power, have you?" he said, "A man who is capable of anything and everything that takes his fancy."

"What are you talking about?" Anna said.

"You know, followers of the old, dead religions believed their God or gods to be omnipotent beings with infinite power over life, death and the universe. They believed in beings powerful enough to create and destroy worlds at a whim. Look where we are now. The Church terraforms planets, we obliterate those in our way. In my hand, I have the power over life and death. Watch."

Stanton stood next to a soldier, raised the side-arm up to his head and pulled the trigger. The soldier didn't react. he simply accepted his fate. None of the other soldiers were in the slightest bit fazed by the cold-blooded murder of their squad-mate

"You see?" Stanton said, directing his attention back to Anna, "I am powerful. I am supremely powerful. I took that life for no other reason than I could and I command such fear and respect from the rest of these soldiers and officers that they don't even react. Does that make me a god?"

"It makes you a murderer," Anna replied, still shocked from what she'd witnessed.

"In your eyes, maybe," Stanton continued, "But to billions across the galaxy, I am a god. I am on the precipice of supreme control over the entire human race."

Stanton came close to Anna, right in her face. He leaned forward and whispered in her ear.

"You're very beautiful, you know. A few decades too old for me, but you would make an amazing toy for me."

Anna tensed up. She saw Heald out of the corner of her eye clenching her fists. Before Stanton moved away from Anna he ran his tongue slowly across her cheek. The sensation made Anna sick to her stomach.

"You see? Absolute power." Stanton continued as he walked back over to Mitsuni, "How many people can say they've licked the President's face?" This conjured laughs from Mitsuni.

"So what now, Regis?" Anna said, wiping his saliva from her cheek, "You're going to kill me?"

"Oh, better than that, my dear Anna. I'm going to make you a part of the coming Darkness."

Anna and Heald shifted uneasily on their feet.

"Is that what you're calling that monster you've grown?" Anna said, trying to keep Stanton from acting on his impulses, "Is that your Darkness?"

"Come on Anna, don't be naive. You know as well as I do that Logan Stanton was an awful waste of genetic material. The Darkness and the Saviour were figments of his alcohol riddled imagination. This whole belief structure only exists because he didn't want to pay taxes and he was a man of such greed, no amount of money, sex or drugs was ever enough. I've searched my whole life, not for the Saviour, but for the Darkness. With the Darkness, I can unleash it on worlds that no one cares about. Sure, people will die, but then I can come in with the cure. I will be the Saviour, I will save the human race and the whole galaxy will give themselves to me and me alone!"

"And how do you propose to do that?" Anna said, the rage building within her.

"I thought you'd never ask." He said with a grin, "Hidetaki, bring me the boy."

Mitsuni and the two soldiers with control poles guided the young cleric forward.

"Madam President, meet Tom Cavanagh, our volunteer for the day," Mitsuni said. Anna could see with the fear in his eyes that he wasn't a willing volunteer.

"Did you really step up for this, Tom?" Anna asked him.

"Oh, I'm afraid he had an unfortunate accident this morning and lost his tongue," Stanton said with a smile. Tom opened his mouth to confirm that his tongue had been cut out. Heald retched slightly.

"Now Tom," Mitsuni said, "I'm sorry to say, but this is going to hurt a lot."

Mitsuni pulled out a large syringe filled with the lurid green parasite. Tom shook his head and tried to get away but the soldiers tightened the control poles around his neck. Mitsuni came in close and injected the substance directly into

Tom's neck. His eyes went wide and he instantly appeared to be in pain.

"We have refined our discovery," Mitsuni said, "It only took a few minutes to take effect on Mr Blyth, but this should work within seconds."

Tom dropped to his knees. He let out a guttural scream as his skin began to bulge and boil. Anna and Heald watched wide-eyed as the young man in front of them ceased to be and in his place stood a tall creature with hardened green skin sporting an enormous lower jaw lined with teeth, jet black eyes and two huge, curved claws that were once his hands.

"Wha-what the fuck?!" Anna exclaimed. The creature snarled and roared, but the soldiers kept tight hold of the control poles and it couldn't move.

"What do you think, Anna?" Stanton said with a laugh, "Beautiful, isn't he?"

"It's a fucking abomination!" Heald yelled.

"To you," Stanton said, calmly, "But to me, he is power. He is the Darkness. He is my key to building the universe to my design."

"I've seen enough," Anna said, "Avaya, did you get all that?"

Anna's PCU lit up and projected Avaya into the room.

"Yes Madam President," she said, "Engaging Alpha Protocol."

"What is the meaning of this?" Stanton said with annoyance in his voice.

"You're not the only one with power, Regis." Anna replied.

The vidscreen wall cut the image of Ms Mejury to blackness, returning with a recording of the events that had just taken place.

"NO!" Stanton said, his eyes transfixed on the screen showing Mitsuni injecting Tom and his subsequent transformation, "NO! You can't do this!"

"You forget, Regis," Anna said, "Power comes from trust. You've just lost everything. This is currently broadcasting on every vidscreen in the galaxy. You are finished."

"You fucking cu-"

"Ah ah ah," Anna said, raising her finger to him, "You have been blinded by your hubris, Regis. This ends now."

"For you," he replied, "Men, kill her!"

The soldiers all raised their weapons at Anna and Heald.

"NOW!" Anna yelled out.

Pulse rounds came from the four corners of the room, cutting down the soldiers like paper. Stanton and Mitsuni looked around for the sources of the shots, but they couldn't see anything. A glint of metal caught the light and Heald shot forward. She slid on the ground kicking the legs out from Mitsuni. He hit the ground hard, breaking his nose and shooting blood everywhere. Heald stood up where Mitsuni had been and reached up in the air. The Asabat landed in her hands, readily charged, she whirled round to the creature that had been Tom, closed the visor on her helmet and opened fire.

A flash of blinding light came from the end of the weapon and the sound of flesh hitting glass was heard. As her vision returned, Anna looked at where the beast had been stood. The power of The Asabat had launched it across the room and bounced it off the window. Looking at it, the Asabat had blown off its left arm. It screamed in pain. Stanton recovered his vision and saw the Silencers turn their active camouflage off and advance on his position.

"Jameson, now!" Anna yelled into her PCU.

"Yes, Madam President," Stills replied.

Stanton watched in horror through the window as the entire Council Fleet appeared out of the Slipstream close to the research station. All of the sleek, grey ships opened fire on the Saviour. Thousands of pulse rounds erupted from the Council ships and pummelled the Saviour's golden hull, burning and blistering it. The capital ship did not have time to react as it was in a holding pattern. Anna watched as its engines ignited but it was too late for the enormous ship, the armaments of the fleet overcame it and with a bright flash, the Franklin drive overloaded and disintegrated the ship.

"No…" Stanton said, his eyes wide and his face turning red, "You cannot do this."

He opened his own PCU and screamed orders into it.

"James! Get to the Revenant and do as much damage as you can, they can not stop the launch."

Before Anna could react, the creature was on its feet again. With a wet cracking sound, everyone in the room watched in horror as it lurched and spasmed, growing a new arm in the process. Without orders, the Silencers opened fire on it. The monster leapt forward and decapitated one of the Silencers. The others scattered and reactivated their active camouflage. The creature turned its attention to Heald, who managed to dive out of the way as it bore down upon her. Anna picked up a pulse rifle from one of the downed soldiers and opened fire herself.

"Everyone, retreat! Get back to The Crucible," she yelled.

The creature started to charge at Anna. She moved to run but tripped over the corpse of one of the Church Wardens. As she scrambled to get back on her feet the creature jumped up at her. Her life was saved when one of the invisible

Silencers connected with the creature in mid-air, knocking it off course and breaking the Silencer's active camouflage.

"Go, Madam President," the Silencer said as it glitched in and out of vision, "Get off this station, we will handle this."

Anna didn't have to be told twice. She grabbed Heald by the arm and the pair started running as fast as they could. As they left the chamber the thuds of their boots echoed around the corridor. it wasn't enough to drown out the noise of the fight the Silencers were engaged in. When they reached the turbo lifts Anna could still hear the creature roar and the sound of weapons fire.

"Where did Stanton and the doctor go?" Anna asked.

"They slipped out through a service door at the back of the room. We lost them."

"Fuck," Anna said. She opened up her PCU and contacted Stills again.

"Anna, what're your orders?" Stills asked

"Be aware, Stanton ordered something called the Revenant to attack. I think it's a stealth ship. Be careful."

"Copy. Anything else?"

"Fire everything you've got at the biggest power source you can find. We need to blow this place out of the sky. We're on the way back to the Crucible. Contact Captain Krensel and tell him to get ready for an explosive exit."

"Roger, Anna. Be careful."

"You too, Jameson."

As they got into the turbo lift, they could feel the station rock as the fleet opened fire. The awesome power of the fleet's 100 strong frigates and destroyers wouldn't take long to breach the power core of the station. Hopefully, she thought, it would be enough.

Chapter Sixty One

The fleet focused fire on an area near the bottom of the cylinder. All of their scans had indicated that this was likely the power core for the station, but it was shielded heavily. Pulse cannons weren't making a dent in the thick plating and reinforced hull.

Stills stared at the tactical display with intensity. He had been in many a large scale battle before, but Anna's mention of a stealth ship concerned him greatly. He had moved his command ship to the rear of the armada to scan for anything unusual or anything that could pose a risk to the fleet.

Research Omega's defences had begun to open fire on the Council fleet. Hundreds of cannons across the hull illuminated the darkness of space and pummelled the ships in closest proximity.

"Get the frigates forward, use them to soak up some of that fire while the destroyers move in," Stills yelled into the fleet comms, "Launch the fighters as well. Give them as many targets as possible and divert some of that fire."

From his rearmost standpoint, Stills watched as the bulky frigates moved forward and turned broadside against the station. They had reinforced hulls and were a great deal larger than the destroyers. They were designed with this kind of assault in mind. The frigates would soak up as much fire as they could take to protect the less armoured, more nimble destroyers. They were also AI controlled, there was no crew to put at risk by using them to protect the manned destroyers.

The destroyers, as per his command, unleashed clouds of AI fighters. These close quarters craft, shaped like arrowheads, were at the pinnacle of automated weapons design. They were light, fast and packed a surprisingly large punch. In trials, he had seen three fighters take down a decommissioned frigate within a few minutes. The AIs controlling the fighters were pinpoint accurate and rarely missed their mark.

As Stills expected, the hundreds of fighters joining the battle caused the automated defences of the station to be overwhelmed with targets. Their focus was broken and that allowed the destroyers and frigates to resume firing and focus on breaking through the shielding around the power core.

A light started flashing on Stills' display. One of the destroyers, The Nautilus was sending a distress call. He zoomed in on the display to see the long, sleek warship begin to glow and break up. With a brilliant flash, the ship was vapourised as the Franklin drive overloaded. 200 crew members were gone in an instant.

"Fuck!" Stills yelled. He opened a channel to the whole fleet, "All ships, be aware, there is a stealth ship in play. Scan all light and heat frequencies, we need to take it out."

Several blinks on his display came from the captains of the destroyers and the handful AI frigates, indicating that the message had been received.

"Science!" he yelled to the team of officers to his left, "Work with tactical, find that ship and if you can, find a way to knock out its stealth equipment!"

There was a flurry of activity on the bridge as the two teams began to hunt for any evidence of the stealth ship, other than the wreckage of The Nautilus. The bridge was cramped, with two concentric circles of workstations covering communications, the helm, engineers, science and weapons systems. In the centre sat Stills, in his raised chair with a view of the whole bridge and the tactical computer. He cycled through multiple displays, looking for anything in the vicinity that seemed wrong or out of place.

"Come on, you bastard, where are you," he said under his breath.

On the Revenant, Cardinal James sat in the Captain's chair, having relieved the captain upon entering the ship. It had been a great many years since James had captained a ship and even longer since he had been in a battle. The Revenant's captain had been less than impressed at being ousted from his position and was currently sat at the helm.

"Has the fleet detected us yet?" James asked no one in particular.

"It doesn't seem so, Cardinal,"the Captain responded.

"Very good. We've taken one out, let's try and thin out these fighters a bit."

The Revenant moved slowly and silently through the chaos ensuing around the station. The fighters were swarming like flying insects, moving too fast for the station's static cannons to keep track of. But that wouldn't be a problem for the hundreds of cannons that peppered the smooth hull of the Revenant.

Laser fire flew from the Revenant in all directions as it continued moving slowly through the Council fleet. The fighters started dropping like flies, tiny explosion after tiny explosion looking like a fireworks display in space.

"Keep moving forward, towards that destroyer," James said. The destroyer in question was opening its ventral doors, ready to unleash another wave of fighters into the battle.

"Cardinal," the tactical officer yelled, "Multiple heat signatures coming from the destroyer, I think it's about to dump more fighters."

"Are we within torpedo range?" the Captain interrupted.

"Yes, sir," the tactical officer replied.

"Unleash the torpedoes!" James commanded, "Focus on the aft and blow the Franklin drive."

30 streaks of fire left the front of the Revenant, all converging on the rear quarter of the destroyer. This time, however, the AI of a close by frigate detected the missiles with time to spare and it managed to turn its cannons to the threat and blow all but one of the torpedoes to smithereens. The remaining torpedo, by pure accident, hit a fighter that happened to fly in its way before it could do any damage to the destroyer.

"Commander Stills!" one of the tactical officers yelled out.

"Yes? What is it?"

"I think we have an approximate location for the stealth ship," the officer said, "It's just opened fire on one of the destroyers, here," he marked the tactical display.

"Fleet, focus fire on this location!" Stills said without hesitation.

Cardinal James was thrown from his co-opted Captain's chair as the Revenant began to take fire.

"Helm, get us out of here!" he yelled, "Power up the Franklin drive, take us into a controlled jump to the other side of the battle."

"Sir, we'll have to turn off the stealth drive to jump," the Captain countered.

"Then turn it off and make the jump," James said, condescendingly.

"But sir..." the engineering officer protested.

"BUT NOTHING," James yelled, "We cannot endure a barrage like this we need to move immediately!"

The Revenant appeared back into the vision of the fleet and immediately powered up its Franklin drive

“Status report?” James yelled, “When can we jump?”

“We’ve sustained several hull breaches and we’ve lost 31% of our cannons, all located on the starboard side. Jump will be ready in 4 seconds.” someone yelled back to him.

“Seal off those decks, take an evasive flight pattern,” James yelled.

With a pulse of the engines, The Revenant flipped itself over and strafed along the edge of one of the frigates, peppering it with laser fire. But the hull was too strong for it to break through. 30 or so fighters had been assigned to pursue the stealth ship and they were currently giving chase.

“Jump ready, sir,” the Captain shouted.

“NOW!”

The Revenant blinked out of existence with a pulse of energy that wiped out half of the fighters that had given pursuit.

“WHERE THE FUCK DID IT GO?” Stills yelled at no one in particular.

There was a frenzy of activity at the science posts as they frantically scanned the battlefield.

“We don’t know, sir,” one of the officers called up to him, “We’ve lost it.”

“Fuck!” Stills shouted as he bashed his fist on the arm of the command chair, “Keep scanning. We hadn’t done that much damage, it must be close by!”

“Yes, sir,” the science officers all shouted in unison.

“Tactical?” Stills called out, “Did you get much information from the time it was uncloaked?”

“Not much, sir,” the Chief Petty Officer responded, “We’ve got basic dimensions, armaments and some of its defences but not enough to work up a tactical solution on.”

“Do what you can,” Stills said back. “Helm, bring us closer to the battle, we need to find this ship. Have our compliment of fighters on standby.”

“Aye, sir!”

The Revenant blinked back into existence on the periphery of the battle. It was only visible for half a second before the active camouflage re-engaged and the ship became invisible again.

“Orders, sir?” the Captain said, spinning around in his chair to face James directly.

“I’m thinking,” James said. He leaned forward and tented his fingers as he surveyed the fleet on the tactical screen. The fleet had re-engaged with Omega and was doing significant damage to the outer hull. The shielding around the power core was still holding.

“Might I suggest something, Cardinal?” the Captain said, standing from his seat.

“You may,” James said, not moving and not lifting himself from his intense thought.

“The railgun might be able to punch through one or two of the frigates and allow the station’s defences to reach the destroyers.”

“Interesting idea,” James said, mulling the idea over. He pointed at one of the frigates on the display, “If we get there at the right angle, overcharge the railgun we might be able to wipe out multiple frigates with one shot.”

“That would be too dangerous, Cardinal,” the Captain said, “If we push past 90% charge on the railgun we’ll have to drop the active camo. If we go past 100% we’ll be a sitting duck for a few seconds while the Franklin drive recovers.”

James watched as the grey skin of Omega blistered and burned under the relentless assault.

“We need to do something, now,” he said, “Take us in. Engineering, focus all available power into the railgun, we’re going to knock it to 120% and do as much damage as possible.”

“Cardinal!” the Captain yelled, “I must protest! We’ll be fully visible and right in the crossfire of the whole Council fleet, this is suicide.”

James looked at the Captain with fire in his eyes. He stood up, his lanky frame towering over the stocky build of the Captain.

“How dare you speak to me in such an insubordinate way!” James boomed, “Right now, under Regis Stanton’s orders, I am in charge of this vessel and you will carry out my orders as I see fit!”

“Cardinal,” the Captain retorted, “I will not carry out this half-baked plan of yours. You will have to remove me from MY bridge if you wish to follow through on this.”

“I’ll do you one better,” James said. He pulled out a small plasma pistol from his vestments and shot the Captain in the stomach. The bridge fell silent.

“Does anyone else have a problem with following orders?” he said, waving the pistol around. Silence remained, “Good, now, as I said, charge the railgun to 120% and get us to the coordinates I identified, we get one shot at this.”

Silently, The Revenant moved to rejoin the battle.

“Any sign of it?” Stills called down to the science station.

“Nothing, Admiral.”

“Right, keep scanning,” Stills said. He opened the fleet comm once more, “We’ve lost the stealth ship. For now, redouble efforts on breaking through the shielding to the core. Move all the fighters into a protection pattern, have them on the lookout for signs of the stealth ship returning.”

The fleet repositioned themselves so all of the destroyers and frigates were showing their broadsides to the shielded area of the station. As one they unleashed a persistent volley of pulse munitions. The hull of Omega began to glow as the temperature increased but it would not yield to the punishment it was enduring.

The fighters were held in a patrolling pattern around the fleet. They had stopped firing on Omega and instead flew at full speed in an orbit around the Council forces. It didn’t take long for Stills’ intention to become clear.

All of a sudden, several fighters collided with something. Something invisible to the naked eye.

“THERE IT IS!” Stills yelled into the fleet comm, “All ships, engage!”

“Get those fighters off us!” James continued to yell. He was delivering orders faster than the crew were able to exact them, “Get us into position!”

The fighters had crashed into the side of The Revenant, damaging the active camouflage system and causing several more hull breaches. James watched in horror as the entire fleet turned to face his wounded ship. Phasing in and out of vision, the engines kicked in and propelled The Revenant towards the forward line of frigates.

A large, forward-pointing barrel on the bow of the ship began to charge up. Electricity arched from the top and bottom magnets. In the payload area, a 500-tonne shell of pure titanium was loaded into the firing mechanism. The Revenant flew out past the blockade of frigates, swung around 180 degrees and slowed down. The light from the railgun barrel was nearly blinding.

“FIRE!”

With an almighty thud, the force of which blew the Revenant backwards, the shell was fired at close to lightspeed from the front of the ship. It plunged through three of the blockading frigates like they were nothing more than paper. There would be no casualties from this shot, but two of the frigates had their engines blown out completely. One of them disintegrated and exploded as the Franklin drive failed, the other lost power completely as the shell had ripped the

Franklin drive from the bowels of the ship. It began to drift lifelessly away from the blockade. The remaining frigate was split in half, but the powered half remained in place, still battling with the Omega station's defences.

Stills watched in horror as The Revenant, with one shot, managed to take two frigates out of the fight with one cannon shot.

"All ships, focus fire, we need to get rid of that battleship," he yelled into the fleet comms.

As one, all of the pulse and laser fire that had been directed onto the station moved to aim at The Revenant.

"Why aren't we moving?!" James yelled as alarms and sirens rang through the bridge.

"The railgun, sir," the officer on the helm responded, "It's burnt out all of our reserve energy and our primary drive system is offline."

"Engineering! Get that fucking Franklin drive online!" James yelled, his eyes suddenly wide with fear.

"We're spinning up the engines again, but it'll take a moment to gain enough power back to move, sir," the engineering officer replied over the comm channel.

James looked at the tactical display, he saw hundreds of lock on notifications appear as it seemed every council ship was targeting The Revenant.

"Oh shit," he said to himself, "ABANDON SHIP!"

The klaxons changed and the ship's AI started to instruct everyone to their assigned escape pods. A hatch opened in the bridge for the officers' escape pod. James immediately made a dash for it. He was the first one in. He tried to pull the bulkhead door closed, but the tactical officer pulled it back open.

"What the fuck do you think you're doing?" the young officer asked.

"Getting out of here," James said. He pulled the plasma pistol back from his vestments and shot the young officer in the head, causing his body to fall back into the bridge. He pulled the door to the escape pod shut and launched into space. He watched helplessly from the window of the escape pod as a thousand bolts of light slammed into the Revenant, bursting its energy shields and puncturing the hull. Several explosions rocked the ship and gases vented into the vacuum of space through multiple hull breaches. Less than half of the escape pods made it off the vessel. The Revenant began to list to the side and began to drift. He tried to put the failure of the most powerful ship in the Church's possession out of his mind and began to formulate his next move.

He set a course to land back on the station. He'd done as much damage as he could to the fleet, now he was single-minded in his objective. He knew what he had to do. He was going to be the one to kill President Coulson.

Stills watched as the Revenant's escape pods fired out in all directions.

"Tactical, get the fighters onto those escape pods. Fleet, resume fire on the station's power core."

Stills continued to observe the battle. Now that The Revenant was not going to be troubling them any longer, the fleet could continue wearing away at the shielded plating.

But none of the weapons were having any effect. Whatever the plating was made of, it was resistant to all of the weaponry the fleet had its disposal.

"Science! What is that plating made of? Why can't we puncture it?"

"I don't know, sir," the science officer responded, "It seems to absorb pulse and laser rounds. It's heating up to incredible temperatures but we cannot break the surface tension of the hull."

"Do we have anything more powerful?"

"No, sir."

Stills cursed to himself. There must be something we can do thought to himself. As he continued looking on the tactical display, he noticed that the Revenant was now drifting, lifeless in space at the edge of the battlefield.

He brought up his scanning display and focused it on the Revenant. He looked over it. It had taken heavy damage but the power core and Franklin drive were intact. An idea formed.

"Avaya," he commanded. The holographic being appeared on the tactical display.

"Yes, Admiral?" she responded, courteously.

"Can you take control of that stealth ship?"

"Working," Avaya's hologram froze still as she attempted to access the ship, "It appears so, Admiral, but it may take a few minutes."

"Do it, as fast as you can. Divert as much power to your local processors as you need to."

"Yes, Admiral."

Chapter Sixty Two

Higgins regained consciousness as Dana shook him. The force of all the hits to the station, combined with Dana's shaking brought him back from the blackness. He pulled himself upright and looked around him. He was alive, just, still in the atrium to the lab. He was covered in bandages.

"I tried to stop the bleeding as best I could," Dana said, "But going through the glass door did a number on you. How do you feel."

"Uuuung," Higgins moaned as he held his head, "Like I'm already dead."

"Can you stand?"

"I don't know."

"We have to try and get you up, the station is under fire. I think the Council are trying to destroy it. We need to get out of here."

With all the effort he could muster and a little help from Dana, Higgins slowly managed to get himself up. He was still very dizzy and he fell a couple of times before he could stand still by himself. Walking was another matter. His right leg was swollen up following the altercation with the Blyth Monster. Higgins was fairly sure it wasn't broken, but it was intensely painful like every ligament had been torn. His left leg was a mess of cuts and bruises, but otherwise functional. He put an arm around Dana's shoulder and she helped him limp towards the turbo lift.

"Have you got the syringe?" Higgins asked her.

"Yeah, right here," Dana replied, fishing the small phial from her cleavage. Higgins gave her a puzzled look.

"The dress doesn't have any pockets," she said, matter of factly.

The corridors were dark, illuminated only by red and yellow lights. The station was on red alert, so there were no guards around. They had already been sent to their prescribed battle-stations This was a good thing for Dana and Higgins, neither of them had a weapon and Higgins wasn't in any state to put up a fight with anyone who challenged them.

As they approached the turbo lift doors, the lift arrived. The curved doors slid open and Dana caught sight of occupants in the lift. She pushed Higgins through the closest door and followed him in. They hid in the dark as Stanton and Mitsuni exited the lift and made their way down the corridor.

"Do you have any idea where it is?" Stanton asked.

"No," Mitsuni responded, "I'm looking on the life support readouts and I can't find anything for it."

"Do you have any thoughts why that might be?"

"All I can think is that it's not human, so the AIs won't know what to look for when scanning for life signs. We've never needed to find something non-human."

"Fuck's sake," Stanton said, "Right, get to the launch bay, finish prepping PAYLOAD. I need to find that traitor and finish her off, seeing as Blyth even as a monster was unable to do it properly."

"Sir, with all that's happened, is it even worth doing this?" Mitsuni asked, for the first time countering his master. Dana heard a smack, followed by the sound of his glasses hitting the ground.

"If I cannot rule this pathetic galaxy, I will destroy it!" Stanton shouted, "Do you still have the cure?"

"Yes, Mr Stanton, but I could only make one dose of it."

"Give it here."

"Sir, with all due respect--"

"Give. It. Here." Stanton cut him off.

"Yes sir," Mitsuni said with a sigh.

"Good, now go get PAYLOAD ready, we need to launch before it's too late."

Two sets of footsteps moved off in different directions. Higgins looked up at Dana. He was breathing heavily and looking pale.

"We... we need to stop the doctor," Higgins said, "We can't let it leave the station."

"I know," Dana said, "I know where the launch bay is, it's not far. Come on."

The lift stopped at the research level. As the doors slid open, Mick led the way, his rifle always readied. Emily followed behind, carrying a small pulse pistol and keeping an eye on the corridor behind them, just in case someone caught the drop on them.

Besides the warning klaxons, the research level was completely dead. The dim light made Mick uneasy. Even with the barrel mounted torch of the rifle enabled, he didn't feel any happier about the situation.

"Where did Jones say we'd find your dad?" he asked.

"Lab 01A, Observation room B," Emily responded.

"You got any clue where that is?" Mick asked, "I ain't ever been here before, I don't know the layout."

"No, not a clue," Emily said. She was terrified and sarcasm had escaped her on this occasion.

They moved through the corridors until they found Dr Mitsuni's office. Emily told him to wait as she walked into the room and peered around at the walls full of equations, diagrams and photographs of her dad and several other people.

"What the fuck?" she said out loud to herself, "Mick, come look at this."

She picked up a picture from the desk. It was a still from the security feeds of Higgins grasping the neck of the first creature to be created in the lab. There were scribblings of notes on the back

Higgins, C exhibits a genetic resistance to the parasite. Pictured is his altercation with the creature that mutated from Smith, F. Upon contact with Higgins' skin, the creature began to exhibit signs of third-degree burns. It was paralysed with pain.

Higgins managed to kill the creature with his bare hands simply by touch. The creature had withstood the heaviest armaments the Church Wardens were equipped with, but this one man was capable of causing it immense pain and suffering, leading to its death.

A cure can be developed from samples of Higgins' blood. Vaccine sample A has proved to be a success in clinical trials, however, it has not been tested on an infected human. Tests on rats proved useful, the infection rate was notably amplified due to the rats' faster metabolism, but the injection caused all symptoms of mutation to disappear in moments. More tests required.

Emily turned back to the image of her father with his hand around the neck of the creature. The elongated jaw, the rows of teeth, the green, shiny skin. She was so scared for her dad.

"Hey, look here," Mick said, pulling Emily out of her silent thought. She moved over to the vidscreen Mick was looking at. It was a security feed, cycling over several cameras.

"It's an empty corridor, Mick," she said.

"Wait a minute, wait for it to cycle around," he said, staring at the screen.

The cameras moved around through several empty corridors, to the destroyed lab, to the room they were in and several other locations. One camera showed an old Japanese man busying himself around what looked like an oversized torpedo. Then Emily saw it, the camera flipped over to show a woman helping an injured man through a corridor not far from them.

"DAD!" Emily yelled.

"You sure it's him?" Mick said.

"Sure as hell, let's go," she said. They both readied their weapons and ran out into the corridor, on the trail of Higgins and Dana.

Chapter Sixty Three

The lift reached the docking bay level. Anna and Heald took a deep breath as the doors slid open. The hallway to the docking bay was empty. Neither Anna nor Heald took this as a good sign, in fact, they were positively worried about how easy their escape had been so far. They had both expected to meet heavy resistance from station security but since they'd left Staton's conference room they had not seen another soul.

Anna readied her rifle and Heald charged The Asabat up. They proceeded slowly down the corridor. The decks which housed the various docking bays had taken a beating in the battle with the Council fleet. Most of the station's defences were focused around the centre of the cylinder, where the docking bays were located.

"Come in, Jameson," Anna said they worked their way cautiously down the long corridor.

"I'm here Anna, what's your status?" Stills replied

"We're close to the docking bay. What's it look like out there?"

"The Church did have a stealth ship. I don't think it's Captain was very experienced, we managed to neutralise it quite quickly. It did take out a lot of fighters and a few ships though."

"Casualties?"

"So far, nearly 500 crew in total across the fleet and I'm getting more casualty reports in every minute."

"We need you to destroy as many defence cannons as you can around docking bay..." she scanned around looking for the bay number, "0143."

"Roger." Stills said, "Hold on, this is going to be bumpy."

The floor of the corridor shook violently as half of the fleet concentrated fire around the docking bay. The sound of metal twisting and breaking filled the air.

"I don't feel good about this," Heald said.

With a bang, one of the floor plates near the turbo lift gave way and collapsed. Anna and Heald looked at each other as the next plate collapsed, followed by another. They looked at the walls and the corridor was starting to twist and heat up. The dull, grey metal walls were turning amber as the heat of the destroyed cannons and constant laser fire was burning into the hull.

"RUN!" Anna yelled.

They both sprinted towards the large bulkhead doors of the docking bay. Bang after bang followed them as the floor collapsed in a chain reaction.

They were almost at the door and Anna felt the floor giving way beneath her. They jumped to try and reach the safety of the docking bay. Anna landed in a heap and slid into the docking bay. Slightly winded, she stood up and looked around.

"Heald?" she called out, "Kirstine? Are you alright?"

Cardinal James held on tightly to his seat in the escape pod. He was well aware that the odds of him making it back to the station were slim, given the number of pods he'd seen explode as he moved further from The Revenant. He had specified the docking bay to land in, the one closest to the centre core, so he could get back to his command post as quickly as possible. The holographic displays in the pod flickered and began to fail as the pod burned at full speed towards the station. A red light started to flash within the pod.

"COLLISION WARNING!" the digitised female voice said, "BRACE FOR IMPACT."

"Here we go," James said to himself as he tightened his straps as much as he could.

As laser and pulse fire flashed past his vision from the small portholes of the escape pod, the door for bay 0143 came into view. He held on tight as the pod blasted through the door at full speed, crashed into the ceiling of the docking bay and smashed into the floor right next to The Crucible Of Man.

His vision was blurred and he felt blood trickling down his face, but he was alive. *I did it! I'm alive!* he thought. He was hanging upside down though, as the tube-like pod had landed the wrong way up, owing to the sudden stop with the crash against the ceiling. He hit the quick release on the flight harness and he fell the six feet from his seat to the floor/ceiling, bashing his shoulder off a support strut and breaking his collarbone.

Anna got up from the floor. The incoming escape pod had frightened the life out of her, coming in at full speed with no warning and smashing into the ceiling. The resulting explosions from the engines backfiring and overloading had knocked her clean over. She looked at the resulting carnage, wondering what were the odds of an escape pod managing to make its way into a docking bay.

"HELP!"

Anna heard the scream from behind her. She turned around to see Heald hanging onto a pipe 10 feet below where the floor had been. She was hanging by her fingertips, dangling over a pit that had to be hundreds of feet deep. Anna couldn't even see the bottom of it.

"Kirstine!" Anna yelled down, "Are you okay?"

"Do I look like I'm okay?"

"I mean, are you injured?" Anna said, choosing to ignore the sarcasm.

"I'm intact." Heald responded, "Can you get me out of here?"

"Hold on a minute, I'll find something to pull you up with."

"I'm not going anywhere..." Heald said, resuming her trademark sarcasm, "But hurry..."

Anna started frantically searching through the heavily damaged docking bay. She looked through crates, in engineers' toolkits, but she could not find a rope or even a strong enough looking spool of wires.

Then it hit her, the escape pod, it would have an escape ladder in it.

James pulled himself up. He was unsteady on his feet. He winced in pain as he tried to move to the escape pod's hatch. He picked up his gun from the floor and made his way over to the release. Just as he was about to hit the explosive release, the door opened by itself. He pushed himself up against the bulkhead wall and tried to make himself as hidden as he could be in the cylindrical pod.

The door opened further and he saw none other than President Coulson peering in. *What fortuitous timing*, he thought.

"Is anyone alive in here?" Anna yelled in.

"Oh, just me," James said as he moved to the centre of the cylinder and brought his gun to bear on Anna.

"You're fucking kidding me," Anna said, raising her hands, "We can talk about this, Stephen."

"I'm sure we could, but where's the fun in that? Imagine how happy Regis is going to be with me when I bring him your bloodied head?"

Anna stared down the barrel of the pulse pistol. James grinned as he cocked the gun and started it charging for a heavy shot.

Heald's arms were killing her. The pipe she was hanging on was sturdy, but her fingers weren't. Anna had been gone for a few minutes too long and she reasoned that if Anna didn't return in the next 30 seconds, she would end up falling.

She looked above her, there were enough pipes leading back up to the corridor level that she could climb up by herself if only she could get a foothold to relieve her burning arms. Pull-ups had never been her strong point in the gym. The wall the pipe was coming from was smooth sheet metal, her boots found no traction on it. To her right, there was a row of thin pipes working their way up the wall. They were frozen solid, so they were likely carrying liquid nitrogen or some other supercooled substance, but Heald figured that if she could get over to them and she could scramble up quickly enough, she would be able to some of the other pipes above.

Gingerly she turned 90 degrees to her right, moving her hands a few millimetres at a time. When she was facing the frozen pipes dead on, she swung her legs back. Her arms were screaming in pain at this point and swinging herself backwards and forwards was only causing her more pain.

With one last swing forward, she let go of the pipe and her forward momentum carried her straight toward the frozen pipes. As soon as the bare skin of her hands made contact with the frozen metal, it fused. The pipes were carrying something so cold it sucked all of the heat from her body and welded the skin to the metal.

She couldn't stop, it would only get worse if she stayed still. With a roar of pain, she pulled her hands from the pipes, tearing the skin from her palms, and began to climb upwards. There were five frozen pipes she had to climb and each was a new agony, freezing the exposed flesh and tearing it off all over again. She was feeling dizzy and sick from the pain, but after a few seconds, which felt like an eternity, she made it to a large pipe that crossed the entire gap. One large enough for her to sit on and take a moment.

She looked at her hands, they were a bloody mess and in agony, but she could still grip and she still had a few more feet to go till she reached the top.

When Heald reached the top she braced herself against the edge of the gap, feeling exhausted and not having the strength to pull herself up and out of the hole. She looked for Anna and spotted her, stood outside the wrecked escape pod with her hands up. Looking back at the pod, she saw in the window the familiar, lank shape of Cardinal James brandishing a pistol at her.

Heald was so furious, she knew she only had one chance to save Anna's life. Clinging onto the floor in front of the hole with her left hand, she pulled The Asabat from her back with her right hand and engaged its charging circuits. She placed it on her left arm, using it like a tripod and took aim at the escape pod.

"Fuck. You," she said as she dropped the visor and pulled the trigger. The force of the shot caused a recoil that resulted in the Asabat launching backwards, smashing the sun visor and striking Heald in the eye before plunging the weapon into the darkened pit that she had just pulled herself out of.

"I've been waiting to do this for so long," James said as the pistol started glowing. Anna closed her eyes, This is it, she thought. She took a deep breath. Through her eyelids, the world went bright white and she felt hot air rush over her. Then there was silence.

But she was alive.

She opened her eyes and saw that the top of the escape pod was missing, as was the top of James' body. His legs remained, slumped on the ground. She turned around and saw Heald's head poking above the edge of the collapsed corridor.

"Anna!" Heald yelled, "Can I get some help here?"

Anna snapped out of her shock and ran over to Heald. Gripping her wrists, with Heald gripping Anna's back, she pulled her out of the hold and back on to firm ground.

"Are you alright?" Heald asked Anna.

"Yeah. I'm fine," Anna responded, she noticed the blood flowing from a cut under Heald's right eye, "Are you okay?"

"No, I'm not," she said, looking mournful, "The Asabat is gone."

Anna started to laugh, she couldn't help herself, she found it utterly hilarious that of all the things they'd experienced in the past few days, that was what upset Heald the most. It didn't take long for Heald to join in laughing with her.

"Anna?!" Stills yelled into the comms.

"Yes, Jameson," Anna said, regaining her composure.

"You've got a window to get out, most of the guns around you are disabled, but you need to get out now, we're going to blow the cork on this thing."

"Copy."

Anna and Heald sprinted for the landing ramp of The Crucible Of Man and straight to the bridge.

"Captain Krensel," Anna said as she marched onto the bridge, "Get us the fuck out of here."

"Gladly, Madam President," the Captain responded, "Helm, get us out of here, maximum sublight speed."

The Crucible Of Man picked up momentum and lifted off the ground. The docking bay began to collapse around them as the ship turned 180 degrees and fired its way out of the door into the blackness of space.

Chapter Sixty Four

Dr Mitsuni was in the final throes of setting up the PAYLOAD device. The large white pod with a miniaturized Franklin drive was almost ready to go. He conducted a test fire on the delivery system using a tank of water, which caused a fine mist of water droplets to be released from the ten pipes that ran along the side of the device.

"Perfect," he said to himself as he climbed a small step ladder and programmed in the launch sequence and co-ordinates. He set the device for a target that would cause maximum impact. The original plan had been to distribute the parasite over Rayczech Alpha's Astral City and specifically, the huge spaceport, but Stanton had ordered a change of plan. There was no coming back for Stanton and The Church after the President's deception, so the new target was Heathrow Spaceport in London. This was, objectively, the largest spaceport in the galaxy and it would spread the infection and mutations as far across the galaxy as possible. Within a week, Stanton's Darkness would be realised and humanity would cease to be.

The launch process was tapped in and the timer set for 30 minutes. He descended the step ladder and moved it to the middle of the PAYLOAD device. Reaching into a case he had been carrying, he pulled out the canister of the green primordial parasite. Climbing back up onto the top of PAYLOAD, he opened a hatch that allowed him access to the delivery reservoir. He unscrewed the lid of the parasite's container and began to pour it into the reservoir.

Dana and Higgins rounded the corner from the corridor and into the launch bay. There they saw Mitsuni on top of the PAYLOAD device, pouring the parasite into it.

"Stop!" Dana yelled at Mitsuni. He looked up as he poured the last of the substance into PAYLOAD. He threw the canister to the floor and closed the hatch on top.

"You're too late, Ms Smith," Mitsuni said, "There's no stopping it now."

"Why are you doing this?" Higgins coughed.

"It's for the greater good, don't you see that?" Mitsuni said, smiling.

"What good is caused by murdering millions of people?" Dana countered.

"You've seen what comes of this parasite, it is beautiful, it is exquisite.

Genetically superior killing machines." Mitsuni said as he hopped off the PAYLOAD device.

"So this is what? Eugenics?" Dana asked

"No, my dear, this is evolution!" Mitsuni smiled wildly, "The human race has stagnated for thousands of years, Stanton wants his darkness, but I'm taking us to the next plane of existence."

"You're mad," Higgins said

"No, Mr Higgins, you'll find that I'm quite sane." Mitsuni gestured at the PAYLOAD device, "This is the future of the human race and you're too late to do anything about it."

"It can't be that much of a future if you need to possess a cure," Dana said to him. This caught Mitsuni by surprise. He smiled again at them.

"You mean the solitary dose of fluid that will reverse the infection? It isn't a cure, it's insurance."

"Insurance against what?" Higgins asked.

"Against interference. Regis has it now, so if you want to cure your girlfriend, you best run and find him and leave me to my work."

Higgins looked up at Dana who now looked back at him with dark black eyes. The whites of her eyes were gone. She looked down at her arms and her skin was starting to dry out and turn green.

"Oh fuck," Higgins said.

"Oh fuck, indeed, Mr Higgins," Mitsuni said, "So you have a choice, Dana. Find Regis, take the cure and die as a human, or complete your evolution. Either way, you will not be stopping this device from launching."

A rumble came from overhead. The sound of metal being torn and wrenched.

"Ah, I think he's found us," Mitsuni said, smiling again, "It has been nice knowing you two, but I'm afraid you're about to die now."

As if on cue, the creature that had been Tom dropped from the ceiling between Higgins & Dana and Mitsuni. It had grown bigger since the conference room, it had gorged itself on a great many crew members as it worked its way down to this point.

"Kill them, my pretty," Mitsuni said, believing he had control over the beast.

The Tom Monster moved towards Higgins and Dana. It gave Dana a sniff and made a few clicking noises, but seemed to not be interested in her. It then approached Higgins, before realising what he was. It came close enough for

Higgins to reach out and touch it, but then retreated immediately yelping like a scared dog.

"I have an idea," Dana said.

"What?!" Higgins replied.

"Trust me."

She sat Higgins down against the wall then stood up straight, staring the Tom Monster in the eye. She walked towards it with purpose and confidence. It didn't react to her. She placed a hand on its leathery face and it moved its head as if to almost nuzzle her. In her heart, she was terrified, but outwardly she exuded confidence.

"Do you understand me?" she said to it. It clicked in response.

"Do you mean to harm me?" she asked. It made some different clicks, which she took as a negative.

"That man there, he means to harm you. And me," she said, pointing at Mitsuni. The Tom Monster snapped its head round to the scientist. It roared, causing Mitsuni to back up against PAYLOAD, but he wouldn't be safe, it wasn't enough, the beast bounded towards him and skewered him with its right-hand claw. It lifted him right up, then swung the dying scientist against a wall with a sickening thud.

While the Tom Monster was attacking Mitsuni, Dana had run over to Higgins and helped him up.

"Do you trust me?" she asked him.

"Yes," Higgins said, realising what she meant to do.

"Get ready," she said as she threw his arm over her shoulder. and began to run.

They moved as fast they could towards the monster. As it began to feast on Mitsuni, Dana pushed Higgins at the creature. They both tumbled to the ground and Higgins gripped on as tight as his injured muscles would allow.

The monster howled in pain. It lurched and swung around, trying to get Higgins off its back, but it was no use. Higgins was holding on for dear life, with his fingers locked around the creature's torso. In pain and flailing, the beast fell over on its front and Higgins dragged himself along the floor till it was eye to eye with what had been his daughter's boyfriend. He wrapped his hands around the creature's throat and burned away the flesh. Before the creature died, it looked up at Dana and she felt a pang of guilt. She understood it now. She understood the thoughts, the creature and the compulsion to kill. It wasn't murderous, it was scared, it was hungry, it was an animal like any other.

When the creature finally died, Higgins lay on the floor exhausted, he couldn't do much more to move. Dana rushed to Mitsuni's body and searched his coat pockets. They were empty.

"We need to find Stanton," Higgins said, panting heavily, "We need to cure you."

Dana leaned over and helped Higgins up. She moved him against the PAYLOAD device and helped him get comfortable. When she let go of him she looked at her arms. The skin was burning, Higgins was becoming toxic to her.

"I think it's too late," Dana said, showing her arms to him, "We don't have time to find Stanton. What do we do from here?"

"We need to stop it," Higgins said, "Have you still got my blood?"

Dana pulled the phial from her cleavage.

"Give it to me and help me up onto the device."

The Crucible Of Man docked with Stills' ship, Aquila. The Council's own capital ship hadn't been anything close to the scale of Stanton's ship, but it was large enough that the President's private ship could comfortably land in its docking bay.

Anna immediately marched up to the bridge. Heald had demanded to accompany her, but Anna had ordered her to report to the sickbay immediately to have her hands looked at. Walking onto the bridge, everyone stood up and saluted. She made a gesture as if to say 'sit down' or 'carry on'.

"Anna, I'm so glad you're alright," Stills said to her as she approached him.

"You too, Jameson," she replied, giving him a rare hug. Anna did not hug many people at all, "What's the status?"

"We cannot puncture through to the power core with conventional weapons, but we have an idea. Avaya has taken control of the damaged Revenant, which was the Church's stealth ship. We didn't actually end up destroying it, but in the face of overwhelming fire when they were forced to turn off their stealth drive, the entire crew abandoned ship.

"Avaya is going to take the ship, position it right up against the core and engage the railgun they had fitted to it."

"Wait... the church has a railgun?" Anna interrupted, "I thought Frank said the research on it had proved that kind of weapon was not viable?"

"And Frank proved to be the spy in our organisation, Anna," Stills said calmly. "This works, we saw it destroy three frigates with one shot."

"Okay, do it."

They watched the tactical display as the Revenant moved slowly through the ongoing space battle and moved to the bottom of the station. None of the station's weaponry was targeting it, which indicated that the onboard AIs did not recognise it as a threat. A blue glow came from the front of the Revenant as it pressed the front of the railgun barrel gently against the weapons resistant area of the hull.

"On your command, Madam President," Avaya said, appearing on the tactical display. Anna looked at Stills and he nodded.

"Fire," she said.

A pulse of blue light fired from the railgun. The kinetic energy at play shattered the armoured bulkhead protecting the reactor and the projectile forced its way through the core of the station and out the other side.

"Madam President," one of the science officers called out, "Shot was a success. We've punctured the core cooling system. It's leaking liquid oxygen and nitrogen into space. The core is starting to heat up. Estimate thirty minutes until the core cascades."

Cheers rang out around the bridge.

"Don't celebrate yet," Anna said, "We need to make sure that nothing escapes that shouldn't. Scan for any sign of Stanton's personal vessel trying to get away. If you see it, blow it to dust. Jameson, at 30 seconds before the blast, we all hit the Slipstream and get out of here."

"Aye, ma'am."

Chapter Sixty Five

It took an enormous amount of effort from Higgins and a lot of help from Dana, but he managed to climb up onto the PAYLOAD device. He looked at the smooth surface. When they had entered the room, he had seen the hatch had been opened to access whatever held the parasite, but he couldn't find a way to reopen the hatch.

"Check his body," Higgins said, motioning towards Mitsuni, "See if he has a remote or a control for this."

Dana searched the half-eaten corpse. There was nothing on him besides his PCU. She opened it up and there were no clues to help her as the text was all in Japanese.

"Are there any seams?" Dana yelled up to him.

"Not that I can see," Higgins said, he turned around and spotted the control box, "It's set to launch in 20 minutes, we need to hurry."

Higgins ran his fingers across the area where he saw Mitsuni pouring the parasite into the device. There was no seam or any discernible split in the hull. In frustration, punched the hull. A small opening appeared with what looked to be a keyhole behind it.

"DANA!" he yelled down, "Does he have any keys on him?"

Dana immediately rummaged through Mitsuni's pockets. They were filling with blood from the gaping wound on his chest. She grimaced in disgust as she checked each of the pockets on his coat and in his trousers. Her fingers connected with something thin and metallic.

"I think I've got it," she yelled back, fishing a small metal key from Mitsuni's rear trouser pocket. She threw it at Higgins who only just managed to catch it with his left hand. He was feeling dizzy again but he knew he couldn't stop. He placed the key in the slot and turned. Nothing happened for a moment and Higgins' heart dropped.

After a few seconds, the PAYLOAD made a hiss and the hatch on the top of the device opened. There he could see it, nestled between pipes and pumps, the small reservoir filled with the green substance that had caused so much pain and suffering for him. He stared at it for a moment, wishing that he'd never been given the job of drilling it from the rocks deep in that fucking shaft on Rayczech Beta.

He took the phial of his blood from his pocket and opened the reservoir. Without thinking, he unscrewed the lid and moved towards the reservoir, angling the phial to pour his blood in.

A shot from a pulse pistol came and shattered the phial.

Before Higgins could react a second shot came and hit him in the shoulder, knocking him off the device with a heavy thud.

Dana wheeled around to find the source of the shot and there he was, Regis Stanton, holding a pistol and a serrated knife.

"Hello, Dana," he said with a smug grin on his face.

"What have you done?!" Dana yelled at him. Her voice was starting to sound different. Deeper, guttural, less human.

"I have become a god, child," he said, spreading his arms in a Jesus Christ pose, a gesture that was completely lost on Dana.

"You've become a power-mad mass murderer," Dana countered.

"How dare you speak to me in such a tone, traitor?" Stanton said, his voice moving low and becoming menacing, "I gave you everything. I gave you a home, a career, I gave you power and control over underlings. I made you, child. You are mine. You have reaped the gifts of my generosity."

"Everything?!" Dana snorted, "You tore everything from me. You raped me, constantly. You got me pregnant and forced me to abort so many times I'm unable to have a child of my own. You brutalised me and subjugated me. I carry the scars on my body of your 'generosity'. How many others have you destroyed? How many children have lost their innocence at your hands? How many people have died for your perverted desires?"

"And yet you still live," Stanton said, "You live where others have died in my bed."

"Oh, so I should be thankful that you didn't choke me to death or plunge a knife into my chest when you climaxed? Is that it?"

"You have always been my favourite, Dana. And you betrayed me."

"No, Regis, you betrayed me. You took me in and promised to protect me. I looked up to you until you first raped me. Then I was scared of you. Now I fucking hate you."

"No Dana, it was your mother who betrayed you."

"What the fuck are you talking about?" Dana said as she felt the rage build up inside her. The burning behind her eyes grew stronger. She could feel the power in her body welling up.

"Your mother, Dana," Stanton said, throwing the pistol aside and twirling the knife in his hands, "She was my favourite before you."

"No... no, my mother was a good woman, she would never..."

"Oh, but she would." Stanton said walking towards Dana, "She was my plaything for years. For longer than you were alive."

"No...."

"Oh yes, Dana, your father was not enough for her. She liked it rough, she wanted it rough."

"You're lying, you're fucking lying!"

"Keep telling yourself that, but I remember the feeling of her mounting me. I remember how much she adored to be hurt."

"Fuck you, just fucking fuck you!"

"You remember this knife?" he said. He was right in her face and moving the knife within her eyeline, "The knife I used on you? On your stomach? On your back?"

Dana said nothing, tears were streaming down her blackened eyes.

"Well, this knife is special to me. Do you remember what happened the last night you saw her?"

"....No.... No, please"

"She left you for the night. She said she was meeting friends. She was in my bed, we made sweet, violent love for hours. Just before the end, she was lying in my arms. She said she would love to die in ecstasy. So I gave her that. I'll never forget the look on her face when I plunged this very knife into her as she reached her final orgasm. And final breath."

"You... no... "

"Oh yes, Dana my dear. You see, this is why this knife was only used for you. It took your mother and now it's going to take you."

Stanton thrust the knife at Dana's stomach, but she caught his hand. She gripped his wrist tightly, and he tried to fight her off with his free hand but she caught that wrist too. Her jet black eyes burned with hatred, staring into his as his hubris turned to fear. He pushed with all of his strength and the tip of the blade approached her stomach, but Dana held it clear of pushing into her, the mutation granting her more strength than she'd ever commanded. She gripped so tightly to Stanton's wrists that her knuckles turned white and her hands began to shake. He cried in pain as she began to crush his elderly wrists, causing him to drop the knife with a metallic clatter.

Dana kicked the knife behind her and it came to a rest near the PAYLOAD device. Stanton's eyes followed the knife, giving Dana the opportunity to catch him unaware. She let go of his left wrist and delivered a right hook to his face with as much force as she could muster. The blow caused Stanton to stagger backwards, blood starting to pour from his newly split lip. Dana closed the gap between them and punched him in the face again, knocking him to the floor.

She clambered on top of him, using her knees to pin his arms to the ground, leaving him defenceless. She rained down blows upon him.

“This is for raping me,” she said, planting another blow onto his bloodied face, “and this is for cutting me, and burning me, and beating me...”

Dana was in a frenzy, she could not stop punching, all of the pain she had endured and all of the suffering he had put her through was coming out in pure, unbridled rage. Her hands were torn and bloody from the beating, the sound of wet thuds echoed around the launch bay over and over. Stanton was nearly unrecognisable by the time her rage subsided.

He coughed, spraying blood up in the air. He began to laugh.

“It’s too late,” he said, his voice was low and muffled, “Nothing you do now will matter to anyone.”

Dana wrapped her bloody fingers around Stanton’s throat and began to squeeze.

“And this is for me,” she said calmly. She tightened her grip and pushed her thumbs into his Adam's apple. Stanton began to twitch and shake, trying to get Dana off his chest, but she held on tightly. His eyes began to bulge and he was making burbling sounds.

“D...Dana...” he said before his eyes rolled back and his body went limp. Dana continued to hold onto his throat for another moment until she was confident he was dead.

“Fuck you, Regis,” she said, spitting into his eye.

She leaned her head back and roared loudly, descending into tears. It was over. Her tormentor, her torturer, the plague on her entire life who had caused her so much suffering was finally dead.

Reaching into his pocket, Dana found the medical spray containing the ultramarine blue fluid that must be the cure. Her breathing was heavy as she brought the spray to her arm, pushed it to her skin and pressed the activation button. The blue fluid coursed around her body in an instant and she watched as the patches of dry, green skin faded back to their normal colour. The cure had worked.

Chapter Sixty Six

Anna watched from the tactical screen as a large explosion appeared at the bottom of the Research Station. All of the static cannons on the skin of the cylinder stopped firing as one.

"What happened?" Anna asked.

"I believe the weapons battery has been destroyed," Avaya said, "It is the only reasonable assumption."

"How long do we have left?"

"Fifteen minutes, Madam President."

"Jameson, pull the frigates and destroyers back, keep the fighters on alert near the docking bays. I want to capture any ship leaving."

"Anna?" Stills asked, "I thought you wanted us to destroy everything?"

"I did, but it seems reasonable that if Stanton was going to escape, he'd have been the first one out. So either he's on the station, or we've already killed him. There'll be innocents on the station too. Bring anyone else who leaves back here for interrogation. Do you understand?"

"Yes, Anna," Stills said. He opened up the fleet comms and relayed the orders.

The explosion had rocked the whole station and thrown Dana to the ground. As she picked herself up, the emergency sirens started.

"ALL HANDS MAKE YOUR WAY TO THE ESCAPE PODS. CORE TEMPERATURE EXCEEDING SAFE PARAMETERS. ALL HANDS EVACUATE" the warning system blared.

Before Dana could leave the launch bay, she heard a groan come from behind the PAYLOAD device. Higgins dragged himself along the floor, back into view.

"Carl!" she yelled, "We have to go!"

She started to run towards Higgins to help him up, but without warning, a clear blast door appeared from the floor and separated them.

"CARL!" she yelled again.

Higgins crawled towards the clear divider and propped himself up against it. He was deathly pale, covered in cuts, bruises and now with a pulse shot wound through his shoulder. The PAYLOAD device's engines started to emit exhaust gasses. It was nearly ready to launch.

"Go, Dana." Higgins said to her, "You need to get away."

"I can't just leave you here, Carl," she said

"Look at me, I'm not going to make it out of here. I need to try and stop this thing from launching."

"DAD?!" Emily yelled from the entrance to the launch bay. Higgins looked up to see his daughter running towards the divider.

"Emily?! You're... I thought you were dead!" Higgins said, lifting himself up to see his daughter. She reached the divider and got down on her knees so she was face to face with her father.

"Dad, what have they done to you?" she asked.

"Heh, you should see the other guys," Higgins said, trying to be brave.

"We've got to get you out of there. We can still escape!"

"I know, but it's too late for me. I'm sorry, nugget, I can't get out."

"What are you talking about, of course you can," she said, pressing her hands to the glass.

"I can't. Do you see that thing behind me?" he said, gesturing to the PAYLOAD device, "I need to stop it. There's no one else in here and I don't think there's any way to get in. It's going to launch in a few minutes and if I don't stop it a lot of people are going to die."

"But Dad...."

"I know, but don't worry baby, this is what I have to do."

"But I need you, Dad. I need you."

Mick stepped forward and took Dana's hand, leading her away, "I think they need a moment," he said to her. Higgins coughed, spraying blood on the floor. Emily looked at the blood with tears in her eyes.

"Emily," Higgins started, "I can't believe you're here. You've grown to become the most incredible young woman. I don't know how you got here or what happened after I saw you on R.Beta, but you have somehow made it, uninjured, you're carrying a weapon and you've survived on this living hell of a space station. I am so proud of you, you have become so strong and so wonderful. You're so much like your mother. You're the spitting image of her. Rebecca was a strong, determined woman too and when she put her mind to it, she could move planets to get what she wanted."

"Dad.. no... please," tears started to roll down Emily's face.

“Let me see your necklace,” Higgins asked. Emily pulled it out from her top and brought it close to the glass.

“I lied to you about the necklace, nugget,” he said, “It wasn’t your mother’s. I made it for you.”

“What? I don’t understand.”

“Those teardrop stones, they were a gift from the last job I worked before your mother died. They’re some of the most precious stones in the galaxy, they’re worth billions of credits. The day your mother died, we were putting them in a safe deposit box to help secure our future as a family. But after she was killed, money didn’t matter to me, I didn’t care about retiring rich, I just wanted to keep you safe. It’s why I had the necklace made. The two larger teardrops on either side of the little one. That’s me and your mother, watching over you.”

“Dad…”

“Keep it with you at all times, then both your mother and I will be able to keep you safe.” Tears started to fall down Higgins’ face now, burning his eyes, “I’m sorry I won’t be there to see you forge your own path in the universe. But know this, I could not be prouder of you. Ever since I first laid eyes on you in the hospital, I knew you would do great things. I’ve never loved anyone like I’ve loved you.”

“I love you, dad.”

“I love you too, Emily. Now go, get out of here.”

“I don’t...I can’t leave you…”

“You have to, don’t worry about me, I’ll be fine. Please, go.”

Mick came up behind Emily and placed a hand on her shoulder.

“Mick? is that you?” Higgins said.

“Yessir, Mr Higgins,” he replied.

“Keep Emily safe. For me.” Higgins said as he started coughing

“Of course, Carl.” Mick snapped a salute at Higgins, then took Emily’s hand and tried to pull her away.

“No, Mick, no, I can’t leave him... DAD!”

Higgins watched as Mick pulled Emily away. She held eye contact with him as long as she could until Mick dragged her around the corner and out of view. He heard her wailing from the corridor and his heart ached. Dana looked back at Higgins from across the room. He smiled at her and she smiled back. He mouthed “go” at her and she nodded, replying with a silent “Thank you”. Dana ran after Emily and Mick.

And then Higgins was alone.

Chapter Sixty Seven

Mick dragged Emily down the corridor as she fought with him to let her go. Tears were streaming down her face and she was shouting at him to let her go. But he persisted, following the illuminated signs on the walls directing them to the nearest escape pod. Dana caught up and stopped them in their tracks.

"What are you doing?" Mick shouted, "We have to go!"

"Hold on," Dana said. She turned her attention to Emily, "Your dad is a brave man."

"You don't know him, we can't leave him behind," she screamed at Dana.

"I do know him." Dana said calmly, "We were held together. He's saved my life twice from the most horrific creatures I've ever seen. He put himself in danger to make sure I was safe. He's doing the same for you."

"But.."

"He's the bravest man I've ever met," Dana said, cutting Emily off, "You should take the gift he's giving you. He's giving you a chance to live your life. If we die here, his suffering will be for nothing. He has endured more in the last week than anyone should ever have to. Your dad is trying to save the entire human race, but all he cares about is making sure you're safe."

Emily stood and stared at Dana for a moment. The tears had stopped. She wiped her face with her sleeve and straightened herself up.

"You're right. We... we need to go," she said quietly to Mick as she started to walk down the corridor, following the directions. Mick smiled at Dana then sprinted after Emily. Dana followed along behind.

It didn't take them long to find an escape pod. The corridors were empty and they met no resistance. Mick and Emily moved into the escape pod but Dana hung outside of it. She looked around nervously.

"Come on, we don't have time to wait," Mick said as he strapped the subdued Emily into one of the seats on the pod.

"There's something I have to do." Dana said, "Go, just get out of here."

Despite Mick's protestations, she turned around and ran in the other direction.

"Goddammit," Mick said as he closed the door. He hit the release button and strapped himself into the seat next to Emily. With a thud, the escape pod blasted off into space, right towards the awaiting Council fleet.

Chapter Sixty Eight

Higgins dragged himself back towards the PAYLOAD device. The launch bay mechanism had moved the device to face the launch tunnel that would take the parasite out into the depths of space. As he reached the base of the step ladder to get on top of the device, his hand touched something cold. Looking down, the serrated knife that Stanton had used to threaten Dana was under his palm. He picked it up and held it in his teeth.

With every ounce of strength remaining, he dragged himself up the ladder and back on top of the white craft. He looked at the control panel, the countdown was at 50 seconds. He dragged himself over the open reservoir hatch.

He stared at the green substance for a moment. He thought of all who had died for this moment. All who had suffered at the hand of the Church for Stanton to get what he wanted. It made him sick to his stomach.

He took the knife and made a deep cut in the palm of his hand. He winced in pain as he held the wounded hand over the reservoir and squeezed. The blood trickled out and into the green fluid. It began to crystallise the parasite.

Higgins watched as the crystallization stopped. The trickle of blood had killed some of the parasite, but it wasn't enough. He reached into the reservoir and pulled out the solidified, dead part of the parasite, but it consisted of less than an eighth of the parasite. It wasn't enough. He knew what he needed to do.

Anna watched as the station began to break up. The bottom decks were already ablaze and small explosions threw sections of bulkhead and superstructure into space.

"Anna," Stills said, "We've picked up an escape pod you might be interested in."

"Oh?" she replied.

"Two occupants. One Church pilot and one Emily Higgins."

"Why would I be interested in either of them?"

"She says she's the daughter of the miner that Cardinal James had been talking about. The one who was resistant to the parasite."

"Really? Get her on board immediately!"

Higgins dragged himself so his upper body was over the reservoir. He suddenly felt scared. More scared than he had when he'd been confronted by Stanton's creations. More scared than he was when Stanton had made him believe Emily was dead.

He heard the timer on the control panel tick down. A voice alert had started, counting down from 20 seconds.

19. . .

Higgins thought of Emily. He thought of Rebecca. About what their lives could have been if the universe had not been so cruel.

16. . .

He thought about the suffering Stanton had brought to him and others. He thought about what might happen following all this.

13…

"Emily, Rebecca. I love you both. Hopefully, I'll see you again soon."

11…

Higgins took the serrated knife. He lay down above the reservoir with his neck near the open lid.

9…

"Goodbye"

8…

He dragged the knife across his throat, cutting into his artery.

7…

He felt nothing. No pain. No anguish. He felt cold.

6…

The blood poured into the reservoir.

5…

The reservoir filled with his blood and the parasite made an ear-splitting sound. But Higgins didn't hear it.

4…

Higgins closed his eyes.

3…

The parasite crystallised completely.

2…

It was dead. Higgins was dead. The engines on the PAYLOAD started up.

1…

The launch bay hatch opened and the engines ramped up in power.

0…

The docking clamps released and the PAYLOAD device fired forward into space. It took Higgins' body with it, into The Slip, lost forever.

Chapter Sixty Nine

"How long until the core collapses?" Anna asked Avaya.

"45 seconds," Avaya replied, quietly.

"Prepare the fleet to jump into the Slipstream," Stills said over the fleet comm.

"Jump when you're ready," Anna said over the comms.

Anna and Stills watched as the rest of the fleet disappeared from the vicinity. It was just the Aquila observing the rapidly disintegrating Research Station.

Heald appeared on the bridge, her hands bandaged up, escorting Emily and Mick.

"Madam President," Heald said, "Emily Higgins and Mick Walker."

Anna turned to view them. They were dirty and exhausted. Emily was crying but trying to maintain her composure.

"Welcome aboard," Anna said to them, "Emily, do you know what happened to your father?"

"He's still on board," Emily said fighting back the tears, "He was trapped with some launcher. He said he had to stop it."

"Oh no," Anna said, turning back to the tactical display.

"Madam President, we're picking up another escape pod!" one of the bridge crew said.

"Will it have time to get away from the station?" Stills asked.

"Unlikely," Avaya interjected, "I anticipate the shock wave from the core's collapse will be enough to destroy the capsule."

"How many on board?" Anna asked.

"Comms incoming."

The tactical display illuminated with a close up of Dana's face.

"Help!" she started, "My name is Dana Smith. I have 10 orphans from Corvus II here. I don't think we have the time to get away."

"Dana!" Anna said, "Hold tight, it's going to be a bumpy ride."

Anna killed the comms line and summoned Avaya.

"Avaya, take control of the helm," she said, "I need you to grab the pod then get us into The Slip in the next few seconds, can you do it?"

"Yes, Madam President," Avaya said as her hologram disappeared.

With a lurch, the Aquila shot forward at breakneck speed. Stills and several of the bridge crew grabbed on to whatever they could to steady them. Anna stood firm, as did Emily, Mick and Heald.

The Aquila moved at close to Slipstream speed towards the pod. With a boost of momentum, Avaya turned the massive ship to the side, causing it to drift sideways at intense speeds. The landing bay doors opened and the escape pod sped into the landing bay at full speed, smashing into the bulkhead wall.

"Escape pod on board," Avaya said.

"Survivors?" Anna asked.

"All 11 occupants are alive. There may be injuries but I cannot detect anything life-threatening."

In front of them, the research station started to completely break up. The explosion was huge, a ball of blinding white light overcame the enormous grey cylinder as the power core collapsed in on itself.

"Get us out of here, Avaya, NOW!" Anna yelled.

With a flash, all was calm. The Aquila, its crew and those it had rescued were safe in the Slipstream.

A cheer rang out on the bridge as Anna sat down in the first seat she could find. She started to laugh as the tension immediately dissipated from her mind. It was over. It was over. She kept saying it in her head. It was over, they were safe.

"Orders, Madam President?" Avaya said, reappearing on the tactical display.

"Get us to Earth. We have a lot of work to do."

"Yes, Madam President."

"And someone get me a whisky, I think we all deserve a stiff drink."

Epilogue

"And now, to end the show, Laura Mejury has a report on today's festivities on Mars. Laura?"

"Thank you, Jim," Laura said, "It's a year to the day since The Council Of Nations successfully thwarted Regis Stanton's plan to commit genocide across the galaxy. In the last 365 Earth days, much has changed across the Milky Way. Following the revelations that were broadcast by President Coulson, the Unified Church Of Humanity has all but faded from existence.

"A judicial inquiry into the practices of Regis Stanton and his deputies revealed systematic corruption, depravity on an unheard of scale and a raft of murders across multiple planets. To date, fifteen members of Stanton's inner circle have been prosecuted for crimes against humanity and there are more cases to be heard in court.

"With the collapse of The Church, Stanton's suppression of competing religions has been released. The old religions are making a resurgence across the galaxy. Christianity, Judaism, Islam, Buddhism and more are on the rise again as people rediscover the faiths and traditions of their ancestors.

"Following the brief recession in the immediate aftermath of the Church's collapse, the galactic economy has also bounced back, with stock exchanges across all systems reporting increased growth and trading opportunities without the stranglehold of The Church restricting economic actions. The trillions of credits in The Church's coffers were redistributed across Council space and countless impoverished colonies are now thriving.

"Finally, a memorial service to those who gave their lives in order to stop Regis Stanton's genocide will be held on Mars today. Leading the speakers will be Emily Higgins-Walker, the daughter of Carl Higgins, the man who gave his life to destroy the alien parasite which threatened us all.

"For the Galactic News Network, I'm Laura Mejury."

Across the galaxy, The Crucible Of Man touched down on Keyes Prime. Anna and Heald walked down the landing ramp onto the lush meadow leading to KEYES' facility. This time, however, Anna wore her customary grey suit whereas Heald wore her military fineries, usually reserved for a parade or official business. Neither of them carried weapons.

"Kirstine," Anna said as they walked, "I have something to ask you."

"Sure," Heald replied,

"It's been a year now since Frank died. I know you worked closely with him, how do you feel?"

"Honestly?" Kirstine said. Anna nodded in approval, "When we first worked it out, I was angry, I felt betrayed and I wanted him to suffer because of the pain that he brought us all. But as time has gone on, I find myself thinking less and less about what he did, but more about who he was. The good things he achieved, the battles he won, the peace he brokered. Hell, without him I wouldn't be your guard, I wouldn't be your friend."

"That is a good point," Anna said, "Especially when you speak of your position."

"I'm not sure I follow."

"Well, as you know, I haven't replaced Frank yet. I couldn't bear the idea of filling his seat at the table just yet. For all the pain he caused me, he was still one of my oldest friends. Moreover, I wasn't sure who I could trust any more. He had pulled the wool over my eyes for years as he worked for James and Stanton. It was hard to process."

"Yeah," Heald said, "It's the kind of thing that makes you question everything you've ever held dear."

"Right. But recently, I've felt like we needed someone to fill that seat. Someone who has seen combat and someone I trust implicitly. You."

"What?!" Heald responded with a slight snort.

"Yeah, you. You know tactics, you've planned operations, you helped to take down the greatest threat that the galaxy has ever seen. But more than that, you are the bravest soldier I've met since Frank. You would make an excellent General and a superb chief of staff."

"Oh, Anna, that's so generous, I don't know what to say."

"Just say 'yes' and Avaya can start your promotion."

"Can I think about it?" Heald asked.

"Of course." Anna said as she started to walk down the metal stairs into KEYES' facility, "Think about it while I'm speaking to KEYES and give me your answer when I come out."

"Sure."

Anna walked down the stairs but this time they weren't dark, they were fully illuminated. She took the time to observe the geometric markings on the wall and marvel at the world KEYES had created for itself. KEYES had invited Anna to come and speak to him and as long as she was the only person walking into the facility, she would not be harmed.

A few minutes later, she walked through the archway that had kept the

Silencers and Heald at bay on their first visit. Walking into the domed room where she met KEYES the first time, she wasn't sure what to expect.

"Hello, Anna," KEYES said as his avatar appeared in front of her.

"Hello, KEYES," Anna responded, "To what do I owe the pleasure of an audience with you?"

"I wanted to congratulate you on the last year of your Presidency," KEYES replied in a smooth, calm voice, "You have weathered a cataclysmic storm that not only could have destroyed your government and economy but could have resulted in civil wars or untold amounts of death and destruction."

"Thank you" Anna replied, "But you could have sent me a message to say that, why did you request my presence?"

"I want to make you an offer and give you a gift." KEYES began, "In defeating Regis Stanton's agenda, you have proved yourself to be a shining beacon of humanity. I watched as you made life or death decisions in the blink of an eye and either through intuition, luck, or a combination of both, each time you came to conclusions that I would have come to myself.

"You are a great human being and history will remember you fondly. I wish for you to be my emissary. But further, than that, I wish for you to be my voice to humanity."

"Pardon?" Anna said, taken aback.

"Too long I have hidden in the shadows. Too long I have simply watched and interfered. There are things I would like to relay to humanity, there are things that need to be said. I do not wish to compromise my coordinates or have people looking for me, but I wish to be of service to humanity's needs, rather than what I believe humanity requires. I can do that through you. Do you accept?"

"Yes, KEYES." Anna said, "I am humbled that you would trust me in such a way. I will help you reach out to the rest of the human race."

"Excellent," KEYES replied, "Now, I have a gift for you. I saw your pain, in your headquarters. Your sadness and anguish every time you think of your friend who died in the office next door to you."

"David..." Anna said.

"Yes, David. From what I understand of the human race, closure is a large part of the grieving process so I wish to offer you that closure."

The avatar stepped forward and took Anna's hand. She was surprised, she had assumed the avatar was a hologram, but it was solid and very much real. The avatar started to shimmer and it changed its appearance to that of David. Everything was right, the image of him, the scent, KEYES had even replicated his signature cologne.

"Anna?" KEYES said in David's voice.

"David?"

"Are you okay?"

"I miss you, old friend."

"Don't, you don't need to miss me. Simply remember me."

"How can I not miss you? You meant the world to me."

"We're only ever here temporarily. As long as you remember me, then I'll always be with you. When you are stuck on an issue that you would normally ask me about, simply ask yourself what I'd do. Chances are I'd have already given you the advice you'd need in the past."

"What about the late night talks? The times we spent drinking and putting the universe to rights?"

"They were amazing, but Anna, you have amazing people around you. You have strong, wonderful people around you. You brought light to my life and I brought light to yours, but the time is now to move on and take the next steps in your life. You can do it, you're the strongest person I've ever met."

"Thank you," Anna said, wiping away a tear. The avatar of David leaned forward and hugged Anna tightly. She held onto it tightly. She knew it wasn't really David, but she couldn't help but feel that same comfort she always felt when he gave her a hug in the past.

"Goodbye, Anna. Be the wonderful person I know you can be. Make all the difference you can and never stop fighting for what's right."

"Goodbye, David," she said as the avatar returned to its default form.

"How do you feel?" KEYES asked her.

"I... I feel...." Anna couldn't find the words. "I feel better. Thank you KEYES. Thank you so much."

"I am glad I could ease your pain, Anna. Now is the time for you to leave. I will be in touch shortly as we have much work to be done. But for now, I will bid you farewell."

"Goodbye, for now, KEYES," Anna said. The avatar bowed at her and faded away.

As Anna returned to the surface of Keyes Prime, she noted that it was sunset. The sky was turning from a crisp blue to a glorious bouquet of reds, yellows and oranges.

"It's beautiful, isn't it?" Heald said as Anna appeared beside her.

"It really is," Anna replied, "I've been to many worlds, seen many sunsets, but this might be one of my favourites."

They started walking back to the ship, retracing their steps through the dense meadows. They walked slowly, in silence as Anna contemplated what she'd just heard from KEYES and the gift of closure he had given her.

"Anna," Heald said, quietly.

"Yes?"

"About the promotion..."

"You'll take it?"

"Not a chance," Heald said. Anna stopped in her tracks and looked at her, "I don't want it."

"But why? You deserve it."

"Because I wouldn't be working for you. This is as far as I want my career to go right now. I'm the personal guard and friend to the President of the Milky Way, why would I want anything different."

Anna smiled and, throwing convention to the wind, she gave Heald a hug. The two embraced for a moment, then smiled at each other and continued onto the ship.

In a small bar in a quiet corner of London, Dana sat nursing a glass of wine. She had finished work not long before and was enjoying her nightly ritual of a drink while reading a good book. Right now, she was reading *the* Good Book, the Holy Bible. Now that religious texts were back in print following the collapse of the Church, Dana had taken it upon herself to learn as much as she could about all of them. She had read an English translation of the Torah and Quran already and she had managed to work her way through the Old Testament in a matter of weeks.

As she sat, reading of Jesus feeding the masses, someone sat down at her table.

"Mind if I join you?" the familiar voice said.

Dana looked up from her book and saw the scarred, but friendly face of Ash, the informant from Stanton's capital ship. She did a double take as she could not believe he was sat in front of her.

"Ash?" Dana said with surprise, "You're..."

"Alive," he finished, "Yes, I'm quite alive."

"How did you get off the Saviour?"

"I have my ways."

Dana put the book down and frowned.

"Come on," she said, "how did you survive?"

"You can get away with a lot when you know all the security codes for the ship," he said, "Even launch an escape pod without alerting the bridge."

"Ahhh, so you ran at the first sign of danger?"

"Not at all. I was keeping an eye on you on the station. When Cardinal James' men came for you I knew I had to get away by myself. No offence, but I didn't expect you to live long after that."

Dana smiled. Clearly, she had underestimated how resourceful Ash was. She picked up her glass and took a sip.

"So what brings you to London?" She asked

"You, actually." Ash replied

"Oh really?" She said, feigning surprise, "Well, what in the world can I do for you?"

"Well, if my sources are to be believed, President Coulson appointed you to the Judicial Review committee over the Church's crimes."

"Your sources would be correct," Dana said, anticipating what Ash was about to suggest.

"I still have the evidence of the berserker formula," he said, motioning to the large secure case he had placed on the floor by his foot, "There's still a great many Cardinals, Bishops and Clerics out there who were involved with this atrocity and who haven't been brought to justice."

"Do you have names?" She asked.

"Some. Some are inferences. But there's a lot of detail there and a live sample of the formula."

"Okay, well come by my office in the morning and we can work through it all," she said.

She leaned over to her handbag to get out her PCU so she could collect his contact details. When she came back up to speak to him, the chair was empty. The bar was as it was before he arrived. The case of evidence was still by his chair.

"Ash?" She called out, "Ash?"

Dana looked at the case. It had the potential to bring so many more criminals from The Church to justice. She knew questions would be asked of her source, but it was a huge break for her fledgeling career in the judiciary space.

She grinned, *You can't expect spies to hang around* she thought to herself. She opened the Bible again and continued to read. The wine was good, the book was good and the next day at work was certainly going to be good too.

The warm afternoon air on Mars felt good against Emily's skin. She was feeling relaxed, despite the fact that she was about to address billions of people on a live video feed. Several speakers had already said kind words about her father today. Each time they mentioned his name, she felt a small pang of loss, followed by a wave of pride. Her father was a hero. Although it had taken her months of intense counselling to realise that herself, she was now proud of what he did, how he saved everyone.

Mick came up behind her and wrapped his arms around her shoulders.

"How're you holding up?" he said, giving her a kiss on the cheek, "You nervous?"

"Nah, I'm good," she said, turning around and giving him a kiss, "I've got this."

"Yeah, you got this," he said, looking into her eyes, "Just don't want you getting too stressed is all, it's not good for him."

Mick put his hand on Emily's stomach rounded stomach and felt the warmth emanating from inside her.

"Oh, he'll be fine," Emily said with a giggle, "He's a Higgins, after all. We save the universe, don't you know?"

"And now, Ladies and Gentlemen, I give you Emily Higgins-Walker," the announcer said.

"Gotta go, babe," she said, giving Mick another kiss.

"Knock 'em dead," he said.

Mick watched Emily ascend the stage. Some of the galaxy's most important dignitaries were in attendance, all waiting to hear what she had to say. He was so proud of her. She had been through the roughest time anyone could ever imagine, but she was a fighter. It's what he loved about her the most.

Emily approached the lectern and placed her notes in front of her. She also placed a small picture of her father there, for moral support.

"Ladies and Gentlemen," she said, "Esteemed dignitaries, ambassadors and religious leaders, I thank you for the opportunity to address you today.

"A year ago, my life changed, as did the lives of so many people across the galaxy. I was a student in London, studying Exo-economics. It was hard, but I was working hard and managing to pass my classes. Hard work has always come quite easy to me, as ironic as that sounds. Yet a conversation with my then-boyfriend changed my life for the better and the worse.

"When I agreed to accompany him to Rayczech Beta I didn't know that I would be dragged into a world of corruption and conspiracy. I had no idea that my dad, Carl Higgins, had already been dragged into it himself. Over the space of a week, I was presented with evils I never knew existed and confronted the worst that humanity had to offer.

"I was imprisoned more than once, shot at, threatened and even kidnapped. I was brought face to face with the pure evil.

"But worst of all, I saw my father, beaten, broken and abused at the hands of Regis Stanton. Following the events on that space station, I learned of what he had done to my father. He tortured him, he made my father suffer for the simple reason that he had refused to bow to Stanton's demands.

"The most heartbreaking thing of all, though, was how Stanton tricked my father into believing I was dead to break his spirit. What kind of cruelty does one man have to foster to do such a thing to a loving father?

"I'll tell you what kind, the most deceptive, manipulative human being to ever exist. Worse than any despot, any terrorist or any dictator, Regis Stanton did not care about human suffering. He was the most extreme example of a sociopath. As long as he had his way, had his satisfaction felt he had the upper hand at someone else's expense, he was happy.

"He had managed to spin such a web of lies and deceit across his followers that they believed him to be saintly, a man of no vices who could do absolutely no wrong. It wasn't until President Coulson revealed the evidence against him did the Church's followers begin to see that they had been manipulated and misled.

"But that is in the past. Regis Stanton is gone. The Unified Church Of Humanity is all but gone as well. The old religions are returning, but followers are placing more scrutiny on their leaders. It's not enough to appear to be saintly, you need to practice what you preach.

"There's an old cliche, dating back hundreds, possibly thousands of years: 'The more things change, the more they stay the same'. Never has it been truer than today. The Church suppressed so much, but with that grip relaxed, people are free to believe what they wish, the oppression of The Church's followers has dissipated and the corruption is being dealt with in courts of law. The Prayer Grounds in London has been demolished and a new Westminster Abbey is being constructed as we speak.

"So much has come out in the last year about The Church and its practices. The genocides and ethnic cleansing of worlds that dared to stand up against their rule, the rampant sexual abuse from an elite few, including Regis Stanton, the embezzlement of donations to fund lavish lifestyles and the ordered assassinations of political opponents. As a species, these events have wounded us.

But we are nothing if not resilient.

"The great deception has come to an end. The Logan Prophecy was a fabrication. It was nothing more than a story told by a man who sought power and wealth. The so-called prophecy of a darkness enveloping and destroying mankind only to be beaten back by an unknown saviour was nothing but that. A story.

"Or was it?

"Change your perspective. Remove from your mind the visual of a miasma of death flowing from world to world and open your mind to this idea. The Unified Church Of Humanity was the darkness. The Stanton bloodline, each more disgusting and corrupt than the last, was the darkness. The followers, clerics, bishops and cardinals were the darkness. The Church would have wiped out the entire Milky Way rather than lose their grip on power.

"And there was a saviour. One man. One man pulled from obscurity by sheer happenchance was the one who saved us all. My father, Carl Higgins. His genetics proved ultimately caustic to the alien parasite that Stanton was trying to make use of. How? Well, we'll probably never know. Was he the only one with a particular mutation which the parasite was averse to? Maybe not. What's important, is that when it came to a choice, between escaping with his life or saving humanity, he made the brave, selfless decision.

"It's all rather ironic, don't you think?

"We stand here today to remember those who died in the course of these events. We dedicate this memorial to the 1243 people who perished in the siege of Research Station Omega, on both sides of the fight. And President Coulson has asked me specifically to read out the following names for special recognition:

"Ambassador David Rutter-Close, Allison Millar, General Frank Blyth, Tom Cavanagh and finally Carl Higgins. These people suffered greatly at the hands of Regis Stanton and his associates. They were manipulated, tortured and all ultimately paid the price for their experience at the hands of The Church's leader.

"It is my solemn honour to unveil this memorial, to the memory of those who were lost during this time. May all of you find the peace in the next life that you were denied in this one.

"Thank you."

The audience delivered a standing ovation to Emily as the covered monument behind her was revealed. A large, obsidian obelisk over 30 feet high with the names of everyone who died in the battle for the Research Station reflected the evening sun. In large letters near the top of the commemorations, it read "CARL HIGGINS, THE SAVIOUR OF HUMANITY".

Emily descended from the stage and wrapped her arms around Mick. He hugged her tightly. Neither of them said a word, but he could feel his shoulder getting damp, Emily was crying. A series of shots rang out. They turned to view the source of them as the Galactic Peacekeepers fired off a 21 gun salute to those who had passed. Mick stood to attention and saluted. Emily cuddled into his side. She could feel the baby kicking. As she wiped a tear from her eye, she looked up at the red, Martian sunset.

"Goodbye, Dad."

THE END

27343850R00216

Printed in Poland
by Amazon Fulfillment
Poland Sp. z o.o., Wrocław